MW00529534

WOMB CITY

WOMB CITY
WOMB CITY
WOMB CITY
WOMB CITY
WOMB CITY
WOMB CITY
WOMB CITY

TLOTLO TSAMAASE

an imprint of Kensington Publishing Corp.
www.erewhonbooks.com

Content notice: *Womb City* contains depictions of blood, body horror, car accidents, child death, death, death of parent, domestic abuse, drug use, emotional abuse, gaslighting, gore, grief, infertility, infidelity, kidnapping, miscarriage, misogyny, murder, physical abuse, pregnancy, rape, sexism, sexual violence, and violence.

EREWHON BOOKS are published by:
Kensington Publishing Corp.
119 West 40th Street
New York, NY 10018
www.erewhonbooks.com

Portions of this book were adapted from the following works: "Behind Our Irises" (*Africanfuturism: An Anthology*, Brittle Paper, 2020); "Eclipse Our Sins" (*Clarkesworld,* Issue 159); "Murders Fell From Our Wombs" (*Apex,* Issue 107); "Dreamports" (*Apex*, Issue 128)

ISBN 978-1-64566-056-9 (hardcover)

First Erewhon hardcover printing: February 2024

10 9 8 7 6 5 4 3 2 1

Printed in the United States of America

Library of Congress Control Number is available upon request.

Electronic edition: ISBN 978-1-64566-076-7

Edited by Sarah T. Guan
Cover art by Colin Verdi
Cover design by Samira Iravani
Interior design by Leah Marsh

To

Omphile and Boitumelo for the fires and worlds within your mouths that have offered shelter, warmth, and laughter.

[Those] who said my dreams were farfetched (and myself for that "fuck, am I crazy? let's quit" moment), I hope you embrace this dream in flesh and word.

You welcome to *Womb City*. I hope you enjoy your stay.

He said to the police, "Don't let her go. She's a criminal, a killer."

And they asked me, "Is what he says true?"

"I am a killer, but I've committed no crime. Like you, I kill only criminals."

"But he is a prince, and a hero. He's not a criminal."

"For me the feats of kings and princes are no more than crimes, for I do not see things the way you do."

"You are a criminal," they said, "and your mother is a criminal."

"My mother was not a criminal. No woman can be a criminal. To be a criminal one must be a man."

"Now look here, what is this that you are saying?"

"I am saying that you are criminals, all of you: the fathers, the uncles, the husbands, the pimps, the lawyers, the doctors, the journalists, and all men of all professions."

They said, "You are a savage and dangerous woman."

"I am speaking the truth. And truth is savage and dangerous."

—*Woman at Point Zero* by Nawal El Saadawi

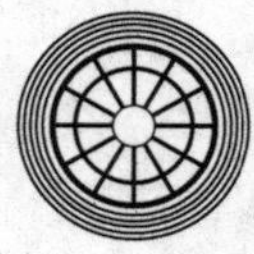

For death and truth are similar in that they both require a great courage if one wishes to face them. And truth is like death in that it kills. When I killed I did it with truth not with a knife. That is why they are afraid and in a hurry to execute me. They do not fear my knife. It is my truth which frightens them. This fearful truth gives me great strength. It protects me from fearing death, or life, or hunger, or nakedness, or destruction. It is this fearful truth which prevents me from fearing the brutality of rulers and policemen.

—*Woman at Point Zero* by Nawal El Saadawi

SUNDAY, AUGUST 2

05:00 /// PURE

In our city, everyone lives forever. But murder hangs in the air like mist.

The morning sun is a still-sparkling eye, blinking through our bedroom shutters when my husband shrugs me awake. "It's time," he whispers.

I toss and turn. Sleep slips, evades me. Eyes closed, the skin of my eyelids is tinged pink as the probing, UV-forensic sunrays seep into the darkest part of my mind, the part that wakes up with me every morning. *Barren. Lonely. Desperate.* I rub the heels of my palms into my eyes.

"Babe." Elifasi's lips nibble my earlobe.

I sit up as my microchip vibrates, sending quivers down my spine. It's my daily reminder for my morning assessment. I already feel so incarcerated in my own bed that the government-imposed reminder makes me grit my teeth.

"I don't understand why you always feel nervous about this daily routine," he says, fluffing the pillow. "You always pass."

"You don't understand what it feels like to lose a body," I bite back. "What if I had a child?"

Child. That grenade of a word in our marriage lands in his heart, blasting out pieces of sadness like shrapnel. The hurt in his eyes is too heavy to hold. But what if I bump into them at the market, and I can't tell that I gave birth to them in my previous life? I do not say these things aloud.

His hand detaches from my face. The cold air fills his place, gripping me. The vast amount of space between us keeps us emotionally light-years apart. My fingers clasp his cotton shirt at the small of his back, where I often draw circles to comfort him, but he shrugs me off. "I'm sorry." The wet whisper clings to my lips. "It's just . . . I wish the Body Hope Facility had given me a body that was at least fertile, given the high premiums I pay."

"We," he says.

"What?"

"*We* pay, not *I* pay."

I make more money than him, and he says I keep rubbing it in his face, and he's wrongfully accusing me of doing so. I wish he would see past that because it makes it difficult to speak to him.

"I'm sorry," I whisper.

"It's a waste of time to focus on the past," he says. "The only thing we can change is our future."

Sirens pierce through the silence in our bedroom. He stands, the bedcovers crinkling. His fingers tease open the shutters as he peers at our garden down below. "Looks like it's about to rain." The city sirens are hollow ghosts, fingering the city along the A1 highway, pulsing through our suburb, Tsholofelo East, toward a culprit.

Murder hangs in the air. The cold clings to my skin. Every Sunday at the cusp of dusk, each police tower in every district coughs up into the skies a puff of human-corpse-detecting chemicals. The rains will come, and the chemicals will detect homicide in our urban landscape. Through the sliver of window to the horizon, far out, is a scenic view of soft hills and sky, a mass of forested land, outstretched.

"It must be the perpetrator they brought in last night," Elifasi says. "He wouldn't talk. Previous forensic assessments failed to predict his criminal intent. But the sun never fails us." Its rays catalyze the chemicals into truth-seeking action. He directs this statement at me. The guilt, the anger bridling beneath all that muscle, those still-murky deep-set dark eyes. A ray of light knives its way across his light-brown skin, climbing up his sharp nose. His hand jerks; the wooden shutters jolt and flick open. The sun glares into my face. *Guilty,* it seems to say.

"Even if the sun fails us," he says, "we can always rely on the Murder Trials to protect us."

I tremble. The Murder Trials, heavily shrouded in secrecy. They're a backup plan for our forensic evaluations and allegedly use horrid practices to catch criminals who go undetected by technology—practices I pray I never discover. They especially scrutinize microchipped people, which means a high majority of women, since female bodies are microchipped more often than male. But I've no idea what they do to people like us or why they target us. How can I avoid what I don't understand?

The Murder Trials are based near Matsieng, a ritualistic site made holy by the surrounding folklore-riddled waterholes, where some crazy people drink its *miracle water* to solve financial problems, infertility, erectile dysfunction . . . I'm no atheist, but I can't believe a whole-ass government would entrust our safety to supernatural gimmicks. How could crevices in the ground aid them in unearthing criminals? Yet even I can't deny it's worked so far, reducing crime over the centuries.

Elifasi pulls me to my feet. "Let's get this over with," he says. I lean in to give him a morning kiss, but he evades me.

"Sit." He presses me primly against the armless cushioned chair. He walks behind me, footfalls softened by our lush bedroom carpet. Crouches by the bed.

"It's chilly in here," I say, bare-armed, bare-legged, in a light velvet camisole and pajama shorts, trimmed with satin.

His hands brush my shoulders, my neck, holding me stiffly. "Shit."

"What?" I ask.

He fingers the Plasma hanging above our dresser. "Ran out of memory. It's not automatically connecting to your microchip. Why can't it find you? Told you we should've gone with a different brand."

"Just plug the cable in," I say.

He yanks an audio-video interface cable from the dresser, wraps it around my neck. "Been naughty or nice?" He chuckles and lets it fall loosely around my shoulders.

"Both," I add for the fun of it.

Reality strikes me. I freeze, unable to move, as a cold draft of fear settles in my lungs, and I realize with rising panic that I will never escape this invasive ritual.

His thumb presses against my lip. "You taste like gunpowder," I whisper.

He smiles, inserts the stiff, cold, serpentine cable into a slim port sitting below the AI microchip that's fitted in the back of my neck. He inserts it the same way he uses his penis: mechanically, thoughtlessly. I jerk from the shock of the cable's cold, abrupt slurping of my memories straight into our Plasma's storage facility. Every morning, I have an AI assessment where my husband peruses my memory files. "That's why I married you—to keep you in line," he'd shoot off, laughing at his own joke.

The cable connects to the Plasma and transmits data recorded by my eyes from the past twenty-four hours, like Sunday movie night. He sits on the edge of the bed, gulps a cold beer, by the glow from the Plasma's screen. He rotates his finger. A silver remote clipped to his index finger fast-forwards through the scenes, rewinds, freezes the frame of a man at a conference, sitting next to me: honey-gold eyes, bronze skin, crew-cut crow-black hair, a tickle of flirtation in his smile. Janith Koshal. A smoking hot motherfucker. I remember his tongue decanting orgasms from my body.

Fuck. I must not think of him or else a detection alert will prompt Elifasi of the memory triggered by a rising heart rate, dilated eyes, and whatever the fuck bio signals are currently being transmitted. I slow my breathing, quickly recall the most mundane episode of taking the trash out from the kitchen, focusing my mind's eye on the garbage bag swelling with heaps of disposed food, the smudge of avocado on the sharp edge of canned beans, the stink of rotting meat—

"Nelah, who's that?" Elifasi asks, heating the air between us with a smog of jealousy.

"Mm, don't remember." I curl and uncurl my toes against the woolly carpet. "Jan-something. VC investor in construction tech. Our firm's using one of his entrepreneurs' products." Our usual chitter-chatter dinner of interrogation.

He follows my conversation with Jan, which echoes throughout our room like the pilot of a drama, cinematography crisp. Jan leans forward, caught in the golden dusk, taps his finger on my wrist, imparting a meeting into my calendar like nanobots into his bloodstream—it appears on the tiny screen on his wrist, and he smiles. "Then why does he want to meet you late at night?" my husband asks.

"Because I run an architectural firm," I say, masking the memory of our rendezvous with the mental image of the garbage bag in our kitchen. Eli stares at me, waiting for more. "It was a meeting for a project, and it wasn't late, it was at 5:00 p.m. He and *his wife* bought a stand in Mokolodi. They're looking for an architect to design an eco-conscious home for their ever-expanding family. And since I won the Architect of the Year Award for world-class sustainable designs, I'm the best architect for the job. Hence . . ." I point to the screen, exhausted from the amount of labor it takes to hide a secret, and sighing at the effort of having to always ad-lib lies.

"Oh . . ." Thumb against the remote, he presses play.

"You're supposed to scan my memory files for undetected infractions."

Elifasi shakes his head. It takes two hours of him scrolling through my memory files as I pass time by fiddling with the hologram 3D design for a museum that my firm will be presenting to a client this week. But I can't concentrate. I stare at him and wonder if every marriage is like ours: microchipped wives watching our husbands disembowel our thoughts and memories, dissecting our every infraction, interrogating us about our glances, our clothes, our conversations. Monitoring us for undetected crimes. Invading our privacy for the sake of public safety. My nails dig deep into my skin as a scream roils inside my throat—the scream, afraid to get out. We're not only losing the power of our bodies, we're losing the privacy our minds. What will be taken next for the sake of safety? This microchip protects our city, but it's the husbands', the city's, the government's tool to get inside us. My husband has the upper hand in our marriage, because I'm the one with a criminal body.

He stares at me, smiling, unaware of the volcano erupting within me. These intimate sessions mutilate my sense of independence; in this murdered church of my body, every molecule is a screaming prisoner.

I face our slim window. The horizon between the hills and sky is hazy as the sun continues burning like luminol through the city's air, activating chemicals leading to an untold crime. Which murderers or buried bodies still hiding in the nooks and crannies of the city will be found today?

It doesn't matter, as long as it's nothing to do with me.

Sometimes it turns me on, the gluey mixture of fear and pleasure in the minimal tactility Elifasi gives me when he connects me to our home system. It's our foreplay. After this, like always, we have sex. Pump, pump. Tap out in four strokes. Cum. Done. Unsatisfactory. My body's sexually frustrated. Elifasi stands, shakes himself out. "Finished. So far, you're pure."

Mxm, bastard. As if it's his dick that purifies me. No, I don't hate my husband—I just casually and occasionally call him a bastard, with . . . love. My thoughts might leak into our home cinema, leading to a long interrogation by my husband, the formidable Elifasi Bogosi-Ntsu, well known at the force for his scathing ability to gouge out the truth from the mouths of perpetrators, and even his wife.

He pulls on a dressing gown. "Next task."

We walk into our spacious closet, fitted with mirrored closet doors. A slim biometric scanner is embedded in one of them. I push aside my curtain of Senegalese braids, exposing the back of my neck and the microchip. He slides his hands down my bare arms, giving me chills, and presses my palm against the mirror. Its surface ripples, fibrillating into horizontal lines that break into patterns of sound waves as the AI microchip assessor's disembodied voice echoes through the closet in a monotone: "Dumêla, Nelah," she greets. "How are we feeling this morning?"

Her voice echoes through the room, but I stare steadfastly into the mirror. "Tired. Please scan my microchip."

The mirror launches into a series of questions that are meant to assess my responses. "Have you been feeling unlike yourself lately? Are you experiencing any sociopathic tendencies?" The vibrant blue sound wave patterns recede into the mirror.

"No," I say. The lines are steady. "No."

"Have you committed a crime that the microchip failed to detect?"

"No."

"Have you recently experienced unexplainable bursts of anger or other emotions?"

"No."

"Have you experienced any problems or malfunctions?"

"No."

"Good. You are required to obtain your next dose of medication from the Body Hope Facility within seventy-two hours."

"Thank you. I will do so."

"This is also a kind reminder that you have your forensic evaluation this Wednesday at 16:45."

How could I ever forget? It's my nightmare. "Thank you."

She's interrogated me before, in the days after I came home from the hospital after my consciousness was transplanted into this body. It felt just like the day after I gave birth to a stillborn child. Everything was sore and raw, my body thin and famished. She has a database of my physiological responses as benchmarks, and my current responses are charted on the mirror by an invisible needle. The needle moves erratically if I lie.

She reports my results: "Your physiological responses are steady and indicate no signs of deception."

I am perfect. I am innocent. I am pure.

MONDAY, AUGUST 10

08:00 /// THE BLACK WOMB

This is my third lifespan.

Since there's no record of an eviction for criminal reasons, the original owner of this body must have willingly evacuated these skin and bones at the age of eighteen for reasons I'm not privy to, but her parents continue to love me as if I'm their original daughter. The second host was evicted for a heinous crime. As per my country's criminal legal regulations, my body is fitted with a microchip that observes my behavioral patterns to deter criminal recidivism. It is an operating system, implanted in my brain stem to remotely control my body during criminal activities.

Privacy violations are rife on such bodies until their assessment confirms their purity, which can take anywhere from a couple of years to decades. My purity test is close, but we're neither given an exact date nor told what to expect, much like the forensic evaluation. Passing the purity test means I could ultimately be free of the microchip. I'm terrified that one tiny wrong move could destroy my chances. I need to be perfect. I need to be perfect. I *must* be perfect.

One day, I'll be free.

But how can I be free when my womb is a grave, killing any new life that tries to form, any seeds that my husband plants in it?

A black cloud hangs over me. We lost the fetus during our first round of IVF, and now we trundle about the house, broken and forlorn, having thrown all our savings at it. I didn't pay the alarming cost for mind transfer reincarnation to receive an infertile body with an artificial arm, even if it is a surgically attached, fully functional bionic prosthetic. I couldn't tell it apart from the rest of my body until my doctor peeled back the synthetic skin to show me, the first day I was revived. But I don't know why this arm was amputated; my parents won't tell me what happened to their first daughter in this body, so I don't know if it's the first or second daughter who lost this arm, or how. I feel robbed. I filed a report against the Body Hope Facility ("The Body Hope Facility. Body hop, body hope; we give every soul hope."), but it's in their indemnity clause, which allows them to supply bodies *they* deem in perfect condition, not what the host considers perfect; there's nothing I can do.

It's back to the old routine now, the ovulation alert waking us to morning darkness. Elifasi thought it'd be exciting to do it in the shower, the one thing we can vary, the only thing we can control in our lives. Suddenly he wasn't in the mood, so I said, "Just stick it in and cum. It's not like you ever last anyway." His mouth puckered. He hammered me. I leaned against the cold tiles, zoning out into an out-of-body experience. I was a robot; the sex was mechanical.

I'll need to work something out so he forgives me for my quippy remark.

I was pregnant before, for five months. Second trimester. We were glowing, more in love than ever. As a parent, all you think about is how you'll protect this newborn once it's outside the safety of your body. That's all we fussed about, purchasing nanny cams, baby monitors, an AI tool that would monitor his little breaths. A surgically installed GPS app tagged into his nervous system, just in case we lost him. I'd read terrifying stories of newly minted parents losing a baby, forgetting them at the mall. Such a horrid thing for a parent to do. That would never happen to us.

But we lost our little boy. Within the boundaries of my body. Inside me, not away from me, not forgotten in some random place, but right beneath my skin, below my heart.

You just never, ever think that your baby could die inside you and you wouldn't be able to tell. To be pregnant for five months—then to come home three nights after an emergency induced labor with an empty, scraped-out womb, holding that blanketed, precious stillborn—is devastating.

01:34, when the dead fetus was removed. Intrauterine fetal death, they called it. I gave birth to a dead child.

I have given birth to three dead children.

What was worse was that fed-up, "I don't know what's going on but something smells funny" look of betrayal my husband shot at me. "Really? You couldn't tell you were carrying a dead baby? *Our* baby. That you've been throwing money at the fertility center to have. Didn't you find it strange *he* wasn't kicking? For three fucking days. Jesus Christ, you killed my son."

The memory of it sends panic blazing through my body. I didn't drink, I didn't smoke, I didn't overwork. I ate healthy, I exercised mildly, I came home early. I did everything right. I paid my taxes, as if that should have a bearing on my fertility. My husband later apologized, but you can't erase what's said, what's done. Words leave a certain damage, just as much as a bullet in the flesh.

I'd stared at the fresh white lilies drone-delivered to our home, tagged with a note: *From the Koshal family. We're terribly sorry for your loss. Our family's hearts are with you. Anything you need, please don't hesitate to call.* Only, I know *he* sent it, not his wife, like she'd give a damn about my pregnancy loss. He must have done it behind her back—she'd never allow him to send another woman flowers. I know he meant it, too. I glare at my husband, and sometimes I wish he was another man named Janith Koshal.

I shuffle into work, sleepwalking out of the elevator. Jan's message is the first to come through. `Morning, had a dream about you last night. Link up?` I ignore it. I need to stay away from him. But we run in the same business circles, so we're bound to bump into each other. I married someone I *need* to stay loyal to. Jan's married, too, with twins, and that's what I envy, what he has, which makes me appreciate the natural way he flirts with me . . . It turns me on, turns *me*—the robot who's been malfunctioning for years—on. I hate to think this but

what if,
what if,
what if
Jan can impregnate me?

I know the doctors at the fertility center said I'm infertile, but that "what if" is making me think terrible things. Maybe, just maybe . . . it's not me who is malfunctioning, but Elifasi.

I lazily press my finger against the biometrics scanner. I yawn as the door buzzes me into the open-office plan of the glitzy Gaborone School of Architecture (GSA). I gulp down coffee that's not pumping any effective caffeine in my system. Most of my colleagues are hyped, but some are agitated about the board meeting regarding student marks, absences, failures . . .

My back stiffens when an early-bird student trudges in, one hand pressed against her arched, aching back. I'm teaching several courses as an architectural design lecturer. On the days I'm on campus, I see pregnant freshmen traipsing through hallways, courtyards, into our offices begging for marks and submitting late coursework. I want to scrape out the fire of pure anger that devours me with my nails and teeth. Because I *hate* it. I hate how easy it is for a child to have a child. They're too young to take care of themselves, let alone a baby. It's amazing how it happens: you just fuck and you're pregnant. The ease and simplicity is so foreign to me. As if my body is made to just have sex without leading to procreation, like I'm being punished for being successful in other areas of my life. In gossip rags that often demonize me for owning a criminal body, they started calling me the "Black Womb."

I came home one day to find my husband yelling at someone, who works at the latest culprit newspaper, over the phone. "So heartless," he screamed. "So despicable and insensitive of you, publishing clickbait articles on our pain, my wife's unimaginable pain, after all the humanitarian work she does."

Mxm, what a hypocrite. Everyone thinks he's the perfect husband, protecting me. It's not me he's protecting, it's his reputation. In the privacy of our home, no one sees him yell at me out of frustration over how embarrassing it is for *him* to have *his* wife's image shamefully spread across these news sites.

He doesn't care about my fucking tears. I'm just cheap, dirty laundry tarnishing his image.

At the table in my parents' backyard during our lunch are my parents, Limbani, and his wife. For the third time in a row my husband's absence is devastating, much to the pleasure of my brother. Jan's text buzzes in. My wrist itches with the neon-blue words: `1 UNREAD MESSAGE.`

> What are you afraid would happen if you responded? I am worried about you. Concerned. Forget my feelings for you. I just want to make sure you're okay.

Our relationship has been solely a two-year emotional affair that was only consummated once. After I crossed that boundary, I resisted ending up in bed with him again, and I thought he'd grow impatient, consider that fuck a conquest, and leave. Instead, we simmered in our reciprocal adorations, making me a sun of his world, his heart. I drew back, afraid of what we were becoming. I used to wonder, "Why's he still here? Men don't do that unless they think I'm an exciting challenge: the married woman who keeps saying 'no'." Even though I know that's never been true of Jan, to push him away, I childishly respond in a fit of frustration:

> Find a fuck-buddy elsewhere.

Just as I'm about to switch my phone off, his message comes through: `My wife started off as my fuck-buddy, I learned my lesson there. I'm not just attracted to how beautiful you are, I'm attracted to your intelligence, the work you've done in this industry.`

My heart stops in my throat when his last message comes through: `I'm getting a divorce. Not for you or anyone. For me.`

So the rumors are true. How brave he is, I think—which is strange.

Why do I think that? Do I want to leave my husband? Am I a coward then, for staying in this marriage?

Pouring himself wine, my brother, Limbani, continues his incessant verbal attacks on me whilst the rest of my family tiptoes around any mention of babies. Limbani was furious when he overheard me call *his* sister's body infertile. I was broken, confiding in Mama. He called me ungrateful, a stupid, spoiled brat for disrespecting his sister. He will never *ever* accept me.

Limbani slices into a piece of his medium-rare steak, and I stare squeamishly as blood oozes onto the white porcelain plate. He scrubs the blood clean with a cushion of meat, chucks it into his mouth, and says, "With the astounding advancement of science—we can even upload our consciousnesses into other bodies!—there's just no scientific reason for a woman to be unable to have kids. It just doesn't make sense. My wife's been brilliant so far. Given me three healthy kids. Isn't that right, babe?" He glances at her with a smirk. She looks terribly uncomfortable, busying herself with getting salad.

"Nana," Mama says as she places her hand over mine, the other cradling a cup of rooibos tea. "Isn't there a way for the doctors to perhaps transplant the consciousness of the stillborn child into another body?"

Limbani laughs, and he's got the yak incessantly flowing in his wine glass, tipsy as fuck. "God, Mama, no one's donating newborns as body supplies! They're too young and not eligible for the process."

"Well, couldn't they transplant your baby's consciousness into an older body? Maybe a teenager's body." She stares around the large table, but everyone avoids eye contact with her. "Aren't they supplying them nowadays, huh mogatsaka?" She turns to Papa, who looks just as uncomfortable as the rest of us, unable to offer her a lifeline.

"Ja nè. Maybe she can't fool her body like she fools us," my brother's voice booms, and I close my eyes waiting for the blitzkrieg. "Maybe, like I've been saying, they pumped a man into my sister's body." His sister's body is my body. *My* body. "I'm right, ain't I? You're a man under that skin. It's all unnatural." He points his fork at me. "And because of that, you angered the ancestors. They must be punishing you by not allowing you to have kids. A life for a life."

"Hae, Limbani," Mama admonishes him.

"Your husband has been childless for how many years now?" Limbani asks, looking up with bright eyes alert with happiness. "No surprise that the poor man's still stuck in the same position while his male colleagues are earning promotions just as much as their wives are churning out babies. No one promotes a man without a family. I'm surprised he's stuck around this long. Probably wise to do so since a divorce may tarnish his image more than being childless."

He hates me more than the devil, but that's low, celebrating the fact that innocent babies have lost their lives. *My* babies. Celebrating the fact that my husband has never earned a promotion, the fact that that has affected us financially, yet my parents *still* won't give me access to my inheritance. Is this what my parents think of me, too?

There's a deep overwhelming sadness within me as everyone avoids my eyes, which intensifies my desperate need to belong and, as a traditional set-up family that has never experienced body-hopping into strangers' lives, my family is unable to understand me—after all, they've created stronghold ties with Limbani since he was a fetus. I've never had that privilege. Even though I was placed into a program at eighteen to socialize with other young body-hoppers to dispel this feeling of loss, loneliness, and family fractures that comes with body-hopping, it still failed to fill in that void and grief that sits between my family members like a sibling. The government was wary that a fractured family creates a fractured society, which creates a destroyed nation. Several local organizations created communities to offer a sense of place for people who were transplanted into teenaged or adult bodies, having lost the pivotal formative years to connect to childhood friends and families and grow those relationships organically. Because we understand each other's experience and lack of roots, we were able to find within each of us a sense of home. It is that very program where I met some of my best friends, like Keabetswe, who I fondly call Kea.

"I mean, look around the table," he continues. "Where's your husband? Always busy. Always absent. Only a *real* woman can keep a man around."

I leap forward, fueled by loss and anger, my knee crushing the center of the chocolate cake. "You misogynistic bastard!" There's a knife in my hand, raised to stab him. My other hand wraps around his throat, which is laced with childhood scars. He cackles. Maybe that's how he got those marks, not from wriggling through a church's fence and getting his neck snagged like everyone says. Maybe, one day, someone got sick and tired of him, and slashed his neck with knives. If only they'd managed to kill him.

Mama screams. Grabs the hem of my dress. "Nelah, please!"

Limbani is startled when tears crawl down my face.

"What? Didn't you think I could cry? I never took *your* sister's life away. Her body was given to me. Live with it."

I walk out and never come back for any more of the family lunches my poor, sweet mother holds.

I am the Black Womb; everything I touch erodes.

Our last hope, our last resort, is Wombcubator specialist Dr. Nnete Senatla, an obstetrician-gynecologist and fertility researcher near Rasesa Village at the Matsieng Fertility Fund, the site of water-well wombs that allegedly influence the Murder Trials.

We're thirty minutes early at the forty-nine-hectare heritage site, so we make our way to Matsieng's creation grounds. Verdant lawns separate it from the Matsieng Fertility Fund. In the distance, koppies lull the land, whilst expansive blue skies are smeared with few cirrus clouds and too much sun. The path we take rises to become the green roof of the custodian's brick-faced office, covering it with veld for the dry, arid climate. Opposite it is the paved food court where smoke rises from sizzling boerewors; vendor stalls fry magwinya, fries, noodles, and stews jam-packed with hot spices as a line of chattering people wait to purchase some bunny chows. We pass by a huddled group of sweaty varsity students who are bickering over their brochures in Seherero. Eli and I make our way done a narrow path lined with thorny trees that leads to the rocky outcropping sheltered by jackalberry trees. The rocks swirl across the site in strata of browns and reds, and punched into them are the deep grooves of shapeless openings. Nearby stands a young man with a patted-down Afro, button-down shirt and corduroy pants tied high above his waist with a worn-out belt. He recites the history of the site whilst pointing to the deep crevices.

"This is where a colossal fearsome female god climbed out of this waterhole," he says in a Sengwato dialect to a family of five Batswana, "bringing with Xem the first ancestors of our tribes, straight from the earth's womb. This is why we refer to these as waterwombs."

Eli leans back, hands deep in his pockets, listening with amusement.

I peer into the chasmic craters, but only darkness echoes back. Matsieng ascended from the amniotic underwater of earth's womb, birthing our autochthonous tribes, guiding their passage as they clambered out of this crater, scarring the surface with their footprints. Most natives, though, believe that it was a large one-legged man and not a woman, whilst others concur that whatever crept from the craters was a non-binary god.

"There used to be only two waterholes, but over the years, more mysteriously appeared already impregnated by unknown phenomena," the guide continues. "People come from all over the world to collect this water, sometimes hued pink, like diluted blood, to sell and use for ritual purposes. The waters are very sacred and are essential to many rituals, blessing believers with miracles."

"Sacred water, nè?" Eli muses. "So what has this water gotten you?" I nudge him because he's staring at the guide in a judgmental way, as if to say, "If this water were so holy, why are you so poor, with a job like this?" Eli sometimes forgets that his privilege obstructs him from perceiving other people's struggles.

"You're one of the skeptics, nè?" the guide asks, staring at Eli with raised bushy eyebrows, flecked grey-white. "Terrible situations often turn people like you into believers. I do wish you well, but let's hope you don't meet that predicament."

His warning sends a shiver trembling down my spine. Eli, however, seems unperturbed. The imprints embedded in the rocks are footprints of animals and people. But Eli wrinkles his nose at the petroglyphs. "Aren't these cartoon sketches made by herdsmen of those times?" The family observes us with irritation; I'm burning in embarrassment.

"He's referring to the other myths that dispute this creation folklore," I say by way of apology.

The guide shakes his head, tutting. "Sometimes if you touch these marks, you can still feel powerful energy reverberate through this rock."

"Maybe I should have a sip of that. I could become a billionaire, nè?" Eli whispers, clutching his belly as he chuckles.

I glance at him in reprimand. "Eish, be more respectful, will you? Besides, the administrators of the Murder Trials believe in this for some odd reason."

Eli shakes his head, rolling his eyes. "Fucked up shit, I tell you." He stops. "Why are you looking at me like that?"

"I'm now realizing why no one would ever take you to church."

The guide raises his hands to an elderly man joining us, the sun glistening on the newcomer's chiskop haircut. "The world of Matsieng's era had neither death nor disease. After some time, Xe returned back to this waterwomb, cursing our vices with death and illness. Despite that, we are tied to this land and, regardless of how far we travel, this land is our ancestors' dialect."

"So this god-thing lies buried deep beneath the earth?" Eli asks with a smirk. "For how many millennia is that now?

Why must women—even powerful ones—always live out our existences buried? Why remain beneath the earth with all that power? Maybe Matsieng's been restrained, or Xe's waiting for something. *I'm crazy if I believe in this.*

I point farther ahead to a secluded path leading to a curved roof supported by tusklike columns, white as clean bone. "What's there?"

The custodian cranes his neck. "The Murder Trials Section, but that's for authorized access only."

"Do the waterholes stretch back that far?" I ask.

He shrugs. "Can't say." He turns, walks away whistling. What do the Murder Trials have to do with the rest of the waterholes? Wisps of shadowy smoke rise above the tree line, and they sound like voices. I shake myself out of my trance. Smoke has no voice. It's only the chattering of the crowd of people surrounding us.

Eli tugs me by the shoulder and we walk back to the Matsieng Fertility Fund, a white-ash building clad in concrete that folds in and around its internal spaces like a shell. It reminds me of why I love architecture, the breath of the past held in the present. From the revolving doors, the specialist waves to us. She ushers us in through the spacious lobby, down wide reflective hallways and into a cavern-like facility.

"My womb is a minefield," I tell Nnete as we stand within the facility's vast underground gestation space. "It blows up any existing fetus."

Elifasi wraps his arm around me. "My wife is a cynic. We wanted to forego the artificial route, but that proved futile."

Nnete gives a warm smile, full of understanding sadness. "Historically, women carried babies to term. That's declined exponentially over the years. We curate an embryo using IVF and transplant the embryo into our Wombcubator, which is our term for artificial wombs." Nnete points out the Wombcubators: minuscule oval spaceships hanging in deep-set alcoves in the walls, each accompanied by an intimate set of beechwood tables and armchairs upholstered in muted colors. Close to a hundred Wombcubators across all floor levels. They glow two colors: amber and blue. The former signals that something is wrong—perhaps a lack of nutrients or technological errors—to the observing doctors and scientists, whilst the latter indicates that the system is functioning perfectly. "The Wombcubator is AI- and human-monitored—nothing ever goes wrong. You'll be able to monitor the fetus's vitals and growth through visual feeds linked to your cell phones and other devices, which will allow you to see and talk to the baby remotely."

She shows us around the facility, adding occasional explanations. "The fetus develops in a controlled Synthuterus environment. We emulate the climate of the womb through controlled dosages and nutrients." She pauses at a station of triplets hovering in amber liquid within their Wombcubator, taps a series of instructions onto its screen and the liquid changes to blue. "Our technology can control the biological clock, speeding up cell activity to reduce the length of telomeres to that of a required age. Our technology accounts for bone therapy and brain development—all very extensive genetic manipulation. Our machinery will sequence your genomes to read and optimize your DNA, to eliminate diseases and disabilities. If you want to fully edit your child, to control how they look and what they like—"

"No," I whisper, tracing my fingers on the cold glass. "I want them to be who they are, not what *we* want."

"But, babe, we could have a genius," Elifasi says.

"God gave you free will. Why must we take it away from another being just because we can?" I say. "That is too superficial."

My husband rolls his eyes. "You need to get with the times. You can't fuse science and religious dogma. We're having an artificial birth—now you're talking about God. We threw God out the window the minute we stepped into this facility." His eyes skirt Nnete's face before he quickly pulls me off to the side. "I only want our child to have a better quality of life, and sons tend to have that more than daughters. Having a daughter is risky, and male heirs fare better in carrying the family line than a girl would."

I lean forward, my eyes gazing deep into his irises to discern the meaning of his words. "Would you love our child less if it were a girl?"

He pinches his nose, closes his eyes tight in frustration. Opens them, clenches his teeth. "Look at your holier-than-thou Bogosi family preaching morality and fairness yet hampering you from your inheritance even though your brother long gained access to his when he turned twenty."

"They said I can only access it when they pass away," I say.

"Oh, for God's sake, woman, they don't trust you. *You* need the money desperately, but your family won't lift a finger to give it to you. This body has changed hosts twice so far—they don't trust you enough to tell you the truth about this arm that you lost," he says, tapping my bionic arm. "What makes you think they trust you'll stay in this body until it expires? They're probably waiting for another host to replace you. That inheritance is tied back because it'll never come to you." He leans in close, his words a soft whisper: "Do you think our son would love you any less because of this? Not care for you when you're old?"

I dig my nails into my palms. I know I will always be a stranger to my brother and parents, hence the sole reason Eli and I wanted to start our own family, one we chose the same way we chose each other, loving each other unconditionally, unlike the Bogosi family I was placed into without their choice. It will bring more meaning to me in this lifespan where all I've wanted was a family that loved me back. To give a child the life I wished I had, to have that love reflected back to me.

I stare up at Eli. "What does any of this have to do with the gender of our child?"

He presses his hands against my arms. "Sons fare better in the forensic evaluations than daughters. Do you want your daughter to go through the same fears you face? Nelah, babe, we have no memories to remember the families we lost in our previous lifespans. Lost memories, lost loved ones—how about we avoid more losses? Having a big family was always our plan. Let's have a son first; we can always have more children once we've sorted out our finances. At least then we know the male heir will always protect his younger siblings."

"And what makes you think that our daughter won't be capable of protecting her siblings?" I ask.

"When we got together, your body was valued low because of its criminal past, this bionic arm, and this microchip," he says, enunciating his words as if sharpening each one and driving it into my heart, and I almost collapse from the weight of it. He continues, "That lowered your chances of marriage—people are never interested in walking into a scenario with a partner who has a wiretapped body that has a criminal past. Such a mother's history will tarnish your daughter's standing in society more than it would our son. She may not be as lucky as you in finding a partner. Women are more forgiving of men than other people are of women, in marriage and at work. I married you. I gave you a chance—give me a son, asseblief tuu."

My mouth slacks open, and my posture slouches, resigning me to disappointment. Disappointment at Eli for stooping this low to use the history of my body against me. Disappointment at me for thinking married life would be perfect and full of unconditional love. I've invested time and myself to this marriage. Should I consider his comment as spur-of-the-moment desperate thinking? We're this close to getting the family we want. Should I let this one comment be an obstacle to that? I can't. I can't. I won't bite back with abrasive banter. I will be the bigger person. For our future child.

"Our child is not even conceived, yet we've already rejected them if they are a girl," I say. "How different are we from the Bogosi family if we'll reject a baby that has no history and has done no wrong except be a girl? Isn't that why we wanted to start a family? To be different from the families we were brought into?"

Eli casts his eyes lower, a quirk of his when I'm winning him over. He twists his mouth, chews at his cheek. "I'm not a father yet, and I'm already doing a shoddy job." He lowers his head, curling his arms around me. "Let's leave it to chance. We'll love this child regardless of who they become. We'll protect them."

In the end, we sign over our entire savings account, a mortgage, and a loan. Although we have received a discount given Eli's government job offering benefits for family planning, maintaining a Wombcubator requires an obscene amount of money. IVF was affordable on both our incomes, which we did three times. The Wombcubator is several times the cost of IVF considering that there are daily running expenses to maintain the fetus for a whole nine months. Besides the sign-up fee, the Wombcubator's running fees are equivalent to paying the operating fees of my firm on a monthly basis. But it's worth it all to have our child. And twelve weeks later, there, our little baby floating in their Wombcubator. I convinced Eli to waive our right to choose the gender so we'll be surprised by the reveal. And it's a girl!

But I still feel the chill of Dr. Senatla's warning: "The Wombcubator has a kill switch should anything go wrong with either the development of the baby, or late payments." That's all I can think about. I can't lose another baby. "Failure to pay the charges and monthly medical bills means you lose ownership of your daughter, which will automatically give us the authorization to either terminate the pregnancy or foster it for the Body Hope Facility's supply chain—that's if it can fit in their annual budget."

Her latter statement sends a chill up my spine. Because there are many consciousnesses on the waiting list, it'd be a waste to discard an original prime body, which is expensive to grow, instead of appropriating existing bodies like mine that fall low on the body-hopping grading scale, given the body's history. So rather than turn off Wombcubators, the government confiscates fetuses it takes from prospective parents, nurtures them for several years, and uses those bodies to increase the body supply and therefore lower the wait times for a new body.

The younger and more original the body, the more valuable it is.

Transplanting those on the waiting list onto our existing bodies is cheaper. Still, the demand for such bodies is lower because, like my body, the problems are numerous: infertile, amputated arm, criminal. Whereas the biology of an original body can be tampered with during the procreation stage, such that it's free of errors, which is a callous perspective. I can only imagine before that as a Black woman, one was oppressed thrice: that they are not white, a man, and worse, they are Black, and add to that the layer of disability, being the third owner of a body that was so young, since the value of a body goes down if it has endured a few consciousness transplants. It's the trite version of women considered sluts because they've had multiple sex partners. Being myself seems to be a life of navigating landmines in my family, professional life, and my marriage to Elifasi.

If we lose our daughter, her body will be fodder for those on the waiting list. If the budget allows, her consciousness will be placed in one of Body Hope's foster homes until it reaches the legal age to be independent to obtain a low-valued body, provided a sum of money, and thrown out into the world to survive. I can't imagine my daughter suffering the same fate as mine because of our misdemeanors as parents, inheriting our punishments for a crime she didn't commit only because she's our child. I can't let that happen. She's not even born, yet she lives a risky life. We'll be out of the grey if life can move smoothly and perfectly until she's born. At least then, if anything happens, the government can't take her away from us; my parents will take care of her.

"Maybe things will start looking up in my career," Eli says, "perhaps *finally* I will get that promotion." I thought our family would be a treasure to my husband rather than marriage and children serving as stepping stones to get ahead in his career. Is that why he got married? Is that why he's only interested in having a child? Is he doing all this for his job? Sometimes, I think, he wields more power than he gives the impression of because his position has no access to that high level of influence. Sometimes I think he can't resist the ease of surreptitiously stealing power in whatever room he finds himself in and hiding it to use later. Oh, how can I believe this of my husband? He's not perfect, but he's not that deceitful, too. No, I won't let my thoughts deter us from celebrating this moment. I know how painful it's been for him to watch his colleagues rise in the ranks and leave him behind. I should support him as he supported me and my firm. Finally, we'll have the life and family we've always wanted. My husband hugs me. "Life's working out for us, isn't it? The baby. Our perfect home. Our perfect family."

It is in my third lifespan, but deep down, I must confide in myself that I am relieved I don't have to carry my children; it removes my fears of pregnancy and childbirth. I used to find it strange when some of my girlfriends looked forward to being pregnant several times. I can't believe I thought it obligatory just because I had a womb and never once interrogated that yes, I had the power to say, "No, I'm not interested in carrying a baby to term." I mentioned it subtly to Mama and she considered me selfish and cold, and she wondered how I could love a child if I were incapable of loving them with my body, and I knew then that it was strange, foreign, and uncouth of me as a woman to think like this, what I shared with her in confidence that she must have told my brother, who added more vitriol by interrogating my true gender.

So what if I was a man before I got transplanted into this body? Is it really that bad? And aren't souls genderless? So I groomed myself to accept this traditional role because I was retrofitted for it. I kept quiet and pretended to love this womanhood that was not mine to wear, that only fit too tightly, leaving me breathless. Is that why I had an affair? Because I had power in something? Sometimes I realize that perhaps it's Mama's grief speaking from losing her daughter; she'd cry sometimes, whispering, "You don't know what we went through, it was hell. She shouldn't have died like that." I wonder if she meant the second or first host, but she'd offer no more information.

Perhaps I'm not that different from my husband. Marriage and having a child protect me from the harsh judgment of society and create an image of me that is respectable and allows me to have it all, and my way of thinking doesn't remove how deeply I'll love my children.

However, I'll grapple with society's idea that I must take time off work to provide childcare for years. I want a successful career, a family, and power. I want it all like my husband wants it all—only he gets applauded, and I get condemned for wanting *too* much. Is it so wrong to want it all because I'm a woman? Am I suddenly inhuman and without those desires? I wish they'd stop seeing me as a woman, and maybe then I'd be free to be what I want.

In our bedroom, I extract a hologram feed from my watch that pulls up visuals from the Matsieng Fertility Fund. I stare at the subterranean Wombcubator pod. Beneath the flesh of the glass lies my little sweetheart's heartbeat. It's like ordering a meal, then fetching it once it's fully cooked. A plaque below the pod glows, reading: *28 WEEKS REMAINING UNTIL I AM BORN*. I trace the edges of the transparent hologram with my fingers and watch my hand bleed through the hologram's projection.

WEDNESDAY, SEPTEMBER 2

16:45 /// AN OCEAN OF SHADOWS

Dark clouds scud the sun's face. My looming doomsday is here: my forensic evaluation. In the gloomy, towering Gaborone Police Precinct.

Elifasi stands with me in the waiting room. Not being helpful, irritated by my anxiety. "Need I remind you how your body is dangerous?" He clinches my shoulder. "It belonged to at least one previous convict, indicted for money laundering, kidnapping, and murder. What if you wake up one night and kill your own child? There are still traces of that criminal inside you."

"Fuck, you make me sound like I'm sick," I say.

"You *are* sick."

Those three words hit harder than I expected.

"Unless . . ." He spins me around, stares at me with hurt in his eyes. "Did you do something?"

"Of course not."

"If you're stuck in a tough spot, it's better we figure it out together."

"Really, Mr. Assistant Commissioner of Police? You wouldn't handcuff me and take my body in, and then have a new wife living in my body the next day?"

They'd be an adult, allowed to divorce him. But what's to say one wouldn't remain married to him, to wear my life and fortune? It is legal, and it terrifies me that I could lose my marriage, my business, my entire life to another woman. Like a side-bitch taking your husband, your body, and kicking you out of your house and business, taking your child as you sit mum in a disk.

He scoffs. "I could think of better ways to revive our sex life with handcuffs than arresting you."

I grimace, sink my mind into anxiety. Our sex life is the least of my worries. A lifespan is composed of several body-hop seasons, each running a max of seventy years. On the 210-year mark of every lifespan, EMTs collect you early in the morning, and a registered doctor suctions out your consciousness onto their Mind-Cell disks. Thereafter, if the body is still young, below seventy years, another consciousness is transplanted into it. Each body-hop season allows the host options to assimilate into their new body's family and to either retain or forfeit their previous season's family.

I met Elifasi when I was twenty-four, got married at twenty-five within our current season. I stare at him, trying to figure out how he's become a cold stranger over the years. This is his fifth lifespan, second body-hop. After he expired the seventy years of his first-season body, he opted not to rekindle the relationship with his first-season family and sixty-year-old wife, which prompted an instant divorce. Instead, he chose to integrate into his second-season family. During one of our date nights, I was utterly shocked when he casually pointed out that sixty-year-old ex-wife to me, an old timid waitress at a restaurant. She had no authorized access to his new identity, didn't know that she was serving her ex-husband a platter of seswaa, loleme, and madombi with gravy.

He has the privilege of memory, yet he forfeited everything—his grandchildren and nephews—said the family was bad news. But how bad could they be to deserve that? Would he do that to me, too? If I fail today, could he just as easily move on tomorrow?

If I could remember my previous families, I'd cling to them with every bit of my soul.

I finger the cold metal in my neck, desperate to scrape it out with my nails. Think of it as a grenade. Take out the top and it detonates. Detonates there in your brain, and you're brain-dead. Gone. No DNR through a consciousness transplant. It's a cold shutdown, a crashing of the system. Some have ended their lives that way . . .

But I'm always so distracted about being mind-incarcerated for a predicted crime that I never stop to think: What if the forensic evaluation predicts me as a victim and finds it insignificant to tell me because it's not as worthy as me committing a crime? We're always valued on what we do and not who we are. Would the forensic panel even reveal to me who might be my murderer? If I'm not blamed for the crime, one day I will be blamed for being a victim. I will be a statistic. Blamed for my own murder simply because I was either underdressed or veiled my skin and boobs.

"One day," I whisper my thoughts to Eli, "I will be at the wrong place at the wrong time and get murdered. It's always our fault. I feel *so* helpless, *so* powerless."

"Times have changed." Eli touches my shoulder, and his thumb grazes my neck, making me shiver. "This microchip's not just for society's protection; it's for your protection, too. You will never be a victim."

"Is it really protecting me or monitoring me?" I ask, anxiety making my voice crack. "Of course, I've to worry. The number of women incarcerated is higher than men, the evaluation is harsher on us whilst men get away with so much shit—"

"Oh, God, don't start with that whole gender equality crap. Don't you think we've lost out as well? Sacrificed to give you what you want: all these fucking rights y'all are always crying about. When will you all be satisfied? Always complaining, always taking. The men are found guilty, too."

"Not often enough," I growl, surprising myself with the coldness in my voice. This frustrating truth never fails to erode my gut.

"If that's how you feel."

"It's not how I feel. It's statistically true. *It* is happening," I say, tears stinging my eyes. "Now we have an AI machine to assess which one of us it gets rid of and which one stays. And who stays, exactly? The pliant ones? The ones who won't fight back?"

"The forensic evaluation gets rid of criminals. *It* has made our city safe."

My voice shakes. "Safe for whom, exactly? The men who can now get away with everything?"

"What's wrong with you?" Elifasi eyes me suspiciously.

"You don't have to fear anything, like a microchip or the Murder Trials," I say, swallowing the sick feeling in my mouth.

"For this type of security, isn't it worth giving a bit of your privacy once a year to the forensic panel?"

The evaluation room: concrete floors, concrete walls, with one glass wall overseeing the misty city. In its center stands a human-sized, onyx-colored glass house, facing a forensic panel. The words on its gold plaque glint: *AI Criminal Behavior Evaluator (CBE)*, notoriously known as a hound that, through simulation, sniffs out traces of sociopathic tendencies in the blood, in the gene. Predicts the crime. Sees the crime. Tells the crime. A reel of motion picture film, reeling out your ocean of shadows and punishing you for it. All because this AI machine tells on you 100 percent without error. What could possibly be worse?

I swallow hard. My footsteps falter toward a workstation, which holds four seven-inch, wrist-sized, thick metal restraints.

A young woman, kohl-lined eyes, black hair clasped into a bun, shakes my hand. "Dr. Farahani. I'll be overseeing your simulation today."

I glance at my distended reflections dancing on the surface of the assessment chamber's compact glass house. I blink. Reflections are steady as hell. My hands have a viselike grip on my arms, my thoughts stick with a clingy anxiety to my skull. I want to flee. I want to ram my head against the wall. I want to slam through the glass walls of the police precinct and fall fifty-five floors down, splat to the ground. Anything to avoid my evaluation. I've seen confident people walk into evaluation rooms only to be immediately evacuated from their bodies because they failed.

Someone clears their throat. I look up. The forensic panel, sat like bored brown mannequins, fits into the shadow of a wall across a long table. The Honorable Judge Rorisang Moitshepi, criminal profiler Aref Sayed, forensic anthropologist Percy Nkile, and prosecutor Serati Zwebathu, overlooking a hologram screen that will transmit my simulation. These are friends, mostly my husband's, who've come to our home for weekend *braais*, chuckling over glasses of wine. These are uncompromising and ruthless, justice-seeking people who could easily sentence their own blood, their own children, to abide by the law. It makes me wary. Close friends will bear witness to the intimate parts of my life.

A young man with dreadlocks busies himself at his transcribing station, which will record my simulation conversations much like a confession.

I grip the chamber's framing, the metal sickly cold. Why did they give me Serati? Her questioning techniques infinitesimally slip through the simulation into the evaluatee's loved ones' speech, using emotion to extract a confession. After all, don't we trust our closest friends with some of our deepest, darkest secrets? The affairs we're having, the car we accidentally veered into in the parking lot and left without notification, the times we had to skive work for a potential job interview. How long would it take you to spill your guts to your best friend, your lover, your confidante because of the inability to endure the overwhelming, unbearable weight of a secret? It's very hard to trust in the real world when the simulation is just the same.

One question. One trigger. And I could spill my crimes. Even those I've yet to commit.

I swallow. Study them. Serati. Shorn hair. Light-brown skin. Bright, wide eyes. No makeup. No earrings. Full, plump lips patted with beige. A soft, quiet beauty often depicted in tones of rage in the media, a beauty that buries us, a beauty that audiences long to replicate through incisions, surgeries, injections.

The ventilation system hums and sings through the glow-lit ceiling as Dr. Farahani clasps the thick rings of metal restraints around my wrists and ankles. They're cold and heavy.

"Don't be nervous," she says, causing my eyes to veer from Serati.

"There are chains inside that will magnetically connect to these restraints. For your safety."

"Or in case I become . . . difficult?"

She smiles. "You've nothing to fear."

"Dr. Farahani is right," Serati says, approaching us. "We do everything through Matsieng. We acquire peace through Xem. Matsieng understands your blood intimately; if you were dangerous, Xe would've flagged you to the Murder Trials. *You* are one of the safe microchipped people."

I shiver. Why is Serati referring to Matsieng as if Xe were a government employee assessing microchipped people, determining which to report to the Murder Trials? "What does my blood have to do with that folklore?" I ask. "What do you mean by that?"

Serati smiles, evades my question. "This evaluation may feel like a nightmare, but from the nightmare comes heaven."

She rejoins her colleagues, but her words leave me cold and empty. It doesn't matter if you haven't committed a crime in the now or the past. The CBE knows if you *will* commit a crime in the future. Which fucks me up every time. You know every detail of your current lifespan's past, but how can you know your future? How can you even prepare to pass this evaluation? To trick it in the same way it tricks reality?

Forensic evaluations start at age sixteen. The original owner successfully passed two, the second host failed one, and I have passed eight. A good record for eight years. A model citizen. Yet why do I have this paralyzing anxiety?

Dr. Farahani tilts her head. "It's protocol that I read you the process of what happens to your body hereafter. If the CBE simulation indicates your future self committing a crime, you have forfeited your right as a citizen of Botswana to receive a new body. Your current body will be considered unusable and a liability to the country's safety; it will be cremated. After our forensic transcriber has noted down your confession, your body will be transferred to the theatre of Utopia Hospital—which is on the sixth floor Wing E of this building—where your consciousness will be transferred to the Crypt Prison, virtually incarcerated, and tortured forever. For the Security of Society."

The Crypt Prison is a tower on the northern side of the city containing mainframes and servers of minds that have been uploaded, some in a virtual prison, others on a waiting list, all in the same building. They are stored in sleek black disks with intricate, honeycomb designs tucked into a wall. What would be my eternal new home.

"But if your crime is minor," Dr. Farahani says, "given the history of this body, you will be provided with one year of intense therapy, after which, should this repeat, nothing can be done except to evacuate you."

I remind myself that as much as the CBE predicts the future, it is not me. I know the real me, not a machine. But what if I don't really know myself? What if using machines is the only way we can find out who we really are? No, I *know* myself.

Dr. Farahani lowers her head, eyes peering at me above the rim of her glasses. "As a reminder, should the forensic evaluation become faulty—which is very rare—we will remedy that."

My knees tremble, and I grab the workstation's counter for stability. This information never fails to spark terror, liquefying my muscles.

She reassures me with a consoling touch to my shoulder. "A body-hop season only occurs on two occasions: once you reach seventy, and any age before seventy when you undergo a natural death or an accident leaves you with only a couple of hours to save your consciousness. Should that happen today, you'll be instantly given a body if you haven't expired your two hundred and ten years of your lifespan."

I have time: 182 years remain before my lifespan expires. But what if something goes wrong in the evaluation and they give me a body with worse conditions than this one? I can't breathe, can't swallow. Something's stuck in my throat.

"Take a deep breath," she says. "It's going to be okay. Of course, you do have the option to forfeit your body, seeing that this is your first season."

I glare at her. Some insane people donate their bodies like they're spare kidneys. Others sell them for monetary reasons, preferring to sacrifice the years waiting for a body. The money would be registered to them, managed by an investor, so once they start their new lifespan, it's with good returns waiting for them. That's the typical strategy of first- and second-year lifespanners as well as first- and second-season body-hoppers and those who turn eighteen, the legal age to sell.

"No," I say, rage seething inside me. "I have an unborn daughter whom I intend to be with."

Dr. Farahani's forced smile is cold and off-putting. I slow my breathing as I watch her tap a syringe filled with an opaque blue liquid. I gasp as she plunges the needle into my neck. Then: "This way," Dr. Farahani says, clip-clopping to one side of the chamber's wall that faces the forensic panel. She points to a slim opening in the cubicle's façade. "Please put your hand here for biometrics data collections."

I steer my eyes from this vitreous den of claustrophobic terror as I slip my hand between the warm LED lights that ferry away my data into her file, updating it of any changed information since last year's session. I stare warily at the glass chamber's venous wiring network sandwiched between two planes of glass. It is retrofitted with amenities: a basic toilet, shower, and bed. You can stand or sleep as it assesses you. The simulation can last hours to months. "Some patients aren't as forthcoming as we'd like them to be," is what they told me the first time. "They need time. So let us in, and we'll let you out. That's the deal."

Let them in, and it's over.

Nowhere to run, except through it.

The doors hiss open. I step inside. The froth of darkness embalms me as the door clicks into place, locking automatically. I jerk back at the astounding number of people inside: women stuck in the walls, staring at me in terror. Women identical to me. I'm surrounded by mirrors. Except it's one-way. I can't see out, only in—within myself. I hate the thought of that. Step back to get out. Only no handle on the door. Just a sheet of mirror feeding the image of myself back to me, telling me this time I can't run away from myself. I ease my face closer to the mirror, inspecting the slate-black wiring running beneath its skin, a delicate system of mechanical arteries that will somehow inhale my essence and provide feedback. It consumes the data that my body emits and shits out a strictly candid doppelganger. It's the place where perpetrators vomit confessions. Sweat prickles my armpits as a charge singes through the chamber. My arms flick downward, pulled heavily by the force of the metal restraints driving toward the chains tied to the ground. I fall to my knees.

A quiet hum. Then a voice and neon-blue lights: "I stare at my husband, and sometimes I wish he was another man named Janith Koshal." I jump at the sound of my voice, rereading my thoughts from two days ago. Fuck. The recording pauses; darkness becomes. Soft anger flows in this voice-lit cubicle; a channel of my thoughts, my feelings, my beliefs feeds through it like the flow of blood. The veins of the cubicle glow neon blue, pulsating to the pitch and pace of my voice as a bomb of thoughts and emotions explode inside me:

what if,

what if,

what if

Jan can impregnate me?

And I hate it. I hate how easy it is for a child to have a child.

"You misogynistic bastard." There's a knife in my hand, raised to stab Limbani.

I am the Black Womb, everything I touch erodes.

Darkness torpedoes the room, plunging me into a swirl of fear.

The walls tremble, buckle, shake loose of today's reality.

I scream, trying to hold on to my reality. "I'm not a criminal. I'm not a criminal. I'm not . . ."

But darkness swells into my sight; an ocean of shadows swallows me into a simulation.

Time has wilted; the day is grey. I'm standing in line at the Body Hope Facility, commonly known as the Body Hop Facility. Everyone moves with the pace of water. The mirrored walls reflect a light-brown woman, Senegalese braids fastened into a top knot. Me. The walls are muted colors and speak nothing. When I stare out the large-paned windows, there is no sun, just clouds skirting by like a massive ice floe.

The line heaves forward. "Your prescription, please," a bodiless voice behind the glassed dispensary compartment says. I press my hand on the screen. A blue light zips up and down, reading the fingerprint-tagged prescription. In several seconds, my medication is dispensed from the sliding glass partition. I step aside, a foggy mind, though something important floats at its bay, a shipwrecked thought I can't seem to reach.

My husband appears, carrying a brown bag of something. "Got it," he says. Though I don't know what. He guides me to the waiting area, sweat flecking his forehead. We sit down, and his hands cradle mine. "Babe, what time did you leave the house?"

I stare at his shiny black shoes. "We left together. Shouldn't you be at work?"

His gold wedding ring sparkles in the sunlight as he twists it around his finger. "No, I meant yesterday."

"Around 9:15 a.m."

"Was our son home alone?"

A headache snaps in some part of my brain that's trying to compute something. "Our son . . .?" I gaze at the windows; soft, golden light filters in like embers of water—there's a flow to it, a current.

"Yes, *our* little boy." His eyes bore into mine, a weight I can't manage.

The headache grows as I try to remember. "He was with the [indiscernible—lowered voice]."

"Who, love?" he presses, looking unusually desperate.

I cringe. "The maid."

"Are you sure it was our helper?" he asks, gentler this time.

"Yes, who else could it be?" I snap.

"I gave our helper the day off that day. Remember? You said you'd stay home and watch our boy. Think hard, baby. Our boy is missing. Someone took him. The first twenty-four hours are critical. I won't be mad if you tell me the truth." His fingers tremble, shaking apart the brown bag. "Jislaaik, look what they have sent me. Look what they have done. His little fingers. Dear God, my boy. The maid, she was killed. A hit and run. What have you done?"

My vision sways. I lean forward. The bag is blood-soaked. The baby. "I only stepped out for a second . . . Everyone thinks I'm guilty." My knees tremble. "What about our daughter? We're behind with our payments."

"Do you feel that you are guilty?" His expression stills of emotion, the room sucked of sound. In the stairwell sits the sound of a crying baby. The sound builds, overfilling my ears.

Tears flood my eyes. "How can you say that? I didn't kill anyone." Unimaginable strength crackles from my hands. I push him. His back smacks the floor, the vertebrae snap. I stand up abruptly and run. The floor gives beneath my feet. The walls collapse from the structure's hold. The roof bulges out. My heart screams into my throat. Cold air grips me, the wind of gravity sucks me out into the empty sky-blue of the world and the soft cries of a baby. I'm falling, falling, falling . . .

I drop into reality. My eyes burst open, sleep-stained, a scream throttled from my throat. My arms flail, metal clasps cutting straight to my bone. The shackles. The CBE evaluation room. The fluorescent light burns into my eye sockets. A shadow; a sharp, angular face peeks into my vision. Prosecutor Serati Zwebathu. Pinched lips. Furrowed eyebrows. "Mm. I understand that you and your husband have been having difficulty conceiving." She's not asking me a question; she's telling me. "How could your newborn son disappear when you have no children yet? Whose baby did you have?"

FRIDAY, SEPTEMBER 4

09:15 /// SCREAM OF A SIREN

I thought I'd flunked my CBE until the prosecutor Serati said, "There's nothing evidential beyond a reasonable doubt that you will commit a crime within the coming twelve months. Although, given your response attack on your husband in the simulation, we will up the surveillance of your microchip until your next forensic evaluation. Otherwise, do have a good day until next time."

I felt light-headed as I made my way down the front stairs of the building, the daylight flooding my entire body with relief. I was trembling with glee that I didn't have to worry about my next forensic evaluation for another twelve months.

Waiting in line at the Body Hope dispensary, I watch everyone. A teenage girl trots by, skin a beautiful, shimmering dark, faux locs tied up high exposing the nape of her neck, unsullied by the glower of a microchip. So free. So young. And not a body-hopper. Citizens in our country who haven't body-hopped are incompatible with the microchip implant; they experience dizziness, migraines, seizures, nausea, and anxiety, so they're only instituted to a yearly forensic evaluation.

To manage the high demand for bodies, the Body Hope Facility finds ways to augment "improper" and malfunctioning bodies with bionic technologies to upgrade them to proper condition. Disability rights organizations find that the real issues can't be fixed by tampering with our biology and replacing it with mechanical limbs. The world should be augmented to make it easier for us to assimilate rather than manipulating us to fit into it.

Papa assumed that having bionic parts would raise the value of our bodies because of their superior functionality, but in actuality, it lowers our value. Bodies like mine are often supplied to those on the waiting list or offered to ordinary citizens since every Motswana is eligible for one free body per lifespan, unlike in other African countries, as the costs of body-hopping are regulated through private and public hospitals.

No one desires to buy or inhabit a body willingly and manage the functionality of its bionic limbs. The only issue I've had with this body is the microchip; that's the disability for me. I've been called derogatory names; the label "improper" hardly hurts me. Even if we changed that language, it doesn't change the real damage weaving itself through my life; it doesn't remove the microchip noosed into my neck, it doesn't remove the microaggressions I encounter in my professional life, it doesn't change what my husband says or does to me. Having an organic or bionic arm makes no difference to me.

I only want to be free.

To live freely.

The line finally inches forward. Up ahead, an older man limps to the dispensary desk, his clothes dilapidated, wrinkles laced into his skin. "Hae mothowamodimo, asseblief, I need help. This is too costly for me to manage," he says, tapping his bionic leg with his walking stick. "It's malfunctioning, and the hospital said I could get it fixed or removed, but it costs money for each treatment. Please, I'm still trying to talk to my medical aid, but they won't fully cover the treatment. What's the point of paying for medical aid if they won't help me? Hae, Jesu. This is very painful; I only want it out of me. Why, why did this bloody country give me this body?"

Hae, monna mogolo wa Modimo, I utter to myself.

The woman at the front desk looks uncomfortable as he's spilling his pleas to her. She keeps uttering, "I'm sorry, malome, I'm sorry. Could I have your ID number? Let me check the system?"

This is not a good look for the Body Hope Facility. The lifespan of a bionic part is a few months to a few years. Some people are lucky not to incur unimaginable pain and functionality errors, and some of the rich can fix those issues with money; the poor who attempt to get out of poverty by selling their bodies can't make a thebe from selling a body with disabilities. The Body Hope Facility will only accept payment for bodies that aren't too disabled, using euphemistic bullshit jargon in their questionnaire to assess the impairment levels of a body. The older man is but a teardrop in an ocean of erasure. No one sees the poor and sick. I've been in that state, asking for help and not being able to get it.

We must pay the cost of the technology the facility put in us. Besides serving the nation's cry for more bodies, what cost do they incur? Our lifespans were cut short because of this pressure. What other repercussions will follow?

I step forward to the older man. "Dumêla malome, what seems to be the problem?"

"Joh, ngwanaka," he says, sighing and leaning onto his walking stick. "Please, talk to these people. No one will help me."

I'm dealing with more significant expensive issues. I can't imagine his costs, which are perhaps an iota of what it takes to fund my firm's monthly operation fees. Such a difference could hardly affect my ability to pay the maintenance fees for my daughter's Wombcubator. Losing such an amount won't make a difference to me, but it will make a massive difference to him.

I lean toward the woman with my wrist outstretched. "Please charge his treatment to my account."

The woman clears her throat, her eyes skimming the screen before her as she taps in instructions. "It will take a couple of days to process," she says, "and once we get the green light, he'll be called in for his treatment."

The man claps his hands into a prayer form and starts sending me blessings and prayers as he leaves, making a call to a relative.

The waiting list system adopted by the Body Hope Facility is supposed to treat each consciousness equally and fairly. Still, news reports declare that they can trace our original identity, and based on who we were, their algorithm decides what bodies we get, which dictates who lives in privilege and who doesn't. Regardless of how you hide yourself from other people around you, the system will know if you are bisexual, lesbian, gay, trans, Black, Asian, or whatever minority. I find it aggravating that a soul's first identity is tethered to it regardless of who it becomes in the next lifespan, and whatever oppression its identity carried, it will enslave it into another oppressed body. That to escape this cycle one has to game the system or earn an upgrade; to consider a change in gender or ethnicity an upgrade is ludicrous, for it is only the materialism of this flesh and the laws of this world that muddy the true calibre of our souls.

There are days I wish I owned three bodies—that of a man, that of a woman, and that of a liminal gender—and could decide which to wear every day. But because I have a microchipped body, I am ineligible for that status afforded to some after intense inquiry. It is far more expensive to transition fluidly from one body to another frequently than on a one-time basis, as it requires highly adaptive technology, cloning of the consciousness, and plugging into and out of these bodies. Only 0.01 percent of the population has this status.

Once the dispensary hands me my medication, I storm down the hallways by the maternity ward because I'm a masochist. Getting a dose of crying, cooing, laughing babies warms my heart, assures me that I, too, will have that one day. In Ward 6, Suite 1, a door's ajar, almost empty, except there's a baby inside the room. I inch my head inside the luxurious suite with beige walls, a strip of windows overlooking Notwane Dam, splaying golden morning sunlight into the room.

"Hello?"

No one but a cot with a baby inside. She's gurgling, blowing bubbles with her spit, her legs folded to her chin, her toe in her mouth, with little chubby cheeks. Soft brown skin, downy black hair just waiting to thicken into a rich Afro. She's so cute I could eat her up. She smiles when I come into her vision, and I smile, too, playing with her little toes. The sunlight doesn't reach her from the window, and she looks like she needs a bit of sunshine. I take a whiff of her smell—it's like cocaine to a drug addict. Lavender baby powder. Baby oil. Soft skin. She's in my arms, chubby cheeks at my lips. Why would someone leave a baby here alone? What would've happened if I hadn't walked in? Poor thing doesn't deserve such parents. *I* will take care of you.

"We could go to the garden," I whisper as she curls her whole hand around my index finger. She stares at me with dewy dark eyes. "Would you like that? Fresh air. The smell of flowers."

I'm out of the suite's doors. My body jerks. An electrifying current stabs my every nerve ending. The baby tumbles from my arms. I fall to the ground, convulsing, waiting for the pain to end. A mass of people clad in scrubs, their clogs squeaking on the vinyl flooring, rush past me to the fallen, wailing baby. *Oh God, did I break her?* I only meant to hold her. I wasn't trying to kidnap her.

I scream, watching through the windows as the blue expanse of the sky burns with a sun of intoxicating minuscule machines that flit about like hummingbirds from their stations at the police towers through the city air to their miscreant owner. One of them, a drone, unhinges from its docking station, splits through the hospital wall like a bullet, and punches into my shoulder blade, wailing the scream of a siren. A drone registered to my microchip.

The microchip is a foolproof, bona fide police forensic tool.

I can't kill, steal, or kidnap someone without it delivering a paralyzing shock to my nervous system.

A drone films me as the burn of electrocution drowns me, and I slip into the dark abyss of unconsciousness.

SATURDAY, SEPTEMBER 5

12:55 /// SHIPWRECKED FROM REALITY

"What the fuck?"

I wake dry-mouthed, eyelids split open by a stream of fluorescent lights.

A booming voice shakes me. "What the fuck were you thinking?" It's my husband. Shouting. Spit flying from his gnashed teeth.

I raise my hand to block the incoming fist of his words, but it's yanked back by . . . metal restraints. "What the . . . ?" A whisper trembles from my lips. I take in the room, my mind fogged. Concrete walls. Concrete floors. The CBE evaluation room—except that the panel seating is empty. No technician.

"No, no, no!" I start to scream. "This isn't happening."

My thoughts slur, slipping through my mind.

"Do you realize what you've done?" Elifasi hurls the words through the chamber's dark glass.

Fear ripples through my body. "Please, tell me what's going on."

The thud of his boots echoes as he prowls in circles around my chamber. "Your initial CBE result was inconclusive, worrying. It hinted at attempted kidnapping and assault."

"Assault? I'd never—" It's my word against the CBE. "*You* have to believe me."

"Ag, sies man!" His lips curl in disgust, matching the words. "They felt you were too perceptive of the simulation for them to get a good reading. You've been in evaluation for three bloody *fucking* days—"

"Three days?" I whisper. "It's not Wednesday?"

"It's a fucking Saturday," he shouts. "Do you have any idea how worried I've been ever since I left you here for work, wondering if you'd actually come back home? They gave you the impression your evaluation was over, hoping you'd slip. And you fucking slipped. What the fuck were you thinking, taking someone else's child?"

They never let me go. The Monday lunch was just like every Monday lunch with my family, my snarky brother, his brutal words the right shape of sharp. Every single detail, every single personality, down to the fiber of Mama's favorite blouse, to the woodsy, cherry taste of the wine, the balmy air sour and sweet from the crushed marula falling from the tree in our backyard. They got everything correct, got me to feel relaxed without noticing anything amiss. To pull the walls down so they could get in. Into me. My subconscious is supposed to be my most loyal friend—how can it do this to me? Just willingly forfeit every detail, every secret that the CBE needed to infiltrate me, to assassinate my faith in it? After this, how can I ever trust my mind, trust myself or reality?

In our city, it is unwise to trust reality.

I have been betrayed by reality, betrayed by my subconscious, shipwrecked from reality.

Now every thought must be deceased from my mind before its birth.

I've been passed like a package from the evaluation room, to the psychiatrist, to the commissioner of police, Rohan Kohli.

The metal chair I'm sitting on bores into my skin. I shuffle around a bit to take out the stiffness from my body. "What happens to me now?"

I ask Commissioner Kohli, whose role my husband's currently being integrated into—a promotion due to Rohan's retirement. Wrinkles are chiseled into his face, and his milky-brown irises hold a steely gaze on me. A desk is sandwiched between us, with his blade-thin computer sat in the middle. A wall full of disks and files surrounds us.

He eyes me through his lowered glasses, hair greying on the sides. "This is the second time your body has committed a crime, first from its previous owner and you—"

"*I* didn't technically commit a crime."

He scratches his grey-flecked beard. Zooming into his glowing screen's text, he reads, "'There's a knife in my hand, raised to stab him. My other hand clasps around his throat.'" I'm gobsmacked as he stares at me, waiting for a response. It takes me a moment to recollect the familiarity of those words—where they began, where they dropped. My face collapses in my hands. The Monday lunch with my family. My thoughts, my confession. What the transcriber put down.

I chew on my nail as he continues, "'She's so cute I could eat her up . . . I take a whiff of her smell, it's like cocaine to a drug-addict . . . Poor thing doesn't deserve such parents.'" Then his voice rests heavily on: "'*I will take care of you.*'"

My confessions aided and abetted by my actions, motives up front and center. I had the means, the opportunity, the motive all tucked into the soft skin of that baby, that hospital room.

I wilt under his gaze, pull the lapels of my cardigan in, though it helps little with how naked I feel. "I know how that could be misinterpreted, but it's not what you think. The relationship between my brother and me is—"

"Complicated," he interrupts, scratching the buzz of grey hair on his jawline. "Your mother said so yesterday. She convinced him not to press charges against you." The lunch with my parents was real, and the baby incident was a simulation, but both have truly damaging effects on my life.

I bring my knees closer together, head down, ashamed. "Yes, I desperately want a baby. Yes, I fantasized for just one second, but I meant no harm. And the microchip stopped me. I mean, that's why they're installed in us. To stop us. Always. So we can remain in this body. So the city doesn't run out of body supplies." My palms are now raw and sore from my nails digging into them.

"How long have you had this urge?" he asks.

"I haven't. I was worried that someone left the baby alone. I've been terrified because . . . we're behind with our payments to the Matsieng Fertility Fund . . . and we might lose our daughter."

"'I'm just afraid that the body will relapse and . . . I don't know, hurt someone.' That sounds like an urge to me," he says, reciting my feelings back to me. Jesus, am I his case for him to remember so intimately the conversation I had with my husband days ago? "The CBE doesn't only look into the future, it peers into your past, the last twelve months of it, in case it missed something in your previous evaluation."

"If it was serious, my husband would have reported me," I respond.

He rubs his beard again, peering at me in an indiscernible way. "The microchip reads into facts, not emotions, because under criminal law, you took a baby out of a room without permission. Their GPS tag set off an alarm: they were being moved from premises without approval of parents or any registered doctor by an entity with your microchip registration code. The GPS tag's AI did not detect any danger or any viable reason that would explain the movement of that baby. Two foolproof, bona fide technologies working together identified you as a threat. And I should just trust your fickle emotions?" He taps his index finger on the desk. "There is something deeply worrying and dark inside you, Nelah. Feral."

I'm embarrassed when a huge lump of a tear creeps out my eye and takes its time crawling down the side of my face.

"Listen," he says, "a body can only have three mind transfers. Three chances and no more. A person in their lifetime has an unlimited opportunity of mind transfers into other bodies. But if they commit a crime, that opportunity is chucked out the window." He heaves out a breath. "You'll be put on probation. You are allowed a year's worth of therapy to remedy your body's fallback and to assess if the problem lies in the body or your way of thinking—but only a year," he emphasizes. "If all else fails, you will be sent back to the Consciousness Bank until we find a compatible body for you."

Before, I was on a waiting list for a body for fifteen years in their Consciousness Bank. It's not a coma, but a limbo state of waiting and waiting and waiting. You feel everything and hunger for a life to fit into rather than wavering around like a vapor of cloud in a blade-thin disk in their servers. No sunrises. No sunsets. No materialism.

Sometimes, my marriage reminds me of that still time stuck in limbo.

You'd think I have the power to claim Nelah's life since it seems more logical for the evacuated mind to be considered dead. But memories are lost during the process of consciousness transfer, a phenomenon that baffles scientists. Nothing about it can be rectified. The only past we can hold onto is that of our body's predecessors. The self resides in the body. It is the self that keeps the relationships that belong to the body. It is the self that carries criminal tendency.

By the time I came into this body, I belonged to the family by name. *As the memories of my old life evaporate from my mind*, goes Body Hope's manifesto, *my mind relinquishes my old life, therefore I relinquish my old family. I am a brand-new person with a new lifespan, a new identity. I no longer walk backward into the past but move forward to the future.* It's part of their contractual agreement when disbursing bodies.

"Next time, the microchip won't save you." Rohan's chair squeaks as he leans back. "I know things have been a little difficult at home, but a few years of the microchip treatment can cleanse you. Just try to stay clean." He's making me feel like a dirty woman.

Criminal habits are tied to the brain, where new minds take up residence, and oftentimes absorb these historied criminal predilections; it is the body and the brain surveilled, but it is my mind that bears the punishment.

"For your husband's sake," Rohan adds. "He works so hard. I'd hate to see what this would do to him." As if it does nothing to me. As if I don't work hard, too.

He stares at me now, waiting for something. "I do feel fortunate. I'm very sorry for the worry I caused everyone. I didn't mean to," I say.

"There was a teenager here the other day. He didn't mean to drink and drive and crash his car and kill two of his best friends. You see where I'm going with this?" I nod. He leans forward, stares at me for a long time as if I might break. "You have friends in high places. But you can't always be a friend and an enemy to God and get away with it. A sin unpaid for grows heavier and hungrier and will satiate itself in ways you'll regret. I'll be watching you." He lifts an object that grates heavily against his drawer. Hands it to me. A black hexagonal disk. "A memento," he whispers.

I stare incredulously at it. It's a jail cell for the mind: a Mind-Cell. "My mind was . . . in this? Was I about to be incarcerated?" Jesus, how or who intervened? My husband. It must be him who saved me. But how did he manage to engineer such a deal? Would he even tell me? I'm too afraid to face him, to ask him.

"You need to be careful about what you do from now on. You can go. Your husband is waiting for you in his office."

The police staff stare at me as I, the wife of the assistant commissioner of police, perform the walk of shame to his office; the Mind-Cell in my handbag grows heavier with each step. Every senior officer's office is separated from the open-plan bullpen by a thin frame of glass. Elifasi is standing behind it, glaring at me, his palm against it gradually reducing the glass's transparency to frosted glass, so no one will see what occurs between us, except for shadow and swayed truth. The heat of his anger fibrillates, suffocating me.

The door shuts behind me when I enter. I inhale the lingering scent of roasted coffee beans, pinpoint an empty mug rimmed with milky foam.

He throws a file on his desk. "You have a file, a case." Underneath his protruding eyebrows, his eyes bulge with anger. I pull the chair aside to take a seat. He shakes his head. "Don't sit. You're not staying."

I stand ramrod straight, arms tucked in, like a pupil being reprimanded for a schoolyard infraction. "It was stupid, reckless, what I did. I'm very sorry. Please forgive me."

"What the fuck were you thinking? Did you think you could cover it up?" he says. "Kidnap a baby, carry it as your own? Should it really have gone that far? You've fucking embarrassed me." He paces back and forth, pinching the bridge of his nose. "I lost a child, too, but I'm not trying to wreck my life along with everyone else's.

"Do you want to kill another one of my children? Does it even bother you that this might fuck our chances with the Matsieng Fertility Fund? That we could lose ownership of our child because you couldn't fucking control yourself? That her body could be prostituted to some fucking stranger on the waiting list? If the Body Hope Facility gets ownership of our child, only God knows whom they would give our child's body to once it's of age."

If parents lose ownership of their fetus, the Matsieng Fertility Fund fosters the child for the Body Hope Facility until it's eighteen, the rightful age at which consciousness transfer can occur. The body is brand new, with no bad history tarnishing it.

My lips tremble, and my voice collapses out of my mouth. "But . . . our daughter's consciousness will still be in her body."

"For fuck's sake, woman, this is business. A fresh body like that is a prime estate for whoever is powerful on that waiting list. These organizations won't care about its consciousness; they'll move it to low-valued bodies like yours!"

"Eli, please," I wail.

"You're not only going to lose us our child. You will fuck up my promotion. Do you think childless men ever get promotions? You're cracking, Nelah, losing your sense of reality. This is not what I married."

Tears crawl down my face. "The baby, she was crying. I only wanted to calm—"

"I don't care if that baby was dying and you were the only one there. You can't do shit like that, just take people's things." His teeth clench the anger against his lips when he utters, "I have a fucking low-life rat that saw my wife's ass."

"What?" is the only thing I breathe out.

I was afraid that after my forensic evaluation, a tjatjarag informant would snitch to him. An affair isn't a crime, but my forensic review is confidential. Obviously, not to people like him who are chummy and colleagues with officials that oversee our evaluation. What exactly did his informant say? Eli doesn't have the authority to go through forensic evaluation footage, especially ones that concern those close to him. How much does he know? I need to stop overthinking this; it's making me look guilty even if I am guilty.

I stifle a gasp. "You make me sound cheap."

"You make me look cheap," he says.

"Bathong, Eli. When we got married, this was not who we were. What changed?"

He stares at me like I dare to speak back, but the glimmer of anger in his eyes buckles. "Life doesn't stay the same. You changed, didn't keep to your vows." Then he eyes me like the barrel of a gun. "You're not going to ruin promotion for me." It stings that it's not the affair that hurts him but that it might jeopardize his career if he couldn't even manage his wife and marriage to success. Of course, childless men receive promotions, but they go no higher than the assistant commissioner or any equivalent role. He won't divorce me as much as I won't divorce him. But do I need him as much as he needs me? "You're supposed to be the perfect wife," Eli continues. "I gave you a chance when no one would. You think men are interested in wiretapped women like you?"

"There's no need for that."

"Whom are you fucking?" he asks again. "It must be someone powerful for the low-life rat not to squeal to me the identity of the bastard you're sleeping with."

"I'm not sleeping with anyone," I say. "The forensic evaluation involved you inquiring about our missing child. That's it, I swear. Whoever you're talking to is trying to ruffle your feathers. Didn't you say it's been tense in the office since you got promoted?"

His eyes slide to the side as he ponders this since people have been talking behind his back, displeased that he received a promotion. Who on the panel would've said something? Or might it be the confessional transcriber? No, maybe Eli is reaching because he's mad.

"Well, they've gone too far," he says, his shoulders relaxing. "I'll see to it that they're reprimanded."

And that's it. No apologies, even if I did sleep with someone.

He crosses his arms, jaws tense. "I saw a huge chunk of money subtracted from our account."

The money I used to help the older man at the Body Hope Facility. I wasn't prepared for him to ask me that today or to exaggerate the amount of money for it does us no damage. He keeps track not only of my thoughts on our Sunday film nights but even of my financial activities. There are seconds of the day that I am wrecked in anxiety, wondering if he is looking through my eyes at that very moment, and I seal them shut, dazzle his voyeurism; to blind him, I must blind myself.

Apologies spill out; I whisper, "I was helping—"

"A charity case can't help a charity case. Remember that the next time you feel like offering a hand, which you don't have," he says, looking at my bionic arm.

Bastard, I want to spit. He knows how my arm is a sensitive topic. I want to hurl flames from my mouth. I want to punch something. I want to scream.

But I will look crazy.

I will seem criminal.

Instead, I nod and say, "I'm sorry. I wasn't thinking."

"Stop saying you're sorry and stop fucking up. I can't deal with you now. Go home. *Stay* home."

15:40 /// THE WIRETAPPED ONES

I don't go home after Eli's exhaustive and intense interrogation. Instead, I go to my failing firm, Pulafela Architects. The office, dark glass, a piece of the expensive real estate sky, Fairgrounds. 190th floor. A large square floor, with three glass-boxed offices attached to the exterior wall and an open office plan in the middle. The elevator dings my arrival onto my firm's floor with its striking view: steel, glass, nothing else but a glutton of wealth slaughtering the city skyline.

Miriam, my receptionist, gives me a tight-lipped smile. "Where's everyone?" I ask.

"The conference room," she says, standing up. "Yemi called and said he can't attend this year's construction site visits." Yemi is a Nigerian architect collaborating with my firm to construct a safari lodge in the Okavango Delta.

"What? Why?" I ask, stunned.

"His work visa has been rejected."

"Based on what account?"

"His stay and intended purposes are not well justified."

"Are you fucking kidding me? We provided all the documentation that the immigration body required, even the nails and blood of our great-great-great-grandparents." I add the latter sarcastically because the regulatory body might as well ask for the skin of Jesus.

Yemi has attempted body-hopping into a South African identity for three years to gain citizenship. Still, the immigration policies are pretty strict, and after five years of waiting, he was rejected. You can't just export yourself into a foreign country's identity through the body-hopping scheme without being duly processed through their border control policies. Most people desire this because navigating their identity means encountering barriers everywhere—traveling to certain countries, turning down opportunities to attend conferences, conventions, or work trips because of that inability to travel freely. The African countries' immigration policies are less strict than European or US border control, but that doesn't make them easier to process. After 209 years of being on the waiting list, Yemi's cousin got approved for a white male British body, a rare occurrence. He'd almost expired his lifespan, which would have automatically ejected his consciousness back into his native country's waiting list, erasing all his progress—*this* has happened to many applicants.

Miriam continues, "Yemi said at this rate, he might as well jail himself into the body-hop naturalization application system to the UK."

"Shit," I utter. "That's the worst place for an African to be."

To obtain citizenship in a European country through the body-hop visa, one must revoke their native body and identity and let their consciousness be placed in the application filing system, which can take weeks to months to decades to get approval or rejection; in addition to this shitload of requirements, they must provide evidence of a year's worth of financial ability to live in that foreign place. If one is rejected, they have no body to fall back into unless they paid for the exorbitant fees for it to be fostered by a local body foster agency. And if you do get rejected, it costs a vast sum of money to transfer your consciousness from their visa application system to your native country's waiting list, which must also be paid upfront. It's worth a whole lifespan of dignity and funds lost.

A Motswana sixteen-year-old girl living in the bundus without money can't attempt body-hop citizenship for a better future elsewhere. However, some lucky few have won the lottery body-hop visas that are issued annually. Others have obtained a foreign body through marriage or employment. This varies from country to country, as some fellow friends from Japan, for example, have fewer restrictions.

"Yemi's quite devastated by the whole matter," Miriam adds. "He feels like he spends all his time applying for visas and has lost many work opportunities because of the rejections."

"Bloody bliksem," I say, "why is it so difficult for an African to travel to another African country, nje? This makes work so difficult."

"Mark van Rooyen says he can step in," she says.

"Of course he can," I say, rolling my eyes. Mark doesn't even need to apply for a visa. He's an American who was approved for South African body-hop access in two weeks. Two weeks. He didn't have to revoke his American body and identity, his consciousness wasn't placed on the application system, and he didn't need to show a year's worth of finances as evidence that he could afford to live in South Africa for however long he desired. He just walked freely into our homeland that keeps its gates locked to us.

There are multiple body-hopping systems worldwide, all similar to Botswana's but with a few variances specific to each country and its regulations. My best friend, Kea, worked on her application for ten years to body-hop to a female British white body—which is much easier than that of a white male. She had her consciousness stored in their application system and sold her three homes to fund the exorbitant cost of the application and the upfront migration fees, and to have her former body fostered in some bougie clinic. She had to sign away rights to her body should she not be able to pay the costs, which would look like she voluntarily sold her body. Kea agreed, praying that the processing time wouldn't take long, but it took forever, and the clinic ended up selling her body to the Body Hope Facility to recoup the expenses.

I kept reaching out to her mother for updates—Kea was rejected. To this day, I can't help but shed a tear when I think of her. Because she had no body to return to, she didn't lose it because of sickness or an accident, so the government wouldn't issue her a free body that every

Motswana citizen is guaranteed, even though she had several more body-hop seasons left before her lifespan expired, so her consciousness was pushed onto the waiting list awaiting a body for a new lifespan, which can take as long as several decades. The devastating irony is that this requirement is not enforced on passport-privileged people. Given their developed technology, they can travel to and fro into African bodies freely and assimilate quickly into an African or whatever identity.

With this being my third lifespan, I wonder if perhaps I also suffered that in my former lifespans. We can never know. Everyone has a reason and a desire to body-hop, whether for pleasure, economic status, the devastation of a country, or the plight of asylum-seeking peoples—we endure the worst of the systemic atrocities employed by international body-hopping policies, which I'd instead not put myself through. As much as I suffer, I have more privileges than my counterparts—I'm not living in devastating poverty or a devastated country. I have a house. I can afford a Wombcubator. The little I have, others can only dream of having a speck of it.

Mama once asked, *Why not just get residency rather than a body-hop visa? Why go to all those lengths?* You are treated for how you look regardless of what anyone says. For some, being in a different body provides them asylum from the trauma they endured. For a second, she'd seem interested in that. Growing up, I'd hear her wake up screaming, she'd have nightmares, and maybe she was enticed by the idea of leaving this body and its terrors and finding refuge in another body. She wouldn't speak much about the nightmares for which she's been going to therapy for years, but I'd realize that she'd be distant to Papa as if he were at fault for the night terrors.

Miriam taps her desk to get my attention. "Yemi said he's been trying to reach you for three days," she says, eyeing me sheepishly as if she can smell that I was in my forensic evaluation for that whole fucking time, triggering me back to that place.

"I was tied up," I say, backing away.

"He wondered if you could talk to someone to clear this up," she says.

I've got a whole shitload of problems barking up my back; the last thing I need is to dip my hand into corruption when my mind was just about to immigrate to a virtual prison. Instead, I say, "I'll talk to someone."

I must always appear duplicitous even if circumstances prove otherwise.

"What should I tell Mark?" she asks. "His receptionist has been calling nonstop."

"We're going to continue working with Yemi, regardless of his situation," I say. I, too, wouldn't want to be dropped from a project because of things beyond my control. "We'll find a way to make it work. Tell Yemi that this decision is conditional on him not ending up in jail to get the UK body-hop visa, yet. Once this project is done, he can file his consciousness wherever he wishes."

She nods. "Got it. Will you need anything?"

I shake my head. Bypass the glassed conference room, quiet with morose interns, interior designers, and architects-in-training who are physically editing the hologram of a psychiatric hospital's 3D design in preparation for a tender submission and hopes of actually getting paid this month. The hologram's blue-tinged glow burns their faces into something sad, aloof, and alien. They're so focused on the project that no one notices me. But their stares sear into my back as I approach the three glass-boxed offices belonging to the QS, the engineer, and me, practicing architect and managing director. I feel marked now, stained with sin like everyone can tell what I've been up to. How will our friends—the forensic panel—look at me when they come over to our house? Will they tell my husband about Jan? I only slept with him once. I ride on the positive note that at least they saw I'm no longer practicing infidelity and that I've rebuffed every one of Jan's advances. I hope no one tells my husband that another man is after me.

I shut the door to my office, and silence screams into my vertebrae.

I drag the Mind-Cell from my bag. Raise it above my head, heavy, throw it against our marble floors—once, twice, thrice—until it splinters into sharp pieces. I run one against my palm. The pain, blood-lit, flows out. I am awash with relief. I press my lips to the jarring cut, and suck. The liquid salt of pain seeps onto my tongue. Who am I? I don't know anymore. I weep into my hands, but the darkness inside doesn't want out. I gather the broken pieces into my handbag.

Faint and dizzy, I lie on the couch, gazing through the picture window. It's deadly quiet. No business. No tenders. Debtors are chasing us. Clients aren't paying. Of course, our lawyers have filed lawsuits against some clients, but suing is costly and takes an obscene amount of time, and some clients use this to stall their payments or cry bankruptcy. I've only been able to process half the salary of each employee for the last six months. I hate myself. They'd have left by now, but the job market's tough. Desperation is a very thin thread that binds them to me. Any blunt blade, such as a potential job, is sure to set them free.

"Screen on," I say, and the concrete wall adjacent to the picture window glows. "Please play the drone footage of the Women Without Borders' eco-city project in Oodi."

I've been eagerly working on this development for five years, a gated eco-community of over fifty homes in the acres and acres of agricultural farmland under the ownership of my original host, meaning it's mine. Limbani was pissed, as if he doesn't have his own inherited land. A portion of the homes is meant to alleviate women's societal adversities through architecture, whilst the remaining homes are for the wealthy.

Our Women Without Borders project, which we submitted to the biannual Architecture Awards Grants for funding, is a play on the without-borders paradigm meant to empower women who are confined by gender, status, or poverty by breaking down those borders and empowering them to their ideal sustainable self by offering counseling and educational programs whilst assisting them with homeownership. They live in a protected, eco-friendly social housing community with a suitable home for their family as they heal and work to reach financial freedom to better their family's future. But some investors have pulled out. Construction issues have set back the timeline.

If this project can work out, the company will be able to float through for a couple of years at least, enough time to stabilize. My husband keeps making his exasperating I-told-you-so argument. "If you'd sold at least half of that land before development, your company, your life would be stable right now." Instead, I divided it: half the farmland designed for struggling women, and the other half for luxuriant, hungry homeowners.

The drone footage swarms above, showing fog-covered steel bones clothed partially by green safety netting. Scaffolding like hands tries to hold it together—a ghost town of parks, what's meant to be the aquaponics center and the recreational area. A huge injection of funds would get this project finished within six months. I perform a holo-tour of some of our projects based in Maun, Dubai, Francistown, but nothing promising there until after a few months.

I spent an hour on the phone with Mama, who was seriously concerned about me and crying on the phone. "I can't bear to lose another daughter. I can't lose her again," she'd said. She lost her daughter's soul, and she can't bear to lose her daughter's body this time. My face, my smile—even though my mannerisms erode them into a different identity—still remind her of her daughter. It's probably why she still loves me. Sometimes I wonder if she loves the real me, not just the shell of her daughter. Papa was also on the call, sounding like he'd been crying. "We love you, just remember that," he said.

Magosi Theo, the quantity surveyor, pokes his head into my office. "Eita. Everything alright?"

"Ja," I lie.

"The CI Conference is today." Silence. "At the Golf Estate Conference? Phakalane?" He squirms under my stare. "You do remember, right?" He comes around the desk, shakes my shoulder. "Are you listening to me?"

I rattle my head. "Sorry about that. Right, the Building Expo."

"No, the Construction Industry Conference," he enunciates. "One of us has to attend, scoop an investor perhaps. We talked about this months ago. I'm flying down to Maun tonight. For a site visit. Remember? I saw you did a holo-tour of the resort."

"Ja, I did. Ja, I'm definitely attending."

He looks at me warily, like I'm a diseased bomb too close to his source of income, but must be desperately hoping he's wrong because he adds, "Well, here's the bill of quantities you needed. For the psychiatric hospital." He places it on my desk, considers, leaves.

Another knock, and I groan. The door slides open again. "I'm sorry." Miriam hurries in behind a behemoth of a man. "He refused to make an appointment. This is Mr. Aarav Koshal from Koshal Holdings Inc.—"

"Koshal." I stand. Cross my arms.

"Greetings," he says, eyes skirting my office, the view.

"It's alright, Miriam," I say. "I'll handle it."

He laughs, this despicable man who is Jan's father. "'Handle'? Izit? Two months I've been trying to appoint a meeting with you, and suddenly you can handle me?"

It's alleged that Aarav's ancestors arrived from somewhere in the northern districts of India nine or ten centuries ago, and established their ties to Botswana through startup businesses in the technology industry before branching out to other sectors and spilling across African borders to international waters, growing the family's outreach and power. Within these companies, politicians had shares and interests. Koshal family relatives and associates from India received favorable work permits from the government, some of which people say included body-hopping advantages throughout the family line that no one knows specifically. As such, it's pretty easy for their firms to hire and transfer people from one country to another, given their international establishments. It's common for a cousin, an uncle, or a grandfather to head one of the branches in a foreign country. Such positions are held chiefly by patriarchs within the family, and the women are given more minor roles to maintain a high proportion of men at the top. In the rare case that a white British man controls some firms, for example, a Koshal man managed to obtain the much-lauded body-hop British citizenship. And Aarav, running the Botswana arm, is the latest in a line of his family who continues to expand the Koshal empire.

Aarav unbuttons his suit jacket and offers himself a seat. "I've a business proposal for your firm. Decided to drop by. It's an offer you can't refuse." He stares at me whilst I seethe. "We're branching out into the construction industry. As you know, our partnerships with highly acclaimed businesses have our tentacles steeped in every industry: manufacturing, agriculture, food industry, technology, fashion, publishing, *everything*. We believe you're the perfect captain to spearhead us into the architectural landscape. We have a plot in the CBD of Mozambique, and we require your design services. Your firm will make millions. It'll put you on the map, allow you to collaborate with powerful global firms."

"I'm already on the map," I say.

"A dying one," he emphasizes. "Don't be a domkop. I hear your firm's flailing about in debt. You *need* this partnership. Your designs have a distinct ethnic flavor, and you've won awards, but now they aren't really paying, are they? We could create something with international appeal. You've seen my firm's work. Culture plays a significant part in all our brands. From the Khoisan brand we did for a textile and manufacturing company to the translation department of a highly esteemed publishing company—my power will open so many doors for you, and likewise."

"Mxm, sies. I'm never doing business with a thing like you," I spit. "You're a rapist—"

"Ag, that dirty word." He teases his fingers together as if something sticky and messy clings to them. "My case was dropped, and *those girls* withdrew their statements after evidence was found showing their duplicitous nature."

Shortly after the sexual harassment allegations lodged against his firm, it grew to manage operations in twenty-nine African countries and is now toasted for its high diversity hiring and marketing strategies. I don't care.

"I don't know what your expensive lawyers did," I say, "but get the fuck out of my office."

His eyes narrow into slits. He crosses his legs, steeples his hands. "Cunts like you always regret saying no. Even the wiretapped ones." The wiretapped ones. Our microchips record everything, but even such evidence can barely bury him.

I sidestep my desk and push his chair. "I said, get out!"

He hoists himself up before the chair topples over. Shakes out his arms, buttons his jacket. "I did try to engage amicably. You are your own ruin." He sweeps his eyes over my office again. Leaves. The door clicks into place.

In the hallways, in the toilets, in the kitchen, nothing counters my anxiety, worsens it only. The voices of my employees flood my mind.

Barbie-cute, killer interior designer Goaletsa Pelontle: *Mr. Koshal was a potential client, and she basically told our literal paycheck to fotseke.*

Architect Sewelo Onkgomoditse: *Getting half your salary for months is just kak. What a bitch.*

Goaletsa: *Mxm, I swear she's used our salaries to fund her IVF treatments. Adopt a kid, get a pet—move on and* pay *us our salary.*

I want to hurl my body into a pit of fire. I knead my fingers into my temple at the onset of a migraine, insanity. My grip on reality loosens, my need to survive disappearing. I slap myself. "Wake up," I whisper. "You're not just living for yourself anymore. Think of Mama. Of Papa. Eli. My baby. My employees. But Aarav's a terrible, corrupt man. Partnering with him is a suicide of our ethics, our moral conduct."

I'll figure something out.

My wrist buzzes. A message. Janith Koshal. `See you soon. Can't wait.` I pinch the bridge of my nose, brushing away the waves of emotion flooding my thighs.

20:10 /// SCARRED REGION OF EMOTIONS

Elifasi's furious that I'm going to "mingle and get sloshed." He's supposed to come along, but he forgot, as usual, trapped at work. He'd appreciate it if I sat at home all day, wagged my tail as soon as he came through the front door.

His caller ID visual is tacked to the back of the driver's headrest, the framing electric blue, displaying him in his office.

"Ag, I don't know how you expect me to just stay at home," I say, sinking into the back seat.

"You're the one that designed the damned house," he says.

The Eli I first met before we married would've never spoken to me like this.

"And I seem to always be alone in it," I respond, "just like these events and lunches where you cancel on me last minute. You don't even bother to notify me anymore."

"I supported you earlier in your career when you spent months working in different countries," he responds. "I sacrificed all my life savings for your firm. It's my time now."

Staring at him, I remember those moon-drunk nights we'd talk endlessly, burrowing so deeply into each other that his thoughts became enmeshed with mine, and we seemed to be one person, tied together by similar dreams and a desire to settle down. We attended functions and made distant memories in places far from our country, on shimmering sands of beachside resorts, and in cities where the buildings touched the skies. For the first time in my life, after ceaselessly migrating from one myriad dead-end relationship to another, I'd finally found a person whose steady hand would always frame mine, whose eyes would leap into mine, the love diving into my body with certainty that I could trust he would always stay. He became the love I'd always desired in my family, a love I would not let slip away. For how long would it take to find another like him? In the years after marriage, the pressures from work inflicted cracks into our perfect lives: me, working months away from home in countries with visa restrictions that wouldn't allow me to bring my husband along as my firm's reputation grew to great success while his stagnant position at work threatened his pride. The more successful I became, the more his balls shriveled, and the quieter he became, reserving himself to the teeth of his thoughts while his glances glazed me with a sweet poison. What appeared as commitment in the past now reveals itself as possessiveness and a controlling tendency to make me stay. His steady hand is now a noose around my neck, and his love is a knife driven into my body, inciting a desperate fear within me never to leave. He can't meet my emotional needs. After all, he doesn't have it in him to be safe for me because he is not safe within himself. I have now become emotionally unavailable to myself. It kills me to know that I am dishonoring myself, and I can't but find freedom in this prison of my body.

When the recession hit our industry, we pooled our funds to keep my firm operating, but that period made it difficult to get projects. We floated in the never-ending money woes he was spiteful of me for drowning us in. Is that when he stopped trusting me or stopped believing in us? Or is it when my parents wouldn't give me access to my inheritance or when we lost our babies? Perhaps he relied on my status as a microchipped person, that I would always be valued less and struggle to rise the ranks, thereby always remaining below him, that when I changed that status quo, it hit him harder than if I were a microchip-free wife. Did all these things also turn me away from him so I could dip myself in Jan, in someone who accepted me and all I was?

"Ja, it's your time," I whisper, the words bitter. It satisfies him that I'm not putting up a fight.

"You should be happy by now," he says. "You have a husband and a child on the way."

"I am thrilled." I repeat the words to his glassy reflection.

"Nelah, I know you're upset about earlier, but can you understand why I was mad and worried?" Eli asks. "Can you imagine how life was before without microchipping people? People killing innocents without any alerts going off? A man could kill twenty people in months or years without being caught. I read a case centuries ago where a man spent years building an underground basement to imprison his daughter as his sex slave for a decade before he was caught. Shit like that won't fly today. Unfortunately, only the microchipped are monitored, and you have to commit a crime to be endorsed with a microchip. The problem today is that not everyone is microchipped, so some crime slips through. Can you imagine how perfectly crime-free our country would be if everyone were microchipped?"

I'm stunned, and his words send a chill down my back. "It's easy for you to say since you're not microchipped," I say. "Maybe we shouldn't receive criminal bodies, because I'm suffering the consequences of someone else's actions. Would you offer yourself, too, if you suggest that everyone be microchipped?"

He laughs. "Come on, babe, government officials hold such sensitive data that adding a microchip would conflict with the confidentiality of our work. Imagine if a body like ours landed in the wrong hands or we got kidnapped and our microchips hacked into. Such a breach of our nation's data could compromise our country."

"Basically, you're against being microchipped," I say.

"For the protection of our people. This is beneficial to us, Nelah. Come on, surely you can see that," he says. "It's the best job in the country. I have benefits that no ordinary citizen has, and having this authority and access to oversee the private lives of our citizens is a huge advantage; having the power to enact change down the line is what I'm aiming for. At least one of us must be the inside man. I want to reach the highest position to implement more policies to ensure that safety remains pure. We can't all be chess pieces the government moves around; one of us at least must have that power. I'm doing this for you and me. For our family."

Elifasi tends to look at things with rigid pragmatism. I thought his passion for public safety and national security was more altruistic than self-serving, and I wonder if he wants to advance to wield this power as his weapon.

"Well, I am proud of you," I rehearse. "I hope it doesn't take them too long to promote you again."

I stare out the window at the blurring view of highways, skyscrapers, malls—headlights slapping my window.

My nerves twist: I'm about to see Jan.

Eli's expression softens. "About this morning. I'm sorry, nè."

"Ja, I know."

His eyebrows rise, surprised, hurt. The call cuts.

My car meanders through the suburbs of Phakalane. Reaches the iron gates of the Golf Estate, where the checkpoint scans me through. A traffic of cars. Glamour and wealth don every bone and flesh. Five-star hotel. International speakers from the industry. Elegant. High-volumed ceilings. Voices swishing with alcohol. Laughter clinking with wine glasses. Lavish décor.

I find my table, mostly men heavily salted with ego. And Janith Koshal. Our eyes meet, that awkward tension I try to tightrope every time. He stops talking to his neighbor and comes up beside me. Pulls out a chair, scans the nametag on the plate.

"I'm sure Mr. Kgorosi won't mind changing seats." He settles down, painting the air with his cologne, unbuttons his suit jacket.

I stare into his eyes, a kohl-dark ring around each dusk-amber iris with hints of green, like an eclipse in reverse. His life's filled with pitch decks, hungry entrepreneurs, crying twins, diaper changes, and a dying marriage, but I'm envious of him.

Janith Koshal is a forensic structural engineer turned VC investor in construction tech, managing partner at J&J Associates. He's acted as an expert witness in court cases based on his analysis of failed structures. The company he invested in runs drones for property inspection and facilities management, which my firm has been using, and that's how I met him, at the company's presentation conference. Our seats were arranged next to each other. I remember him arguing with his wife on the phone.

Intelligence turns me on. His taut-muscled body is packed with it.

He leans back into his seat. "There's news about you on the grapevine."

My heart rams into my chest, hiccups, silences. The panic must show in my eyes. "About your firm," he emphasizes.

"Oh." My shoulders relax. A glass by my lips. Cold water down my throat. My trembling hand settles the glass back down. "What about it?"

"Sometimes a business needs corruption to survive," Jan says. "But another alternative: just cry bankruptcy and go back to the drawing board. Failed businesses are learning curves to a successful one. Consider this one a stepping stone."

The lights dim, the stage lights up, the food arrives, and silence falls as introductions are made on stage. I'm not listening, but staring at my food, poking at it, trying to push it down my throat.

"You look like you need a drink," Jan says, getting up, guiding me out of my chair and out of the conference room through thick, carpeted hallways into the open air of a restaurant. Frogs burp into the night, the thick scent of fir trees. A golf course sprawls, blanketed by dark. And a pond, the silver glimmer of the moon on its surface.

A waiter arrives with two glasses and wine, decants it into our stemware. Its warmth slips down my pharynx, sends chills to my arms. I forgot how drinking numbs reality, incites the magic of the ordinary in my body. I run my fingers through my braids, untying them, letting them weigh down my back.

Jan eyes me intensely, turns serious. It disarms me. "Honestly, how are you?"

"Eish, I really don't know where my life is headed right now," I say bluntly, the wine loosening me up. It gets tiring, locking things up, being careful, especially with the recent betrayal of my subconscious mind. Even if I was still in the CBE, there's nothing wrong with talking to Jan. "My marriage is messed up, and we might lose our daughter because we're behind with payments, and I just don't want to think about it."

"Shouldn't your husband be worried about that, too?"

"Ag, he has a laissez-faire attitude toward life. Believes things have a way of working themselves out, meaning me. I work out everything."

"Jesus," Jan says. "Why'd you marry him?"

I twist the wine glass stem in my fingers, watch the light flow through it. "To be honest, I was scared, terrifyingly alone. I wanted to settle down, and I kept thinking about the good parts of him, which lately I'm struggling to recall." I lean back into the chair, sighing. "I just thought our issues were fixable. But I'm the only one who's willing to work on the emotional breakdown between us."

"Why the hell do women do this?" he asks, leaning forward. "Stay with someone when they deserve better?"

I sigh. "We're having a baby. I can't just leave. He's really not all that bad."

A breeze tousles his pitch-black hair. Jan shakes his head. "You sound like my sister. She blames herself for all the bad guys she gets. She's sticking with this one fucking asshole because she's thirty-one, and she's terrified of getting back out there, having to deal with one new horndog after another. Rather the devil she knows, which is *kak*, I tell you. She still has a hundred years left until her lifespan expires. But she just won't hear it."

Every citizen can accumulate 210 years per lifespan through a minimum of three body-hop seasons; it used to be 420 years per lifespan, but it was cut in half due to body shortages and the need to afford others an opportunity. Once those 210 years elapse, they're registered into the Consciousness Bank until a body becomes available. This is the first body-hopping season of my third lifespan. As with every delivered death, my first and second lifespan memories have been erased. But you still remember the basics: how to ride a bike, drive, cook . . . like dying and waking up as someone else.

With the amnesia of reincarnation and its confidentiality clause of the past, it frustrates me that I don't know what I left behind. What am

I without my memories? Am I a completely new and different person from my past life? Do I carry the same habits, thoughts, and predilections? Or have I been reincarnated into someone completely different? Who were my previous parents? Did I have any children? I'm grieving for things I can't remember, which is the injustice of consciousness transfer because what else are we losing that we don't know?

Although, some lifespans carry more than the allotted three body-hop seasons since there are instances where a citizen needs to go through more than the minimum number of bodies. Suppose we become sick or get into a car accident such that our current body is too damaged to suffice as a refuge for our souls. In that case, every Motswana citizen is offered one free body per lifespan, unlike other African countries. Body-hopping is commonplace, and my parents and brother are in the minority who opt out of it. "Then why are we drawn to body-hopping if we can't remember ourselves?" Mama asked me once, completely dumbfounded by this fascination. It's seen as a solution to wealth inequality that Africans have endured, to curb Black tax and conjure generational wealth that you can accrue from selling your body since many African families have never had access to affluence that only a touch of immortality can bring them.

But if you commit suicide, you revoke that right. First- and second-year lifespanners adopt this strategy, selling off their 210 years, which is mainly obtained by foreigners with passport privileges who can declare citizenship through this form. Chinese, Indian, British, or American people possess some of our people's bodies. Most of the Batswana I see walking in the city, I wonder what white souls colonize their bones.

"There is no future with such a body," Yemi told me. "Hence this body is dead. We are born in dead bodies that make it easier to bury them, revoke them, and claim ones that will give us a better future."

Many Batswana have successfully migrated overseas using this scheme with less struggle than other African natives, given that Botswana historically had low migration compared to other countries.

Besides, you retain your memories if you body-hop within one lifespan. It's only when you transition from lifespan to lifespan, separated by the limbo stage of being on the waiting list, that amnesia happens. There's no science to back up why we lose our memories, but some say that the limbo stage is where the memories disperse in that disembodied state of being. I had to wait for fifteen years before receiving a body, as my memories eroded in that gap. Maybe technology will advance in the future, and we'll be able to retain our memories.

"This whole thing of not remembering previous lifespans," Jan says, "you could be meeting a relative from a past lifespan and sleeping with them without even knowing it."

I raise my hands. "Ja-nee. Technically, it's not incest since the bodies aren't blood-related, but still."

Jan winces. "I've met people who have ten lifespans. That's two thousand years in this world!"

They're the elite one-percenters: entrepreneurs, celebrities, business moguls, judges, and lawyers, and they can maintain this status and protect their interests by exploiting advantages that are open to them. I often wonder if one of those benefits is that they keep their memories, which keeps them still clinging to their fame. After all, what would be the point of wealth if it wasn't guaranteed in the subsequent lifespan?

"Your father's had eight lifespans, so you don't have to walk far to know one." He tilts his head, annoyed. "Everyone knows about your father, Jan," I add to smear that curious look off his face.

Some say that when the grandparents die in powerful families, they bypass the waiting list and are shuffled instantly into a teenage body introduced as a child of so-and-so within that family. So how could I begin to have that power as an individual to retain my previous identities and memories when those in governmental positions are primarily men, who supposedly say our memories are lost, which puts us in a vulnerable position to control, who microchip us to keep us in line, while they keep their positions to themselves in reincarnation. As successful as I am, how could anyone with less privilege achieve this feat?

Jan muses, eyes surveying the few dining clients at the far end. "My nephew is my-great grandfather, who 'passed away' last year."

My mouth hangs open.

"Yes, the rumors are true," he says. "Perhaps this will persuade you of how important you are to me that I will divulge family secrets. It's quite easy to explain it off and to create birth certificates of a new family member."

"Were you an ancestor of the family?" I ask.

He shakes his head. "Not every relative has the same privilege, and not everyone in our family gets this advantage. You must prove your allegiance to the family to earn such rights. I was just recently born compared to our ancient relatives. And given my recent activities, those benefits were rescinded from me even though I enjoy some."

"How do you show your allegiance?" I ask.

"If the family wants you to destroy a certain company, you do so. If they want you to marry a certain someone, you do so. If they want you to kill, you kill, without question—that has never happened. It's just a way to show you how much of yourself and your values you must sacrifice for the family."

His casual tone is bizarre and keeps me silent. If my affair with Jan, who's from a very powerful family, is exposed, it will have devastating consequences for me. I drink my wine to melt the fright away from my body.

A blank look. Jan rubs his jawline, shakes off the disturbing remark. "That's another reason why my sister wants to be a carer now. Thinks life will be easier that way, that she can be free and choose who she wants to be with. She's met some carers who are in stable, long-term relationships, with good jobs, good homes, and a welcoming community. Says they're happy people who look to settle, unlike our one-night-stand society."

The cut-off age for a body is seventy years, at which point it's taken over by a carer's consciousness at a retirement center, who will routinely care for the body until death sets in. During this period, the body donates organs and biological material for stem cell research and to the cloning bank desperate to resolve the body shortage supply. It's nothing fancy, being a geriatric; when the body's on the brink of death, the carer's consciousness is removed and placed into another geriatric.

"Eish, Jan, I'm so sorry."

Jan leans forward. "I know it's scary to start again not knowing what's next or when you'll finally be happy. But you can't reach happiness if you choose to remain landlocked in such a terrible situation. I hate to see you both choosing lesser-than because you're afraid. What if choosing your husband destroys the perfect future you could have? With an intimate, caring partner?"

"I'm not afraid," I lie.

"Right." He taps the table. "Do you really want such a man to be the father to your child?" I look down at the wood grain of the table. "Your desperation to have a kid gives him power." His hand brushes mine to soften the cold words. "Don't tie your self-worth to his opinion. Be careful. Sometimes the wrong reasons keep us clinging to the wrong relationship. If you want to use him to have a kid, sure, but remember there'll be consequences. There's nothing shameful about getting divorced or being a single mother whether you're thirty or two hundred."

The realness of his statement sobers me. But he wants me, and men can be very convincing to bring you toward them. What if he's just saying all of this to bring my walls down so he can sleep with me, use me, then discard me? I'm finding it very difficult to trust anyone because it feels like kindness is extinct nowadays.

The light dazzles his irises, a smile tickles lips. "One question: Who wouldn't want to be deeply intimate with you?"

It stills me. I take another sip, ignoring his tempting flirtation. "I hear you. But everything is crumbling around me. Just a bit much this morning. Nearly got arrested. Almost flunked my CBE. For kidnapping." His mouth drops. "A baby."

His intense eyes grasp me. A tingling feeling vibrates up my thighs.

"It's not true," he whispers. "You lost four babies." At this, he touches my hand, only slightly, to soothe the blow of that statement. "That will always be used against you." He leans forward conspiratorially. "Is your microchip recording us now?"

"You're checking to see if it's safe to talk to me," I say. "No one feels safe talking to a 'wiretapped person.' Isn't that what they call us? A walking, snitching police tool." I swirl the wine glass, the light slipping in it. "I understand. That'd fuck up your divorce proceedings if someone illegally got hold of our conversation, *my* footage. Media would have a field day: VR investor fucking the Black Womb."

"Don't. *Ever*. Say that about yourself." He clasps his fingers beneath his chin. "I was more worried about what would become of your life if our recorded interaction got into the wrong hands."

He scans our perimeter, finds no one close by or watching. Fishes something from his suit pocket: a black button-sized object with a red LED light.

"What's that?" I ask.

A smile lurks upon his face. "It's safer if you don't know, but I want to tell you something without someone listening in." He rests his thumb against it, and it lights up blue. "Now, where were we? Right, in regards to your evaluation, the CBE doesn't read through the hazy, complex emotions. It just computes fact into motive purported by your past, the most painful events shaping your modus operandi."

"Eish, I don't know, Jan. It just all felt real."

"How could it not? It fucked with my self-esteem when I was a teenager. I went for therapy. To help me trust myself more than I trust what the CBE tells me I am. Don't believe anything the CBE tells you. Don't." His thumb rubs my hand. "Your subconscious is bloated by your anxiety, your trauma—and the CBE magnifies that into something dangerous. You're not dangerous. You just need to heal. The city has so many broken people whose consciousnesses are being sent to prison. But, God, I want to see you heal."

"I killed my babies," I say, flicking hot tears from my face. "They died inside me. I don't deserve to heal. What about them, Jan? Who's going to heal them back to life? And that baby I took from the hospital. That was going to happen."

"Because your need for a child is greater than your need for life. That infested the CBE. It wasn't your fault," he says.

I stare at his hands, moon-pale. "Izit? What did the CBE tell you about yourself?"

He leans back. The cool air quickly replaces his warmth. He stares at the sky. "My father married this woman, his second wife, after my mother . . . passed away. I was only twelve years old. I've never considered her a stepmother—she's not a step closer to a mother. My father was always busy. He thought she was looking after me, but she was abusive . . ." He gulps. The sharp protrusion of his Adam's apple scurries up and down his neck. "Sexually."

I gasp.

"I never understood why abuse victims felt ashamed until I felt that shame and guilt." He stares long at the table's edge, draws inwardly into his memories. "I was ashamed, a boy growing into a man, and this wasn't supposed to happen to men. Something was wrong with me. She'd spike my drink to overpower me . . . and . . . she'd point out my body's response as me having fun."

I touch his hand, brush his face. "It's okay."

He clasps his hands into fists. "I never wanted shame or guilt to silence my truth. Fear destroys people. The world tells us to bury our emotions, use masculinity as a weapon. I wanted to be both strong and soft, but . . . I struggled." He watches me intently, checks if this is okay for me, this place he's taking me. He's more worried about me than he is for himself, which both pains me and seduces me with his kind, noble act, his emotional transparency. I want to stay in this, in him, this safe horizon. I nod for him to go on. "I felt so violated, so meaningless—I erased myself from the world by terrorizing my wrist with a knife."

I clasp my hand to my throat, wrap my soul around his heart, his pain. "Yoh! You were a Suicidal?" I stare at his wrist—it's clean, without scarring.

He pulls back the sleeve. Covers it. "Ja, that's how the CBE feels. That's what it does."

The light by our table flickers. My elbows burn from the pressure of the table, and I realize we've leaned closer to each other. "If you were a Suicidal, how are you still here?"

Jan takes a breath. Peers into his wine glass. "My father bought a body from an eighteen-year-old Punjabi intern at a Kenyan firm."

My throat tightens. "What?" I lean back. Stare at his body. The crow-black hair. The whiskey-gold eyes. Not originally his.

"The kid . . . had a lot of debt," Jan explains. "His papers were arranged, and he was transported here. I was . . . mad at my father. After a couple of months, I left home, and went to varsity. Became depressed. Anxious. All the time. It was exhausting. People couldn't understand it. They'd tell me to chill out, and go for drinks—only drinks and drugs made it worse. Then I didn't know how to handle them, now I do. For my evaluation, I was no longer the abused; I was the abuser. I was immediately evicted from my body and processed to be sent to prison."

"A second time? Mara, if you're virtually incarcerated, you're never let out." Except me.

"My Mind-Cell was on its way to incarceration." He looks down, bristles with shame. "My father . . . intercepted it. Bought the body of a twenty-two-year-old Bengali in South Africa whose family wasn't doing well. You'd swear he has a roster of these desperate kids. He didn't care if the body didn't match our identity. He was this close to getting me an Afrikaner body until my grandfather stepped in to take control of the situation, given that this body and the children it procreates would be heirs of the Koshal name. And my grandfather wanted something that looked valuable. Regardless of what body he got, I feel strange, not belonging to this family. I feel lost most of the time. I don't know if perhaps there are lingering feelings the original owner left in this body."

One would assume that the powerful lose access to their relationships and identities from previous bodies, but reports suggest otherwise. They retain their wealth and stature through each lifespan through the connections and favors they pull from the government, thereby fortifying their power. After all, Jan's father was able to obtain not only one but two bodies for Jan across our borders, who still recalls his memories and keeps the Koshal identity clinging to his bones.

My mind swims in anger, confusion, and hurt. You can only sell one or several bodies, equating to thirty years per lifespan. Otherwise, everyone would over-sell and destabilize the economy. Even if you sell your body before your 210 years expires, you've forfeited any remaining years. This structure is so unfair to the destitute—they're desperate for money and survival. Those poor boys lost their years to people like Jan, who cleared away their problems with money. And it's so unjust because Jan's lifespan didn't expire; he didn't accidentally die. He was a Suicidal, yet he's possessed two bodies illegally?

"How did your father intercept your imprisonment?" I ask.

He sighs. "One of two ways: he owns highly established companies in which some politicians have shares, or he might've called in a favor or bribed someone." He shrugs. "It happens. He just never told me how."

"You escaped incarceration through illegal means."

"My *father* intercepted my incarceration through illegal means," he corrects me.

I've seen the back of his neck, and it's naked, free of any metal parts. "How come you don't have a microchip?"

"My case file was destroyed. My forensic evaluation was edited to construe innocence and purity."

"*I* have a microchip."

"I know. It's not fair. I'm privileged because of corruption. Whilst women are easily predicted as future criminals for the tiniest thing. And we get away with every illegal activity."

"*I* have a microchip because the previous owner committed a crime," I continue. "I'm suffering from this infertile body with its surveillance system because of *their* crime, but *you* get to do all that and *still* be free and have kids."

"I am sorry. I am *so* sorry." He peers at me, eyelashes touching the ridge of his brows. "Do you hate me now?"

I'm taken aback. He stares at me, *hoping* that I will hate him. If I hate him, I'm a hypocrite. I was on the same journey today, and my husband intercepted it. "No," I answer. "I'm jealous. I shouldn't hate someone because of envy."

His eyes widen, first with confusion and then with relief. "Thank you."

I stare at him, wondering if the rumor is true that some men are exempt from the amnesia we suffer from when we begin new lifespans. "Do you remember your previous lifespans?"

His eyes slide sideways. "Not like the others, the guys I know. Just some parts here and there, like déjà vu sometimes. A twenty-year-old kid that may be my son. I saw him at an expo I was invited to. Started talking to him. He had this scent that hit me hard and I felt this deep connection to him. So I've been sponsoring him since then."

"This is bullshit," I growl, "because I'm stripped of things that could trigger memories—at least *you* have something. I have nothing that connects me to my past."

What if I had a child, a child who could get that same opportunity from me, but is suffering because we're separated by this amnesia wall?

Jan casts his eyes downward, unable to offer anything better than an apology. "I know relatives who have that privilege, higher men in society, higher than my father. But they're legally bound to not speak of it, else they'll lose their memories."

My eyes bolt out at the incredulity of it. "They get to keep their memories just because they have balls and a dick?" I stare ahead, empty. "I wish I was a man. I have no interest in being a man or a woman—I'm not one. I don't know what 'me' is supposed to be because no matter my label, the world will treat me based on how I look." A sharp grief slashes its way through my chest, suffocating me with the desperate need to remember the people I've left behind in my previous lifespan, as if a chasm separates us and all I need to do is jump and reach them. But there is no chasm. My memories have been yanked out of me.

Jan twiddles his thumbs. "I think it serves a dark agenda. I've heard some locker-room banter reveal they prescribe women amnesia so they don't remember what was done to them. That and other illegal activities."

My hands clench into fists, grip the anger fibrillating through this cold air. "We'll never, ever be free, will we?"

Jan strokes my hand. "I am so sorry, love. I just heard whispers. Something about Matsieng's blood, the Murder Trials—I don't know."

"Matsieng's blood?" I ask, shaken by this revelation.

"The waters in the Matsieng's caverns are bloodlike and have properties that the Murder Trials committee often finds new uses for."

"What do they use Matsieng's blood for?"

"According to one of my father's informants, it helps the committee with the ceremonies to test the microchipped people during their purity test. They say there is too much power in Matsieng's blood, that a drop of it could kill a person or change the body's properties—what that change involves, I have no idea."

"Is that true?" I ask.

"Religious people from various countries come to Matsieng's blood to cure diseases and problems in their lives, but I never believe in such propaganda." He shrugs. "Not even my father knows. I've no idea what he did to get his sexual harassment cases cancelled. *His* name is my name." He clenches his teeth, flexes the muscles in his jawline. "*I* have to carry this shameful name that he wears proudly for the things he's done. *I* carry that. Work tirelessly to clean its reputation, but that's all people remember: the Koshal Rape Files. As if I performed that evil. I wish he could feel my anger, that it could teach him a lesson, kill his invincibility . . ." He teases his fingers into his scalp; the vein on his forehead protrudes, throbbing with anger. He slows his breathing, catches me staring wide-eyed.

Tension locks me into place, something pulses in my ears. "Your hatred, Jan, I never thought you felt that way about your father."

He swallows. Stretches out his hands from their folded rage. "Better not speak about him, else the devil will hear."

I tremble because I know he's referring to his father as the devil, and I wonder if Aarav has ever abused or punished Jan to keep him under his thumb.

Jan exhales, shifts the conversation elsewhere. "Anyway, I know it's illegal to body-hop from a non-dead body to a purchased one but, if you want, I could make it possible for you."

My chest becomes light, and I stare at him, shocked. "How?"

He takes hold of a salt shaker, says, "Things could be put in place such that"—he topples the salt shaker—"you suffer an accidental death." The salt spills from the cavernous body of the shaker, and he pats at some salt crystals with his finger, transferring them to a napkin. "We'll have a body ready for you. The body *you* want." His eyes flick to me.

My mouth hangs open. "You mean you'd design my murder and procure me any body I want?"

He nods. My mouth runs dry from the sickening, delightful offer. My hands are sticky with sweat. A rational thought hits me. "You'd give a body to the woman you've been pining for, who won't ever give you her body nor the relationship you desire with her? Is this because I won't sleep with you now that you think you can buy *me* with a new body? Perhaps you feel that once I'm no longer tethered to this body, I will be free of the husband and any attachments this body has, finally giving you the free rein to conquer me. I've been fucked over by Eli, and I won't walk blindly into another situation. So, what is your true agenda? What game are you playing?"

"I don't understand it, either," he adds thoughtfully. "I only care to see you happy."

"Bullshit." I shake my head. "I know I'm desperate, but no, I won't resort to corruption."

He smiles. "I know." Takes off his jacket, and I realize I'm cold when he wraps it around my shoulders. "Sometimes you think you've healed, but the past returns in the form of your wife. That's why I'm getting a divorce." His eyes bore into me when he emphasizes, "I can only heal if I stop the pattern from repeating—as difficult as it can be."

He's inside me, and I'm scared, but I want to be as courageous as him. I clear my throat. "That was brave of you to relive everything by telling me. When people share intimate stuff about themselves, I don't feel so ugly. I feel like I can survive because they did."

"*You* can survive."

Is this what they call emotional infidelity, this scarred region of emotions that we walk through to immerse ourselves into waters we willingly swim through? I've never had a man be this transparent about his scars, his thoughts and emotions before. Is this the bright future I could have with someone? Or is it the honeymoon phase of a relationship before it burns out?

Jan stares at me for a long time without speaking, his eyes soft, musing, and it feels as if I'm lying in calm but dangerous waters. I want to drown in him.

He folds his arms on the table, leans in, eyes focused on me. "I wish I'd met you before Mel. It'd have been much easier for us, don't you think? We're both ambitious, family-oriented, deeply passionate people. Imagine the life we'd have built, the empire we'd have created for our family. I don't think your husband realizes the woman he has; he doesn't know how to handle the power that you are—he's losing the point. You are not something to handle. That's just limiting you. I don't know why people like us must have such obstacles, no?"

I go for the jugular. "If you hadn't met Mel, you wouldn't have your twins."

"I was talking about Mel, not my girls," he corrects me. "I wouldn't lose them for the world. I still want them to be part of my life. I want to be a part of your life, too. It'd still be much easier for us, getting rid of the deadweight. If you weren't married, you wouldn't hesitate."

"*Mara,* don't you feel like you're still repeating patterns?" I ask. "You're attracted to damaged women. I'm damaged."

"Damaged women who don't want to heal. *You* want to heal," he says.

I push aside the flurrying feeling of a man wanting me, a man I want. "There's no point in talking about that. I'm very loyal."

But my muscles are sore, the headache slips away, the vague taunt of tension rests on my shoulders. The restaurant's almost empty, and soon I should go home. I'll find it empty, my husband only coming in at four or something. I'm thinking again, the last thing I need. I wish to switch my thoughts off. I don't want to go home. I don't want to be alone in the dark with my thoughts.

His eyes are flaming gold, intense. "We can do it according to your rules. Meet occasionally to chat, have drinks. Anything you want. You're in charge."

Power. I am in power for once.

"Book one of the hotel's suites," I say.

His eyes widen. Smiles.

I wait by the bank of elevators as he pays for a room. I won't kiss him or do anything so disruptive to my marriage. I'll just harmlessly lie in his arms. That's it. That's all I need.

I feel bad as we make it upstairs. I feel sorry for him. That he likes me. And I'm using it, especially after what he just told me. And this could be a vulnerable time for him, his crumbling marriage, and that he doesn't mind being used if it affords him some tiny pleasure. But what pleasure can a man get from lying next to a woman he desires? Maybe we're using each other, then.

We pour out into the hallway, he uses the keycard, and we flow into a luxurious penthouse with picture windows peering into the dark speckled with lights.

"Let's be dangerous," he says. Tucked in between his fingers, a plastic sachet of white powder.

I step back.

"What's wrong?" he asks.

"They're going to see this." I chew on my lip. "My microchip's footage will be part of my next CBE. Our friends were the forensic panel in my last one. They don't even visit anymore. My microchip, it has a backup recorder. It will legit film us, *our* sex tape. Oh God."

"Shh," he whispers. "Stuff like that is confidential. They don't disclose *anything* to anyone. Not even friends."

"And the drugs?" I point to the sachet.

"Don't worry about that. I'll handle it."

"Even if we muted our voices somehow, they have professional lip-readers who'll use the footage from the EyeCam. What if the next CBE, they tell my husband about you?"

Jan purses his lips. "I'll handle it. I promise." He kisses my forehead, the tip of my nose, cheeks, and lips. I believe him, given the fact he's gotten away with two illegal body-hops. "I want to meet you more in a way that no one—not even an AI machine—will flag our meetings," he whispers. "I'll make that possible. You're safe. You'll always be safe with me."

Acquiescing, I yank my heels off, soak my feet into the thick carpeting.

He tilts his head. "I'm glad we're back to business."

He removes his shoes, tie, cuff links, and I fold his jacket onto the couch. Stand at the edge of the bed. My dress whispers against my skin as it falls. His arms slide around me. I haven't been touched with love in such a forever time. My hands find bare skin beneath his shirt. His breath halts.

I must be forgiven for today.

"You drive me crazy," Jan whispers, voice a velvet rope slipping around my neck.

I feel him in and around me. My shriveled lungs hang dry on my rib bones, my breaths desperate to escape into his mouth, his lips, his hands. "I missed you," I whisper.

He is the skyf I used to smoke. There are parts of me that still don't belong to me, that belong to him, scattered in reds and blues. I bite my tongue, knock back the desire, only it poisons me from inside. He smirks, sees the emotion bleeding from my eyes.

Karma meets me on my knees. I burn on his tongue. We tear our skins off, soul-mix on a bed, on a table of heated drugs until we're bone-fused. We stay like that, hour upon hour, as a peaceful sleep enthralls my body. This quiet moment stokes the growing embers between us.

But who will it cremate?

MONDAY, OCTOBER 5

06:30 /// MY EYES

It is said that women used to get raped in post offices, family homes, and public spaces. They couldn't walk at night without carrying their keys in a way that could serve as weapons to defend themselves. That they couldn't walk in peace. They couldn't feel safe in some homes when an uncle, father, brother, or nephew was sliding into their bed. That men faced the same fears and couldn't speak out for fear of being called less than a man. That those whose genders weren't accepted were forced to bend and break at the violence throttling them.

We leave our doors unlocked. I can walk at night without looking over my shoulder. I can leave my drink unwatched without fearing that it might get spiked. We can leave our children unattended. Men can transition into women's bodies, and women can transition to men's bodies with ease and the aid of gender-affirming clinics in collaboration with the Body Hope Facility. There are no hijackings, robberies, or hit-and-runs. Botswana is a utopia of peace, and it is worth the privacy we give. No one would dare commit a felony against a microchipped body. I am always safe wherever I roam.

The world is considered a crime-free place because crime is immensely lower than before. Given the number of people waiting for new bodies, the government has faced such pressure to meet their demand that citizens are criminalized for minor infractions and their bodies recycled for new souls who face strict surveillance and latent criminal tendencies. Souls who have committed low-level crimes are ineligible for a new body and must either serve an extended sentence of punishment trapped in limbo before they can be loaded into a new body or serve eternity for the highest degree of crime committed. I've heard worst-case scenarios of people being evacuated from their bodies for offenses such as shoplifting, burglary, and petty theft, so there's one more body to supply those on the waiting list. This will be my fate and worse: the loss of my daughter and her loss of her body.

The upside is that a person will think twice before groping a woman, breaking and entering a house, or committing an act incited by their ill-will thoughts to another lest they lose their body; as Mama always quotes, "'If your hand causes you to sin, cut it off. It is better for you to enter life crippled than to have two hands and go to hell, into the unquenchable fire.' A body that sins must be cut off from the owner."

And I wish to utter to her,
my mouth has sinned,
my body has sinned,
and might my daughter be dismembered from me?

It takes a lot to make a perfect world that bleeds crime at the seams.

The Mokolodi townhouse, painted charcoal black, with off-white roof sheeting. Jan, a car aficionado, stands by the garage's slate stone cladding as I park my car. He pats the car's body: an SUV by a Kalanga automaker he invested in. "Let's hit the road."

"Eish, can't. He's expecting me any minute now," I say.

"He got you on curfew?"

"Ja, something like that."

Jan steps forward, teases his fingers into the waistband of my pants, tugs me forward, and I have to lean my head so far back to keep eye contact. "Love, you shouldn't be chilling with babysitters." He tips his head to one side. "Got some stuff to turn around our day."

"Don't be dom. I don't just hang around you for the sex and drugs. Quit advertising our dates like that to entice me."

He pulls back. "You're the one who keeps calling me a side-bitch."

I look away. "It's a joke."

"Why'd you even come?" he asks.

"I wanted to see you, even for a second. *Sober.*"

He shrugs. Moves back. "Well, come in. It's your house, too, after all."

The house we're renting, well, technically, that he's renting for us. We're halfway official. Damn. I follow him past the front garden, up the steps, and into the foyer of our home, serenaded by a shimmering chandelier. Jan waits for me in the kitchen.

"I have a gift for you." He opens the drawer with the utensils. Inside sits a box wrapped in a chiffon ribbon. "Happy anniversary."

No. No. No. I swallow, step back.

"It's not what you think," he says sadly. "Open it."

I untie it. Sitting on a cushioned tiny pillow is a circular grey disk, small enough to fit in my palm, with a blue LED light in the center. I raise it to the light. "What is it?"

"I want to have sultry, dirty conversations with you without getting flagged." He traces my microchip with his thumb. "I got this for us. When we're together. Got it manufactured in Malaysia by a tech expert I shared undergrad classes with. He helps with our firewall and technological breaches."

"What does it do?" I ask.

"I promised you I would protect you," he says. "This tool interferes with the microchip's transmission signal, the recording interface that dials back your conversation to the police monitoring towers. You just need to press the center to activate it. When it's on, it's blue. So if you were snorting coke, the flagging sensor wouldn't control your microchip to, say, stop you or report you. Ergo, no drone will be activated to find you."

We got away with it before, the drugs and all. There's this secret gentlemen's club of some sort, in Lobatse, a haven for microchipped men. Its walls are retrofitted with a substance that manipulates surveillance and allows the men to get loose with sex, alcohol, and drugs. Jan used to take me there, to one of the private rooms where we'd get up to dirty deeds. But this device he's offering is flexible, portable, and offers privacy from prying eyes.

A tiny tool that can serve as a cushion for my thumb.

I touch my face. "But my eyes."

His thumb brushes my cheek. "Your eyes are beautiful, love. You could walk into a bank and rob it, but as long as a warning alert is intercepted, their monitoring towers won't flag you. Only flagged visuals are assessed; the others get drowned in the noise of every wire-tapped person's stored footage."

"But the footage will still be in their servers of, say, 'me snorting drugs,'" I say.

He nods.

"That's still dangerous," I add.

"It's better than nothing."

"I mean, anyone can search my profile and analyze my footage."

"It's AI monitored. It's illegal for any human—"

"And you believe that? That's a lie the government probably tells the public."

He steps closer, rubs my arms. "Even if it's a lie, they'd have to reveal their lie if they were to prosecute you."

I used to wonder why people committed crimes even though they were aware they'd get caught. Men who'd rape and murder. Women who'd steal and murder. People who laundered money. Couldn't they just restrain themselves? How stupid can one be to give in to a temporary impulse that will destroy their lives permanently? It's all about control, restriction, and discipline. But the amount of sacrifice is too heavy a weight to carry. At some point, you break under the pressure, you give in. And I realize impulses aren't temporary. Jan is an impulse I've had for years. What's the point of life if all I'm doing is restricting myself from living? Having an affair isn't a crime. I'm not killing anyone. In fact, the forensic panel are bound by the confidentiality clause. If one of them so much as breathed out the affair to my husband, they're done for. It wouldn't be that difficult to trail it back to the snitch. But the drugs. Oh, the drugs. There's always a loophole in every system. No matter who you are, which part of the world you live in, there's always a fucking loophole you can squeeze through.

Jan hands me the remote that will manipulate the signal into an innocuous one. "But," he says, "the remote has to be on—blinking a blue light—during the event. Otherwise, it's ineffectual."

I stare at him, unable to take him at his word. Am I naive to fully entrust my life to Jan? Some days, I think so when I call him randomly, and he drops everything to meet me. Some days I think not. I don't have too many options, nor do I have the energy to find them. Am I repeating my mistakes with men? From the emotionally unavailable Elifasi to Jan and his promises? Am I repeating history with Jan? How do I know if I've picked a lousy seed again?

Eli and I got married full of promises that are comatose now. I'd be selling myself short, trusting Jan, giving him full access to me while having no evidence from our past to show me that he could protect me.

Jan. I stare at him, his thick eyebrows, deep-set light-brown eyes, and his summer-set brown skin glazing in the sunlight. I press the tips of my fingers against his sharp jaw and his lips, memorizing the shape of his face, his breath a firelight against my skin. "It's easy to make promises, not so to fulfill them," I whisper, placing the remote back into his hands. "I have much to lose, and you've nothing to worry about."

He looks sadly at the remote before putting it into his pants pocket. His breath is warm against my face when he whispers, "If we're going to have a serious conversation, let's at least relax a bit."

I raise an eyebrow as he uncorks a bottle of wine.

"Isn't it too early for a drink?" I ask, reaching for two wine glasses.

"I've been up since 3:00 a.m., work shit," he says, walking toward the fireplace, pressing a switch to ignite it. We sit in the lounge, and I watch his Adam's apple bob up and down as he takes a long sip.

"There's a cost to trusting you, Jan," I say. "Losing my child, going to prison . . . Any slip-up will lead to that. As you've revealed, your family is exempt from what we ordinary people experience."

I have a terrifying fear that although Elifasi may have the power to protect our child, he wouldn't dream of wanting it, for it would mean him being a single parent should I be imprisoned. Would he truly let her die because of that? He'd instead find a new wife and start a family from scratch; after all, he completely cut ties from his previous body-hop's identity. No, I can't think such things, for it'll only give them life and jinx death into my daughter. It's only real if I say it out loud, and my husband would never abandon me or his child like that.

What kind of life is this that my freedom is infinitesimally restricted? Should I wait a hundred years until the law tightens or loosens its noose around my body? Should I consider investing my entire season in relocating to a place that treats women better, like Canada, where my other best friend immigrated? There is no perfect place for a person like me.

“You know I would never let anything happen to you,” Jan says.

A laugh escapes my mouth at his naivety and audacity. “One thing, Jan, that you don’t understand is that you haven’t lived as a woman in this place, so it’s easier for you to make promises,” I say, leaning onto my knees, grazing my glass across the table’s edge. “I know married friends with men and women like you. Promises, promises, promises—being used, and when the price gets too high, we’re discarded. My friend in Cape Town was microchipped, single, and got into a relationship with a wealthy woman who promised him marriage and a perfect life. But marrying a microchipped man would destroy her career and image, so she bought time by asking that they be private. When they were photographed together, landing in the gossip magazines, she took only a few hours to toss my friend aside and find someone ‘respectable’ she could marry to confirm her reputation. His career suffered, and hers is still intact.”

“It’s been two years, and you think I would do that to you?” Jan asks. “I’m the one getting divorced.”

“My husband is dangerous.” The words are projectiles propelling from my mouth before I can stop them. They land on him with shock, and his eyes widen in surprise. Perhaps now he will feel the risk. “Eli monitors me in the house and can monitor me outside the house. What’s to stop him from logging into my feed? From seeing us in this instance, watching us? Nothing. He can find a sneaky way to do so, and his colleagues will surely protect him if he’s, say, caught in the act.”

Jan’s perplexed look turns into worry. “Well, he hasn’t said anything, has he?”

“The thing about Eli is that he knows how to use resources available to him to his advantage, even people he despises,” I say instead. “He hates one of his colleagues, but you would think they’re best friends when you see them together. It scares me sometimes how Eli’s calculative on the fly when unplanned events occur for him to use to his advantage. It would take a while for a normal person to see that they can turn a situation in their favor. And honestly, he can be very patient waiting for the outcome knowing that it'll be fruitful and hence worth the discomfort he has to endure."

"Discomfort?" Jan asks.

"If he knows that I had an affair, for example, he'd keep his mouth shut to keep me comfortable or docile, so I don't see what he has planned for me, so I don't mess his promotion up. He'll probably wait to get to the top position before he kicks me to the curb. You're only valuable to him for as long as you're useful."

Jan sighs. "That's petty."

"Angazi, but Eli has an eye for spotting strategies in the most minor scenarios. His brain is always on, ticking, and working, processing the environment and the people in it like life is a never-ending chess game. Sometimes I can tell by the shade of concentration in his eyes that he's scheming something. I was a chess piece bride, probably. Eli is not the man you give an office in a powerful organization and expect him not to go snooping around lured by the power of access. To you, you wouldn't see him step foot out of those boundaries, but he's long left the room and already using that power on you to blind you from seeing his steps."

"You think he's using the technology at work for his benefit?" Jan asks, shocked, which is surprising for someone who's the son of an unscrupulous businessman.

"Probably. He'd never admit that to his wiretapped wife. Trust no one. Not even dead people. He says, 'Secrets always come out if you bury them in people. So bury the secret in yourself to keep it safe.'"

Jan leans back, thumb to his chin, musing. "Perhaps I shouldn't quite undermine a man like your husband."

"He interrogated me after my forensic evaluation about an affair I'm having, but nothing came of it. After all, I'm behaving as he'd like," I say, pondering. "Well, I'm behaving to a certain extent. On paper, he's a family man, has the package of a wife and child—he benefits from it as long as I uphold that image, too."

Jan clenches his fingers around his wine glass. "Nelah, why are you still married to him if he's dangerous to you?"

"It's less dangerous in the marriage than out of it," I say, gulping my wine. "Don't you get it? You don't just book out from dangerous men who wield such power."

"Does that mean you're planning something?" Jan asks, his voice heavily salted with excitement.

I ignore the question and ask, "You say you can protect me, but do you have the power to protect me from a man like him?"

A breath hitches in his chest, and he stares at the fireplace, the flames reflecting in his irises, mesmerizing him into a far-off memory. "When I graduated from university, I started running one of my father's subsidiaries in South Africa and Dubai. Our businesses are all kept in the family, and my father groomed me to head these companies. You don't negotiate with my father. You follow his instructions. That's how I grew up."

"Why are you telling me this?" I ask. "It's in no way related to what I just said."

"You asked me if I have any power to stop a man like your husband," he says. "May I continue?"

I nod, drinking in his words rather than the wine.

"If I disobeyed him, I'd lose everything, be disowned," Jan says, twisting the stem of the wine glass in his fingers. "My father made sure to remind me of that threat. If he needed something, I had to drop everything I was doing to satiate him."

I recall the times I spent with Jan. He'd get a call from his father and leave immediately. It frustrated me that he was at the beck and call of his father, dropping everything, regardless of what we were doing. We'd argue because I never understood why he allowed himself to be his father's slave.

"Initially, I was blinded by my privilege until I couldn't stand it anymore being under his thumb," Jan continues. "I worked hard to separate myself from him, but he had informants everywhere and would block and threaten me. It took two hundred years plus to navigate without him finding out—"

"Two hundred?" I ask, perplexed. "This is your first lifespan, no?"

"Well, by the book, yes. But it's my second."

The anger struggles to flow in my body, for I am fed up with their intoxicated privilege. "What does this mean? You're not his real son?" I ask.

"I was his son in my first lifespan. We were known as an uncle and son of the family," Jan says.

I gape. Close my mouth, stare at the passing scene outside our tinted windows. "Fok maan." I turn to him. "Have you ever been on the waiting list?"

He looks ahead and steeples his hands between his legs. "No," he says quietly. I think I misheard him. "No," he repeats. "But, unlike the rest of my family, my memories were erased when I entered this lifespan. My family met many obstacles this time, so I wasn't the only Koshal who endured this loss."

"What was different this time?" I ask. "The power of the Koshal name unable to be effectively corrupt?"

Jan shakes his head. "I've just caught whispers about the embroilment of the Murder Trials, Matsieng, and memories. I don't know how those link together. But whoever they were dealing with couldn't allow them that much privilege because Matsieng is dealing with a deficit of resources."

"Deficit of resources? Why would Matsieng need resources? What type of resources?"

He shrugs. "I was never given access to that information."

A cold breath escapes my lips, and I curl my fingers around my wine glass. "Your secrets are of no value to me," I whisper. "If you think that's how you'll coerce me."

Jan continues, "I had to be careful of what I said, whom I spoke to, and whom I was headhunting for the companies I wanted to start. Of course, when I started my second lifespan, I had to start from scratch and reconnect to the people I was secretly talking to. I had to strategize on whose identity I'd use to register and front companies. I had to use technology that obscured my identity in meetings and calls. By the time I got out, he was too stunned, he admired my skills, and he was surprisingly calm."

"That doesn't sound like Aarav," I whisper, suddenly cold.

He stares deep into his wine. "There's something I never told you. Before, you used to ask why I allowed him so much control over me.

It isn't for the money and power of the Koshal family. It's because my identity, the body he gave me, is controlled by my father."

Terror fills my lungs. "What does that mean?"

"He has me hostage in this body." Jan breathes out the weight of his demise. "My father has a trail of evidence that could destroy my life if it were revealed. He got me the first and second bodies illegally. The evidence will only incriminate me and not him. If I don't follow his instructions, he will use all that documentation to expose me to the authorities. After all, he colludes with politicians and the government. It'll only be easy for him to ensure that even my being a Koshal won't protect me. So I minimally find ways to satisfy him without forgetting myself, which is a difficult balance."

"Jesus, have you tried to destroy the evidence he has?" I ask.

A sad smile spreads across Jan's face. "Love, you have a dangerous man in your life, and so do I. It is less dangerous to be his son than outside that kinship. And he's been here for a long time to know how to protect his evidence."

"Fuck, Jan, if I'd known."

"I didn't want to burden you with that," he confesses. "I've thought about trafficking myself out of this identity, but I have children and people I love. Divorcing myself from this identity is as difficult as you divorcing your husband. I despise my father. Sometimes I fantasize about killing him, but . . . I'm not capable of murder. Do you think it's beautiful that my privilege comes from the crimes my family commits? No, it comes at a cost, and I wish to be free of the Koshal family."

I stare at my wine glass, unable to consume anything. "I feel terrible for how I treated you when it came to him. I didn't know—"

"That we are victims to men?" he says, a sad laugh escaping his mouth. "I may not know your life as a woman, but even powerful men abuse me."

"What's your plan?"

"For decades, I tried finding trails that would connect him to his illegal body-hopping scheme he got me entangled in, but he's been good in keeping his hands clean of the deed. If the people he worked with haven't disappeared or died, some aren't willing to speak for fear of the

Koshal name. I've considered incriminating him for other things, but if he falls, he'll take everyone down with him."

"These men can't be that untouchable," I say.

"Well, it seems they are. For now."

The fire dances in its furnace. "Then how can you promise to protect me from Eli when you can't even protect yourself from your father?"

He swirls the wine glass, watching the dark red liquid spin and spin before drinking it to its last drop. Stares at me. "Love, my father is more powerful than Elifasi. I do have my advantages being within the confines he has me in. Elifasi is nothing but an ant compared to him. I come from the most powerful family in this country. Your husband is easily disposable. I will use my family's power to protect you if I must. We are effective and fast." He pulls the remote from his pocket, placing it into my hands. "Do you trust me now?"

I am moving from one powerful man to another. Which one is more dangerous for me? There's a thrill of excitement knowing that I could ask Jan anything, and he would do it. He's observing me as if he can see my thoughts forming a line in my mind.

"Would you prefer if your husband got promoted or demoted?" he asks. "Remember that promotion will give him more power. A demotion will inadvertently affect the finances of your marriage. Or would you prefer a microchip-free body today? You do understand that my words mean nothing without evidence," he says, tapping his wrist to project a hologram and mentally tapping a series of texts I can't see. Within a minute, he gets a call and nods, whispering, "We'll be there in thirty minutes."

My mouth falls open. "What did you do? Where are we going?"

He takes hold of my hands and guides us to the car, which cruises past Phakalane's tree-lined streets, the sun a gilded eye in the sky. It takes half an hour of driving through graveled back roads into Oodi, shadows of thorn bushes slurring against the windows as I'm swallowed by the leather seats, alcohol simmering in my blood.

We come to high wooden gates and a tall fence singing with electricity. A groundskeeper waves as we drive into a vast land of trees to a white-washed farmhouse juxtaposed with an elegant-looking warehouse with the backdrop of an orchard.

"What is this place?" I ask.

"It's one of the body-fostering agencies that our family owns and runs to assist in storing bodies for those whose minds are held up in immigration application systems," Jan says, driving the car into the garage.

A dissonance in my mind as I watch dust unravel behind our car's trail. My life before arriving here feels like a distant mirage. I open my door and slide out into the serenity of the outside, the air cool against my skin. A dog barks in the distance.

"This way," Jan says, jerking his head to the right.

I follow him toward the warehouse, which appears metallic with a glassy surface. Inside, it's sophisticated, with reflective surfaces and without many openings or windows, as if the intrusion of sunlight would deteriorate the building's innards.

A doctor approaches with quick steps, smiling and shaking Jan's hand. "Mr. Koshal, seeing you again is a great pleasure." His eyes skim mine, but he mentions nothing about my presence as he leads us to a set of doors with the words AUTHORIZED ACCESS. I capture nothing of his face except his white coat, hairy hands, and shiny shoes.

Past the doors is a room similar to the Matsieng Fertility Fund, dark as if subterranean with bodies stored in glasslike coffins, eyelids slid over the eyes peacefully. The doctor, who has no identity card for me to know his name, guides us toward one metallic-bottomed coffin where a body lies waiting, naked, face up—a woman's body.

"We have the theater ready for the mind transfer and the documentation you need, sir, which we procured with some difficulty, but under these circumstances, we've done everything in our power. We also have a host to take over her identity and the associated risks." The doctor's eyes skirt mine when he says this. "My partners are still working with our associates at the Matsieng Fertility Fund to transfer ownership of the fetus to Ms. Nelah Bogosi-Ntsu; that may be highly unlikely, but we are trying."

I gape, shock hanging at my ribcage.

"That will be all," Jan says. The doctor nods, taking that as his cue to leave. Jan turns to face me. "I know you don't want this, but I wanted to show you what I can do. Your husband will receive the promotion. Do you trust me now?"

"This is impossible," I whisper, grazing my fingers across the coffin's façade, thinking about my best friend Kea, who may have been in these places while waiting for naturalization body-hop approval into a different continent. Could the Koshal family have hosted her body and sold it?

"This is one of our businesses," Jan says. "Of course, we follow a set of regulations, but there's always a loophole in how a business runs."

"My friend, Kea—"

"I remember you talking of her, and I looked into it," he says, and my eyes cling to his face with hope. "Our agency never fostered her, but one run by another businessman did. Unfortunately, her body was sold to a private buyer. From thereon, I've no leads."

"Does that happen often?"

He nods, folding his arms. "Her body can be written off as damaged goods and cremated when it, in fact, was sold."

"For what purpose?" I ask.

He raises his eyebrow. "Illicit motives of traffickers."

My nails clasp my lips. Oh, Kea. Shem skepsel.

He takes my hand, walking us back to the outside and sunlight, and I take deep breaths of the flowery scent saturated in the air. Push back the thoughts of Kea, of the devastation, as Jan waits for the calm to claim my body.

Finally, I say, "If my microchip fails to record any part of my day, it will get flagged in the monitoring system, and I will be immediately hauled in for a chip repair or replacement by the government."

"The microchip will send a technical failure notification if the recording has no moving pictures or if it's completely blank," he says in agreement. "This device will manipulate the images fed into your microchip into a sanitized version, say if you're taking drugs or driving a knife into someone's flesh."

"Bathong, Jan!" I exclaim.

"I joke, I joke about the last part," he says, raising his hands in surrender, then strokes my cheek. "You wouldn't hurt a fly. The changes implemented aren't that drastic—the device blots out the illegal parts of the visuals, or if the change requires too much an edit, it augments a new scene using images from your archived footage, but it never changes the scene's location. Otherwise, that will contradict your live real-time coordinates and set off an alert to the surveillance system. Now remember that your story has to correlate with the manipulated images fed to your microchips if your morning assessor interrogates you about your whereabouts."

I stare at him, unable to find my words.

He places the remote into my palm, and perhaps for the first time, I trust him.

The peace this will give me, the freedom, what I could get away with. I stand on my tiptoes, press my lips against him. "Thank you. You've no idea what this means to me."

His lips smile against mine, words leaking into my mouth: "This is also for you. When you want time to yourself. Away from everything. The surveillance. Your husband. Me."

I step back. Brush my braids over my shoulder. "Never you."

"Funny you say that when you won't even remember *us* last year."

"Ag, Jan," I moan.

He tucks his hands into his jeans pockets. "We've been together for close to two years, but for some odd reason, you pretend as if the year-and-a-half never happened."

"It *never* happened."

"You just disappeared."

"I had a miscarriage."

"And now you're back."

"Jan."

"S'tru. Don't look at me like that, ja. If you stay married to him, this can only go so long until I find someone else. Then this will be over. I mean it."

"So it's okay that I cheat for you, but you can't cheat for me?"

"I *have* been cheating for you, too. I'm divorcing my wife."

I swallow the tension, the room chills. "You're mine, Jan."

A panic grips me when he says, "If I am to take this risk, I must say this: I can't be yours forever if you won't be mine forever."

THURSDAY, OCTOBER 8

10:40 /// MISOGYNISTIC PRINCIPLES

"I knocked off early yesterday, visited my cousin," Elifasi says over our supper of takeaways, a supper I wasn't able to make due to a late meeting. "As soon as I sat down, his wife served us food and drinks. Without instruction."

I rest my chin on my palm, twist my fork into the chow mein. Thinking about my daughter, it pains me. "Ja nè. She's such a good wife. If only I was good as her. But I had to spend more time at the firm to make payments on our house and that marble counter you're eating off of that you so badly wanted."

He chokes on his chicken. "Mxm. Keep reminding me of how this is your house. I'm sorry I don't make enough money."

I don't have the energy for this tonight. We both have our watches on that show us the feed of our growing baby, its vitals and health information, which are very promising. I took a snapshot of her little raised foot, perhaps what would feel like a kick, and showed it to my husband, who didn't show the faintest interest, putting me in a sour mood. I'm terrified that he's lost interest in our daughter. Ever since the day I almost botched my evaluations, he's kept distant, as if to avoid loving our child, which would inevitably make it challenging to survive another heartbreak should we lose our daughter. What does that mean if we don't lose our daughter—will he open his heart to her? Does he still like being a father, or has it forever changed, and am I to blame for that? Will I always be the one interested in our child, doing most of the work in raising her, and him only enjoying the pleasanter parts of showing off fatherhood to his colleagues, our family, and the rest of the world? How can I rely on his love if it's this fickle, if he's now whittled our daughter's significance down to a status symbol? This became his pattern after the beginning of our marriage, when we were full of hope and ideas; as those dreams shattered, he drew further and further back, as if to believe in something was to plant a land mine he'd rather avoid.

We weren't supposed to give up so easily. He's completely different now from the man I married, and I must protect my daughter from him. With motherhood, I will ascend to the matriarch role I never, until now, thought I'd desire this badly to shield my daughter from harm.

"What's with that look?" he asks.

"I don't know when our idea of family changed," I say. "We wanted the same things—I still do, but you no longer do."

When I was transplanted into this body when it was eighteen years old, I was enrolled in a program to help stifle grief and loneliness. The government has tried to maintain the spirit and cultural pride of Botho, which relies on the interconnections of people since the traditional family setup is fractured through amnesia per lifespan transitions. Community programs have been integrated into schools, recreational activities, apartment buildings, dating sites, and apps that can pair body-hoppers with platonic or marriage partners, and they are free to accept or reject that recommendation. They would be advertised on radio shows, TV, and media, using influencers and actors as ambassadors to drive the message of connection. These programs help those placed in pubescent or adult bodies. Since they've lost out on the formative years of creating ties with family or childhood, body-hoppers feel broken and untethered to society; this assimilation process helps root body-hoppers into a community. Beginning just a few weeks after being planted into the Bogosi family, I met weekly, for over seven years, with a psychologist who created activities to encourage a relationship with my newfound family. There was someone I could speak to and a group of other teenagers who remained lifelong friends, like Kea. We'd interact and talk, creating a sense of belonging.

A dating app recommended Elifasi as a 100 percent compatible marriage partner; we met and clicked and continued clicking until we married. Maybe that void of social isolation never went away entirely, and I fully relied on these programs and married Elifasi—it felt perfect.

He just can't seem to understand what serious financial straits my firm and our lives are in, or perhaps he doesn't give any more fucks about my firm given the dire loss and hit it's taken and to think more about it aggravates him. Maybe this is his way to make it hurt him less, for he miscalculated in investing his savings and this firm is now a symbol of his failure. I tease my fingers into my temples at a gnawing headache, wondering what Jan is doing and if I can manage to sneak out tonight to see him.

Everywhere around our dining table is darkness and loneliness, save for the chandelier hanging above.

"My cousin's in a dark spot," Elifasi says, chewing.

"Another one? They taking turns now?"

He glares, and the devil smolders in his eyes. "Watch your tone, ek sê. This is *my* family you're talking about."

I stare at the clock. "I apologize."

"Need to loan him some cash, chop-chop," he says.

Fucking Black tax, the ruin in his family. "Which one?" I ask.

He pauses, his fork and knife mid-air. "Does it matter? He's family. We care for family."

But I know which cousin it is. "You mean the same cousin who lost his job because he stole from his boss, then continued to lose many more jobs? Why do you keep enabling him?"

His nostrils flare, and he stares steely-eyed at me, black depths in his eyes. "You always turn everything into a fight. My family has been dirt poor for years. I don't have the same privilege you have: being downloaded into the daughter of a rich family that hardly spends time together. I got downloaded into that of a poor man, yet his family took care of me. Is it because I have two more lifespans than you that you look down on me because I haven't made it?"

It's his weakness that he has over 900 years, yet I've achieved more than him in half the amount of time. He's left with 110 years before his lifespan expires. The upside, I have an extra 82 years to be free of him.

So I retort, "You're the one that keeps reminding me you're on your fifth lifespan—"

"They'll blame you if I turn my back on them. Is that how *you*"—he points his knife at me—"want my family to view you, as my wife?"

"No." I tiptoe on eggshells, afraid to crack one. A tsunami, a nuclear explosion will occur. He'll turn into a sour mood for days, and I won't know how to correct it. This is always our evening routine or whatever-time-of-the-day routine. I stare at my wedding band, a gold prison wrapped around my finger. Fuck this. "Do *you* understand my firm's experiencing a low?" I say. "Clients failing to pay, credit cards maxed. We're still waiting for the results from the Architecture Awards Grants—"

"Aren't the results coming in tomorrow?" he asks. "That would do us some good."

"And if my firm doesn't win? There are bills that can't wait—like our baby girl. I'm so terrified of losing her, yet you want to be an ATM for a man who refuses to be responsible."

He waves his hand. "I told you, I'll talk to someone. I'll eventually find the money to recoup all our costs."

"You keep saying that."

Deadlines are noose-tight, and he's too chilled. Today, I was scuttling through the city, scrambling through associates to family, trying to borrow money to pay for our rising bills due at the Matsieng Fertility Fund.

The night is dark and empty when we go to bed. I plead for him to borrow money from his other cousin, whose media business is experiencing a boom. He glares at me. "Nelah," he enunciates beratingly, "I don't want to bother my family, ja. What's strange is your persistence yet you won't even try to convince your parents to authorize your access to your inheritance."

"They gave me land for my firm to develop. Don't you think it's too much to ask for money that doesn't belong to me?" I ask.

"If they're going to keep showing you off as their daughter to their friends and relatives benefiting from your image and hard work, they owe you," he says. "It's a two-way thing, and you are fully entitled to that inheritance."

My parents will forever struggle to accept me as their daughter. I may only access my inheritance when they pass away, and perhaps they feel that once they've passed away, it's better to give the money to their pseudo-daughter rather than a stranger, for they love this body more than they do me—this body that symbolizes the image of their original daughter. But I have the strange feeling that there's more to the story, especially regarding how they became wealthy and where they got money to start their businesses. They constantly avoided eye contact and looked at each other in signaled gazes, which made me feel like an outsider for years. But when I became an adult, I realized that there's shame and guilt in those glances. Not only do I value my parents based on their wealth, but now it's as if we're waiting for them to die quickly so we can get the money. No, I can't let Eli manipulate me into thinking this way about my family.

"Is that all my family is to you? Just a place to get cash from?" I ask. "Is that why you hardly came to our family lunches?"

"I stopped for the same reason you stopped going to those sweet old lunches." He narrows his eyes at me. "You're always making me into a villain, yet I'm the one who also mortgaged my savings to fund that little firm of yours, which wouldn't have risen to the heights it did if it weren't for me. Your career wouldn't be what it was if it wasn't for me taking a chance on you. Where was your family then? I bankrolled you thinking we'd live a financially comfortable life. Look where that put us, so even my salary alone isn't good enough to sustain us, this Wombcubator and child you so desperately wanted, and the ability to support my family. So what if your firm got us this house and the cars and partly the Wombcubator—when was the last time you earned something? I am entitled to that inheritance as much as you." He draws out his hands. "Great poverty we'll be bringing our child into."

The reality of his words sends a cold chill to my skin, that he believes he owns my career because he helped me. It's the level of hate in his words, the anger—does he now regret marrying me? Will this affect how he fathers our daughter? His spiel spills rage into my body. I'm possessed by the overwhelming thought to end this marriage, head to my parents' home, and beg and plead for them to help me.

God, what am I thinking? Divorce? How can I bring a baby into a broken family? I'm certain that, like many traditional men, Elifasi believes raising our child is solely a woman's job and won't participate. How, then, will I raise her alone? How has everything become this disastrous? There's a baby we risk losing. No, I can't let that happen—these are just the pitfalls of married life. Surely every married couple has these types of arguments and gets through them. Perhaps these are the same fights my parents hid from us as teenagers, and they've been married for thirty years and are still going strong. Eli and I can do this. I have to trust my husband, for my daughter's sake.

But as religious as my parents are, why won't they help us if they know that an innocent child might suffer the consequences?

Before I even have the chance to respond or do anything, Eli turns onto his side, switches off his lamp, and falls asleep, snoring, with his back to me. A jolt of anger rushes through me, burns my eyes. I want to strangle him. To plunge a knife through his body, so he can feel what I feel. I want to punch the pride out of him. I am begging my husband to sacrifice his pride for *our* daughter. The traditional role I've roped around myself. The misogynistic principles from his family that I wear like a straitjacket for this bastard. This. Bastard.

How could I have been so stupid? To have been engulfed by his charm, sacrificed for him. I'm panicking and desperate. A black hole sucks me in.

FRIDAY, OCTOBER 9

04:40 /// BLOODY HELL

There's been a rerun of our firm's video application to the biannual Architecture Awards Grants playing on every TV station, my voice playing over the drone footage of our Woman Without Borders eco-home gated community—we won! It's a grand accolade, especially in an egregiously male-dominated industry.

I never thought I would regain my winning streak. Earlier in my career, I was considered a "paper architect"—an archaic term since we no longer use papers for construction drawings—because my designs never made it off the paper. They were too experimental, the forms too surrealist and daring. Some people deemed them alien spaceships, impractical for habitation and unconventional for our traditional construction industry. It was with the luck of snagging a few small projects in places like South Africa, China, the UK, and Tanzania that I established myself on foreign soil. Surprisingly, my designs won awards abroad for their functionality, creativity, and loyalty to identity. This helped me, garnered the attention that I needed, proving that I wasn't just a paper architect, and more organizations became interested in working with me. At the apex of my career, I returned home to focus my work here. Then the recession hit—which meant fewer projects, politics, corruption, and lack of luck coming into play—adversely affecting my firm. I wondered why I ever came back.

I was considered too opinionated. My designs were criticized so that the comment, too, demonized my culture, whether it was the traditional materials I used or the form that was considered primitive and distasteful. One former classmate told a reporter that I only passed in design school because I gave “lascivious” smiles to my male professors; it made him feel safer to believe that I surpassed him based on my looks rather than my talent. I was a top student highly focused on getting the job done, just the same as I was as a professional in the industry. In time, my persona was relegated to a bitchy abrasive person too focused on work and not family. My behavior was often criticized, and I was often told I was selfish. I struggled to base myself overseas. Trying to make a home in the body of a daughter of a family that would never accept me was already tricky. I struggled to belong abroad as a Black woman in a body I felt I didn’t deserve. If I stayed, I could have fought harder, and my company would’ve climbed sheer heights, but it’d have destroyed my mind.

My phone buzzes a special ringtone that sends vibrations through my cranium.

I slip out of bed, out of the bedroom, and into the guest bathroom. “Aweh, side-bitch,” I answer.

Jan laughs. “Congratulations on the big win, love. Are we getting high or what?” His baritone voice slides titillating vibrations up my thighs. Fuck, I miss this goddamned motherfucker. He’s my little secret. Maybe not so little. I giggle and lean against the double sink. “Name the crime, drug, and location, and I’m your victim.”

He laughs. “Man, do I love myself a good victim. I have the merger meeting this evening, just finalizing some shit. Should be done at 6:00 p.m. The townhouse. I’ll get the braai started, the gin, and of course, the *goods*. Then we’ll drive out for an adventure, a good old celebration.”

“Now I can put your gift to use. Silence this bloody microchip.”

“On a real note,” he says, “I’m really happy for you, Nelah. I know you’ve overworked yourself stiff to get where you are. To build this legacy for your daughter. And for other women. You’re a legend, love.”

My husband swings open the bathroom door. Bloody hell, I forgot to lock it. He thinks marriage equals a total lack of privacy. "Ja, that's the council regulation, but we'll see what to do with the building structure setbacks," I say, feigning a highly important meeting.

"Got it. Cheers, love." And Jan signs off.

My husband folds his arms. "It's time."

I am perfect, pure, and innocent. Well, except tonight.

19:40 /// GOD, I'M SO HIGH

Dinner date with the side-bitch, and I'm the bad bitch. Jan's fingers cuddle the remote that will hamper my microchip's recording of our time together, the little LED light is a smiling blue light—if it's not capturing what I'm doing, my activities won't get flagged by the police monitoring towers. I'm officially offline. Been popping pills since noon. Can't tell the time, how it clip-clopped from hot noon to sin-cold night, from office to the townhouse, home of our affair, paraded by the hooves of up-tempo music. But I'm here, night-clad, skin off. Elevated. This shit so good. Freckles of sweat skip my eye. Deep bass sways my vision. I swear the edges of my body fray. Skin more porous than usual. Mind lifts, slips through the skull, and Jan's milky way trickles down my neck—how'd I get down so quick? Fuck it, the universe is glorious.

Time jitters.

Jan's taut muscles writhe in his arms as he works the sommelier corkscrew into the wine bottle. Pours another glass under the warm glow from the valance lights. I'm dancing with the devil on my left side, God on my right, ain't sure which way I'm tipping by the end of tonight. But I'm a motherfucking god tonight. My foot daggers the air, clips a vase, shards sing the fucking night. Jan is somewhere, his voice a beast. It tremors through my uterus, and oh my God, I'm on my back.

Time is slayed, a dizzy bitch.

On the living room sofa, Jan's head's tucked in between my thighs, lips whispering to my lips, drives me heaven-high, tongue changes gear, strokes the G-spot, revs my heart. The night pushes my head back, and through the windows, it shows me the dark sky's broken into splinters of glittering stars.

My mind is racing, racing out of me, out of time. Light shimmies, buries into my sight.

"Joh, is that the sun?" I ask.

Jan kisses me. Gin on his breath.

I could be dying, but my orgasm straddles the constellation's reality. Husband only likes the devil in me. Not the sad. Not the clingy. Just the glitz and sin, the woman he fell in love with, cremated in marriage, exhumed by my lover. Vision sways, swimming in and out of my body. Lover stands, muscles licked by light. Walks to the glass table, skinny whites as its centerpiece. The moon's dead, caked and crusted into powdered stone; Jan rakes his face through it, inhales the crisp pulverized bone. Exhales. Swipes tongue along teeth's edge. Kisses me, I suck him high. He draws me one line. Guides my face. Nose slips some powdered moon into me. I skid into death's lane, smoke my lover high. I am his cigar, his lips rope around my orgasm. Cigarette sex. I love this man. Death tastes delicious, so another line. Palms to skull, I try to hold my mind in, but it's gone, it's gone, it's gone with God or the devil. The music's dancing, the room is shaking, gravity eclipses my entire being. Murdered the pain, I'm so numb, I'm invincible, I could kill a bitch. The music scratches, my soul stirs.

"I'm a notoriously excellent driver," I say.

Jan looks up from the table, where he's fixing a line, and smirks. "If the lady wants to go for a drive, then we're going for a drive."

I lean back. "I've driven in a worse state, way over the limit, never hit anything. We're safe, love. No accidents under my belt. I wouldn't jeopardize our future."

"Careful, don't get too cocky with that."

"Ooh, cocky."

He returns to the table. Mixes pills, mixes demons, fuck it.

My larynx works: "We shouldn't be mixing." But my voice speaks from the far side of the room—it laughs and tinkles.

Jan burns something on a spoon, that ceramic gold, a sinful taste of death—

Darkness, lock-jawed. Where'd we go?

I wake up in the driver's seat. Hands twisted around the wheel. The fast lane, a twisting sordid road, cut sharp by a speeding night. The speakers hush out cold, air-conditioned Afro-Mexican house tunes. Birdsong ripples through the music, cumbia tugs the beat forward, alchemizes the dark. We're floating in a dream; I'm just beneath the surface, the charango-flute current blurring me. My consciousness pulses, grows out of my body. The weightlessness of the world, perfection. The strings of the charango, its fingers across my skin—

"What's a charango?" Jan's eyes on me.

My voice laughs, catches our thoughts torpedoing from our mouths. "Charango, it's an Andean guitar."

He nods. "Where'd you get this music from?"

My voice crushes the dashboard, roadkill spiel: "An ex. From college. He was a DJ. We had a bad breakup. He took my virginity, so I stole his stack of music. It tore him up, more than the breakup did. It was good revenge. He had no backups." My throat snickers.

Jan nods his beer stein at me. "One would think you're a stickler for bastard boyfriends."

Again, time's a dizzy bitch. I feel the sun screaming in some part of the world, moonwalks to now. Dashboard: we meander off the A1 highway, through the Oodi-Modipane Road. No self-driving, no quantum computer steering the wheel. Just my love, a smooth tarmac, that svelte sky. The back road connects us through Ruretse to the Tlokweng border road.

How'd we get here from the house? Memory teeters, moves in reverse. Its sound system echoes into my head of an hours-back scene:

We barreled to the car, giggling and tripping over domestic paraphernalia. Then the road. A carbon-fiber body slew our rush; the machine, a classic 600-horsepower supercharged V16 engine, 722 pound-feet of torque of high, so high. God, I'm so high.

Me: "Where's my head?"

Jan: "It's here, babe." Hands me a joint.

Can't breathe.

His hand stops the window going down. "Don't, we're hotboxing." Hotbox, we're burning. Someone gonna dox us.

No guilt. No pain. Nothing. Taste for speed. The devil trickles through the vents, simmers with the tangling smoke. "You good?" Jan asks.

My voice: "Work hard, party hard, *ja*."

"I love you," he whispers.

I turn onto a graveled road, stretch my hand out to him, tease his five o'clock shadow. He kisses my fingers, curls his tongue around them. I sigh into the leather seat. His free hand reaches for my thighs, moves my black lace dress up. I moan. He pushes my panties aside, whispers, "You're wet."

I could have him right here, sex in a 200 km/h drive.

He tips the amber drink into his mouth.

The road is slick with rain, a horned devil.

The car sails through the ocean of dark.

The world spins. Distorted arms of trees snag the night.

"We're flying!" I shout-scream-cry.

Lightning blasts an avenue of trees into fluorescent ghosts.

The sky falls—

A dark shadow meteor-drops into the windshield. Its weight rolls, pinwheels against the hood onto the ground. A snap, a swerve. Bone-crunching.

"Jesus!" I scream. Swerve. Tires spit bits of rock to the side. Something catches in the wheel, it snags, swerving the car. The car swallows a lump on the gravel's tongue. Another lump. Skidding, my head snaps against the window, neck cracking at the base. Jan's hands slam into the dashboard, holding him steady. My eardrums pop, like the little sugary crackle sweets my niece eats. I hit the brakes. The car comes to a halt. My heart slams into my chest. My shoulder into the window. A standstill. The engine roars, sizzles. Hands braced against the wheel. Knuckles pale, snagging my skin taut. There are no speed bumps on this gravel. No wandering animals, except, perhaps, humans.

Jan's hand hits the dashboard again, breaths chugging from his chest. "What the hell was that?"

"Jan?" My voice is hoarse, pinched. My braids have escaped their bind, soggy wet at the temple. My hand returns into my vision dark red, not wine. My blood. "Jan?" My voice a squeaky scream.

I turn to Jan, eyes wide. He blinks, hand still on the handbrake, having killed the motion of the car. "What was that?" Jan whispers.

"That was a cow, right?" I ask.

"It'd have bashed the screen in," he says. "But a skinny cow wouldn't do that." It'd be a joke in a different scenario.

"I hit a skinny cow," I plead. "I hit a skinny cow." I hope. "I hit a skinny cow." My hands shake, unclasp the seatbelt after several tries. A gravel road. Farms too far off. Thorn trees. Dusty air. My fingers slip against the door latch. It won't open. I thumb the power lock, slide out into the heart-pounding dark, crumbling to the ground. I snap my head both ways, the dark giving forms to nothingness. Someone will grab me. Someone will grab me. A crunch of stones startles me. My heel snaps as I stumble to a stand.

The passenger door dings open as Jan exits the car. He walks to the back. I check the front. I exhale a sigh. We're safe. Something must have fallen—but I look up to find nothing suspicious, just an empty sky bearing down on us. When I look back, the car is undamaged. No shrapnel crack on the windshield as I thought I'd seen. No blown-out airbags. The night, dead silent. I open my mouth, my windpipe blowing out a chilly smoke into the air. I rub my hands together, cup them against my warm breath, and stagger onto the sandy road. I drop to my knees, cough, splurge blood onto the ground. Nails grip through mounts of sand.

"Let's get out of here," I say, but Jan is suspiciously quiet.

My feet crunch on sharp rocks and soft sand as I head to the car's rear. Jan stares at me, taillights red in his bloodless face. He's staring down. Two cones of light probe the dark, the smoky road. On the ground, a torso burns from death, gargling its last breath. I stoop. I scream. I cry. She lies there, eyes wide, staring at me. The engine hums. I stare up. A lonely moon fog-tied to the sky, looks at me: *I know what you've done*. A sob crumples my mouth. A silent sky, no drone, no AI eye. The moon is unencumbered by forensic science.

Around us, sand still swirls around like smoke. Pain singes my lower neck, where the microchip's retrofitted into my body. I snap, touching my arms, my body. "What's going on, Jan?" My body goes cold. There's a dead woman on the ground. I killed a person.

My microchip has seen everything and has prompted a warning alert to the server towers. Any minute now, a minuscule drone will spear toward me. I look up through the windscreen. Something's wrong.

The sky, a machine-less moon unencumbered by science and forensics, is no alibi, no witness. The microchip didn't stop me, didn't control me, didn't paralyze me with electrocution. It let me kill a young woman. No drone rips through the night to offer CCTV footage of me, to debilitate me further. I am unbound. I am a murderer.

SATURDAY, OCTOBER 10

01:34 /// A TERRIBLE MOTHER, A SLUT, AND A MURDERER

The last smoke of dust trails into the dark. Silence settles on our shoulders. Thunder booms, murdering any sound, any life. Jan moves forward, feet crunching earth. A wind ripples through. Jan drops to his knees, devastation a gloom in his eyes. An owl hoots from the cumbia music in the car, making me jump.

I close my eyes, rub them, try to rewind time. I look down: a slung Barbie doll, tossed by a tantrum-run death, skin finely dusted in mild melanin. Tire marks on her face, her torn jeans. My gut convulses. I turn, and my vomit spurts onto the road's shoulder, muddled with shrieks.

I lean over. Two locks of black braid stuck in the fender, congealing, bloody flesh stuck to it like a clot of sticky jam. Dizzy. The world's moving too fast. On the ground, she lies. I see her. The pain licks at the jarring bone protruding from her elbow, a piece of white beauty sticking out, sharp as a sword. Jan kneels next to me, his hands around my face, the blood, the pain. "Are you okay? Did you get hurt?"

Nothing sobers you like a murder.

My microchip records my every waking moment; it's supposed to respond to a person's intent and actions. Whether I intend to commit murder or end up in an accident, my microchip is supposed to stop me either by electric shock or by taking control of my motor neurons and alerting the police monitoring towers, triggering my drone and the authorities to locate me. I tap my wrist, checking the functionality of my microchip on a projected hologram. Microchip outages are rare, but they do happen, but mine doesn't show any diagnostic errors or failure. If no alert is transmitted from it to the police towers, the government will assume nothing of note is occurring.

In a panic, I stare at the car's console where the remote control lies. Its LED light blinks blue, meaning it's been intercepting my microchip the whole time, meaning this accident hasn't gotten flagged, meaning I'm free for now. I take a deep breath, relieved. God, so I can trust Jan.

"She's still alive. Jan, call the police, an ambulance," I say. I kneel, touch her head like a fractured egg. "Oh my God, sweetie. We'll get help, hang on, okay? You'll be okay. We're going to get you out of here, okay?"

Her eyes reel to the side. She gargles blood instead of words. "Help . . ." she manages, raising her hand to my face, smearing it with blood. Her nails scrape my neck before falling back to her side.

A twig snaps. I look up. Jan. Doing nothing. Just standing there. A dangerous panic in his eyes. "What are we going to tell them?" His eyes are listless, and I stand up to make him concentrate, to make sense. "She touched you. Your fingerprints are all over her," he continues. "Your DNA is beneath her nails. Your tire marks are on her face." I step back, fear collapsing into my lungs. "We're high and intoxicated—pumped with drugs—caught in a negligent accident. What's *she* going to tell them? No, fuck—what's *she* doing in the middle of nowhere late at night?"

Breaths chug out from her chest.

I attempt to touch him, but I'm too afraid. "Jan, sh-sh-she's still alive."

"I . . ." The girl struggles to say something, words blanched with spurts of blood. "I won't say anything." Something protrudes from her chest. A chunk of metal, winking back the lights from the car. She's impaled. A grisly image. Biblical undertones. But priapic insinuation. Fingers gnarled, I step forward, something cushy beneath my foot. It's her thumb, the soft tissue gorged. The taillights are lurid red on her body. Her small body. Her thin fingers. The light in her brown eyes. Her braids, caught in the spinning wheel, peeled off her scalp. Her braids. Her skin, the layer folded back like the peel of a fruit. Jesus. What a painful way to die. I turn, vomit again. She: Loose designer denim. Boots. Parka jacket. Braids running down like a rope for strangulation.

My first reaction: I reach for my phone.

"Stop. We're high and drunk," Jan repeats. "We're over the limit. This is no slap on the wrist. We'll be virtually incarcerated. We'll never have a chance of getting transferred into another body."

Fuck. No.

Jan touches my shoulder, eyes bloodshot, hair amok. "Incarceration was fine eons ago, get some bigshot lawyers knowing we'd get a few years' jail time, get a couple of visits from family, friends," he says, tone acerbic. "Not now. Not anymore. You're thrown out of your body. Incarceration now, you're sure as dead. At least with death, you get the chance to go to heaven or hell or something. But now, there's no coming back into a new body. You're gone forever. We can't lose three lives tonight. Better we lose just one." He looks at her, cringes. "Death picked her. Not us. We have a chance to save ourselves. To see your daughter grow up, her graduation, her first job, her first marriage . . ." He steps forward. "Nelah, this is your third body. We have to take this opportunity if the microchip didn't snitch on you."

"Maybe because it's faulty, they'll go easy on us," I say.

"You've been drinking, smoking a joint, snorting cocaine—you're fucking high. I can smell it off you, and you killed someone. It's negligent. It's a crime." He stops pacing, holds my shoulders together as if to keep me in place. "What will women think of you?" It confuses me, and I'm lost in time, but he continues: "Public opinion. What will everyone think of you—not me, but *you*? Out with another man. Leaving your own husband at home to get high and drunk with another man. Just for sex. The news media will eat you up. They will scandalize you. Use your name to get famous for their racy stories, for their bylines.

They will objectify and scandalize you. Women will hate you. You will be the most hated woman in the world. Because you left your own unborn child and husband to have sex with a man and ultimately kill a woman. Your reputation will sully your daughter's life—it will follow her everywhere."

He's hit me where it hurts. "Fuck you!" I push him. "Fuck you!" I scream.

"Is this woman—doing God knows what in the dark—really worth saving? Is she really worth sacrificing your family, your business, your reputation, *your daughter* for?"

Two things hit me at once: That he's a bastard for manipulating me. That he is right. He's a man. No one will shit on him for leaving his twins at home. No one will shit on him wanting to loosen up for once. Because he's a man and I am a mother, straitjacketed into a cliché-ridden role I must live. I'm not supposed to be a person. I'm worse than a woman; I'm a microchipped one. I'm supposed to be at home, always, as a prude wife. The shame. I feel embarrassed; how could I be those things, the way he says them? She's my baby—going out doesn't mean I love her any less. "I only wanted to go out, to have fun."

"That's not what they're going to see," he says.

Jan's right, because it won't matter what I feel or why I wanted to do it—they will shame me for being a terrible mother, a slut, and a murderer. Who would want anyone to think they are something they are not?

She starts crying, squeaky, soft, high-pitched voice. How the hell is she still conscious? "You don't have to take me to a hospital," she says. "You can keep me somewhere—I know a doctor who will help with my wounds, who won't say anything. He'll just want money. Please, I won't say anything." Her voice is pureed softness, delicate and fruity. She sobs again, blood instead of tears. Her screams mix with blood.

"To bring a witness who'll blackmail us for more money? No." Jan folds his arms, not looking at her.

"Why are you so suspicious? Jan, she's just a young woman. She could be your sister."

His eyes soften. She stares at him, eyes wide with fear, grips my leg. Me, her only hope.

"I'm sorry." She starts crying. "Please, please, don't kill me. I'm scared. Terrified of the dark. Don't leave me here."

"But you were here. In the dark. Alone," Jan says. And it seems suspicious. She shouldn't be apologizing. He grips me tightly. "Honestly, babe, you're lucky that you went undetected in your microchip assessments. If it weren't for your husband influencing the forensic evaluation verdict in your favor, your mind would be incarcerated in a MindCell at this very moment."

"How did you know that my husband did that?" I ask.

"I know everything, love," he whispers, as if it's romantic.

I shiver, wondering if there is anything of me left that is private to myself without Eli or Jan knowing.

"My family's name has protected me thus far," Jan continues. "The Murder Trials will go easier on me than you. We know women don't fare well with them."

"You fucking promised me, Jan, with all your power, that you could take care of anything," I shout.

"Anything didn't mean murder," he emphasizes.

"I can't believe you. How was I stupid to trust you? I fucking trusted you!"

"Listen to me. I'm taking care of us now. This is how I can do it."

I clutch my mouth. Stagger back. Sick swirls onto my tongue. I swallow. "Regarding the Murder Trials, what exactly happens to the women? You know something I don't?"

"The Murder Trials don't reveal the involved parties, do they? Well, except the ones they mind-incarcerate, which is a high majority of women. Neither do we know the details by which it processes undetected criminals. Even if we get caught, I could get away with this scot-free. And you—a married woman cheating on her husband, worse, you're wiretapped with a criminal history—you'd take the fall for everything." He strokes my cheek, voice gentler now. "I don't want that to happen to you. But if you want us to report it, Nelah, knowing what the stakes are, then there's nothing else I can do. I will come with you, I promise. You decide: Do we bury her or hand ourselves in?"

I back away, shaking my head, fearful.

"Then," he says, "we have to bury this secret."

I look down. "Bury the secret, bury the body."

"Do you have any tools in your car?" Jan asks, not wasting time like I am.

"A helmet for construction site visits," I say distantly. "Boots."

"I'll try to use the helmet to dig a grave." He quickly opens the trunk, pulls out a helmet, hurries into the woods, starts digging.

Her head is cushioned on my lap. When did I kneel beside her? I don't know why or how that happened. Tears streak down the blood drying on her face. "Please don't let him bury me," she cries. Then, "Mama, I'm scared." She sounds like the daughter I want, that I could have. She cries for the womb, and I weep for her.

"I'm sorry." Blood trickles down her cheek, face pale, like she's bleeding melanin as she keeps passing out and coming to.

Almost an hour and a half later, Jan stops digging. "That's far enough." He appears out of the woods, disheveled, wet with sweat. "Let's carry her."

"Jan," I cry.

"We don't have time," he says. "What if someone drives by?"

If we're caught, I'll never have the chance to see my baby girl. I can't have that happen. My baby girl growing up without me, without a mother. Worse, having a microchipped mother who was committed for murder will destroy her future. I can't leave my child alone. I'm too terrified to commit a crime, kill a fly, but I've killed a woman.

I hoist her beneath her shoulders. She wakes, shrieking in pain. Her eyes ricochet until they meet mine. Back-turned fingers cling to me. She sees Jan stoop to pick her up, kicks him in the chin. "Help me, please!" she screams. "Please, I won't say a word. I won't tell anyone. Please don't let him bury me!" High-pitched voice. The air frigid as a morgue. This young woman could destroy my whole life, yet her eyes stay focused on me, only me—I'm her target just because I have boobs and a vagina, like her. I feel imprisoned by her skin-tight fear. I've seen it all before. She'll be on the news, paid copious amounts of money for a tell-all, and she will continue to destroy my life and *my* daughter's.

"You don't understand," I say, throwing dirt over her—I can't remember having carried her or buried her into Jan's makeshift grave. "If you don't die, I die. If you die, I live. I have a baby. My fear is bigger than your fear of dying."

I'm frantic. What if someone hears her screams? A rock. I smash it into her face. Just to keep her quiet. Her hands, viselike around my own, I have no choice. With the last minute, I press my palm into her mouth, wrap my other hand around her throat, siphoning her last breath, closer to my hope. Her hands tussle around with my face and neck. "I'm sorry," I cry as Jan throws soil over her. "Please forgive me."

She uses the last beats of her heart, a mordant whisper thrust into my ears: "You're . . . going . . . to . . . regret this." She's gone. Buried. Into the dark. Into the dirt. Our lungs heave sighs of relief. But. But. But. My DNA beneath her nails.

Jan's not pouring any more soil. "Fuck."

"What?"

"Her wrist. There's a cell phone signal in it, blinking red." He swipes at the sweat dripping from his forehead. "We have to remove her watch to stop it from reading her dead heartbeat. Kill the signal. That happens. Phones die all the time. We'll leave the cochlear aid in."

I back away, falling onto my butt. "I can't."

"I'll do it," he says. "If her body is found before we come back—"

"Come back?"

"Her body will eventually be found. We'll have to transfer it, find a way to get rid of it." Then he looks away sheepishly. "The tire marks on her face will lead them to you. To us."

It hits me. We must get rid of any leads. I grip his arm. "No, Jan, don't."

"We have to take her skin," he says. "It's the only way we can *still* protect ourselves."

"Just wipe her face, damn it. We're not that gone," I shout.

"You can't wipe out dents or bruise imprints," he says.

"Jan, you're scaring me right now, the things you're saying, what you're willing to do, and I don't like that. Please, this is enough. Please." I wipe the sweat from my face, mixed with tears and blood. "Please, Jan, that's horrible. Please, you have daughters, a sister, a mum, *me*—how can you do this to another woman?"

I sound like a cliché, and I hate it, hate it when you always have to associate the woman they're damaging to some woman in their life for them to understand that what they're doing is *actually* wrong as if they can't realize how wrong it already is. She's a person, and I'm here raising that gender-based-violence-against-women statistic, pushing it along the factory line of crime.

"It's *because* I have daughters," he enunciates. "Aren't you willing to do anything for your daughter, your life, your career? If not, we can just walk into a police station." I hesitate. "Exactly." His knife unfolds, slitting the dark, the moon's eye licking its sharp edge. I grip his arm, shaking. He pauses. "It's fine. You killed her. I'll do this. You don't have to worry about this."

I stand up, walk to a line of trees, and wait for my lover to flay the skin off a young woman's face. A young woman. I'm a hypocrite. A disgusting human being. I promised to protect women. I touch my face to make sure my skin is still there. It's wet with tears, blood, snot. I'm wide awake, and rabid fear singes my eyes. This could be my daughter.

The dark is huddled up too close to me. There's something in the dark, watching me. Her voice is still in my ears, crying to her mother. I just killed some woman's daughter. I keel over. My stomach convulses, but nothing comes out. Something's not right about me.

Jan returns, shirt off, scrunched up in his fist, soggy wet, embalming her skin, and in his other hand, he carries a backpack or something I can't quite make out in the dark. My mind swarms, the ground punches my head. Jan runs to me, helps me up. "I'll drive," he says. "I'll drive."

"I feel sick, Jan," I cry. "I feel like I'll be sick forever."

"Burying it is the easy part," Jan says, "now we have to keep quiet and not let our minds run loose, not let our minds snitch on us. You got that? Things like that, when they happen, it's very hard for people to keep them buried. But we have to keep this secret, fight our consciousness from trying to convince us with guilt, you hear me? In the coming days, our consciousness will be our enemy, but don't fall for its tricks."

"Jan," a shivery whisper, "have you done this before? Killed . . . someone?"

"No."

"It's just . . . you sound like you have."

"I have guilt from the past, not from murder. It's logic. How can a sane mind be okay with killing someone? I'm just trying to be proactive. It's not going to be easy for me, either."

I realize then that he's trying to convince himself to comfort himself, the only way to save our skins.

"Your eyes." Jan nears me, knife bloody and slick in his hand. "Your eyes. They've recorded everything." *Your eyes,* he used to say, *your eyes are beautiful.* But now. Everything inside me collapses, and I stagger away from him.

"Your remote, Jan," I cry, staring at his hand. "It blocked my microchip from recording everything."

He stares at his hand, realizes what I'm thinking. He drops the knife. "No, love. I'd never hurt you. I just meant . . . your body is a witness. I forgot about that remote—good, it bought us time." He wraps his arms around me. "Shh," he says. "I'm sorry. I didn't mean to scare you."

I can't stop crying. He kisses my forehead, hands bloody and cold. He wanted to marry me. *This* is marriage by murder. We'll never, ever be divorced from this nightmare. Sweat drips from my face. Jan and I pack ourselves silently into the car, our minds still pinwheeling from fear to exhaustion. It doesn't feel over. The shadows of the night cling to my heartbeat. I feel eyes crawling all over my skin. I itch from guilt. The trees flanking the road are graveyard-still.

He's right. My body is a witness.

"Jan," I whisper. "Your device protected us tonight but I have the microchip assessment tomorrow morning. There won't be any more running." I sniffle; rub the sleeve of my shirt across my nose. "But Jan," I whisper, "what if we're under the CBE's simulation?" There's no way to run. Reality has us hemmed in.

But he's not listening, eyes tense on the road. My face is wet with hot tears.

"We had no choice," Jan finally says, a mantra of conviction. "We had no choice."

04:44 /// THE DEVIL'S TONGUE

Jan's at his home somehow. I'm on my street. My family home's driveway. Engine still humming. The roar of the garage yawns open, its lights flare on. The car gently revs itself inside. I'm too terrified to touch its steering wheel; I whimpered in the dark as it drove through the winding highways, taking me home. I give it my thumbprint to switch off.

"Don't forget to switch off the remote. It can't intercept your microchip for more than twelve hours," Jan had reminded me before we parted.

I stroke the tiny device that saved my life tonight, press the center, and the light turns red. I'm back online, and my microchip sees everything now. I swing the door open, topple out of the car. I gasp at the house opposite ours, its deep shadow looming toward ours. A man's silhouette in the dark. From where he's sitting, he's got a clear view of me. The streetlight pours light across my body. He watches me stagger out of the car, covered in blood. Intoxicated with the stench of death. Neighbor. Donald. Up on his balcony. Can he see? No. It's too dark to see. He's up there, cigar red-lit in his mouth. A whiskey glass in his hand, his nightcap. Even so, the blood may gleam under the light, but he can't discern it as blood. Maybe some liquid. But not blood.

But this memory will be a snitching witness, a field day for the CBE's simulation when I go under. No. I have at least eleven months to worry about it. Eleven months to un-fuck my life. Quite sufficient, I think.

I smile, half-wave, pretending everything's hundreds. Donald doesn't wave back, never does. His company has lost tenders to mine; he's always second to me. Still, the darkness sways in my chest. Don't panic. You overreact when you panic. I won't apply for the next tender. He's sure to win then. Let bygones be bygones. Maybe call him up for a chat, throw him a piece job. Should shut him up. Better an ally than an enemy who won't lie for you. Corruption is a crutch sometimes. And I need a crutch, something to lean on.

I get into the house at the witching hour. Burn the bloody clothes in the braai stand, in a way my husband won't notice, out by the laundry room. The microchip can't report me; there's nothing illegal about incinerating clothes. Every piece of the fabric's ash sweeps away into the mouth of the breeze. I drench myself in a cold shower, sneak in beside him, spoon against his peaceful-sleeping body. It's this thought, this thought that terrorizes me: God, what have we done? My brother was right about me, something's not right about me. My soul won't stay for long; something will pocket it soon enough. My mind jerks backward, rewinds to my forensic evaluation day and Serati's words strike my bones coldly: "Matsieng understands your blood intimately; if you were dangerous, Xe would've flagged you to the Murder Trials." My blood has committed murder, and it's mysteriously connected to Matsieng, who is connected to the ever-suffocating existence of the Murder Trials. What does this mean for me?

I can feel the devil's tongue on my shoulders, my neck, making my hair stand on end. Something evil lives inside my body. Something even Matsieng could not see.

10:44 /// ICEBERG OF A SECRET

In sleep, the words drift into my dreams clear as day: *Nelah Bogosi-Ntsu, you are not obliged to say anything or act in any way, but anything you do or say, any of your actions, may be used as evidence . . . Where were you on Saturday between the hours of 1:00 a.m. and 5:00 a.m.?*

I wake with a jerk, with terror, and realize the reason for my dreams. I've slept ceaselessly for only five hours. My husband must have let me sleep in, with him starting his morning late, too. So I slip back into sleep. Morning light slits my eyes open. Nature is so nauseating, so disturbing. Dread. I'm choked by dread. Like I've done something wrong. It couldn't just be a hit-and-run, could it? No, you had to dump the body.

The alarm hammers against my mind, disrupting my chain of thought. My neck aches. A blood-pumping headache beats behind my eyes. Bloody migraine. I envy his being at the Matsieng Fertility Fund last night, looking after our daughter, little Naledi, our name for her. If he loved me better, if our marriage wasn't so parched, last night wouldn't have happened. I hate myself the same way I hate him. But I can't blame him.

I can hear him downstairs. Chuckling. Chatting on a call. Happiness gliding through his body. I am drained, shaking, trying to get up, but the bruises yank me back. Dry tears tremble down my face. The shock drags fear into my body. Last night. Jan and I just went out. Had a couple of drinks. A few drugs. That's it. Everything else has to be a nightmare. A hallucination. I check my phone. Dead. Covered in mud crusts. Evidence?

"No, go away." I scrape the mud crusts off. My voice is hoarse from all of last night's screaming, arguing, negotiating.

What to do, what to do?

Bloody bliksem, *my career.*

Bury the body, bury the secret.

That's a human. A life. That's someone's—

It doesn't matter. What matters is we have drugs in our bloodstream. We're fucking high and drunk.

Life, a wretched bloody poem. *Bury the body. Bury the secret.* No. I'm not a murderer. Silence and light shadows intermix, a misty body invading our bedroom. Every sound muffled. The long stretch of window overlooks our garden's trees, which are normally fresh and green. But today, they are blank, bleak, and grey as the storm-cast sky.

"It's raining." My voice startles me. I didn't realize that it's raining. "She's out there, lying in the rain. In the mud. The cold eating at her skin," I silently whisper in shame. I'm here, in this fluffy bedding, this warm home that cost us an entire year of my business's earnings to acquire. That feeble thing of a girl. Out there.

No. It's her fault. What was she doing there in the middle of the night? Just standing there. In the way. Toying with us. Toying with death. *She* wanted to die. And she got us roped into her morbid plans. Couldn't she have offed herself with a gun, a rope, or a knife? Why use us as her props? Stupid. Stupid girl. Jesus. My heartbeat won't fucking shut up. I can't have this. Not this morning. I have a meeting. A business to run. I have an unborn daughter. A beautiful daughter who needs me. Bills to pay. What obligations did she have? Clearly nothing for her to stand in the middle of nowhere like a ghost. She's haunting me now. But the silence . . . no sirens, no murder-mist in the air.

I scramble across the comforter, throw a couple of pills down my throat. Please silence these voices. Please silence these voices. Please silence these voices. Evict her from my memory, her small body. Her thin fingers. I lean back against the headboard, and pain strangles my neck. I pull up my gown to conceal traces of where her fingers scraped me. The morning is quiet, so is the sun, its rays not raising fumes leading to the body we buried. Only on Sunday, in sixteen hours.

I can imagine how it'll go down tomorrow morning: a scent that emanates from the dead, grows potent, grows through the soil, a plant seeking daylight. The blossomed pheromones hover eagerly above the crime scene, above the makeshift grave, above the dismembered body parts, the loose tissue thrown amok, the bone tossed aside with reckless abandon. The scent will hover, grow citywide, waiting waiting waiting for the sun to wake up, for a particular building exterior to breathe.

The perforated outer façade of the Gaborone Police Precinct building is retrofitted with a storage of chemicals, automated to hiss and exhale these noninvasive chemicals into the air. We will breathe it in. Dead bodies will breathe it in. Even dead bodies lying fifty meters below ground. Chemicals will come into contact with the corpse's pheromones, and the sun, in his clear, cloudless haven, will burn this tousling fusion into a cloud-like sapphire blue, and this flame of a serpentine trail will light up the city, twisting through the highways, the narrow neighborhood streets to the outer edge of the city, the place where we buried her, where our DNA lies. This is the new cadaver dog, and on its trail will be the police, news vans and news drones and EMTs.

Murder is a toxic beauty against the sky's skin.

The CBE may fail.

The microchip may fail.

The sun will not.

I *will* be found. Exposed. The crime I've committed.

Sunday is tomorrow. Sunday is tomorrow. Sunday. Tomorrow. Will Jan and I have figured things out by then?

I'm about to conduct an online search of how to erase the scent released from a dead body. Then I remember a digital trail is just as damaging as DNA left at the crime scene. I wonder how it used to be to kill someone before, to hide it in the earth, and it might go unnoticed for days or even years. What a privilege. I close my eyes, hating myself for thinking that. What if it were me, placed in the earth, in the dark, in the forest, all alone?

"Babe?" Sticking his head into the room, my husband asks, "You alright? You came in late last night, ja."

He can't even tell, can't smell the death clinging to my skin. It's part of his job. The police staff's olfactory organs are surgically fine-tuned to the perfection of a cadaver dog's. Perhaps it's good that he can't detect my immoral acts. I have time to right things.

"Jesus, what happened to you?" He sits down on the bed, touches my cheek. It hurts.

I stab the charging cable into my phone and switch it on. "Mxm, fucking work drunkards. Had me drinking more than I could," I lie. "I fell. Have another meeting this morning." *I helped you pay for my lobola. What have you done since then besides chow and chow?* I hate panicking. It sends out all my demons. All of my anger. I snap at anyone.

He tilts his head, leans against the headboard—stares too long. "You're overworked." He crawls onto the bed. *It's your fault. Yet you don't have blood on your hands.* "Let's go on a holiday. Get some rest. Last night, you were talking in your sleep. Clearly, you're overwhelmed."

Bloody bliksem, even my mouth is snitching on me. "W-w-what did I say?" I can't let him see my eyes, the fear, the hatred, the anger.

"You were talking about someone." He chews the inside of his cheek, always when he's analyzing a situation. Eyes scanning, rolling back as if to see the memory printed into his brain's archives. "Some woman. You kept telling her to get out of the way." He pinches my chin, turning my face toward him. In the opaque stillness of dawn, his eyes are dark, unreadable, scanning my face, his skin a still, quiet brown. "Every time you have a nightmare, it always reveals something that you've been hiding."

I hate my nightmares. Little snitchy bastards that infiltrate our minds and thoughts when we lie unconscious, use our lips like their vuvuzela. I thought the sleeping pills would knock me out cold—yes, even on top of the cocaine—seal my mouth shut. Kill the nightmares, at least.

His fingers tighten around my chin. "Who is this woman? Do I need to be worried?"

Something's stuck in my throat. Won't get out. My lopsided smile, I twist it up my face. "My mistress," I joke. *Attagirl. Look cool. Look normal. Look hundreds.*

I squirm, getting away from his grasp. His lips turn down. I hate it when I hurt him. I'm exploding. Overreacting. Losing control of my boundaries. Breathe. Stay intact. Stay in control.

"Just . . . things are complicated right now," I whisper. "The project I'm working on is a bit of a headache. I'll be done soon, and then we can go on holiday."

"I'm here for you, nè?"

Tell him tell him tell him, my thoughts erupt.

In comfort, he rubs my knee. Always *seeming* understanding, baiting me for the catch, to reel me in.

Still leashed to the charger, my phone buzzes. Instead, I glance at my wrist. A text blips across my skin screen:

Janith Koshal: It's raining. What if the thing washes out onto the surface?

A knell tolls in my chest. The iceberg of a secret, tipping up, lulling above ground. It must be sunk.

11:11 /// MY HUSBAND'S GUN

The stillness in the bedroom is stuffy, silence cocked into my neck, alternating with the intermittent buzzing of my phone. My phone, blade-thin, see-through. I reach for it, again, before Elifasi does.

Janith Koshal: Bloody *bliksem*! Aren't you the queen of architecture? The grave is in a construction site! How did you not get wind of this? It's in the same fucking industry as you! The same fucking ballpark. Parked in your backyard. Are *you* trying to get us caught?

Expletives as intense as his passion. Unlike him. His morning messages used to be *Morning, love, last night has stained me. You drive me crazy. I miss you already, the taste of you.*

Anger distorts him. Probably why he's going through a messy divorce.

Janith Koshal: Oh, God, what if she's microchipped?

Janith Koshal: Fuck, fuck, fuck! I forgot to check.

The phone's screen clicks to black. My trembling hand sets it face down on my lap. If she were microchipped, her drone would've appeared, but it didn't. Unless it was intercepted like mine. If those construction workers dig up that land, we're screwed. Someone might have seen us nearby. Our number plate. *My* number plate. I want to rewind last night. We got high. My body was laced with drugs. We were naughty. It was supposed to be fun.

My husband cranes his neck. "*Who* is that?"

How does a man of such high intelligence leave evidence in my phone? Connecting us. Bloody hell. Get yourself caught, not me. What if his wife finds the messages he's sending me? She'd rat us out to fuck him over in the divorce. Of course, I live this life of dancing around every oppressive law fine-tuned to my microchipped world that only a man as power-drunk as Jan storms through freely and stupidly. He said I could trust him, yet he's already fucking up. Wait, Jan navigated his father's control the same way I maneuver through this world, so he wouldn't be so stupid to spill our secret on our phones unless . . . I stare at my phone, and the messages have disappeared. There's no trace of them. I shiver from Jan's calculative mind of keeping our trails hidden. So I can trust him.

Makes no difference, anyhow. Our phones must've pinged to the cell towers—little fucking snitches—when we drove by them.

"My secretary," I whisper.

My husband's eyes are searchlights, appraising me. His scientific gaze grips me without noticing the woman in me. I cover up without wanting to. I exhale in relief when he looks away, stares at his wristwatch. "It's time."

My heart races at the equivocal moment the microchip vibrates in my neck. Now it's suddenly a tjatjarag thing when last night it was quiet? I stare at the jangle of keys on the dresser, sharp as knives. I want to run them like blades down my nape to extract the piece of microchip metal, the barcode in my neck—removing it would kill me.

His abrasive stare washes over my bruises from the girl's hands. "I fell down outside my office building, scraped my whole body against the brick wall," I quickly respond, a reflex to his constant interrogations. Duplicity is no longer required—just his stare makes me talk. If I don't, we go down a labyrinthine path of arguments, and I end up not recalling what we're fighting about anymore, except that I'm wrong. I'm *always* wrong.

I scramble across the carpeted floor to our walk-in closet, paneled in mirrors. I stand in front of one mirror, embedded with the AI assessor. I reach out, hesitate. I shield my eyes. The smoke, the glare of headlights. Handprint against it. Palm against it. But the mirror pays homage to last night: a bruise stapled to my neck; love bite, I can still feel Janith's lips, still taste them, that deep, raw hunger in his baritone vibrating through me. A landmass of bruise marks across my chin. A deep scratch down the side of my neck. She has my skin cells trapped beneath her nails. Fuck.

My husband stands beside me. I scrunch up my gown around my collarbones. *Tell him the truth. For poorer or for worse. Maybe he can save me. For once, trust him.* But I can't read his eyes, so deep-set, lying under the dark shadow of his protruding brow. I feel uneasy, and I shrug out from his grasp. "Do you always have to watch?"

It's impossible for last night to have happened. My microchip was supposed to send red-flag signals to one of those bot controllers in the police towers. Someone was supposed to stop me. To stop us.

His hand presses into the small of my back. "I'm not your ordinary public servant, babe. Better to have me as your witness as commissioner of the police force." He kisses my cheek. His teeth flash, lips thin and cold. Alibi doesn't get any better than that. His profession offers him immunity, doesn't it? As if he's Jesus, incapable of criminal acts. I'm the unhappy, mistreated one who ends up with blood on her hands, but he gets everything.

I inch forward. The assessor will tell him what I did last night. He will fetch his handcuffs and send me for processing. His moral loyalty toward his profession supersedes his love for me.

"My daughter," I blurt. "I want to see her."

He narrows his eyes, nudges me forward. "Let's determine if you are pure first."

Fear clenches my gut. I grip my mouth as bile rises into it. I take a deep breath. My daughter needs to be safe. *I* have to be safe for her. “It must be nice to be you, nè,” I bite back. “Every police officer has the privilege of a body with no criminal history.”

“Babe.” He tips his head toward the mirror. “It’s time.”

“But honestly, if I did do something terrible, would you arrest me?” I ask, staring deeply into his eyes.

His dark-brown irises waver in the sunlight pouring through our windows. “Never.”

And I know he’s lying when he adds for humorous effect, “I’d pack our bags and flee. We’d live an adventurous life on the run. I, of all people, know all the tactics we can apply to evade the law successfully.”

He’d sacrifice me rather than his badge, I know that for sure. He wouldn’t want to look stupid in front of his colleagues. He wouldn’t want them to know that I either hid a crime from him or I somehow *manipulated* him into covering for me, which only emasculates him. Because women’s vaginas are so seductively nefarious, according to the euphemistic news reports regarding the tiny blobs of crime in the city. But what would I do if we switched places? Would I keep his crime a secret? Go on the run with our only still-in-the-Wombcubator daughter? When I look at it like that, I don’t think I’d do that to my daughter. She comes first, before saving our skins, so I understand why he lies to me, to band-aid my anxiety. Maybe I’m desperate to believe there’s still someone loving under there. He may not love me the way he did in the past, but he cherishes my daughter. And that’s all that matters to me. I’d flay myself to keep her warm from a cold, evil world.

“Ja nè, you’re right,” I say, which always cheers him up.

“Exactly. Now chin up. Do it.”

My heartbeat paces fast in my chest as I plant my palm against the mirror. My microchip can’t read my thoughts until my husband peruses them for our weekly Sunday movie night tomorrow. I have some time. I must pass this test. My heart rate must be even, my breathing, my body calm. I love my husband. I love my daughter. Breathe in. I did not kill someone. Breathe out. I did not kill someone. Concentrate. I believe the lie. The lie is the truth. The lie is the truth. The lie—

"Good morning, Nelah. How are we feeling this morning?" The mirror's surface ripples, sound waves appear as the AI assessor speaks.

My neck burns. Breathe. Relax. Maintain eye contact. "Please scan my microchip."

I still my heart, I slow down my breathing, and I blink only naturally, not too rapidly, not too slow, for I know what comes next.

"Are you experiencing any sociopathic tendencies?"

Cold air plagues the room.

"No," I say, though my voice comes out squeaky. My husband stares. "No," I say, steadily. Focus.

"What were your activities yesterday?"

My husband's gun is in the third set of drawers to my right. In a safe. Code: 3967. Can I get there before him? I mean, if it came down to it, would I let him just take me in? No, I can't have gunshots fired off in our home. My daughter will grow up with that story noosed around her entire life. He's unaware that I know his passcode. I feel safer because of that fact. No, of course, I'd never shoot my husband. I'd never do that to my daughter, leave her without a father. Here's the deal: If the mirror reveals to him what happened last night, I'll fall to my knees, cry and plead with him to keep me safe. Sell my soul to him if I have to. Promise to do anything that he wants. Surely, that'll move him, right?

My husband nudges me. I zoned out, terrified.

"I'm sorry, I didn't hear the question," I say. Relax. Focus. I love my husband. I love my daughter. It is a beautiful day.

"What were your activities yesterday?" it asks. The microchip wasn't recording for nine hours because of Jan's device—instead, it received manipulated data of our activities last night, the cleaner version of us. I recall Jan's words: "Just remember that your story has to correlate with that of the manipulated images fed to your microchip if your morning assessor interrogates you about your whereabouts."

I stare at the sound waves drawing in and out, wanting to swallow me. Act normal. Act normal. "I was at work from around nine in the morning until late, preparing for my firm's award this week. I later attended a work party to celebrate with my colleagues and returned home in the early hours of the morning."

Technically true. Jan is a colleague in the industry, singular yes, but with his fleet of companies, one could consider him as equal to several colleagues. We did go out. Killed someone. "Shut up," I blurt, trying to still my thoughts. "I mean, I had to shut up one of the male employees. He was overly drunk and pestering his female workmates." Jan was pestering me deliciously. My husband smiles at this, squeezing my arm. I must add this because my movements are tagged into the car's GPS system. "Then I drove out of the city. To survey a site. Take note of prowlers."

"Have you been feeling unlike yourself lately? Are you experiencing any sociopathic tendencies?"

"No," I say. The lines are steady as hell.

"Have you recently experienced unexplainable bursts of anger or other emotions?"

"No." I need to live through the full term of this body before being consciously transferred again. I want to make certain that my daughter and I will always be together. I must act normal. Act normal to keep this life. Breathe in, breathe out. Focus. I believe the lie.

"Are there any problems? Malfunctions?"

"No."

"Have you committed a crime that the microchip failed to detect?"

"No."

"No."

"No."

I hardly compute the questions, but the AI assessor sure is analyzing them. God, what's the verdict? The wait tortures me, the air tightening around my body although I keep my breathing even, my heart steady.

Elifasi tilts his head. "Mm, it normally doesn't take this long."

My knees buckle. I open my mouth to sing, but I believe the lie, I believe the lie, I am the truth, I am the truth, I am the—

The assessor's voice stitches into the air. She reports my results, "Your physiological logical responses are steady and indicate no signs of deception."

I'm shocked. Elated. Scared. But shocked.

She's a lie detector, and I'm a self-taught pathological liar.

12:44 /// GUILT IS A GUILLOTINE

"Now that wasn't hard, was it?" My husband kisses me on the forehead. "Oh, my cousin dropped off his daughter yesterday. Was babysitting. Trying to learn how to be a father whilst I have the time," he says, smiling. "I'll get breakfast ready. Join us, will you? She missed you last night." He disappears, and I'm finally alone.

"I may need a replacement for the AI microchip," I tell the AI assessor quietly. My tongue is thick with lies. "This one's been burning through my neck these past days." *What the hell am I trying to do? Get myself caught? Let it go! This fucking guilt.*

"Please turn around," the microchip assessor says. "Remove any material in the nape area that might obstruct the scanning session."

I move my braids to the side, turn around and expose my microchip to the mirror. The scanner's LED light is warm as it zips up and down my neck. Maybe the microchip really did malfunction. Crime can be annihilated, but its energy will always find ways to trickle into our country. This body of mine *is* a liability to the country's safety.

"Scanning complete," echoes the assessor. "There were no errors detected in your microchip. No replacement is required. If you feel unsatisfied with my assessment, please alert me to set an appointment with Gaborone Police Precinct."

My stomach sinks. That can't be right. The Gaborone Police Precinct's tools are considered infallible. Does that mean body-hoppers throughout the city are getting away with crime? If I bring this up, I'd have to snitch on myself to provide proof of how wrong their AI microchips are. I don't want to be caught, but I don't want to bring up my family in a place where danger breeds without detection.

"Thank you," I whisper. "No, that won't be necessary. That will be all."

If my infractions aren't caught by the AI assessor, they'll certainly be detected by the forensic evaluation, which I'm due for in eleven months. I've dodged the bullet this round, but not for long. For surely, within one day, the body will be found.

"Have a good day, Nelah," it says. The sound patterns dissolve, and the mirror reflects a young Motswana woman with a very disturbed expression.

The marble bathroom is too white, too sterile, too stark. I sit on the porcelain edge of the bathtub. The water swirls, clear of guilt, translucent. My reflection catches me weary. My head aches. My scalp itches. I lean into the toilet bowl and quietly puke. I want to breathe. I *need* to breathe. The bathroom mirror studies me. Prints lack of sleep beneath my eyes, dark shadows eclipsing bloodshot eyes. Gilded dust motes dance in the sunlight pouring through the window slats, painting my skin the same tone, light brown saturated with dawn. I need to wash up. I spill bleach all over my body, exorcising yesterday from me.

I open the medicine cabinet. A handful of pills. Don't know which ones. Doesn't matter. I'm ready to *look* human today. The woman who no one can read. The woman who everyone thinks is a bitch.

I have to look normal, like my usual self. I don ash-black, high-waist cigarette pants, a grey top, and a black hooded overcoat with a lavish gilt-and-emerald Ankara print on the underside, an overwhelming size like a shield from everything. I part my braids in the middle and let them hang to my shoulders, curtaining me from the world. Line my eyes in kohl. Pat my lips in rose. Roll my shoulders back and forth. Exhale. Stand back to stare at my reflection. In media, they say I look like a sharp-boned model. No, I look like a dagger that stabbed someone yesterday. “I am okay.” My voice ripples across my lips; the brown in my eyes shimmers in fear. “Relax. Everything is fine.” I rub sweat from my shaking hands onto my pants.

I skim by my home office, third floor up, beneath an oval skylight, phone-snatch some contractor briefs digitally pasted to the wall.

Downstairs, the chef’s kitchen island is splattered with spilled cornflakes, a glitter of laughter. “Aunty Nelah!” my niece-in-law, Pearl, screams in joy. She holds a red crayon in hand, scribbling on a paper.

My husband tickles her. She giggles, kicking out her tiny legs. Like her. The woman I murdered last night. She jabbed me in the chin, colored it with a bruise entombed under foundation. She’s going to swim out of the mud, swim out for air and scream my secret out, her gills stuffed with my DNA. Shit. What other parts of ourselves did we leave on her body? We must check. Guilt is a guillotine, and it has my head and soul.

I swallow and say, “Morning, nana,” and kiss her cheek. Her hair’s plaited in wool, and I stay in that hug for years.

The TV. Morning news. My face on the screen. A heroine advocating against poverty and violence against women through proceeds from the built environment. I’m a renowned, haloed angel, sometimes. Granted prestigious real estate and humanitarian awards. Yet, how could I do that to the girl from last night? I’m so ashamed of myself that I slam the remote against the counter. The screen flicks to black.

My husband glares. “When’s the ceremony?” he asks.

“It’s this Monday,” I remind him. Again. “7:00 p.m.” Two days left. How can I be in a celebrating mood after what we did?

“Oh, sorry, love,” he says, scratches his thick, rich Afro. “Everyone at the office keeps telling me what a lucky husband I am.”

You love the idea of me. That’s it. You needed me in your bed, wrapped around your finger as marriage.

"Will you sort out my suit for the ceremony?" he asks. He's a king. He must look dapper. The queen is just a trophy he raises to the limelight. In all the magazines, at all the events, no one knows his name. He hates me for it, that he's referred to as "Nelah's husband," not by his real name. Not even his well-known professional status as Assistant Commissioner of Police. He's eye candy, but he's nothing compared to me. That's what he said. *You're the smart one, anyway. You make all the decisions.* I tried to make him feel better, to feel bigger, smarter. Gave him a stake in the company. Invested in his ideas. I tried to make myself small for him. Too small for myself. And Jan . . . He let me be me. And now we've killed someone.

I nod and cuddle his ego against my breast like a fucking newborn. "You'll be the hottest man at the ceremony." The words dry my mouth.

I have other things to worry about, like the girl from last night. He's going to have to take this pity party elsewhere, which he doesn't. He stands by the doorway, the light sharp around his body. Steps closer to me, and we're concealed from our niece, her quiet chatter, busying herself with her drawing. I feel his mood switch ever so fast, as usual. He's waiting. I can already hear what's coming next. Please don't ask. He's holding a butcher knife. If only he could stab me to death with it.

"I'm horny," he says. I stare, clinging to the past-perfect version of him, not realizing he'll never return. *He could be nice*, I'd tell Mama. *Treats me like a queen. Loves me deeply. Once in a full moon.*

"I'm tired," I say, wearily.

"Ag, you're always tired." He turns his back to me. Just as he is leaving the pantry, about to walk to our niece, my neck burns, and my hands pull him by his tie. In seconds, I relent. I'm against the shelves as he silently pummels into me, our niece playing at the breakfast table, unable to see or hear us. Who am I anymore? How do I want and not want sex at the same time, hours after I killed someone? There's something terribly wrong with me, worse than the previous owner of this body. We're both twisted. The microchip fibrillates heat into my nerves. When Elifasi comes, he muffles his shrieks, dropping a black remote.

"What's that?" I ask.

He grabs some serviettes, wipes himself down, and zips his pants. Picks it up, shoves it into his pocket. "Remote key for my office." Walks away.

I clean myself up, take several breaths, and follow him into the kitchen. Pretend everything is normal. My niece pretends a piece of cornflake is a mermaid that she dips in and out of her milk. My eyes tear up, and I brush the tears aside.

"You'll take her to school this morning?" I ask, pushing aside my thoughts. My head's not straight. Better I drive alone, just in case. I can't trust myself with her. Can't have another accident. I stare at Pearl's little neck, my fingers around it. Clasp my eyes shut. My niece is *my* niece—she's not her! The girl from last night. A force yanks me back. My husband. I clasp the neck of a wine bottle instead. Just like I did her throat. I drop it. Its blood splutters on the beige tiles.

"Ao? Drink? This early?" He fiddles with his Vandyke beard, considering locking me in our basement, a sub-street maisonette—before we rented it out. It's worked before, a little isolation to surface me back into society, into normalcy. I shake my head and mop up the spilled drink.

"I'll take her to school," he says. "Have a good day, babe." He kisses me. How does he so easily mood-switch like that? From anger to nothing-happened joy. He lifts Pearl, play-acts she's an airplane. "Just you and me this morning." She stretches out her arms, screaming in joy.

The front door slams. I jump. Too much noise. Desperate need of quiet, to sully my guilt to nothing. Take the attention away. Outside, in the driveway, he's sealing her into the child's seat. He waves to our neighbor across the street. Donald, from last night, in his gown, in his grey-stoned double story. Watering the lawn.

I thumb-press the garage remote. The garage door slides open. The daylight sniffs around, clambering all over my car. It shows me what I didn't see in the dark. My SUV, a dent on its side, a slur of blood across its headlight, the lamp broken. I hit an animal. I hit an animal. I hit—

My husband slams his car door shut. Shouts a goodbye, but I spin around panicked. "I hit an animal."

His eyes widen, color with terror. He skips toward my car, inspects. "What type of animal? Why didn't you say anything? Take my car, I'll have yours fixed. Maybe you should take the day off, too. You look . . . faint and . . ." My husband caresses my face, and I'm overwhelmed with disgust when I look across the rosebush-lined road. "What's wrong?"

I point a finger. To something walking—no, limping—up the street. My husband turns, faces in the direction I'm pointing. "What are you pointing at?" he asks, shielding his face from the sharp morning sun.

"Can't you see her?" I ask.

"Babe, there's nothing. It's just the Viller family watering their lawn."

"But . . . but," I whisper, trembling. "There's a girl. Coming up the street. She . . . she looks hurt. Who is she? Oh God, someone help her."

He blinks, focuses. Sees nothing. Irritation ruffles his face. "Bona, I don't know what's going on with you today, but I'm not dealing with whatever mess you have going on. *Again.* My niece is here, for Christ's sake. Just for one day, can it not be about you for once?"

But a young woman. A stranger. Unkempt. Bathed in dirt. Unlike the crowd in this bucolic estate. Mbinguni Estate, a little utopia stretching its limbs alongside a pseudo-beach. Security wouldn't let anyone of that sort bypass their access gates. I see her, her skin marred with muck. Her clothes ragged at the joints. Her skull, dented on the left side, weeps blood down the side of her skinless face, slurring her leftover brown skin. The sun, a halo in the sky, blinds her sight as she sways to and fro.

I'm about to open my mouth again, but I realize the inconvenient truth.

She's a secret shone by sunlight.

It's the girl from last night.

The girl we buried.

13:18 /// ECLIPSE OUR SIN

This vision of the girl from last night can't be real. She's supposed to be dead, not walking—limping across the street. Toward me. Toward us. She is a macabre evil, wobbling down the peaceful lanes of our estate.

My niece's high-pitched laugh sends me reeling. I can't let that dead girl near my family. I shove my husband into his car, the driver's seat. I stare at my car, its broken headlight, the blood, the fucking evidence. At the corner of my eye, a shadow flicks above our garden's marula tree and melts like burned colors, like a picture still developing, still rendering. A bird lifts off the branch, dragging my attention with it. I'm suddenly alone in the driveway. Husband and niece gone. Good family. Perfect family. Perfect homestead.

The dead girl's closing in now. If my husband couldn't see her, then she's not real. This is just paranoia playing out as a hallucination, some sick reminder. Jan said this would happen. That our conscience would lean too heavily on our guilt-soaked selves. But I didn't think it would be to this extreme.

Tonight, Jan and I will use the dark to cover us, eclipse our sin. We'll exhume her body. Take it somewhere else. Suffer for salvation.

We'll be free. Free to live our lives. After tonight, everything will be solved, the affair annulled.

I scrub off the blood with tissue and crumple it into my pocket.

Donald steps toward me from his front garden, his bald head shiny against the morning light. "Nelah, is everything alright? You look . . . like you've seen a ghost."

The ghost's getting closer. Passing house 6302. 6303. 6306. I am 6309. Wish I was something else. I yank open the car door, key the ignition—panic attack, déjà vu when my hands make contact with the wheel, but I need reassurance, a sense of control. I race off. Exhaust fumes puff up into the air. She sways, turning to one side as I blur past her, her lower jaw hanging. The window's down. A whiff of last night: muck, smoke, fear neon-lit by a string of headlights.

A scream, wet with desperation.

13:53 /// FEET OF TIME

In our city, going to prison is the same as dying.

There are no visitation rights, nor the ability to communicate with the incarcerated. It's immortality in hell. I don't want to live in a petrifying virtual reality. But there she was, the dead girl. The victim. The one who will make me the 5.9 millionth prisoner. I'm going crazy, a guilt distilled from my nightmare.

How do you kill someone you've already killed?

The mirage of Botswana's homicidal heat glistens on the tarmac as I race in and out of traffic. The sun was manufactured in Botswana, and hell particularly loves it; I can feel it on my skin, burning my fear into a hardened layer. During a mid-drive call, my intel provided me with info regarding the construction site we buried the girl in.

"Mosadi, tell him who I am," I say, standing at the reception of J&J Associates, the city skyline pouring through their glass walls. My hands are deep in my silk pockets, trembling. But my body stands still, dominant, not betraying the tornado swarming inside me.

The secretary looks at me. Beady-eyed. Fifth secretary he's gone through.

"We really can't allow anyone in who hasn't made an appointment with Mr. Koshal," she says, voice lined in a Shona dialect. Her glossy desk is surrounded with the cliché décor of ebony African masks and vases, standing waist-high.

"He will want to see me."

She buzzes the intercom. The mahogany doors swing open. Janith Koshal. Handsome. Oozes sex appeal that he drizzles all over himself every morning, makes you want it for breakfast, but I dial it back, tie my thighs together because I know it won't end there. Look where it got us already. His hands, gloved. Of course. Expensive suit. Dapper. Fresh. Not a scrape across his skin. Why was she grabbing at me, begging me, with big teary eyes, as if I were the one in charge? She left a fucking mark on me. Janith smiles uneasily. Reaches for my elbow. A miss. I jolt for his open doors, leaving the glitzy, smooth reflective surfaces of the reception area, air-conditioned cold, and it's a culture shock of stepping into the woodsy hues of his office.

"If anyone calls, tell them I'm not here—postpone my meetings," he instructs his secretary. The door shuts.

"You're a side-dish for a reason." Deep baritone cascades over his office. "You're not supposed to be on stage, in my fucking office. You want to screw with my divorce?" Suited. Palms out. There he is.

"Ehe? Now I'm a side-dish?" I throw my handbag across his ox-blood leather sofa.

His office's bathed with his cologne that's stained with notes of botanicals, something woodsy and sensual, and it spikes my memory with the balmy taste of his kisses, his warm skin, the memory of his tongue roping around me. Then I check myself, reorient myself to our circumstance.

I fold my arms, trembling inside. Is it safe to speak here? What if someone in his office is listening to our conversation? The microchip—it's always listening in, except last night, otherwise it'd have responded. I press my finger to my lips, and Jan shuts up immediately. I take out the circular disk from my purse without my eyes seeing it, and click the dent in its center. The LED light clicks from red to blue.

"Clear up your schedule," I say. "We have to move the body. Now."

"Eh, with a snitch of a sun out there to display us in its glory of daylight?" He points his arm toward his picture window.

"Not really. The clouds will conceal it. The construction site is the burial ground. The ground is too rocky to do a formal excavation. They're going to conduct rock blasting on Sunday, 7:00 a.m."

He sits at the edge of his mahogany desk, relaxed. "Great. The blasting will cremate the body."

"Once an explosion is initiated, it'll be raining dismembered limbs."

"Fuck." He makes for the alcohol rack. Unscrews the top. Whiskey, four fingers. Neat. Downs it. Pours another one. He sits back. Stubble shadows his jawline. An insane laugh punches his mouth. "Mel's gonna love this one. With this ammunition, she's definitely getting custody of the kids. The house. My money. My career will be destroyed. Jesus, my name, not just my name but my father's name. I'd rather die than face my father's wrath."

Beside him, a picture frame of his blue-eyed wife and brown-eyed twin girls, a thicket of dark-haired curls cascading to their tiny birth-marked shoulders. They're laughing at something as he stands behind, barricading them with his muscled arms from the world and its shitty ways. I'm filled with a deep-burning jealousy at how everything looks safe—their smiles, the joy in their eyes, the love that used to be. He slams his family picture face down. Guilt spreads broodily across his face.

"Mxm, we're in the same fucking boat, Jan."

He delicately removes my coat. Strokes my prosthetic arm. I've no sensor to his touch. He always knew that. "Ten years of martial arts. You bludgeoned her with this blitzkrieg piece of work. Metal. Caved her head in."

Defensive wounds.

I stare at the traces Jan's fingers make on my bionic arm. Although Mama won't talk about the history of this body because it's too painful a memory, my brother often growls that I've no right to that information. However, Papa dissuades me with loving words. I still wonder about their original daughter and the countless ways she could've left this body. There are about three ways that could lead to this:

1. someone willingly forfeits their body to be a carer; consequently, their body is donated to a host on the waiting list. This is highly difficult to affirm since that information is

legally withheld under "the right to be forgotten" law to the original owner. Their privacy is maintained by making the following host an Original;

2. someone commits a heinous crime, thereby instituting their eviction from the body; or
3. an accident severely damages the consciousness, but the body is still in perfect condition for a host to be transplanted into it.

I doubt the original daughter left this family to be a carer. Why would a daughter from a tight-knit wealthy family donate their body to be a carer? Only religious people or people with financial issues or other personal reasons opt for that route. I've thought worse things, that perhaps the Bogosi family were like Jan's father, trafficking bodies to host their child—they are rich, but they are not that powerful to make it as clean a job as Jan's father did to override immigration laws. Besides, I've seen photos of this body from when it was a baby until I woke up in it.

While living with my parents for years, I scavenged through the house looking for archived documents or digital files in their personal technologies. I produced no results; most things were hidden behind heavily protected security. It all felt futile and emotionally devastating. So I gave up on the inquisitions, the hunting for answers, and dealing with emotional turmoil from their disappointing lack of willingness to tell me the truth. Instead, I found a new pursuit to build my own family rather than force myself into the Bogosi family. I will never belong in this family if they don't let me in; I want my own family, made from me, not one that I've been brought into as a stranger, one that I will grow within this lifespan.

I flinch, shaking the thoughts from my mind. Put on my coat. Right my facial expressions. "It was a reflex. I was . . ." Scared.

"What else can you do with that arm? Turn concrete to dust?" he probes, leaning against the window. The light sways about him. "Are you even human? Peel that skin off, let's see."

Before, it was his romantic phrase. Peel that skin off. Peel that clothing off. Now it's an insult. The sharp point of a memory stabs me: Jan, paring her skin off last night. I step back, swallowing the bile.

"You always said it was a car accident that took your arm," he says, the drunkenness setting in. "My bet is you sawed off your arm to save yourself from whatever sticky situation you put yourself in."

I take his glass, chug it. Bitter. Burning. "I have a child, Jan. I'm not a devil." I raise his hand, yank his glove off. "You hit her. Bruises from last night. Weapon, no?"

He side-eyes me. "Story is I went too hard on the punching bag." He scrapes a hand through his hair, revealing a throbbing vein across his forehead. Breaks into a spatter of Bengali. He looks at me now as if I am a specter. "Look at you. Up and early. Fresh makeup. Designer clothes. Strictly business as usual. Impassive. Intense. Calculated. Nothing stirs you, does it? That cold, poker-faced glare. That mystery that got me attracted to you. Russian roulette it was. You were my fucking bullet." He looks down at his whiskey glass, reconsiders. "Seems like Mel was, too. Perhaps I should swing the other way, try my chances again." I stare at him. "I'm sorry," he says. Removes his cuff links. Loosens his tie. Stands across his picture window. The 164th story of Khumô Tower, a piece of the expensive real estate sky. Gaborone CBD. World-famous buildings stare back at us, steely and grey, impervious to our stress.

He storms to his desk, rummages through his drawer. Throws a thick-padded object at me. I dodge. "You think I'd hurt you?" His alert, bright-brown eyes narrow into a pained expression. "It's her wallet. And her backpack. I thought she was an undergrad working herself stiff to pay for school. Thought I could do something nice for the family. Sue me for having a heart. Her name's Moremi Gadifele." Moremi, one who hews with an axe.

"No, I'm not touching her things."

Jan raises a finger. Buzzes his secretary by tugging his earlobe, eye-scrolling to speed dial her. The door clicks open. "Boss?" She clip-clops in, towering on sky-high heels. Eager.

"Moremi Gadifele," Jan says as she scribbles it down on her notepad, a very astute and sterile interaction. "Vet her. She sent in a resume. I need to know if she's suitable for our company. No special report, just whatever quick background you can collate. I need this as in last year."

"On it." She spins, blond weave of her ponytail arcing, disappears excitedly like a dog thrown a bone, in a whisper of flowery perfume. I suppose in a fast-paced workplace, she's used to such requests calling for expedited results.

From his desk, Jan extracts white latex gloves from a box and snaps them on. Hands me a pair, to which, raising my eyebrow, I follow suit. He crouches. From a black plastic bag beneath his desk, he removes a wine-red crocodile-skin backpack, gingerly raises it upside down over his desk, and pours out its contents with a noisy clink and a heavy thud from a brass humidor.

I inch closer. "Is this hers?"

He nods. I expected jewelry, perfumes, and cosmetic stuff. There's a sleek white laptop, a nude lipstick, an energy bar, a half-full 200ml bottle of vodka, a screenplay by some famous director of some famous movie, heavily highlighted and with multicolored sticky notes in it, genre: horror.

"Maybe she's a student," Jan says.

I flip through a worn-out leather journal, and, inscribed in a fine-tipped gel pen, are names of people, places, heritage sites, backgrounds—and in question marks is the word "NIGHTMARE." Highlighted around each webtoonesque character drawing is "MEM CARD" titled in consecutive numbers with curt background information.

"What does it say?" Jan asks, leaning in.

I read one of her notes: "'Sometimes when I blink, I wake into a different reality, a different time zone, and I realize we're here again. At the beginning, again. And then it slips out of my skin away from me. And I can't remember anything. I'm unstitched, caught in a state of unrest. Caught in a loop.'" I put it down, shiver. Something about the text reminds me of the CBE. "What does that mean? This is no use to us."

Jan wriggles his nose. "This is pointless. Let's see if we can find something useful."

"This doesn't fit the budget of a student," I say, observing a perforated, silver-grey quantum computer, small enough to be enclosed in my loose-fisted hand. I peer into its several ports. Something's lodged deep inside, and I press my thumbnail against it. The quantum computer spits it out onto my palm: a shiny, unbranded microchip. Inscribed on it is the digital number 1.

"Jan."

"Nelah."

Jan holds up a minuscule, sage-colored chiffon pouch holding opalescent pills, concave surfaces as if embedded with crystals winking in the light. On the table, toppled onto its side, is the humidor, belly vomiting out brand-new microchips. Ten of them. I lean in closer to inspect them. Gasp. "These are from dead bodies." Shiny vessels of dead bodies.

"What gives you that idea?" Jan asks.

"My firm designed a mortuary, and their process involved discarding microchips from corpses into their refuse chute for recycling, which was strangely unsecured. Look." We lean into each other, inspecting the scaled-down writing. "She tried to scrape off the registry numbers."

"Shoddily," he adds. "You think she stole them? But why? Is it possible for someone to access the refuse area of a morgue?"

"Only garbage collectors and staff." I add, "And any morbid person who doesn't mind jumping over their unguarded security walls into the stench of dead-and-burned bodies."

A short, disgusted sound from Jan. "That's how they save on security costs, huh? That's why security doesn't matter there—because no one does that."

"Only law enforcement prescribes and dispenses microchips, but if someone's desperate to get their hands on one, I guess this is the only way. You can't steal one from a live human being without killing them."

Jan leans forward, palms spread out on the desk. He coughs out, "Jesus. This is some serious kak we're in." Kak; it's all shit, really.

We eye the quantum computer. Jan presses the power button. It glows mauve, asks for a code. "Fucking hell," he quips. "Tell me something: What makes someone's microchip valuable to a stranger?"

"It's a mine of data—or rather, a swamp of nightmares," I add, pointing to her inscribed journal. "It's a voyeur's heaven. All those secrets like diamonds."

"That's a fucking security breach on personal data. Why the hell aren't these destroyed? I mean, what if we're in the middle of some fucked-up corporate espionage? What if we have more dead bodies on our hands?"

"Special disposal and storage procedures are followed for politicians, persons of importance, and business people—"

"But not the ordinary citizen."

I nod. "What was she planning to do with these?

His leonine eyes peer at me through a thicket of lashes. "She was far out in the bundus, alone on a dark road, heading somewhere with intention. Could she have obtained serious intel that threatened her life?"

A knock. We jump. Jan yanks his drawer open, and with one arm, sweeps the items into it.

The door clicks open. The secretary. "Boss?"

"Come in," he says mildly, arms crossed. He stands, a tense six-foot-two-inch boulder, his jawline gnawing at anger. She senses something off, a tiny doe-eyed pigeon, tiptoeing on spindly legs, head bobbing to us. He cocks his head. Gentler now, he says, "It's alright, Sam. What's up?"

"Moremi Gadifele?" she says, still assessing if he's a grenade she might trigger with poorly done homework. I see myself in her as a once-timid intern getting yelled at by architects on a construction site or scuffling through the office preparing tenders and making mistakes. I stare at Jan and try to see him from her perspective. Unapproachable. Assertive. Alpha-male persona. And me, beside him, the bitch-on-wheels architect. *Intimidating*, I think. *That's how people see him, ruthlessly quick-witted like his notorious father, like last night.* And I think that scares them. You don't know if you're walking through a landmine or a meadow, but something about that—and I don't know how dangerous it might be—attracts me to him. He is mine, my land mine, my meadow. Terrains I tightrope with abandon.

"Well." Secretary Sam clears her throat, holding her tablet as a shield. "I found some info on her. She goes as Moremi professionally."

Jan. "That fast?"

"She has a website, and some feature articles from elite magazines—*Disculture, Blackstream, Arlo & Dusk, City Scoop*. Anyway, she's all over the internet."

I bite the inside of my cheek, salt spools on my tongue. If Jan's nervous, he doesn't show it. "Continue." He nods, muscles writhing in his forearms.

"I doubt she'll be available to work anytime soon. Yesterday morning, at ten twenty-three in Café Dijo, she posted, quote, 'going on a two-week *sabbatical* for my incubation period of story-mining,' unquote. She emphasized that post with a winking smiley and a selfie with a mocha-choca, chips, and salsa." Sam looks up, waiting for a star to lick her forehead. She peers into her screen and scrolls through Moremi's profile. "True to her word, she's gone—digitally comatose for sixteen hours and counting. No responses to her followers or comments."

Jan stares straight ahead, cleaved from the moment by some thought. "What else did you find?" I ask.

"I found it strange that her name sounded familiar, so I ran it up online, and a couple of articles came up. Moremi's a notable horror film student. Just turned twenty-three." I'm five years older than her. Ten years I've had to live and establish myself, and I cut her life short. Jan's thirty years old. We killed a child. A child. Saliva swims into my mouth, my gut tightens and my vision blurs. I slow my breathing, clench the hem of my coat.

Sam, suddenly comfortable, strides past the potted fern plant, stands close to us. "Here's a quote from her, listen to this: 'Why do we dream of the future when our dreams are nightmares telling of crimes? I imagined crimes captured by a TV-like device, so everyone can watch the terrible deeds we do like eighties films. That thought came into my head during my transcribing internship. I was working long hours, pressured by varsity coursework and a side-hustle. I had insomnia. The only time I could sleep was filled with such horrid nightmares that I literally stopped sleeping for a full week. I had to quickly come up with a project for class. I woke up in the middle of my sleep and had this line circling in my mind: The feet of time rest in the future; its body gathered in future-dust bends backward to collect the past and gather it in the center of the present. And I thought, the future, past, and present are one body, which is probably why the CBE can predict our ability to commit a crime. Instead, I took what we dream, our worst nightmares, and turned it into a profitable, entertaining product that, in a way, became exposure therapy, helps us deal with our fears, and allows us to have fun with it in a light-hearted manner. Dreams are so murky and confusing, but in their midst they are real.'"

Sam looks up wistfully. "My ex took me to one of her horror viewings for our first date. I was in his nightmare. It's so strange the way dreams work. His nightmare was a revolving cast of angry clowns and dolls that followed us everywhere, trying to kill us. It was always dark, and I could hardly run, and each time I tried to scream, I had no voice. I was never afraid of clowns and dolls, but I hate the sight of them now. It's an adrenaline rush, those viewings. But it's not for me."

My stomach tightens. I scrape my nail against the desk, wood chippings falling to the ground. "So . . ." My voice comes out squeaky; I clear my throat. "Is there a picture of her?"

Sam turns the tablet toward me. The face looking at me is a light-brown-skinned face, braids falling to her shoulders and wrapped in clear beads. She's beaming, a gap between her front two teeth. Bliksem, that's her. It's the girl we . . . killed. Shem skepsel, she's so young.

My hands tremble, and I try to still them against my silk pants, leaving hand-marks of sweat.

"Her mother's lifespan expired when she was a one-year-old. Raised by her father. But now she's an orphan," Secretary Sam says apologetically. "Apparently, her entire family has been convicted and sentenced for *possible* identity theft and—*Jesus*—homicide."

Possible. Means they didn't commit it. So the CBE caught them before they acted out their crimes. I stare at the screen. I can't breathe. She didn't want to die. She was working. But who goes out alone into nowhere? At night. Is she crazy? Yes, she's crazy.

In our city, everyone lives forever.

But for a chance at immortality, we're government entities, our bodies rated according to the value they bring to the economy. Moremi is of good value to our city's creative industry; therefore, we've not only damaged a body, we've committed a crime against the government by destroying their property's ability to transplant another consciousness into her body and maintain her empire. We're more fucked than before.

"Oh," Sam quips. "She had a short stint at your father's firm when she was twenty."

"What?" Jan's jaw tightens, and she leans back.

"She'd just graduated. She did admin work and graphic design. A year later, she left. No reason given."

Sam stands, waiting for, what? A treat, a thank you? "You may leave," Jan says in the same breath as a mourner. When she's gone, Jan shakes his head. "We've truly fucked ourselves over. She's a popular freak-show artist from a family of criminals, and she's in cahoots with something dodgy. She worked for my father, too briefly to have created any lasting relationships, but still . . . which one of those bullets is going to kill us first?"

A shadow washes over my face, a cloud eclipsing the sun. I feel faint. Jan hands me a glass of water, which trembles all the way to my lips. I nudge my fingers into my braids, wanting to rip them off. The silence is a taut one to walk through.

I cover my face in my palms. "So in her current life, she was a voyeur, and now she's a voyeuristic ghost." Worry grooves Jan's forehead. He stares at me as I speak. "She's following me."

"What? She's still alive? Oh my God." He spins around as if to flee the building. "No, no, no. Babe, it's your conscience playing tricks on you. Did she say anything? Were you alone?"

I shake my head, holding onto his arm. "My husband was there. And our neighbor. I don't think anyone else can see her. I don't know, Jan, it's so terrifying. What's going on? I'm scared." I peer up at him. "Haven't you seen her at all?"

"It's just guilt." He pauses.

I lean away from him. "It? *It* is a woman."

"Didn't seem like that last night when you were badgering her."

"Mxm, she wouldn't shut up," I say.

"That's what happens when someone hurts you. You scream. For God's sake, you cry out."

I grip myself by the elbows. "I don't know what will happen if she touches me."

He shakes his head, takes hold of me. "Love, what happened last night was traumatizing," he whispers desperately, bending slightly at the knees to be at my eye level. "It's only reasonable that you feel this way, but we need to be strong to get through this. We'll get through this. We've made it this far, and we need to be proactive and alert to stay free."

"But, Jan, what do I do if she comes again?" I sink my head into his chest. "The way she was looking at me, Jan. We were horrible. You didn't see what I saw. You only saw her in the dark. I saw her in the light. We massacred her body. We deserve to be in hell."

"Love, please don't cry. We need to think, love."

"I swear the devil has sent her to me. I can't live if she follows me everywhere!" I grip his shirt, crying into it. "She kept calling my name last night. Oh, what does she want from me? I nearly broke down in front of my husband and told him everything."

He pulls me back, stares hard at me. "This is a cruel world, and people die. The sooner you let that sink in, the faster we can act. Something terrible happened to us—that doesn't make us bad people. If we're indicted, *your* consciousness will be forced out of your body, and someone else's consciousness will be downloaded into *your* body, sleeping in *your* skin, enjoying the life you fought tooth and nail for. The police precinct will have someone reputable take over your lifestyle and run it. Personalities like ours are good for the country. Whoever that is will take your daughter and your husband, whilst you're stored in their dingy prison banks, simulated with terror and experimented on for eternity." Gently now, he adds, "We buried her so we can live. If we fall apart now, that girl died for nothing. Would you prefer that? For her death to be meaningless? For your daughter to lose her mother?" I shake my head. "We're not like those sadistic killers." He wipes my tears with his thumb as I nod. "We need a game plan. What's our most impending doom?"

"The body and the Sunday chemicals," I add business-like, sniffing, and he hands me a tissue. "Our most worrisome detail is the scent her corpse is releasing. If there's a way to erase them from the air so they don't interact with Sunday's released chemicals, then we can delay the body being found. But even if we tried, we wouldn't be able to erase every microscopic detail."

"But?" he notes.

"I passed my AI assessment this morning. That doesn't mean I'll pass it tomorrow."

He checks the time on his wristwatch. "So, we have fifteen hours to figure that one out," he muses.

I'm surprised he remembers that detail I told him a month ago.

"Three problems on our hands: the body, the AI assessment, and your husband." He crosses his arms, one hand stroking his chin.

Pressure tightens the air. I stare across at an alfresco pool in the adjacent building—well, part of the same building—its rippled back gleaming under the light of a cloud-cast sun. Someone swimming laps. A bird flits by. Dips for a sip of water. Arcs back into the sky, rain-quiet. A creaking metal sways, the scaffolding attached to the façade. Maintenance workers repairing one of the large-paned windows.

"Even if we move the body, it'll still get found," I say. "What if . . . no."

He turns. "Say it."

Relief expands my chest. "Maybe we only have two major problems—my husband and the AI assessor—and two manageable problems—her secrets and her body," I say, pacing back and forth. "We need to crack open her quantum to read these microchips. Her fingerprint's roughly thirty kilometers away, but it'll give us access to her quantum and answers to why she's in possession of these microchips. Also, I think we are at an advantage here. Judging from her identity, she's not a body-hopper. This is her first lifespan, her first season. And a huge plus: her body is microchip free. Which means the detectives won't be able to identify the culprits if there's no footage to assess. Even if they perused the database and assessed the location of microchipped citizens to flag those within the crime scene's vicinity, my microchip, with thanks to your device, says I was at work and then at a work celebration. And your alibi is whatever you need it to be. So," I say, facing him, "we already have a dead body on our hands. Let's find her a new killer."

14:43 /// BED OF BONE

"You're diabolically brilliant," Jan says, grinning. "This could actually work."

"But how are we going to find a killer to replace us in fifteen hours?" I ask. "Maintaining this charade with my AI assessor, how long will that last before our truth shatters?"

He yanks his coat from his swivel chair. The chair spins around. He puts the coat on. "You have no idea what people will sell their lives for."

I rub my temples with my index fingers. "How do we even pick someone? Who will it be?"

"Your husband." His topaz eyes light up, and hell is a giggling audience. "Two birds with one stone. Then we have the assessor to deal with, which it sounds like you handled brilliantly this morning. Your husband understands the behind-the-scenes, and with what you've mentioned, it already sounds like the culprit knows the loopholes in the system, like your husband."

"No."

"But—"

"I said *no*." I step back. He's always wanted my husband out of the way. But he couldn't have predicted that the idea would come through my lips. Who can I trust? Who do I blame?

Hurt smolders in his eyes as he stares at me. "I can see it in your eyes, what you're thinking. The answer is no," he says, running a hand through his hair. "You stared at me like that last night, as if I'd hurt you. Up till then, you've always trusted me."

"I saw a different side of you that scares me."

"I see a different, *diabolical* side of you, but I'm not letting that redefine what you mean to me."

I push the conversation aside. "We need to bury the killer's DNA in her body, so the detective's tools pick up their DNA," I say. "Do you know someone we can use?"

"Ja, a bunch of people. On speed dial." He narrows his eyes. "What do you take me for?"

"Well, Jan, you seem to have a bunch of corruptible tricks in your bag and those bodies in your family's foster agency."

"Empty shells, love. The doctor at our agency in Oodi can still transfer you into one of their bodies and have someone take the fall in this current body of yours."

I muse. "We need to see my family first, and then we can consider that."

"I've an idea of who can take the fall," he says. "Your husband—"

"How about your ex-wife-to-be?" I interrupt. "I mean, you're done with her, might as well be done with her completely." His lips clamp shut. "Exactly."

He surrenders his hands. "Good point." Takes a deep breath. Steps forward. Hands delicately on my shoulders. "I'll put up my wife, if you put up your husband."

The air leaves my body. Just as swift, a creature-quick movement sweeps through the closed door. A woman. The dead victim. *Our* victim. Moremi Gadifele. She limps toward us. I fall back over the leather couch. My breaths come out quick. "Oh, Jan, she's here. Blocking the doorway."

He stares at the door. Drags his hand through his hair. "There's no one there. Love, it's just in your head."

"She's right there." I point. I get to my feet. Grab my handbag. "I need to get out of here."

Jan nears me. Places his hands on my shoulder. Frames my face, and only my eyes revolve to the side. "Love, we're in this together. I understand. What happened last night was too, too much." Moremi steps forward, a meter away from us, and I freeze. "And it's understandable you are tormented by what we had to do. No one should have to go through that. Now." He spins me, remarkably faces me toward the doorway, to her. "You need to face your fear. It's a hallucination. I guarantee you, if you touch her, your hand will slip through her, and she'll fade. That's the thing with nightmares. Face your fears, love. Trust me, they're not real."

She leers.

"No, I don't want to," I mumble like a child, try to step back but he holds me steady, my back against his chest. Moremi leans to one side, the side with the twisted foot, facing in the opposite direction. I grimace, close my eyes, but Jan's lips are at my ear, his voice dripping into me. "Love, if we don't face this now, it'll only keep following us, and we won't be able to operate. I'm right here." His hand rappels down my arm, tangles with my fingers, raises my arm, and I lean back as he raises it toward her. "I'll do this with you."

She hobbles, her brown skin smeared with blood. On closer inspection, her face—the revealed muscle, the bit of bone, the crucified eye, sunken into a bed of bone and tendon—sneers at me. "Ja nè, I told you you'd regret burying me, and now you're trying me again."

I struggle to let the words out. I mutter, "Moremi, listen—"

She looks surprised that I know her name.

Moremi's voice gasps through her split lips. "Why?" That's it. A simple question. "Why did you do this to me? *You're* the one that took my breath away." Her eyes are big like last night but with the venom of anger. She stands sentry at the doorway. Her left foot is missing a couple of toes. The other is too flat, pointing in the wrong direction.

"I have risen, fed by your greed, your pride, your fear," she croaks, sounding like an old woman on her deathbed. "Fed by your DNA beneath my nail beds."

Jan stretches my fingers. Her heart-shaped face is not decomposing but fresh and gleaming in the morning sun. We're the same height. Fingers inch away. She tilts her head, beckoning me. I shut my eyes tight. My fingers near the edge of her face where the air turns hot, dip into her eye socket, glimpse the bulb of her cheekbone, glow with a pain full of sun. A death, velvet in its flow, wages through my veins.

I tip back, a broken volcano, a molten mountain, buckled from its stance. A pain so unfathomable, it burns and rebirths me. A scream scrambles from my larynx, claws the ceiling, bangs the windows, breaks the world. A bit of air, a gap of safety. No more contact from yesterday's death. Air flows around me, a running stream of life, but I'm suffocating, suffocating, suffocating, and spinning on the last remnants of life in my lungs. Jan heaves and heaves for oxygen that no longer speaks our lungs' language. I punch my chest, gobble bits of air. The first intake, sharp and cold. My eyes water.

"Get me out of here!" I scream.

Jan wheezes, eyes me, can't believe what he doesn't see but feels. Still doubts, as if it's electricity that's somehow leaked from a broken appliance. Moremi blocks the doorway, Secretary Sam beyond, wavering on pinpoints of heels, staring through Moremi at us, a debacle.

Jan edges back. "Bliksem. There's no other exit."

I'm trapped. My eyes ricochet. A sharp, bright glisten disturbs my eyes. Picture windows. The reflection of sunlight screams across all the glass in the room, drowning me in it. The glass windows are nonoperable. But I stumble over the coffee table, knocking down décor books. Punch my arm against the window. Nothing.

"Running only makes it worse for you." Moremi heaves the other foot forward. "Let me touch you."

The window is cold against my back. Jan stares at me, can't see how we damaged her body last night. "No!" I shout. My arm, I swing it against the window again. A crack flicks across the pane like lightning.

"You're going to hurt yourself! What the hell are you doing?" Jan shouts.

Again. I bang my arm against the glass. Pieces of skin-flannel fly off my arm, exposing grey-steeled bone-metal. Again. An explosion of cracks spread across the window. A meteor. Shards spray against the floor into a song of crystals. The wind screams through the open wound. Wind cranes inside, gropes us. Outside, all the buildings, the architectural marvels, stand like huddled pistons firing into the sky-squad.

"Stop!" Her hoarse voice pierces me like a bullet riddling through flesh. "If you walk away from me, someone else will die."

Jan wraps his hands through his hair like a madman pulling at straw. "Don't!"

I don't think. I throw myself into a mouth of air, tongues of wind wrap and lick me.

I hit the steel mesh of the scaffold. It smacks against the façade.

My prosthetic arm indicates the speed of the wind. Not safe. Tallest building, high vortex. I step onto the scaffold, frightening the maintenance workers. It sways. The ground beneath sinks and swells in my vision. *Don't look down.* Moremi drags her battered body to the window. Rain and wind buck down on me.

I lunge, arms waving as if trying to grab a curtain of wind, use it as rope, and swing across into the pool. Held by nothing but air, the wind wheezes through my ears. My lungs contract, fear trickles in. I spin my arms as the air holds me wary. Screaming, I crash into the swimming pool across the lane dividers, a cold, biting feeling. Joh, I made it. I'm caught between maddening laughter and hyperventilation.

I look back. Moremi's standing on the horizontal metal frame of the scaffold. The wind does not graze her. No need for physics—she launches herself off the scaffold as if it's a trampoline and lands an arm's length away from me. No splash. Chlorine tangles into my scream as the tight molecules of water restrain me from moving faster. She walks through water as if it's air. Fuck me. I drag myself across. Her broken fingers hook into my braids. A burn sears into my shoulder, her hand. I scream, striking out with my nails bared. I stumble, swallow more chlorine. Gasp. Choke. People stand by with their kettlebells, watching me scream for help. The density of the water is unrecognizable to her form. Her blood colors not the waters. I crawl-swim to the edge, remove my coat; a necklace gets lost in the depths of the pool. The cold winter hugs me as I reach for the edge, haul myself up. I stumble about, the sun dizzying around me. I collapse onto the concrete paving, panting and coughing. I swat away assisting hands, wipe the pool water from my face.

I limp on one stiletto, kick it aside. Past the reception desk. Punch the buttons to open the elevator doors. It's taking too long. The stairs.

Standing in the pool, she stares at me; evil gloom drips across her gashed lip. I push gymgoers aside. She paces toward me. Down the stairs I go, careening from banister to wall, the dark shade clinging to me. Stumble down the stairs. Throw a scream out like a missile. No one's there. I take a breath. My backbone clicks. Blood trickles down my pants, peeking out at my ankle. I touch my thigh. Pain. I cringe, get up, water eclipsing my body, making it harder to maneuver without slipping. Make it downstairs.

Jan hurries through the entrance doors, the wine-red backpack strapped to his shoulder. People's eyes cling to us. In a fit of apologies, he carries me into the elevator, punches B for basement parking. Bloody hell, I'm crying. "I'm burning," I shout, trying to remove my blouse. "She burned me with her hand."

Jan holds me in his arms. "Shh, it's okay. I'm here. I'm sorry." He gently sweeps the blouse down my shoulder. Crumples in sadness. The smell of burning skin stings my nose. I twist my back to the mirror. A hand-mark burn boils into my skin. I clench my teeth from the scathing pain. Her touch can burn me. She is beyond powerful—what more can she do?

Jan's lips press to my forehead. He tucks wet braids behind my ear. "We'll fix this. We'll fix it. I promise."

The elevator doors ding open. Moremi stands there. Too late for my scream. She throws Jan aside, against the concrete column. Headfirst. Knocked out. Blood trickles from his head, fans out. I jab my legs at her. Her hands, three fingers less, grip sharply into my shoulders, her mouth cranes open, thick blood pouring onto my chest. A light flickers. We're surrounded by sixty or so stationary cars. At the far end, near the exit, is a security guard. On the other end, by the other elevators, a couple push a cart toward their car, away from us. I'm about to scream, but Moremi punches me in the chest.

"I will kill you the same way I died," Moremi bellows, rippling the cold air into a burning sensation. "I'm going to cave your head in the same way you did mine. My existence is built around your DNA. An automatic GPS route to you. No matter where you run, I'll always find you."

"No, no, no, asseblief," I cry.

"Yes, yes, *yes*," she says. Her fist flies forward. Pain. Pain explodes in my forehead. She drags me out of the elevator by my hair. How can this be the end? No, it can't be. It won't. My arms hustle around with her, tackling her to the ground. My legs shoot outward, wrap themselves around her. She slips out, this damaged body more powerful than mine. She raises her fist, the other crunched around my blouse's collar.

"I'm sorry. Please forgive me," I cry. "Asseblief, just give me time."

The shadows of the basement shift between our faces. Her pupils yawn and pulsate, ravenous and rabid. "You would like to borrow some time?" she asks, which stuns me. Am I even allowed? What are the rules? *Are* there rules?

I'm talking to Satan, so I pause, thinking. She seizes my throat. Her palm is a Venus flytrap, smashing my face into the cold, dusty concrete floor. The undeniable speed and pressure of her grip crushes the sound from my scream. Sparks of white and dark light dance before my eyes.

"Yes, yes, please give me more time!" I scream, slurring words.

The security guard turns, can't see me down on the floor. I hear his footsteps as he tries to find the source of the scream. But he's going in the opposite direction, toward the couple who are just as confused. I'm too scared to scream again.

Moremi's damaged lips attempt to smile. "How long did I take to die?"

"W-w-what?"

"How long. Did I. Take to die?" She enunciates every word so it terrifies me.

"I-I-I don't know." She has the upper hand. Anything to delay.

"You buried me alive. Snuffed my breath. Filled my lungs with muck."

"I-I-I'm sorry," I plead.

"How many family members do you have? Close relationships?" That's her question. My daughter. My husband. A brutal brother. A quiet father. An optimistic, caring mother. No other relatives. Close relationships—Jan, my lover.

She lets go of me. Traces my footsteps as I hurriedly take the opportunity to drag at Jan's body. He wakes, leaning against me as I guide us along the long path to the car. I extract the key from my handbag. Drop it twice. Unlock the car with sweaty fingers as Moremi stares, smiling beguilingly. Jan drops into the back seat and I follow suit, yelling for the car to engage self-driving mode with the door still open. She reaches in casually, hands gripping the sides of my abdomen, her body scraping against the concrete floor, as the car's tires squeal in high-octane speed.

"Five relatives and one lover; six lives. All of them," she says, her legs striking through a column as the car turns to the exit. I cringe expecting impact, but she shows no pain, knows no pain. "Be careful what you wish for. The time I took to die is the time left until someone you love dies," she whispers, letting go, her body falling to the ground, a rolling thud beneath the car—a speed bump. I look through the back window, see her body roll to a still. She disappears like a hazy sunset into the swaying smell of burnt tires.

15:17 /// DEATH'S ABYSS

We're driving through narrow streets, neighborhoods, the outer lanes of the neighboring Phase II development shadowed by the concrete-and-marble husks of buildings.

On the flyover, our car meanders through slow-moving cars and veers northeast onto Nelson Mandela Drive. We pass a spire of a building, distilling fractured light and shadows from its criss-cross façade onto the sidewalks and roads. I'm anemic-faint. Every facial recognition scanner of every doorway of every home, office building, restaurant, hotel knows the history of my body before it knows me, the real me.

My skin, my DNA categorized into the system as "potentially violent" for transparency and security purposes. But my reputation has been my messiah. My work, my name stands higher than the damaging history of my body, which is why others don't look at me funny.

A sparkle of light smacks my eyes. The top body of a car. A woman in a restaurant, the light skimming her glass of water, the windows of storefronts—reflecting me, seeing me, recording me. I suddenly can't breathe. Too much reflection. Too many eyes unwittingly capturing us, potential witnesses.

"Dim the windows," I direct the driver-assist, the car's computer. The windows darken, shushing out the sunlight.

"I detect bodily harm," the female driver-assist says. "Life Gaborone Private Hospital is two-point-two kilometers away—"

"No, go to my parents' farmhouse."

"Heading toward Bogosi farmhouse." I sneeze as the water from the swimming pool drips from my braids down my back. I smell like chlorine. I pat myself dry with a towel from the gym bag that I store in my car.

Jan's lying in the back seat, and I jab my knee into the car's console and grab tissues from the glove compartment to dab on his wound. Flanking the roads are buildings that smear past our windows in blots of grey.

"Please buckle your seat belt," the driver-assist voice says, "we're entering a restricted sixty-kilometer-per-hour zone—"

"Don't slow down!" I shout.

"Estimated time of arrival is forty-one minutes."

"Drive faster. We don't have time. *That* is a command." I turn to Jan as I buckle my seat belt. "Jan, are you okay?"

He ruffles his hair. "I believe you now," Jan whispers, dazed. "I felt like I was being struck by electricity. What the hell is that thing?"

"Quick, how long did she take to die?"

"What?"

"Jan, my family is going to die! That's how much time we have to save them." His eyes color with shock. I grab his collar. "How long did she take to die last night?"

"I wasn't timing her death," Jan says. "She talked to you? What else did she say?"

"She blames me. Only me. Says I'm the one that took her breath away. That it's my DNA, my fear that woke her up. If she can do this to you . . . Oh, Modimo. Car, accelerate!"

"We're entering a section of the A1 highway often patrolled by police," the driver-assist says.

"We don't have time for that. Bypass through Sebele Valley!" I shout. The steering wheel swings left by the traffic lights—and we swing right, sweaty and anxious—into the agricultural district of Sebele Valley surrounded by palo verde trees. "Conference-call my parents and brother. Put it on speaker, no visuals." The dashboard fills with their caller IDs and photos. It rings, and they answer.

Mama. "Nana, what a surprise."

Papa. "Hello, my babygirl?"

Limbani. "What the hell do you want?"

"This is an emergency," I say. "I'm on the way to the farmhouse. We need to meet now. I can't say much on the phone but please, if you see a strange woman nearby, whatever you do, keep away from her. Don't help her. Lock your doors, asseblief." Wait. Only I can see her? Fuck.

"What's going on?" they say at the same time.

"I'll explain at the house. It's very urgent that you're all there. Hanging up now."

The line cuts. "Oh God, what if she can walk through walls?" I ask. "I need to warn them—"

Jan tugs at my hand. "And say what? That the woman we killed last night can walk through walls?"

"A crime has been detected," the driver-assist says. "Calling police."

"Stop," I shout, and the dashboard blackens. "Please update terminology settings. 'Kill' in this context is synonymous to winning at something or doing something excellent."

"Use of slang updated," the driver-assist says.

I glare at Jan. "Watch yourself. Driver-assist, discontinue listening to our conversation."

"Conversation detection disabled," it says.

"If this car was a chatterbox last night, we wouldn't be in this shit," I moan. "I mean, why didn't the car detect anything?"

"That's what I'm thinking." Jan taps his chin.

"Hand me Moremi's ID," I say, withering inside. He hands me the backpack from the floor. I decant her purse for her ID, an electric-blue, translucent, self-powered augmented card. The digital text glows ghost-white upon contact. I tap her headshot, her lips read:

MOREMI GADIFELE, 23

O-RIGINAL (ceased)

LIFESPAN 0

BODY-HOPPING 0

Jan moans. “She’s not microchipped. Thank God.”

“Ceased?” I feel faint. I scroll as a din grows in my head.

Sex: X (she, her/they, them)

Nationality: Motswana

Height: 154 cm / 5 ft 1 in

Weight: 51 kg / 112 lbs

Blood type: O-

Location: Nelson Mandela Drive

-24.636474, 25.916249

Vitals: Health App (disabled)

Date of Bodily Death: [01:34] Saturday, 10 October

Cause of death: AUTHORIZED ACCESS ONLY

Words dribble from my tongue. “Jan, they know she’s dead.”

“Who?”

“The Department of Immigration and Civil Registration. They have her cause of death listed on her identity card, but I can’t access it. Do you have access to it, since your father has tentacles in places we can’t reach?”

He winces. “His power is corruption. He could connect me to someone, but that could lead back to us, which is not what we need.” Jan swipes out his wallet, ID card, scrolls through his ID details as I pull mine out, comparing the two, silver and gilt-edged.

JANITH KOSHAL, 30

O-RIGINAL

LIFESPAN 0

BODY-HOPPING 0

Sex: Male (he/him)

Nationality: Indian

Height: 189 cm / 6 ft 2 in

Weight: 97 kg / 214 lbs

Blood type: A-

NELAH BOGOSI-NTSU, 28
LIFESPAN 3rd (430 yrs)
BODY-HOPPING 1st
BODY CONDITION: CRIMINALLY PRONE

Sex: Female (she/her)
Nationality: Motswana
Height: 160 cm / 5 ft 5 in
Weight: 60 kg / 132 lbs
Blood type: AB+

"Nothing suspicious on ours," Jan says.

My eyes bolt out when I notice the location listed on her ID. "Oh God," I say, "get rid of her ID—it's tracking us."

He thumb-presses the window's button and throws it out into the wailing mouth of the wind. Botswana's notorious heat rushes in with the riff of kwaito music from the side-street vendors and guzzles every bit of coolness we have. Grey clouds stir above, so perhaps the rain will cool shit down. I stare out my window, watching pantsula guys on the pavements with their ankle pants and spottie hats, doing stunning footwork dances to the deep bass of a gqom track as a woman sing-songs, "Woza, woza!" The contrast stuns me: life moves on merrily outside, whilst ours remains stagnant as the dry-arid air of Gaborone.

"What the hell is going on?" I yell, smacking the cards onto the seat. "If immigration knows that she's dead, shouldn't their systems flag the absence of a death certificate? Shouldn't their system notify them to alert police to this discrepancy?"

Jan pinches the bridge of his nose. "If they know when or where she died, they could have tracked her body to her last active location. By now, we'd have heard something—*anything.* Why is her cause of death hidden? Could it be because her family's incarcerated? Hold on. Something's bothering me. I need to call my father." He stares ahead silently as if steeling himself, adjusting himself, righting his fury into something calm. He speed-dials Aarav. He pulls up holo-call visual, but Jan's disabled our visuals.

"Son," his father says. "Show yourself."

"I can't, Ba," he says with a disgusted curl of the lip, as if the latter word is sick in his mouth. His repulsion for his father is a sticky tangible particle of the air and it paints his cheeks a gloomy color. "Quick one. A young woman worked for you three years ago. Moremi Gadifele. She did admin work and graphic design."

"Son, women come and go in our firm. I hardly recall their names or how they look."

The ropes of veins in Jan's fingers writhe as he tightens and unclenches his hands. "I've seen the same women in your firm for the last three years."

"What's this about?" A note of suspicion in Aarav's voice.

"I thought I could take you up on that offer you made me," Jan says.

"Why *specifically* her?" He seems suddenly attentive, voice barricading the words he'd like to say.

"I saw her looking for employment at one of my associates' firms and recognized that she worked for you," Jan says.

"Today?" His voice perks up. "Is the young woman with you? I want to speak with her."

"Unfortunately, you just missed her."

"Oh," he muses, a good thought lighting his brown eyes. "She's still alive." My body goes cold. "What's that joke running the grapevines? Anyone who says 'no' to me ends up bewitched." He laughs. "Son, where's your humor today?"

"My humor is alive as she is," Jan says sarcastically. Of course, his humor is dead. "Anyway, she looks interesting enough. The divorce proceedings are tightening the screws on me, and I thought I could blow off steam so that Melissa won't catch wind of the affair."

"Well," Aarav muses, laughing in relief, "if the girl is the one I'm recalling, she was a highly astute and talented girl. She didn't stay with us for long. Though, I've sent my employees to headhunt her with irresistible offers that she unfortunately declined. Now, seeing that you owe me for clearing up the unsightly mess of that 'wiretapped' architect you keep pissing around, I believe you can talk to this associate of yours . . . that's if they hired her, to offer the girl to me."

I stare at Jan, and his eyes bolt out. "No, Ba, I don't think I can do that. It seems my associate wasn't interested in hiring her."

"That's unfortunate. She's irresistible, isn't she?" he asks.

Jan rolls his eyes. "Well, she's something."

"Apparently, Ms. Gadifele's gone AWOL, which is unusual coming from my team. You know how thorough their surveillance is, which goes to show how off-the-grid excellent her skills are. But I have a couple of our girls I can offer to you. I'll have my secretary send you a list."

Jan. "Right, I look forward it. Well, I have to go. Talk soon." He hangs up. Evades eye contact, and I wonder why? What does he truly think about his father?

"Your father and his cohorts raped women then hired some hotshot lawyers to clean it up," I say, a bad taste in my mouth. "He's ruthless in his business transactions, which sometimes doesn't work out for those in partnerships with him. Some say you have the same acerbic touch."

"Through fair strategies, not backstabbing and manipulation." Jan hangs his head down. "It sickens me that I have to act chummy with him. But he's my father."

"So," I say, staring at him full-on, "he knows you're pissing around me? Did you tell him I was infertile? Is that why we got a good rate with the Wombcubator?" I ask, angry. "I don't need your father's corrupt network anywhere near me."

Jan nods, more with relief than sorrow. "I'm sorry. I despised going to him, but I had to." He scratches his forehead. "His former colleague saw us at that dinner function, told my father about it. My father became fascinated with you. He wanted to bring you on to his team for the design of the cultural precinct skyscraper. I told him to stay the fuck away from you. And once I asked for that Wombcubator favor, he asked me to sign you over as a deal. I agreed just to get it done, knowing I'd have to think something up because he's not one to let things slide, especially significant deals like this. So I've been stalling, and he's getting very impatient lately. Soon, he'll punish me again. I've backpedaled before on a promise, so he messed with our Tokyo clients, obliterated our merger to teach me a lesson. It poisoned my relationship with my managing partners at the firm."

I keep quiet, feeling guilty.

"I'm not like my father," he spits. "You keep looking at me the way I look at him, as if you don't know me." He focuses his eyes on me, burning golden-brown irises. "Do you really think the same of me as of him?"

I touch his shoulder, feel ashamed. "You just scared me last night. You didn't seem like the Jan that I know. The things you were saying . . . You had no regard for that young woman. I couldn't think straight, but you . . ."

His eyelids crush closed. "He's in my blood, his way of thinking in my brain. I just wish I could get him the hell out of my DNA." His fisted hands jam into his jaw. "I think Mel's sleeping with him. After me, she had to move up. And now you . . . What can I do to prove myself to you? Should I burn myself—?"

I wrap my arms around the boulders of his shoulders so crippled with emotional pain. "No. I won't let you go down that rabbit hole. I'm here, nè. You are you. Look at me." He lifts his eyes to mine, and they shimmer with vulnerability. My breath fiercely grasps his, takes him in, secures him on my mouth, my tongue. I pull back, look deeply into his eyes. "You mean a lot more to me than all that's happened to us. I have trust issues. I fucked up by thinking the wrong things. But *you*? You saved us from going to hell, and it's not like I'm innocent." I kiss his forehead, his hard jawline, and his lips. He relaxes into my arms, and we rest into our breaths.

"Okay," he whispers. "Now we need to save your family."

"Good."

"Maybe try killing her again, then she'll stop."

"She's powerful, Jan!"

"Sorry."

A message beeps into his wrist. He opens it and sighs.

"Is that the list of women from your father?" I ask, watching him type a series of texts back.

"You understand why I had to act complicit, right?" Jans asks. "He was very suspicious, which makes me very suspicious. I'm wondering whom I can talk to to find more information on Moremi's history at my father's company, but he has such a tight leash on his social circle that no one would risk being a whistleblower. For now, let's deal with the matter at hand, Moremi."

Jan strokes his chin, then his eyes flicker with realization. "The timeline. Moremi's ID card stated her time of death at 1:34 a.m. I think we left the townhouse around 11:00 p.m. I got home around 4:45 a.m. That's five hours, forty-five minutes. I mean, we drove for a bit before we . . . hit her. It took a while to dig the grave. Check the time log on the car."

"You're right." I click the side buttons on the back of the driver's seat, press the GPS location on its computer display, and scroll back to yesterday's destination routes. "We left the townhouse at 11:59 p.m. We covered the fifty-six kilometers to the Oodi-Modipane Road—which is where we . . . buried her. Got there around 1:11 a.m. We got off onto some unnamed gravel road and hovered there for a bit. The car shows movement at 4:14 a.m. The car is logged at your Tsholofelo East home eighteen minutes later at 4:32 a.m. Then my house at 4:44 a.m."

"So our window of time is 1:11 a.m. to 4:14 a.m.," Jan says, finger to his lip. "She must have died sometime when the car stopped moving. We spent roughly three hours at the site. Much of that was bickering and digging, which felt like forever, but the grave was shallow. Her ID says she died at 1:34 a.m." He swallows. "We may have taken twenty minutes or so . . . killing her."

I swallow. Twenty minutes. That's all it took to end twenty-three years of life in her. As if years stacked in a body make someone invincible. Why is it so easy to die?

"Everything happened so fast," I whisper, leaning into my knees, staring at my hands, how they had blood last night. "How could it be that quick?"

Jan checks his watch. "Given the estimates, it'll take her twenty minutes to kill your loved one. Jesus. But how long will it take her to get to them? Wait. Does twenty minutes refer to when you struck the deal with her or does it speak to the length it'll take to kill . . . your family?"

"I need a skyf." I rummage around the pockets of the seats as if I'll find something, although I'm not a smoker, except for those wild-youth years. Jan balls his tissue in his fist. "This is driving me kad mad!" I shout. "I need to be home now. Car, activate FlightMode."

I work the screen. Enter: FLIGHT PREPARATION

Destination: Bogosi Farmhouse
Distance 15.7km

Walk	**Bike**	**Drive**	**FlightMode**
3h 26min	1h 9 min	24 min	12 min

I press the FlightMode icon, activating hyper-drive. Mechanical parts turn and revolve, changing from drive mode. The car jerks, heaves forward above the traffic into the less congested air roads, and air-pods shoot by like bullets. In FlightMode, the screen depicts air lanes and traffic lights invisible to the naked eye. Only the air vehicles whizzing in and between skyscrapers are detected.

"Jan, what if we're stuck in the simulation?" I ask. "How can we tell if this is truly reality? The CBE tricked me before. What's to say they're not doing it again?"

"No, they'd have woken us up when we buried that girl."

"How sure are you of that?"

He looks at me, deadpan. "Why make us go on?"

"I just want it to be a nightmare—the simulation."

"The consequences are real, not just nightmares."

"I know, but we wouldn't have murdered someone," I cry out.

"But we'd be put away for it because of the CBE's prediction."

"What we did was wrong."

"You have to decide. Make a decision. You're either good or bad. Your actions must align. You can't just choose the middle," Jan says. "Good is reporting yourself. Bad is saving yourself. Sticking in the middle is being a liability."

I hold my mouth shut. Too much is spilling out of me. "How come she's not following you?" But she didn't scratch Jan last night. It's my DNA under her fingernails, not Jan's. Is that why and how she's targeting me?

Jan shifts. "Maybe you're the architect of your story."

"Mxm. Fuck off." I swat his hand. "Seriously."

"You think I planned to have a murder on my hands in the middle of my war-zone divorce? I don't know how this works, either."

"But you killed her, too." We stare at the dashboard. Silence.

"*You* took her last breath." He jabs the air before me. "*You're* the real killer. So technically, she's haunting you, not me."

Anger. Anger. Blazing anger. "She wouldn't let me go. You still took her halfway to death. I'm not going down alone. We're in this together."

He sighs. "Of course, we are, sweetheart."

"What did you do with her skin?"

"I burned it in an oil burner over and over and over and dissolved the ash in my morning coffee and threw it like caution to the wind."

"Jan, if she can burn me with her touch, what else is she capable of? Wait, do you think this is the work of Matsieng's blood? You said it was powerful. Can it revive a dead body? What if Matsieng steps in if the microchip fails? I mean, we are being haunted by the crime we committed. What if Matsieng is the backup plan? Serati said, 'We do everything through Matsieng. We acquire peace through Xem. Matsieng understands your blood intimately.'"

"Love, please, let's not allow our minds to run us into the ground."

"It has to be Matsieng's blood. If Xer blood is this powerful, what else can it do?" I say.

Instead of answering me, he says, "You didn't call your husband. Does that mean you've selected him as a killer by proxy?"

I stare silently at our views as the car cruises past the ridges and hilly terrain surrounding the highway, the sun's eye tracking us in its cloud of mirage, time felled by the second.

Twenty-eight minutes in, and we're in view of Tshele Hill, its oil storage facility. It brings back memories of the day I was released into this body. The Bogosi farmhouse. Driving through the wide gravel road to their sprawling four-hectare farmhouse, a land untouched by the greedy mouth of urban sprawl's concrete jungle. The veldspan fence hums with the clipped ticks of electricity. The kraal out front, the borehole pumping water. The fields with long stalks in a wispy-yellow wave in the breeze. Tswana cattle graze in the distance, various breeds of chickens in their coop. I remember my consciousness sim-transit architect's sleek car coming up the quiet werf's estate, thick trees, sky swollen with blue, the punch of vivid green in the rolling gardens, the sharp peace of quietude, chalets for visiting relatives, where I'd escape to, verandas full of light, warmth, and air, filtering into the house with its high-ceilinged beams, the gardens up the driveway.

Everything was somber and heavy with death the day I was released from the Body Hope Facility into a new body—the Bogosi family's daughter's body. The engine stalled.

She smiled, unclipping her seat belt. "You ready to meet your new family?" She was the first person I saw when I woke up, in her crisp white cloak, to suggest pointers to acclimate into my new body.

Fold-away doors, rammed-earth strata of brown-red colors, clay bricks, the traditional setup of a Setswana setting in a modernized layout—I took it all in, in awe at the immensity of their wealth. The car door slid open for me, the fragrant air mottled with the perfume from flowers and . . . and the smell of sadness in the air, pity swindling my homecoming. Two male workers carrying a slaughtered cow dropped it, mouths agape, staring at me. Everyone stared at me as I walked into the house, the hallways, the large gathering room, where everyone sat, black-clad, coffee cups by their lips, confusion amok in their eyes. A pinprick. A gasp. Against the floor, a cup cracking like a skull. The body that I'd just entered the room in, its deceased owner's spirit had been buried that day. That day, they saw the deceased's body walking around willy-nilly.

"This is wrong," my brother shouted.

"It's injustice," Papa said.

You don't choose your family; the system picks it for you. The system picks randomly which consciousness slips into which body like cloth. Allegedly, no discrimination of pre-identities. And I'd just been delivered into a wealthy family. Lucky for anyone. Yet I wanted to flee. The rejection was hot against my face. The cotton around my skin sharp as pain. There was no turning back. I was delivered to a family who didn't want me and yet had a moral duty, obligation, to take care of me.

The first day my brother saw me was the day of the funeral. How did the sister die? No one wanted to talk about it. I didn't know, otherwise I wouldn't have come to the funeral, wouldn't have desecrated such a special moment.

That day was supposed to be my homecoming into a real world after waiting for a body for fifteen years, they said, and Limbani robbed me of that. "Who are you?" he spat at me. "Who the fuck are you?" Someone squealed and collapsed. "This is disgusting!" he exploded. "She's not my sister. We don't have to take her in. It's our right."

"Honey, what's the worst that could happen?" Mama cried. "We can't just kick your sister's body out into the cold." I was just "the sister's body."

"And if this *thing*"—he jabbed his finger in my direction—"fell in love with me? We've heard the stories of incest, of what things like her get up to. How far are you willing to go to accept this thing into our family? How many of your ideals and beliefs are you going to sacrifice for this thing before it's too late? Will you sacrifice your god for this thing?" He stood before me, walked around me. "We can't tell if this thing was even a woman before. If it was Black, like us."

Papa stormed out. The room was full of shadows. Everyone kept quiet. The silence fraught with tension. Body-hopping nonbelievers forget that we're also human, just looking for a home. Everyone's eyes shifted toward me. For a fraction of a second, doubt flickered in his mother's—*my* mother's—eyes, and just as quickly, the poor woman grabbed me into her arms, desperately hoping to smudge out this irrevocable pain and decision. But I felt it then that I would know no love that their daughter knew, and as much as Mama welcomed me in, I would always stand at the periphery.

My brother jumped forward, had his hands tight around my neck. Manual strangulation, the forensic authorities would call it. Here I was about to die on my first Body Release Day. They pulled him back. The veins strained in his eyes. He spat at me. Called me a thief.

I "stole" the body of his dead sister, and he would never forgive me. So what if he found a way to punish me? I'd waited so long for this day, and now I had to promise this family—my new family—that

I was worthy of their child and sister's body. Today, I have desecrated that promise.

We've arrived, and Jan perks up. The farm's iron gates wind open for our car. One of the farmer boys looks up, shields his face from the sun, then familiarity lights his brain. He smiles and waves. I'm squeamish.

Three exclusive cars are parked out front, red, black, and white. My parents'. Limbani is not yet here, and a cold chill curdles my blood. Mama's car should be parked at the airport, unless Papa had taken her to catch her flight.

"If only we knew how long she'll take to get here," Jan says.

"Jan, she disappeared into thin air," I say. "She could just as instantaneously reappear at my family's home. I don't know the rules to this, either. We don't know what we're fighting."

He pinches his nose. We're thinking the same thing: If we'd never had an affair, would this be happening in a different way, or not at all?

"Stay here," I say, as the car door slides outward.

"But—"

I slam the door shut, cutting Jan off.

The helper, Kesego, opens the front door and welcomes me into a high-ceilinged foyer, the staircase rising toward a chandelier. "Would you like some tea, mma?" she asks in a soft Zambian accent.

I shake my head, making my way to the living room. I follow the quiet jazzy notes of mbaqanga, which paint the air warm, syncopated with Kalanga chants. I take cautious steps through the arched hallways into the dining room, which has a spacious dinner table with a Persian rug, a veranda overlooking the luxurious garden. Honeyed light flows through the wooden windows, charging me with tension. Mama's standing by the bay windows, inspecting her garden. Her body is covered in a luminous, electric-blue tint. She's on call. Holo-call. It's the only way she can be present. She's currently in Dar es Salaam in her hotel room, and parts of her background are static lines, a fuzzy network. Through her window, I can see the steely ribbed outline of towering buildings and the glittering spine of the harbor. She turns when my knee knocks against a coffee table laid out with oven-baked phaphatha, a terrycloth kitchen towel, and a teacup half-filled with the shimmering gold color of rooibos tea.

"Nana." She's startled. "What's the emergency?" Joy is starry in her eyes. That's all I remember, her arms warm around me as she pulled me into a hug, welcoming me into the family despite her son's hot-arid anger toward me. I stare at my watch. Thirty minutes since I last saw Moremi. Nowhere in sight now. *When* does she pitch up?

"Which hotel are you in, Mama?" I ask, craning my neck to take inventory of the other rooms in the farmhouse.

Mama's travels reminds me of my work trip to Morocco, which lasted a month, and the laws governing microchipped women there are so stringent that I felt blessed to be a Motswana. Their microchips alert the authorities and administer electric shocks to their bodies if they enter places that women aren't allowed, if certain parts of their bodies are not fully robed, or if they have sex with a man while they're unmarried. In Nigeria, Uganda, and other African countries, many LGBTQIA people are microchipped. If they enter same-sex relationships, their microchips alert authorities, ending in a virtual prison sentencing and the loss of their bodies. Such bodies are rated low and cremated to avoid tarnishing the souls that would otherwise fill them. Only wealthy people can navigate these laws, while these laws devour the poor. The rich can buy new identities, smuggle their way out. Some parts of the world are disgusting, intolerable places to live.

Her eyebrows furrow since I'm distant. "Golden Tulip Dar es Salaam City Center Hotel," she says. My husband and I went there for Valentine's last year. "Nana, it's so beautiful here. The air, the ocean, the people—you should come back here for your anniversary. How's your husband doing?"

"Ma, what time's your flight?"

She rotates her wrist, checks the time. "Soon. At three forty-five."

"How long's your flight?"

"Roughly three hours."

Three hours, she should land at 6:45 p.m.

"I took the ferry out to Zanzibar," Mama continues. "Look, can you see the harbor from here?" She points through the black-framed picture windows. "And there's St Joseph's Cathedral—you'd love it here, nana."

"Mama, please, are there any layovers? Are you certain it's three hours?"

"Nana, I'm coming from Dar es Salaam, not China. It's a nonstop flight. Although there was that time from Rabat-Salé, and those tedious connecting flights and—"

"And which airport will you be using?" Lounge, empty. Study office, empty. Kitchen, empty, except for Kesego.

"Julius Nyerere International," she says. "It's the closest, of course."

"I know, Mama, I just wanted to make sure. Ma, listen to me. I'll pick you up from the airport, nè? Come straight to me."

Folded arms. She's a bit perturbed by my interruptions. "Where else would I go if you're not in the waiting area?"

I hustle toward the windows. There's no one except our dog, Rabi. Mama's safe. Three hours safe, to be exact. I'm certain Moremi can't teleport to Dar es Salaam or a plane in flight. Then again, there are no limits to Tswana supernaturalism—not that I've experienced any, only heard stories through word-of-mouth, which are bizarre and anachronistic in this digital age. This byzantine phenomenon is not heavily documented like other cultures with surprisingly serious avidity in museums, archives, the internet; instead, it sleeps in geriatric minds, which are now our museums of folklore, and supernatural entities. Prisons of cultural stories. That's the demarcation of the old and millennial: knowledge is separated by the physical realm of our skins. I regret being ignorant of old-folk tales. Can't exactly cross-check a guidebook for a what-to-do list. I've never believed in shit like ghosts and hauntings, but Moremi has duly baptized me into Ietsism.

For now, Mama's one person off the list. I slouch against the wall wiping sweat from my forehead. My heartbeat slows down.

"What's with the interrogations?" Mama asks.

I need to know where everyone is and keep track of them. That way, I can situate myself near them to avoid Moremi touching them. Now the only people I need to concern myself with are my husband, brother, and father. Three, that's manageable.

"What's the emergency?" she asks with raised eyebrows at my silence and harried look. "Oh no, is it the baby? Did something happen?"

"No, no, no, she's fine. Let's wait for everyone to gather," I add. "Where's Papa?"

"He's using the bathroom," she says.

Papa enters the room, whistling a matching tune to the mbaqanga music, head almost skimming the top of the doorway, making him always have a stooping figure. A gait to his walk, arthritis chewing through his bones and nerves. Wrinkles and crow's feet deep in his light-brown skin, woven like leather. A handsome face still lit with joy. I did love the nobility of the family, how together they were. Watching him, I suddenly feel ashamed. How will he protect himself from Moremi? She's a demon, and they're in their late fifties. My brother is only five years older than me.

Limbani enters the estate in a cloud of dust, tires spitting grit and gravel. If he saw Jan parked out front, it's the least of my worries. The main door bangs open against the wall when he storms in. He has a farm farther out north, though he heads a newspaper in the city centre. He'd put me on the front cover, fuck conflict of interest. Everyone close to me is here—apart from my daughter, who is in the safest place in the world, besides her father—nearby where I can take stock of them to conduct a calculative strategy.

"Who are you to summon me?" he asks.

Mama rolls her eyes. "Eish, calm down, please. Has anyone been watering my plants? God, Rabi looks waifish. Are you all feeding him well?" Rabi lies in the garden, perks his ears up, comes trotting to the window, a greeting bark to Mama.

"Mama, you've only been gone for ten days," Limbani says. "We're not sadists."

Papa chuckles, stroking his beer belly, asking her to point out which of her plants is experiencing malnutrition, and she takes the joke seriously as she points to a bed of azaleas. Under the shade of a large baobab tree, something stirs. A trick of the mind, shadow and shade intermingling with the moving sunrays. I take a deep breath, press my palms against the glass dinner table. Now that I have gathered everyone here, I don't know what to say, but I need to quarantine them from her wrath.

"Well?" My brother folds his arms, studying me. I scan his face, his eyes as if I'll find something telling in them. "Who is this woman you mentioned on the call? What does she do? What does she look like? What does she want?" he barrages me.

"She . . ." She has no skin on her face. She is dismembered, she is dead—how do I spin that into something more normal? "She's dangerous, and she looks quite rattled. Her body, her face is . . . distorted. Just—you'll understand what I mean when you see her. Just keep your distance from her."

Limbani narrows his eyes. "What exactly did you do to her?"

"Like I said—"

"You're lying," he says. "You've stolen every mannerism of my sister, and now you've turned her into a liar."

"Your sister is dead. This is my body!" I yell, and I'm loose, the screws unturned.

"Oh, not today!" Mama says, anguished. "I won't stand for another argument. I won't be on my flight worrying about you two."

Papa huddles near Mama to hug her, forgetting that's she's not here physically, so he slips through her holo-form, bumping the wall. Steadies himself. "We're here for you," Papa says. His tenor slides warmly around me, making me breathless with comfort. "Family sticks together." He puts on his reading glasses from the table. "Is your husband doing something about this?" My husband in quotes it sounds like, and if I told him, I'd never maneuver his interrogations.

I pat my braids to mask my trembling hand. "I . . . Well, I just found out today, and I came straight here because . . ."

"Because?" Limbani throttles forward.

I need to be careful of what I say in front of my brother. It would do me damage to have the owner of a distinguished media company as a witness. Given the size and important international positioning of my brother's media company, its reporting has real influence. His news media is unlike the vitriol of gossip rags, and its reports criticize my firm's designs and ethos with such a journalistic flair that sometimes even I'm convinced that my designs are useless to society. I didn't let that destroy me. Instead, it only motivated me to advance further than him, and outdo him internationally, which emasculates him sorely because I've proven him wrong. So he takes out that jealousy on me through biting remarks targeted at my weaknesses—my marriage, my infertility, everything. If Limbani finds out about my crime, his company would be the first to investigate and report it in detail.

"Well?" my brother asks, tapping his foot.

"Because she talked about my family. So I felt you were in danger," I say.

My brother raises an eyebrow. "In such imminent danger that you didn't notify your policeman of a husband?"

"Jesus, why isn't she on the news?" Mama asks.

Limbani steps forward, enunciates again: "Who is this woman? What does she do? What does she look like? What does she want? What. Have. *You.* Done?"

The noise swells around me like an ocean current. And déjà vu pummels into my brain. My forensic evaluation. The waiting room at the Body Hope Facility. My husband carrying a blood-soaked brown paper bag with fingers inside like soggy sweets, interrogating me. This is an interrogation. Is this my brother or a simulated version, a prosecutor's puppet? I block my ears and scream. Like the CBE simulation is tormenting me. Is this the prosecutor Serati using my brother as a bloody pawn? But she'd know he'd be the last person I sing to.

I scream and scream—*it's not real, it's not real*—as if screams can shatter the glass walls of a CBE simulation, and I expect them to buckle and dismantle like the day I spent at the Body Hope Facility. What if I'm still sleeping, inundated by the serum of the simulation? That was a month ago. They couldn't have kept me under for over a month, could they? Who am I kidding? Time is different in the CBE simulations. Years can pass by in minutes, regulated or sped up by the forensic panel—pushing as hard as they can to squeeze out a confession or an act of terror from us. They lied before because I was too aware of the CBE. What if they continued to lie the day I woke up to a yelling husband?

God, what if, what if, what if there is *no* baby at the Matsieng Fertility Fund? A way for them to make me weak. *Let's give her a daughter, the thing she's always wanted, threaten her with losing that and see if she'll still be pure,* is what they'd probably say to test me, which is hardly fair. But they'll risk anything to create the purest society, which is impossible. Humans can't be 100 percent saints, not like Jesus. What if the forensic panel is keeping me under for their own reasons? What if Jan is part of the simulation? What can I use to tell if I'm in reality or their modulated unreality? Maybe to take control of the situation, I should act differently than my natural self. But how do I sever myself in two parts that act as polar opposites? And how can I be objective enough? Maintain that objectivity?

Even now, the microchip doesn't stop me.

The sun doesn't expose me.

I'm out here, a murderer, frolicking about. I want to break reality, shatter it to pieces, find the truth somewhere in its mangled body.

What if

What if

What if

I can push back just as hard, terrorize the CBE simulation—*if* I'm stuck in it—and break it?

But how? I stare at every little mottled fabric of this room, and for the first time interrogating it, its presence—*them*, my family, the streaks of brown in their irises, their mannerisms. This time I get to question things, not the other way around. I will shine a light on hidden secrets and the unknown crevices we've squeezed parts of ourselves into.

Everyone stares at me, a dangerous, alien creature. Papa raises his hand to a male worker behind me, one who was slowly approaching me to subdue me. He bows, leaves. A smile twists up Limbani's face. Ja nè, he's been waiting for this for years. For me to crack, the outer shell to reveal the horrid Matryoshka doll inside me. *There she is, look at the evil leaking, she can't hide it,* I see his smile say.

"What happened to her?" I ask.

I feel everyone's thoughts step back, surprised, confused. Mama narrows her eyes. "Who, nana?"

"Nelah," I say. "The first daughter of this family. The amputated arm," I say, raising my prosthetic right arm.

"No, no, no. Fotseke!" Limbani rushes forward, towering over me, his finger pointed at me as if it can shoot bullets. "*You* will not do this. *You* will not do this." Spit strikes my face.

Somehow, I've never been afraid of him. His masculinity like a bomb doesn't seem to terrorize me, yet it sends others away, dismantles them, makes them bend for him, makes his wife submissive. The alpha male that sees an alpha male in me, perhaps. It scares him, I see that fear flicker in his eyes, and his machismo bulks, expands to take up space, to push me out of the way, to *prove* something, although what I don't know. Patriarchy is just like racism, a glutton for power it won't share, for sharing power means loss of power to them, a form of weakness—*if we give them space, where will we sit? What will we do? Who are we, then?* Fear, the most poisonous animal that stands between them and enlightenment. I'm a woman, a power-hungry woman. I've seen it and I've felt it. And now I punch it out to another young woman; I'd rather remain in the privilege of power than deal with my emotions, my consequences—at least I admit this to myself. That fear, that emotion in him, Limbani doesn't want to recognize it, has too much pride to give in to it.

Yet it is his weakness. He'd rather be a "man." Perhaps the problem was his sister's sweetness, a passivity that made him feel superior. Then I came. Inquisitive. Competitive. Hardworking. Pushing through adversity. Riding higher than him, younger than him, me a "little girl." *She's just a little girl, brah, nothing to be afraid of, joh,* he'd say in a macho coolness to his mates when they came over to fawn over me, aroused by the confused mixture of their fear and attraction to me. *There's a man trapped inside my little sister's body*, he'd say to his relatives. I remember how I used to dress in skimpy clothes just to prove I was a woman. How stupid, when I think back. Because this is who I am, this is the gender I align with, with all its femininity with or without the vagina and breasts. *I* frighten myself as if I have masochistic tendencies. Why must I be the one ashamed? Why must I always tolerate? I didn't question so many things out of courtesy, kindness, and guilt. I've been so afraid, treading the paths carefully—today, I make my own path.

I am selfish. A selfish bitch.

I turn the inquisitive mirror back at him: "Where is she? Who was she? What. Has. *She*. Done?"

Papa buckles against the table. "She was so young."

The threads of this family unspool. I burrow myself into the tissue of their emotional scars. "What are you all hiding from me?" I throw the question at them. "Why won't anyone tell me what happened to her?"

I'm shameless, trying to lay blame on someone else—that I murdered someone because of your actions. Boo-hoo, poor me. *Fuck me.* Staring at death's abyss, there is nothing to lose. I feel powerful, invincible. I need to be the one in control—for my own safety.

"A talk," Limbani demands. Gathers me by my arm. Drags me to the adjacent room, the study office. He spins. "Jou bastard. Who the hell do you think you are? You have no right. You are not a part of this family just because you wear *my* sister's body. My parents are kind people who let you in."

I stretch my hand out to him. "These scars," I say, "why won't anyone explain how I got them? You make me feel dirty, but something tells me your sister was far dirtier than I."

He slaps me, and I'm shocked. But then again, I'm not shocked. I cradle the pain on my cheek. "You're afraid," I say, realizing his expression. "You look very scared. What? Am I getting close to the truth?"

He steps back, ashamed. "Why would you make me do that to my sister's body? You destroy everything you touch." He stares at his hands for the abuse they've left on my face.

As long as I am near my family, no harm can come to them.

I stare at Limbani, and I struggle to reconcile the two ideas of him: the owner of a fast-growing media company with the man who is so antagonistic to me that it makes him appear immature—of course, he's never body-hopped given their religious beliefs to opt out of it, so he doesn't have hundreds of years stacked up in him, like me. That's probably why I repulse him as a body-hopper, why he can't help but be antagonistic to me. He's my older brother, but this is my third lifespan, an accumulation of 430 years to his thirty-two years. He appears to behave respectably toward me in front of other people, in public, and at galas and events. Still, behind closed doors with family members where no public eye can anoint itself with his image, his resentment is gaudy and draws with brute force damage against me with pure obsession. His resentment that I've replaced his sister is something he can purely entertain as he continues with his established career. Unlike Jan, who's shackled to his father, Limbani's a loose cannon mollycoddled by our parents, who are at his beck and call when he needs any form of support for his business and any other endeavors. After all, they consider him their only child, and I'm just a stranger holding their daughter's body hostage—they're only being kind to me out of respect for her body.

Limbani is the heir of this family and seems to have no concerns that his resentment might affect his inheritance because he knows it won't, based on the confidence with which he considers himself the only child of this family. After all, I have no access to my inheritance until they pass away, and each day, he's working on our parents to write me out of their will. This has become his second job. I may understand where he's coming from, but I hate him. I hate that he might be right, that I will always be a stranger, that I am no heir of this family, that they will never consider me one of their own, that I'm just a thief waiting to snatch their wealth.

My brother shoves me against the bookshelf. Takes me by the neck. "You destroy everything," he spits. I am a truth he wants to smother. He's never touched me like this, but I'm unafraid. I pressed the wrong button. The six-foot-two of bulk, tense muscle, and power packed into him slackens my resolve. *How am I supposed to fight a man when they're born with more horsepower than us?* I used to ask my trainer. My brother's greed and hunger for power flows in and around me as I struggle with him, trying to see what's going on in the other rooms.

Through the open door, I see glimpses of my parents like a different track shot. I hear their voices, keeping earshot of everyone. The windows: outside, a sky's constipated with clouds, drizzles rain. Muffled voices through the walls. Shadows in the window. Clothes shuffled by movements. I eye the doorway.

Papa nears the window. "What's going on out there? Haebo, do we have a new worker? There's a woman. In our backyard. Staring at us." He steps back, a grimace twisting his face. "Oh my God."

The mbaganqa rises in tempo, the Kalanga switches into a dizzy, witching speed, and I can't breathe, I can't breathe with the fear smothering me.

I crane my neck. Mama focuses her eyes, squints at the view. "I can't see anything." A pause. "Did you take your meds? You can't keep forgetting."

Something breaks. Glass. Ceramic. "Kesego, what's going on?" Mama asks.

"Let me go," I say.

"Sorry, mma," Kesego responds. "I dropped a plate by accident."

"Mothowamodimo, that better not be my mother's china," Mama says.

The dog barks, yelps. Papa steps back, a grimace twisting his face. "Oh my God. Mogatsaka, call the police."

"Let me go," I shout.

But my brother keeps repeating, "You destroy everything." Pinning me to the bookshelf.

I peer through the window. Our dog, barking. Papa cups his mouth. A scream culls the serenity. "Jerusalema, moloi wa mosadi," he whispers in Setswana: witch. "There's a witch, a witch in our yard."

16:29 /// STALKER'S HEAVEN

The scream shuts us up first. I raise my right arm, ram the elbow down my brother's arm that's strangling me—skin-clothed metal cracks against skin-clothed bone. He yells out in pain. I shove him back into the office desk and run into the dining room. I balk in the arched doorway, the screaming Kalanga chants drowning me. Opposite me, the French doors are closed to the patio. Behind them, Moremi stands in the garden. Without shadow, without skin, Moremi is no wind. Her form disturbs no plant, disturbs no structure, but treads through it without a ripple. And through the wall, she moves. Her skin blisters, forms bubbling boils, as if its singed by her overwhelming fury. Then it settles down into a flat fabric across her skeleton once she pinpoints her target.

Papa jumps back, falls over the couch. He makes a cross over his face.

Moremi chants, pointing fingers. "Mother, father, brother, lover, absentee husband? Your unborn daughter? Who will I pick?"

Panic screams into my spine. No, no, no.

Mama stares at Papa, startled. "What's wrong?" Moremi whacks her arm at Mama before she turns to see her, startling her holo-form from static-white to nothing. She cut Mama's call off. Limbani comes up short behind me.

"The gun. Get a gun now," I shout, quaking with fear.

As if wisdom flows into him, Papa says, "Our family is bewitched. No guns can protect us." He moves with a slight gait to his steps, gathers a Bible from an adjacent display cabinet, and starts praying.

"What the hell?" Limbani asks, helping Papa up. "Papa, are you okay?"

"Can't you see her? Satane o tlile. She's finally here: the devil's come to collect my sins." Papa points a shaking finger at Moremi.

My brother looks in her direction. Turns to Papa with worry. Shakes his head. "Let me take you to sleep. Give you your meds."

It hits me: only the person she's about to kill and the person who killed her can see her. My mother, my brother, and Jan are blind to her, but not Papa. He's her target. She sweeps through the dining table, slaps my brother's shoulder, electrifying him with astonishing force. His body jerks and crumbles to the ground, unconscious. Five relatives and one lover: Those are the people she can touch.

Moremi beelines toward Papa. Yanks him, drags him into the living room. "Witnesses abound," she shouts. She raises her hand as if she's giving an oath. "You killed me last night." Papa's eyes ricochet, stare at me. *You did what?* his eyes seem to say. Shame overwhelms me. "Your fingerprints cling to my skin. Your father dies by your hand."

"Papa, run!" I shout as I dash to his study. The safe stacked into his wall. I run my finger against its scanner. *FAILED: ACCESS DENIED.* "Fuck!" I take two deep breaths. Press my index finger perpendicularly on the surface. *FAILED: ACCESS DENIED*. "Damn it, relax."

Someone screams. Dread quells my heartbeats. I swipe my sweaty hands against my pants. Try again. It chimes: *OPEN*. The tiny door flicks open. I grab the cold, sleek handgun and a box of shiny, gold bullets. Spin the chamber out. Jam in seven bullets. Silence.

I edge into the hallway. Moremi stands over my father. I aim the barrel at her head. Only four fingerprints can automate the gun: mine, Mama's, Papa's, Limbani's. Press the trigger. The bullet spins through the air, strikes through Moremi's right shoulder, cracks the glass panels of the French doors. The gun recoil forces me two steps back. The smell of gunpowder stings my nose. The bullet splits no bone, tears no skin. It streams through her as if she's a fabric of air. No! I fire two shots.

Again and again. Bullets done. Bullets gone. Wounds in the wall behind her. I should know better. Supernatural elements are intrinsic to our culture—praying, herbs, juju shit should work, as I've been told. But Papa's praying proves futile, and I've never dealt with this force before.

Moremi sways, gaping. A rage of anger splits her torn mouth into fury and I step back terrified as the air swarms with her breath. "You bitch. You have some balls," she says. "I function by no law of living humans. Death can't touch an already dead body."

Kesego, other maids, several farm boys, and Jan appear at the broken French doors from the gunshot noise, stare down at the shrapnel glass. I lower the gun. Jan catches my expression, sees my father with his leg raised by something invisible. One of the farm boys, Ofentse Olebile, looks at me, attuned—something in the air, something that Moremi perfumes the air with, turns his nose in her direction. He is highly skilled at deciphering the language of this scene that others can't read, and he steps forward as if to do something. Moremi takes a step toward him, and the air tenses with an electrifying threat—he stiffens. Stretches his hands out to the others. They step back. See the black crust of dust on the ground from the coagulating death shed from Moremi's body. Hands to their chests in shock.

"Go na le moloi fa," one says.

"There's something evil in here," the other reiterates. "What the hell do police know about this? There's no law enforcement to assess witchcraft-related crimes. Sorry mma, but we have to go," Ofentse says in Setswana. They scurry away in shouts and screams. Jan stares at me, perturbed.

"My brother," I say. "Save my brother."

"I won't leave you," he says.

"Take my brother," I shout. "If I'm not out in ten minutes, leave."

"No."

"Jan, please," I cry. "You're not much help here, only a liability. *You* can't even see her." He wavers. "Please," I shout. He shakes his head, dashes to Limbani, heaves him onto his shoulders, and walks out through the front door.

"Kneel," Moremi commands. "You're my bitch now."

I kneel before her, next to Papa, who watches, frozen with fear. I place the gun by my knees, trembling, breaking. I still my hands, praying for mercy.

"You are terrible at taking warnings. All you do is run. I warned you: be careful what you wish for. The currency for this wish is his life. You took my life; a debt must be paid." She punches Papa. "And paid over and over and over again."

Papa groans, hand out to stop me.

"Please, stop," I cry.

"Last night—when you bashed my head in, when you tried to bury me—I scraped the DNA from you. Your essence stayed in me. Enabled me to know the people you love." She pauses, looks up through the foliage to where the car's parked, Jan inside, waiting, biding his time.

"You never gave me time last night. Time to run. Time to escape. Time to say goodbye to my loved ones. Why should I afford you any?" She drags her left foot forward. "Look what you did to me, you animal. Look at my face. At my foot. I have no toes." The scalp is peeled from the skull and hangs over her left eye, obscuring her vision. Dear God, we were animals.

"You risked your own father's life to test my warning. You are truly evil. I will continue to kill until I've erased every drop of your family's genetic inheritance, including you, before my final passing," she continues, arms straining to scratch my face.

My father stares at me like I'm a stranger, and I don't know myself anymore. That can't be true, no. My father's eyes glisten, filled with disappointment, pity, and resolution. And guilt. But why guilt? It's not his fault that I feel this way.

I close my eyes. "I'm so sorry, Papa. It was an accident. We didn't mean to."

She stares at Papa, head cocked to one side like a bird. "Your 'sorry' cannot purchase my forgiveness or your freedom." She pauses. "Come here. To save your father, let me kill you, instead."

"I . . ." I falter.

"Exactly." She mauls him with her three-fingered hand. "When it comes down to it, you will choose yourself over anyone. This is where we really learn who you really are." She stares at my father, who looks up at her. "Not your little girl. She is the alien you feared she was."

She looks at me now. “You’ve had doubts about your family, haven’t you?” she asks, and I’m stunned, not sure where this is going, but she has my essence in her. “Your brother is blatant about it, treats you like a pariah. But your parents—they’re conservative and such do-gooders. You’ve wondered if their love for you is more of a servitude to their daughter’s body rather than you. Deep down, you feel they don’t really care about you, that if they could choose between you and getting back their first daughter, of course, without a doubt, they’d choose her. It’s made you feel like a sham, huh?”

I evade Papa’s eyes, ashamed and embarrassed. I feel brutally naked and guilty now that he knows the fears I’ve worked so hard to keep captive inside my head. I never wanted them to know, to be hurt by my thoughts.

She tightens her grip on my father’s neck. “Yet the real truth is, it’s reciprocal. You despise them. You don’t treat them like family, like blood. Deep down, you don’t really think of them as family. You only love them at surface level. A defense mechanism to protect yourself. It’s easier to get hurt by someone you love than by someone you don’t. Point check: easier to kill me last night.”

My father stares at me, a look of betrayal. “We took you in. Is it true? Was nothing between us real?”

“No,” I cry. I’ve had my doubts about them, how truly they loved me, but what if I unknowingly stayed at arm’s length myself, packed away to avoid being hurt? “I love you all. You’ve made so many sacrifices for me.”

“Ag, save it,” Moremi says. “They’re not even your parents if you look at it. You hate your brother, well, sort of. If your parents die, you receive your inheritance. Seems like a great deal to me.”

Body-hopping from one lifespan to another, I’ve lost countless families. Although the Bogosis are just one in a line of broken family connections, I have a moral obligation to them. Despite the distance and the complications, they cared for me when they could’ve thrown me out, for I was of age, and they had no obligation to take care of me. But they did. Enrolled me in the top-tier schools, funded me with great opportunities that enhanced my career, and cared for me with tender, loving hands that ensured that I, too, grew attached to them, loved them even at a distance. So how could I discard them, leave them to ruin when I love them this much? When I want to bring a daughter into this world, what would it teach her if she saw me treat my parents like this, that she too could do the same to me? If I let Moremi destroy my parents, my daughter will have questions, just as much as I have questions about the history of this family, and it's because of secrets that this family has been severing. I don't want to repeat that with my daughter. Because if I allowed secrecy and murder to continue, it would appear to her that family is easily disposable, and I want my daughter to have stable family ties. If this family were cruel, maybe it would be easy to let Moremi murder them, but they are not.

"Tell me what to do to stop this," I whisper.

Papa flinches, stares at me. "You can't run from something like this. Only God can protect us," Papa says. He leans into the wall. "My punishment has come. I will be redeemed for my sins. I knew this day would come . . . eventually." Then he turns to me. "You grew on me," he says, voice barely a whisper. "You became my little girl, my princess. I do love you. Both of you, my two girls. You are both my daughters. I don't know what to do to make you believe how special you are to me. It's not your fault—please know that. I love you." He takes the gun from my lap. Before I can stop him, he aims it to his head. "This is your second chance."

An explosion. A spray of blood on my face. A crunch of bone. The thud of a body, weightless of life. Papa, gone in a blast, soggy with death. So much in a span of seconds. A deafening ringing noise in my ears. I'm screaming, knees submerged in his flowing pool of blood. My limbs slick against this blood-spill, the gun, his body.

How could he do that?

Why would he do that? But I know the answer already: so the crime scene wouldn't point fingers at me.

He's still trying to protect me. But his blood can't pay for my sins or wash them away. But why would he save me, save someone who would sacrifice their own family? What about his wife, his son—his true family? Doesn't he realize that me staying alive risks their lives? I want to yell, to wake him up from death, because I don't understand why he did this. I don't deserve any more chances, any more lives.

He's past death, but a tear slips down Papa's face. His eyes roll back. His eyelids slip over his eyes drenched with death, face pale brown.

"He's dead," I shout and push at Moremi, who drags him by the foot. "What are you doing?"

"You think I'm going to let your father save you? Last night, you listened to my screams, helped death rape me. Squeamish all of a sudden? Not so last night, huh? Now, you're going to pay." She raises a hammer of a fist and bashes it into my father's face. She exacts that retribution on Papa. Her body, a fist of a vehicle, pumping at him. The impact is astonishing. I can't watch. I scream. Glass and flickering light sprinkle onto the floor. Papa, the skin of his face, unwraps.

She starts dragging my father's body.

"Where are you taking my father?" I shout, leaping forward.

She half-turns. Smiles. "To bury him where you buried me."

I cry to God. "There's no need for this." I cry the same way she cried last night, unheard. Now my father pays for my sins. The devil licks my feet, slurps my transgressions.

I'm the only one that can touch her. So I ram into her, punching, kicking, scratching, and my nails dig and dig and dig, scraping, and something metallic clangs onto the concrete floor, but I don't loosen my pressure. She pins me on the ground. On top of me. We freeze mid-fight.

Her gaze follows the trail of the metallic object as it circles to a stop like a coin; the sun serenades it in a slow-dusk song. It's like the one in my neck. A microchip. *Think of it as a grenade. Take out the top, its body, and it detonates*. My microchip's been extracted. I double over, screaming, waiting to die. My fingers brush my neck, expecting broken skin, only to meet smooth skin intact in its fabric.

It's not my microchip.

It belongs to Moremi, an Original. Every part of her ghost body is a detailed replica of her physical one, so this microchip is incorporeal.

But Originals are never microchipped.

Moremi's staring as if trying to understand it, a trigger to a memory. This is my moment. She's trapped in a trance, mechanically performing a deep scan to recognize this object that was once in her live body. I'm betrayed by her harmless expression and her slack grip.

I crawl out from under her. She seizes my throat. Her palm smashes my face into the cold terrazzo floor. She's supposed to be a ghost, but I feel her bones, her flesh, more real than any live human.

"What is that?" Her voice is deep and raw, jaws bared to my cheek. She could bite me. "What did you put inside my body?"

I look up at her with my left eye, the other crushed to the floor. "It looks like a microchip." My voice squeaks through my tight throat. "But it wasn't me who put it there."

Her nostrils flare into a snarl. "What was it doing in my neck? It shouldn't be there. I am an Original."

Her grip tightens, so I add, "Someone must have put it there without you knowing about it. That's illegal, if it's not the government."

She inches her head back. "Who would do that to me? And why?"

"Angazi. I've never heard of a case where an Original was microchipped. It just doesn't happen."

She stares at me.

"Wait, wait, wait. Please." An idea weasels itself into my mind. Maybe this is how I can save my family.

What if

What if

What if

someone was using it to watch her?

She might be motivated if she realizes she wasn't just *our* victim. I say, "In the wrong hands, the microchip is a stalker's heaven: watching you, controlling you through it. That's what it's used for, to stop someone from committing a crime by controlling their body."

"Yours didn't stop you last night," she snarls, closing into my face, nails digging into my bones. Her mouth smells of decay like a donkey died on her tongue, in her throat. "What game are you playing?"

"You want to know what happened to you," I say, reiterating what she asked me last. "Why you? You want to know why it's you."

"Are you trying to manipulate me into thinking that I was someone else's victim before I became yours?"

"I killed you, not them. So you're following me, not them." I shove against the pressure. "But we can use the microchip reader to see your memories and find the first culprit."

"How will you get the reader?"

"Your quantum computer." She doesn't seem agitated at the fact that I know she has something she shouldn't have. These aren't things you can purchase over the counter or in hardware stores. "If you can give me the code, it'd make it a whole lot easier."

She eyes me intently. "I'm not here to spoon-feed you. Your daughter. If you're lying, I will kill her next. I have no tolerance for liars after what you did to me."

My blood turns cold. "What? B-b-but you can't do that. She's just a fetus."

"Even if she was just a toe, I'd kill her," Moremi says.

My entire being collapses. "Take me instead," I plead, heart banging against my chest.

She pinches my arm, twists it, and flips me onto my front, her knee cocked into my back. Too much tightness in my chest, like she's punctured my lung. Blood and oxygen fill my mouth. "I have a choreography of all the things you did to me last night that I am confined to, and I will exact that same retribution on that little fetus of yours. Find out who put that *thing* in my neck and why."

"If I do that, will you stop killing my loved ones?" I slur.

"Nothing will stop me from killing them," she says, expressionless. "You can't un-kill me. You can't change the past, ergo you can't change the future. I am here to avenge all the wrong that has been done to me. Unfortunately, they still have to die."

"Then why should I help you if everyone *still* dies?"

She eyes me. "If what you find is worth saving a life, then I will leave your daughter out of this."

"*If?* No. *When* I get you that intel, *you* leave my daughter alone. No ifs, no buts."

"It takes effort, you know, to keep myself from killing you now, to manage the power of Matsieng's blood running through my body. Xe must be fed."

"Matsieng? Is this how the Murder Trials use Matsieng?" I ask, stunned.

"Matsieng is no man's subordinate," she says. "If you desire certain benefits, you must sacrifice to the god's wants. The memories, the killings, the women—oh, it keeps Xem satiated. It consumes me." Moremi leans in. "I could punch my hand into your chest, squeeze your heart until it pops, chew it like a sweet, then kill that fetus of yours. You are in no place to negotiate. Make this intel worth my time." I stare overhead, behind Papa's body, at the doors. She knocks my head into the floor.

I'm faint with fear. "I'll do it! Please, just let me go."

"Good girl." She digs her knee deeper into me. "Your mother is next. That is the only name I'm giving to you until you find out who put that thing in me."

Why not take my brother instead when I love my parents more than I do him?

She pulls my arm, taps my watch, distracting me from my thoughts. "My first task is to bury your father. You have two hours. If your mother switches locations, it takes another hour for me to reach her regardless of where she is in the world. Don't try and be smart and manipulate me. If you fuck with me—"

"I know, I know . . . my daughter. Trust me, I won't."

Two hours. I can do it. I wriggle from beneath her but she holds me steady. Something's wrong. "Why are you still sitting on me?" I moan. Oh, God, is she playing a joke on me?

Her torn lips smile. "I can't stop myself from killing you; the law is bound in my bones." She smashes my head again, and pain spits through my nasal cavity, screaming darkness into my eyes. I blink several times to correct my vision as the agonizing ache dissolves its way down my chest. She has to be active in her goal; I suppose if this continues for long, it will be what they call a slow death. "I attack with the same violence I endured last night: hit by a car, my fingers and toes dismembered, strangled, skin peeled off. To stall my killing you, I must cause you the same pain. Those are your options. Choose. Or I can choose for you."

My heart pounds against my chest. I stare in disbelief, shake my head. She can't honestly think I'll agree to picking what part of my body I lose. I tremble from the coldness stalking my skin, imagine the nails of her evil licking it off my bones. My voice staggers from my throat: "No, no, no."

Moremi grabs me by the neck. She aims the jarring bone from her elbow, sharp as a knife, against my throat. "If you don't decide, I'll kill you." With her free three-fingered hand, she squeezes my throat tight, and maybe I should let her, but if I do, no one will save my family.

There is no time. I have to choose the least painful one. "The skin on my forearm," I shout. "Just take it!"

I close my eyes tight, nuzzle my head into the rough-hewn terrazzo floor, hold my breath, clench my teeth, as if that'll anaesthetize the pain that's to come. Her electrifying smile creeps along my arm, causing the hair to stand on end. Her teeth scrape my wrist, and in one quick motion without readying me, she rips my skin like a piece of cloth. A lava of pain singes my arm muscles as she drains the floundering screams from my throat. Groaning, I look up sideways and see the tendril of my skin hanging from her teeth. She flicks it aside, licks my blood from her lips and stares greedily at my arm throbbing in agony.

She takes her weight off me. "Don't be such a crybaby. I went through worse."

I scramble from underneath her, whimpering, and cradle my bloody arm against my chest, but the pain won't keep quiet.

"You have two hours." She smiles. Sucks my blood from her lips. Steps forward. More. She wants more of me.

My heart hammers. Tears flood my face. My voice will not wake. It is not mine. I stare at my father lying on the ground, limbs askew, the gun beside him. I pocket it. I grab the tea towel from the dining table, wrap it around my blood-drenched arm. I adjust Papa's body, arms by his sides, head facing up. Cover him with a shawl. Kiss his mangled forehead. An apology can't fix the evil I've brought this family. There's nothing I can do except to save my daughter.

The steely body of the microchip winks in the dim sunlight. The gun is heavy in my coat. I pick up the microchip, my heavy breaths fogging it.

I stare at Moremi's body, sunlight, a fury around her form.

Soon she will rise again.

And I wonder: Is my father going to wake up like a vengeful ghost?

17:39 /// THESE DARK THOUGHTS

Pistons of skyscrapers cram into the skyline as the highway curves into the city center, where the horizon is grey and mist-covered. Rain slashes against the windscreen. This is the life I'm living.

Gunshots.

Blood spatter.

Danger at every corner, and an ever-escalating speedometer.

My brother's knocked out beside us in the back seat, clipped back by the seat belt. Myself in the middle, between him and Jan. My brother's blindfolded, legs tied, hands tied, still unconscious. A flurry of worried texts from Mama. She boarded a flight two hours ago. I sent her reassurances that Papa was suffering mild symptoms of dementia and that we put him to bed. To dead.

Papa's dead. Papa's dead. Papa's—

Jan shakes me. "Did you hear me?" My arm burns in pain. He unbuckles my seat belt, holds my face in his hands. "On the bright side, your family's consciousnesses will be transferred into other bodies.

They'll be back before the end of week, tops. Back home. It's murder. Not suicide. So they're guaranteed a body."

My father just sacrificed himself for me. For my crime. There's a secret in this family burning us into molded corpses, our skins wilting into each other like flower petals.

"I'm so scared," I whisper, hyperventilating. "All I wanted was love, intimacy, a body to hold, someone to have my heart. I just wanted connection. Why was that too much to ask? Our affair has done this, Jan. Our affair is killing people."

Jan rubs my cheek, and I realize I'm crying. "He'll be back home sooner than you know it." He taps his chin as doubt fizzles in. "He did keep up with his premium subscriptions, right? Made sure to stay connected?"

The air tilts, sweaty and claustrophobic. The three-tiered health plan only benefits the rich. Premium earns you less time on the waiting list, around ten years to receive a donor body. The second level and third level, you wait twenty to fifty years, cheaper, but at the expense of your family members becoming far more separated.

On the far-left side of the A1 highway towers the crematorium, a bland concrete block. Its smokestack sticks out like a poorly done joint, and every evening it lights up and breathes out the smoke of burning flesh into the sky that's turning gloomy. I watch the pyre smoke of burning flesh rise into the sky, the heavens smoking it up. Lightning flashes on the horizon, across Gaborone Dam. If it was way back then, the crematorium chamber would be his bed tonight. I stifle a breath, and Jan holds my hand tightly as if he can hear what I'm thinking. Papa preferred traditional interment at our family estate grounds, and each time he drove me to the prestigious university that he and Mama paid for with their mortgage, he'd glimpse that smoky shroud obscuring the treetops and mutter an, "Mxm," and say, "God is smoking all these assholes' sins." I was only twenty. I didn't understand how you could be religious and still commit blasphemy by putting "God" and "asshole" next to each other. But I took it as an expression of his overwhelming anger. There are others like my family, but they form only a minority of our population that is against body-hopping.

"Look," Jan says, putting his arm around my shoulders. "He'll be back."

"No," I mumble. Grab a water bottle from the car door's pocket. Unscrew its top. Wash the blood from my face and hands, jittery.

"What's that?"

The wipers squeak back and forth against the windscreen.

I take a deep breath. "The day I came home in his daughter's body wasn't my welcome home party—it was the funeral for their daughter. Papa stormed out the back door. Took off. We didn't hear from him for a week. Mama kept reassuring me, comforting me, because that's just who she is. I couldn't understand why he hated me so much. He came back three weeks later, gaunt. It took him two years even to have a normal conversation with me, to look me in the eye. One time, we were in a jammed elevator, stuck between floors. He had no choice but to face me. We got into an argument. He said I'd stolen his daughter's body, 'because she didn't want this, she wanted cremation, but the government refused.' Accepting me was like rejecting his daughter. That conflict tore him up."

I seal my eyelids tightly, trying to keep the tears away, the white noise of rain unable to silence my thoughts. "Jan, the government took her body. Notified the family that their 'revived' daughter was alive and home now, dropped me right on their doorstep like a fucking package. They were waiting for her ashes to be brought home—not her body with a stranger living in it. Can you imagine preparing a funeral rite for your own daughter, only to be told the government took her body and did what they pleased—that they didn't cremate her, they didn't respect her last wishes? That's how the institutions are resolving body shortage issues. Can you imagine how many families this has happened to? This body lost its rights the day its host committed a crime." The tears tremble out, and a sob escapes my lips. "Can you imagine how he felt? How strong and brave my mother is to consider me her daughter. To still love me."

Jan reaches over, traces his fingers on the back of my neck. "And there I was sleeping under their roof, needing healthcare, school fees—I could hardly swallow their food without feeling guilty. Began starving myself." I grip my hands together. "I hated this face. Hated this body. Misused it. Until I almost drowned and realized I was desperately clinging to life. No matter how many lives you have, you're still afraid of dying. I've been guilty since then. Guilty. The people who loved me, cherished me. How the hell can I repay them like this?"

Jan stirs. I never told him this. Never told anyone. Not even my husband. I've been pushing it away, burying it for years, never allowing it to surface. "I owe them, Jan. And these aren't the type of people who are paid off by money. Money is easy. It comes, it goes. But real courage, real bravery has to be demonstrated to them. And look at me. I'm a coward. I'm a damn coward who won't sacrifice herself for a family that have sacrificed themselves in a heartbeat."

I reach into the gilded folds of my coat where the gun lies. Stroke it. The flicker of lightning gleams across its metallic body. Jan attempts to take it, but I tighten my grip.

He eyes my fingers, the weight of his eyes too heavy to bear. "You have a daughter." He exhales. "You're not selfish to consider her."

"My mother has—*had*—a husband, has a son. Two people she loves. Don't they matter? I killed her husband—*my* father—for fuck's sake. Left him there alone." My fingers tremble. "The whole family, Jan, the whole family doesn't believe . . ."

"Believe what?"

"This is no make-believe death, a death postponed," I say. "My family opted for no-resuscitation via a donor body. Papa's never coming back. He didn't believe in this type of reincarnation shit that's manipulated by man and the government." I pull my knees to my chest and chew my nails, thinking hard. "People like my family believe that our ancestors are reborn, that reincarnated people come from the ancestral realm following a natural order of things, not this 'artificial waiting list' our consciousnesses are held up in. But the beliefs vary regionally on how one becomes an ancestor, informed by what that person did during their lifespan and how that person died. If that person died by suicide or an accident, or they were killed, their spirit lingers on earth, unable to transcend to the ancestral realm. That's what some people would call ghosts, no? Is this what's happening to us? If I look at what has happened since the accident, Moremi's spirit is trapped here, terrorizing us until . . . I don't know, she's appeased? Moremi mentioned something about Matsieng's blood flowing through her. Is the structure of our body-hopping reincarnation based on our culture's belief in reincarnation? Does that mean that the government has interfered with the order of things and that there are devastating consequences resulting in this horrifying phenomenon of a powerful ghost? There is an equal and opposite reaction for every force in nature, no? Our country is using science to imitate our cultural reincarnation, enmeshing it with the spiritual dogma of Matsieng. That fusion must have brought about absurd results of this terrorizing ghost. The Murder Trials are based near the Matsieng site, why? In what way are they disturbing that site?"

"Love, let's not bury ourselves in conspiracy theories, okay?" Jan says, stroking my face.

"What if the Murder Trials are demonizing the power of Matsieng, and we're the ones getting punished? Maybe that's why families like my family don't believe in this manipulated reincarnation. Perhaps, based on our people's varying beliefs, more than our souls gets transferred into these bodies with residues of sin and things we may not know, things they'd rather not get mixed up in."

"Nelah, look at me," Jan enunciates, framing my face. "We will figure a way out of this and find our answers."

"Nothing feels real anymore. Are we real?"

"Yes, we are."

"How do you know we're not stuck in a manufactured reality? If I can understand how this works, I can understand a way out of this mess," I say. "Papa's gone. He didn't want to be in a stranger's body. It's against nature. Against God's will and his belief to be reincarnated by our institutions. My father opted for cremation. The whole family did. If they die, they are gone forever. Imagine taking in a stranger, loving that stranger, only for that stranger to commit familicide, to peel the skin off your bone. Imagine the betrayal that must be." I stare at my brother.

There's a portion of our society that doesn't believe in body-hopping. Because they are original owners of their bodies, they decide what happens to them, unlike those who have opted into the body-hopping schemes; that's where the institutions have the authority to determine whom to supply their bodies to. We have coexisted this way for a long time, and of course, there are loopholes where the government can slip in: when the original owner donates their body, they're automatically opting into this scheme, thereby affecting any hosts who inherit their body.

Jan swallows, realizes just how dangerous things have become. He lunges for some sense of hope. "Let's look at our options because the rest of your family can't die."

The car lurches forward and last night sneezes into my line of sight: darkness folds over the windscreen, a blur, like she fell from the sky against the car's hood. My reflexes snapped. The car spun out of control, jostling across a bump and coming to a still on the side of the road. Dust smoked into the flare of the headlights, panic froze in our blood.

The gun leaps to the floor as the car comes to a sudden stop behind a car that unexpectedly cut in by the traffic lights. The driver eyes us through his rearview without a sense of remorse. I could aim the gun at him and shoot his brains out. I squeeze the sides of my face, desperate for my cranium to cave in and expel these dark thoughts.

Jan cloaks me with his broad chest. "It's alright. We're okay. Nothing happened. Take a few deep breaths, ja."

Minutes pass as I attempt this breathing exercise. I gather the gun from the floor and sit back, staring at the line of cars beside ours.

"The quicker we figure this out, the sooner we can save your family," Jan says, rattling my thoughts. "It's Moremi's first microchip in a body she owns. In cases like this, when she was still alive, she should've experienced the common symptoms: nausea, migraines. How would she forget something like that?"

I shake my head. "How could she not know that she had a microchip in her body? Unless death's affected her memory."

The silence thickens between us. I watch Jan's Adam's apple throttle up and down. "How long do you think she's had the microchip for?"

"I don't know." I reach to the back of my neck, massaging the soreness that's been flaring irregularly.

Jan observes Moremi's microchip and her quantum computer. "She wants answers. We just need her fingerprint to access her quantum computer to read her microchip. We can experience her memories before she died, so we know who did this to her and why she threw herself in our path. Your mother is next. So, where the hell are we going?" he asks, exasperated.

"The office," I say. "If this has happened to us because we killed someone, then it must have happened to other murderers."

"Other murderers who are in prison," Jan repeats slowly to himself.

"Police headquarters was extended three years back by our firm," I say. "We have a storage of prisoners' interviews, basic case studies that helped with our design process. Shells of their personas exist in our storage. Our advantage: one of them has answers that Moremi won't give."

17:50 /// A MONSOON OF SCREAMS

Jan parks the car in the basement parking, and after checking that there's no one, we place my brother in the trunk. When I arrive at my office building, Miriam is already tucked into her desk. The modern design open-office plan is buzzing with real estate staff, the glassy walls plastered with digital notices from the property market. Everyone hushes, lowers their heads, their gazes slide and slip, following my every step. Can they tell I did something? Did Moremi's ghost leave a mark on me? Jan's wearing his suit jacket to cover the blots of blood on the white of his shirt. A sheen of sweat eclipses our skin, our rabid eyes barely masked by our pretense of normalcy. At least my black overcoat covers the blood on my pants and top, the hood concealing the gristly crust of blood in my braids. So I steady my voice when I ask Miriam, "What's going on?"

"They found a body," she whispers. "It's all over the news."

The floor, cold. My legs. I can't feel my legs.

"Are you okay?" Miriam asks. Jan's by my side, trying to hoist me up. My handbag lies on its side by my legs. I'm on the floor, back against the reception desk.

"What didn't you mean to do, love?" Miriam asks, which confuses me until I catch my mouth blabbering, "I didn't mean to."

"Turn that down, will you? A bit early to be a downer with such news," Miriam says to someone. I crane my neck. One of my employees, Gwen, approaches the wall paneled with the news channel.

"Wait, don't," I blurt. "Turn it up."

He shrugs, presses the side of the wall, and the reporter's voice washes over the room. "Earlier this morning, a young woman's battered body was discovered by two joggers in New Naledi and rushed to hospital."

My blood pressure normalizes, and I exhale. It's not our victim's body, far from the suburbs of New Naledi.

The reporter continues, "Doctors were shocked to discover, through the ID Consciousness scan, that her consciousness matched identity records of convict Lauren Molaodi, incarcerated two years ago, whose mind should have been uploaded to Crypt Prison as claimed by her records." Jan and I stare at each other with widened eyes. "Upon reporting their findings to the police department, a High Court representative receiving medical care in the same unit recorded allegations made by the young woman. The victim claims to have escaped torture from a makeshift jailhouse in the police department and alleges that, unbeknownst to the public, other prisoners are unlawfully pitted against each other under inhumane experiments to advance the AI CBE. Military officers were seen hours later securing the woman—"

I'm not listening anymore. Advancing the CBE to do what? What would that mean for me and Jan? How—no, why are they torturing prisoners whose bodies should have been donated to those on the waiting list? If I'm caught, what will the police do to me? All of this to eradicate crime completely? The secrecy suffocates me. Even if I asked my husband, he'd never reveal anything to me.

My neck is sore. My fingers come across the throbbing microchip, escalating to hot-plate stove temperatures. Is it the stress? It feels familiar, the memory of the pain. A desperate itch runs through my body. I rise as Miriam beckons me to a meeting with the quantity surveyor.

"I'm dealing with an urgent matter. Cancel all my meetings," I say over my shoulder as Jan and I wind into the *AUTHORIZED ACCESS* entry, through a dim, cold hallway into our project archives, storage of every project's research my firm has done. Exclusive to my firm and highly confidential, it is set like a library with aisles and aisles of onyx-black server units, standing tall like shelves, an industrial look with intricate architectural design.

Jan's brows collect sweat. "I hope we find *helpful* answers. Each thing we discover seems to make this city appear murkier and murkier, and we are swimming further into its dark. Why torture prisoners when the prison is built to be their virtual hell? I'm almost afraid to find the police authority's motives. How does this work?"

"What's contained here is only the voice of the mind, a huge storage of recordings," I say. "We can interrogate them only to the extent of how far they lived before they were caught and incarcerated."

The digital files are arranged alphabetically on a slim drive, each requiring only the head staff's biometric scan to access them. I run past the rows, then spin into row C, looking for Crypt Prison files. I slow down, wiping sweat from my forehead. Holding on to the black framing of the servers, I press my thumb against the scanner, widen my eyes for a biometric scan. It glows green, authorization accepted. A holographic tray folds out and hovers at eye level like a slim plasma screen, translucent, with sleek electric blue lines. I shuffle through the menu with my hands. Each category is tagged according to the prisoners' crimes. I pick "homicide" with a list of alphabetically arranged names. I pick a random name, Lingani Tshekiso, and a short summary follows, glowing under the fluorescent lights:

On the morning of Saturday at 4:30 a.m., a 33-year-old man, Lingani Tshekiso, handed himself in at Borakanelo Police Station and confessed to murdering eleven people, pleading that they save his son. His son was found battered and dismembered in a locked closet at the family home in Moshupa. Defensive wounds on his arms were evidence of him fending off his attacker, but there were no signs of forced entry, no bloody fingerprints on the doorknob.

There's a ► sign next to the summary, and I press it. Sound crackles, and his face appears, pockmarked with pimples and scars. "A warning call to a relative won't stop them," the beady-eyed serial killer, Lingani Tshekiso, says, grief thick in his mind-voice. "Try staying in a room with no doors or windows—*they* will still get inside. Them, the victims who refuse to die." He heaves a breath, and my skin has me hemmed in as I remember Moremi cornering me in Jan's office, the scalding imprint of her hand on my shoulder blade, the sharp explosion of pain as she cracked my head against the concrete floor of the basement parking, imagining the havoc of her terrorism if ever we were locked in a room together.

I close my arms around myself as Tshekiso continues, "The killing started in the closet and ended in the closet. The victim I killed ended up killing my son. My heir."

Jan shakes his head and reads the summary: "'Reports reveal the suspect was under the influence of drugs and suffering from hallucinations as he claimed to being chased by dead people who were forcing him to kill. But preliminary investigations dispute his claims, revealing that the suspect went on an eighteen-hour killing spree after learning that his microchip wasn't working. The following morning, with the assistance of the Sunday chemicals, detectives were led to the shallow graves of the suspect's eleven deceased victims located in Mochudi Village."

I pace back and forth, burning with questions. "Hallucinations?" I say, shocked. "B-b-but we're not hallucinating Moremi. I *felt* her. She attacked my father. She attacked *you. This* is not a hallucination."

"His microchip failed, like yours," Jan says, pale. "It can't be a coincidence." He continues reading the report: "'The suspect was charged for the murders of the eleven victims and his son. The severity of the crime prompted the need for the daily AI microchip assessments, which were nonexistent prior to the case; this stringent surveillance measure became significant in catching crimes that went undetected.'"

"So that's how the morning assessments came into place?" I say. "But my morning assessment failed to detect last night's crime." I direct my question to Tshekiso's hologram. "Why do the victims return as revenge-seeking ghosts?"

Tshekiso says, "Access denied."

Jan raises his hands. "What the fuck?"

"If a suspect reports themselves, will the ghosts stop the killing?" I ask.

Tshekiso says, “Access denied.”

“No, no, no!” I punch my fist through the hologram. “Give me something, for fuck’s sake! How do you stop them?”

Tshekiso: “Access denied.”

“Why are the police torturing prisoners?” I ask.

“Access denied,” Tshekiso says.

I crouch down, press my forehead into my knees, and muffle my screams. *If you walk away from me, someone else will die,* Moremi’s voice taunts me. My AI assessment didn’t reveal me. My husband couldn’t smell the death on my skin. My car didn’t stop the accident from happening. Moremi’s body was infiltrated and hacked by a microchip. And now the police are possibly torturing prisoners with a secret motive?

I look up, staring at the rise and fall of the sound waves as he speaks. “I am innocent.”

Tshekiso’s gruff voice echoes through the room—he sounds as if he’s embarrassed. “I’m innocent, please. I tried stopping him, the victim, from . . . sodomizing my relatives. I tried, but I was too late in confessing to the police. Too late.” He breaks into sobs, and the recording ends. I grimace. Tshekiso sodomized his victims. Moremi mentioned she kills my family the same way Jan and I killed her. So it has to be that Tshekiso’s victim sodomized his relatives only because Tshekiso committed that very act to the victim. God!

I slap and punch the hologram, but my hand skims through it. Moremi’s hellbent on killing my family. She’s only offered me a delay to find her vital information regarding her microchip. That’s my only way to stop her, to save my family.

“Let’s listen to the other recordings,” Jan says in a panic, scrolling through names. But we only find similar accounts: Convicts pleading their innocence. Investigations claiming the killers’ theories are hallucinations and drug-related crimes.

I shove the screen onto its shelf. “How the hell will I persuade her to stop?”

The silence gathers up around me like a tornado. I take a deep breath. When I release it, a sob erupts from my lips. I tighten my fist and press it against my teeth to shut myself up.

Jan paces back and forth, hands clenched into fists. He shakes his vehemently. Focuses his eyes intensely on mine. "Something's wrong. This was a bit too easy for us, don't you think? Too convenient that we find exactly what we're looking for in the first report."

"Bloody bliksem, Jan. What could be so bad about having it easy in this kak mess?" I whine.

"Easy things tend to camouflage shitty things."

The words crawl along my spine and I feel so, so cold. I wrap my arms around myself. No, I don't want to think how worse this might get. I need to focus on the most imminent problem.

My wristwatch strikes 6:03 p.m. "We only have an hour left to drive across the city to the grave site, excavate her body to use her finger to unlock her quantum computer, read her microchip, and make it to the airport before she gets to Mama."

"That's not enough time," Jan says.

"If I can get to my mother, I can keep changing her location so Moremi doesn't touch her. That will certainly pause the murders."

"I thought you said she warned you not to manipulate her conditions."

"I'm only buying time so I can find out who put this microchip in her," I say. "I don't exactly have a way to negotiate. She's not the negotiating type."

A sound screeches from my phone. Gwyneth Kgotso, Estate Awards Committee. Fuck. I swipe across the screen. The hologram extracts from the phone, hovers above me, obscures my identity, but displays her form: chubby face, bob-cut braids, dark-skinned.

"Dumêla, mma," she says: Hello, ma'am. "I'm so glad I could reach you this morning. Congratulations again! We admire the humanitarian work you've done for communities locally and worldwide."

I perfect a smile, feel bile fill my mouth, watching Jan as he stands behind her. "Thank you. Is there a problem?"

"Well, how do I put this? The documents you submitted were inconclusive, and as per our regulations, the awardees are required to undergo forensic evaluation."

"I did. A month ago."

"We know, but we need further assurance, so we sent in a request to the police department to redo and expedite your forensic evaluation," she says, "which will qualify you for the award."

"Qualify me?" I chew my lower lip. "So . . . if my evaluation results determine me as a criminal, you will disqualify me, and someone else will receive the award?"

"Unfortunately, yes. This is not to offend you, but after last year's mayhem of awarding to a citizen who subsequently failed her evaluation, we've had to review our selection process and criteria." She brushes her braids aside. "Awarding a professional who is criminally prone is really against our ethos and principles. We want to avoid the same mistake recurring. But we're not worried. You wouldn't hurt a fly—you'll ace the evaluation. We believe in you." The way she adds the latter is overly enthusiastic and desperate. I wouldn't hurt a fly, but I can kill someone.

I swallow. "Yes, I understand." My mind slips elsewhere. "We actually have a family matter . . . and I'd like to forfeit the award."

Her face dissolves into a horrified expression. "Well, I don't think we can allow that. Even if we did, we'd still have to process the forensic evaluation. Such a request is a cause for concern. This is an award that not only benefits you but all the women out there."

I'd rather not mention that my previous evaluation took days, and if I act otherwise, it'll be suspicious.

"No one is free from this analysis, not even the politicians, not the president, nor God." She chuckles at her joke. Cold dread trickles through my veins, not blood, but fear, torpid fear flows to my heart. "We tried reaching you last night, and instead, we caught your husband," she continues. "Such a kind man—he did us the favor of quickly arranging for your forensic evaluation to be conducted tonight."

Jan's eyes widen. He doubles over.

"Tonight?" My nerves tighten, and I scrape my nails against my palms. *That bastard.*

"At 10:00 p.m. Isn't that amazing?" She beams.

I stretch out my lips into what I hope is a convincing smile. "I'll be there. I have to go. My meeting just arrived."

I hang up before she says goodbye; the hologram disappears in a flash. I hurl the phone aside. "That bastard. Why didn't he say anything?" I shout. I sink my head into my hands. This leaves me with only about four hours to fix this fuck-up. Would I even be able to rig the system, hide the body? I chew on my nail, try to think of a way to fix this without it sullying my family's image, my daughter, my reputation. My reputation is the legacy I want to leave her. Think. Think. I wish I could use my family name to my advantage to get out of this mess. My family is wealthy, but their power has no political affiliations that they can benefit from, like the Koshal family.

I start rambling. "If I die, my husband gets a million from insurance, a billion worth of my estate which is completely tied in my inheritance, and my shares in the company—no, I need to scrap that. Change the will, leave it all to my daughter until she's of age; he'll be her proxy until she's eighteen. If I die, would the police force really have a record that I'm a criminal? Unless . . . I mean, without my body, there is no corpse to analyze. I'd have to completely disappear. To make certain that my body doesn't appear on the radar, I'd have to be in it, alive, always taking it far, far away. But my baby. Could I just leave her? Leave her alone with him? To grow up without me? Taking her with me would be considered kidnapping. And even if I kill myself, I'm no longer eligible for a body in this lifespan."

"Hey, hey," Jan says, holding me in place. "We have four hours. *Four* to figure it out."

The project archive feels like my jail cell. Small. Tight. I stagger out into the hallway, open the windows, and wind screeches in. The faint scent of rain and mud enter. The smell of last night. I can't escape. I just dumped her body. A woman. A woman like me, who probably has a boyfriend or someone looking for her. Or a mother. Or a father. Or a child.

"Every action we make is a memory stained into our mind," I say. "We're basically our own CCTV, recording our own crimes. If I undergo the forensic evaluation's simulation, it will snitch. I thought I escaped it for twelve months. If the microchip assessment was a walk in the park, this will be a ride to hell. There is no way out of this, Jan."

Jan stands, paralyzed by the news. I could pull the microchip. Shut myself down. The noise in my ears, a ringing sound, rises, rises, rises, swallowing me, revealing the threatening order of Moremi's killing spree because the truth is:

"She's picking randomly who to kill next," I whisper, and Jan looks up at me with furrowed brows. "This only makes it worse: I can't predict who she'll go for next."

I scramble about, grabbing my handbag and coat. I'm running out of time. I dig my nails into my palm. Take deep breaths. Hyperventilate. Walk back and forth. Close my eyes. The room shakes. A monsoon of screams and insanity ravages the air. Last night's drugs. The murder. The shock. My body is breaking. I feel my skin tear, my consciousness splatter as vast as a constellation of stars. I expect to wake with Serati Zwebathu peering down at me, smirking. I'm whole again, but not so whole, standing inside my body like there are a million of me unable to escape the skin and bone of me.

18:23 /// SHARP SPLINT OF BONE

Jan jerks his head back, stifled by the uncanny flow of events. I press my wrist, speed-call my husband. The ringtone cracks the silence like the sharp splint of bone.

"Hello?" Elifasi answers. It's cemetery-quiet on his side.

There's no emotion in my body; it's bone-dry. A numbness swallows me. "Where are you?" I ask.

"I'm just at the bookstore. Don't laugh, ja." *He* laughs. "I bought a bunch of nursery rhyme books. Going to Matsieng to read and sing to her. I know it's a bit too soon for our baby to have developed sensitivity to sound, but I want her to *know* us."

Relief balloons in my chest. How could I have ever doubted him?

"I'll probably be here till late, nè." Silence. "Almost forgot, Gwyneth Kgotso called me regarding your award. Put in a favor at work to speed up the reevaluation, so we have tomorrow to prepare for the award ceremony."

Tomorrow is Sunday, the day the sun burns and exhumes our heinous secret. Jan raises his eyebrow.

"I wish you'd told me sooner," I whisper. "I had other plans. Can you reschedule it for tomorrow?"

He sighs. "Uhu, why? I went through a lot of trouble to get this processed. Please, let's not have another baby-kidnapping episode. Rohan has been indirectly giving me flack for that. Be a good girl and show face."

I avoid looking at Jan because I can imagine all the hateful things he has to say about Elifasi.

"Anyway, that's the least of my worries. I feel strange today, like someone's following me," Elifasi says, and my ears perk up. Could it be Moremi? Only the one who's about to die can see her. But she said Mama was next. Instantly, guilt torments me.

"Following you?" I ask. "Who? A strange woman?"

"A strange woman?" he asks. "What gives you that idea? You know I only have eyes for you. I've lost my touch to cause such attention."

"Are you sure?" I ask.

"What's going on? You sound . . . off."

I swallow deeply. I feel vacant, like my spirit has fled. "I'll . . ." He said I could trust him when I'm in a difficult position. If I broke down and told him the truth, would he save me? Jan sidles up to me, wraps one arm around me, and I'm thankful this is only a voice call. I'm too scared to reveal everything to my husband.

"Nelah, babe, you can talk to me. Is everything okay?" my husband asks.

I have nothing in me left for him, but if my daughter is left without a mother, at least she'll still have a father. I'd never leave my daughter without a father. I couldn't do that to her. It's already certain there is no future for me. My husband loves her. Even if he won't sacrifice anything for her, he'd never sacrifice her. That surety keeps me calm, makes me certain that she'll always be safe. I have to protect my husband in order to protect my daughter, even if it kills me. I am lucky he wasn't number six. Maybe I do love him more than I realize.

"I'm just tired," I say. "I'll be home late. I have to drive down to Mahalapye to oversee a project. I just need you to stay with her until you hear from me, please." My voice trembles.

"Okay."

"Promise."

"I promise," he says. "We're not going to lose this baby. Never."

"I mean it. Don't leave her for one second until I'm back."

He chuckles. "Well, I get to have more time with our daughter. But let me know as soon as you arrive. If it's too late to drive back, do the evaluation there and rest in a hotel, *ja*?"

"Ja," I say, trying to hold my voice steady.

"Love you, babe."

"Love you," I whisper.

The call cuts. The digital face of the time fills the screen: 6:29. Mama's flight lands at 6:45. We have sixteen minutes.

"You have a strange expression. Is everything all right?" Jan asks.

I scratch my head, pondering. "Eli has never shown this much interest in our daughter. Suddenly he's going to spend time with her? Read to her? Why does fatherhood suddenly matter to him?"

"I've never trusted the man," Jan says, "but that's the last suspicious thing that should be our priority now."

Either Eli has suddenly become fatherly or . . . or what?

I speak without looking at Jan. "What are the chances they will capture the memories of the crimes a corpse has committed? Nil."

Jan narrows his eyes. "Why is that important?"

"Moremi said to me, in your office, that she has risen. Fed by my greed, my pride, my fear. What if the opposite of those emotions can wipe her out? What if I have to be brave and selfless to stop her?"

"Where are you going with this?"

I don't trust Jan with my daughter's life; his loved ones' lives aren't on the line.

"I've made up my mind," I say. "Tomorrow morning, the sun will reveal directions to her grave, where by now, Moremi's buried Papa. I can't harm Moremi; if I touch her, I burn. We have sixteen minutes until Moremi comes for Mama. Then an hour before she kills again. Moremi is the most pressing concern; secondary, the forensic evaluation, which is in less than four hours. If Papa was first to die, my daughter could be next. I'll hold on to Mama and my brother until my forensic evaluation tonight. But if we don't solve this within four hours, I'll kill myself."

Jan flinches. "Hold on a fucking second."

"Surely, that's what I fear the most," I say. "I don't want to die, but killing myself stops everything. *Everything*. If I kill myself, I lose all the information. A body is not like a hard drive. The ability to recover the information from my corpse would be near impossible for detectives. But I know I'm not eligible for a new body if I kill myself. I know I will die the only way non-body-hoppers die. It'll be a real death. My soul, my consciousness, will be gone forever. How terrifying that this is how people used to live, without reincarnations. Moremi did say she would continue to kill until she's erased every drop of my family's genetic inheritance, including mine. Maybe that's what will stop Moremi since every drop of me will be gone from this world. What would be the point for her to continue without my existence driving her rage? Perhaps wherever I transcend to, she will follow, and there's good in that it saves my family."

"Then get yourself into a car accident so that you're still eligible for a new body," Jan says.

"The authorities may retrieve what's done archived in my consciousness," I say. "I can't risk that."

"I do not agree with this plan," he says. "There are far easier ways of doing this. I'll get you another body, another identity, migrate you to God knows where—to fucking Mars if you want. Nowhere in hell will I allow you to kill yourself."

A sad laugh escapes my lips. "How will you swindle a Black female identity like mine through a racist immigration policy that can sniff us out? Did I ever tell you about my friend, Kea? She was a successful businesswoman. She worked for decades to try and body-hop immigrate to the UK. She sold her body, paid the exorbitant fees to register for a British body—not to buy one, but register one—gave up her entire life to comply with the immigration application that required her consciousness be placed on hold to establish a lack of ties to her home country as an intent to demonstrate her want of residence in a foreign country—after all of that sacrifice, only to be rejected." I scoff and stare aside. "The hate for the Black identity is infinite, an ocean of wrath forever raging. All these great countries may have slogans and laws that stipulate not identifying consciousnesses to avoid discrimination, but only a few pass through their racist sieve."

"Listen, I can fucking buy you privilege," he says, "I can get us two Swedish bodies by tonight—they have one of the highest-ranking passports, which will accrue us many benefits. If that is difficult, I can get South African bodies to buy us time as we look for new bodies with a better future. We're tied down with so much illegal shit that one more illegal shit makes no difference."

"What about our families?" I ask.

"Our future is already dead," he says. "We will find ways to return to them in new identities. That is definite. The only way we can preserve their safety is to preserve us, *our* future."

"Why is it easy for you to commit crimes to solve problems?" I say, stepping close to him as a shadow of clouds skirts across the sun's face. I stare up at him and press my finger beneath his chin, stroking it. "You can't keep using your father as a scapegoat for your criminal instincts. This isn't your first body, so *your* criminal instinct isn't genetically inherited from Aarav." I tap his temple as if trying to get into him. "What's in that mind of yours? Doesn't it alarm you that you have criminal instincts in your own right, apart from your father?"

His pupils dilate, wanting to swallow the entirety of the sun, shadowed from us. "I didn't want to kill anyone. At that moment, when the accident happened, there was no recourse I could think of; everything happened fast, and I mishandled it. In this place, there's no reward for morality. Surviving is the game, and the cost is cheaper than if you stayed a Samaritan in the lower caste of society to be fucked by the government and these discriminatory policies that only serve the upper echelons."

"The game has changed with this immortality bureaucracy—do our souls ever transcend to heaven or hell, or do our governments pocket our souls-slash-minds for further control?" I ask. "Moremi is not dead. She's hunting us. In whichever place our souls and minds go, depending on what you believe in, there is always a god or devil that governs that place—right now, a devil governs your reality—so who punishes the god of this reality of ours—us—we are getting punished for the crimes of this god. How many versions of us exist out there? How many realities do we exist within? Is this reality a construct of the government? Who are you, truly? Where are you, really? This skin is a networked fabric of lies." I tap his forehead, the glass of the façade of our building. "This wall, whose mind does it belong to? Who's mind are we in now? What reality are we in now? A bloody ghost is chasing us! There is nothing realistic about our reality. Pure truth no longer exists in our reality."

Jan nods. "Exactly. The game has changed. I'd rather collect pebbles of power in my palm through each lifespan to maintain a fortune of truth millennia later. I may be an agent of my criminal instinct, but you are an agent of oppression that you'd rather keep manufacturing for what? Morality? Religious belief? Isn't that criminal, too, if you think about it? It also destroys lives. You can't change or destroy the system, but you can sure as hell make sure it doesn't destroy you or your lineage. A criminal thought is a construct based on who says so. In everyone's eyes, you'd be viewed as a far worse criminal than me. So who is truly guilty? It's the foundation of how the world runs," he says. "Is our consciousness carrying genes of our parents? Could I blame my father for my criminal instincts if I continued to act them out? I only acted this out to protect *us*. I've had many bodies, not biologically related to my father, yes, and my criminal instincts are still there, so maybe the truth is that I am a bad person. We're all bad people."

"I . . ." I falter to say.

"Let me tell you something: there are many more powerful families like the Koshal family. They skip the waiting list, most of them retain their memories, and they get to choose the bodies they inhabit. The patriarchal ancestry has never been women, and the women have never been men—even that power is restrictive, and I want to create my own powerful family. I don't give a fuck, and you need to stop giving a fuck because the world doesn't give a fuck about you. You need to claim your power the way these powerful families do, and in that way, can you protect the people like you?"

"Jan, we killed someone; nothing will ever make that sound holy—nothing," I say.

"I suggested we hand ourselves in beside a few other options, and you opted not to. Being silent is just as criminal and complicit as what I did," he says. "I'm not justifying murder. I'm justifying the next steps we take."

"The bodies you want to accrue, have you thought what the hosts went through to lose those bodies? Like the impoverished souls your father bought the bodies you inhabited from."

"As long as we don't pick brown people's bodies, I've no reservations. Minorities have suffered too much for us to add more onto that."

"It doesn't make it right. We're just recycling unjust acts."

"How else, darling, do you expect to claim power? Do you think any agent of this government had any scruples with placing you in this *holy* body you have? You're a chess piece. Accept the moves until you're the one making the moves. Why are you trying so hard to be good? Nelah, you don't need to hide yourself from me like you do with your family and husband. I won't silence or criticize you, so be you. There's nothing wrong with wanting everything, wanting power."

"I wish we could save Moremi," I confess. "She got roped into this. I don't want to continue to be bad to her as the system has been bad to us."

"Love, she's killing your family."

"When pushed far enough, monsters reveal themselves within us just as it has in you," I add. "How else can we survive this system if we aren't bad people? It's the system that made me a bad person, no? I committed a crime by using a device to intercept my microchip. I'm the bad guy, not the institution that placed me in a criminal body and invaded my privacy with voyeuristic technology. No, that's not a crime because we swallow that shit up because our country is crime-free. What about my unborn child? Whose rights are waiting to be snatched up, should I fail, then evicted so her body can be used. What do you think will become of her after to survive this world? We're born into this world with a noose around our neck, tightening, tightening, tightening at every narrowing law, then punished if we react to that."

"The system is bad, and you have to be worse to play it well," Jan says. "I am unlike my father, who's hungry for blood, sex, and power and is microchip-free, unlike you for never having committed a crime before getting this body. His wealth projects his image onto news sites as a good, successful man. He has expensive lawyers. He has everything. I only want freedom and safety, and protection. Unfortunately, the cost is a crime."

I stare at my fingers and this body I've worn for ten years. "Do you think it'll stop this horror if you transplant me into a different body?"

"I'd like to fucking try rather than opt for suicide," he says, palms up.

"Do you think we can retrieve Moremi's consciousness to transplant it, too? Is it even possible?"

He blinks, processing my request. "She's a shark, hungry for death. Indifferent to the science of this world. She won't be docile for any treatment, and I doubt any would be compatible with her."

"How long does the transplant treatment take?" I say, raising my hand to pause him. "Five to eight hours, give or take. By then, my whole family will be dead." Jan opens his mouth to say something, but I shush him. "You can buy me privilege, but you can't buy me time. But," I add, and a smile sprints across his face, "it doesn't hurt to have a backup plan."

Jan smiles, pressing his wrist to automate a direction to one of his subordinates. "God, I love you when you're not reined in."

I raise my hand, making him pause. This time, I get to decide where I go. "Get me a white man's body. About time I have me some fun with that nonstop service of cis white male privilege," I say, observing him with his wide smile, "*unless* you have a problem with that."

"I can swing anywhere for you, love. Although, best I take a woman's body."

"Are you sure about that? It's a hard life."

"You'll give me the cheat codes," he says, winking.

I wait for him to make his call and forward his instructions, and he concludes by saying, "The doctors can only manage to gain access to two low-profile white South African bodies on short notice. If we haven't solved everything by 10:00 p.m. tonight—that's what? Three-and-a-half hours left—we'll hide as my doctors process the transplantation. By the time the authorities find our bodies, we'll be long gone in new identities. We'll be able to navigate the city freely and easily."

"We need to sort out protection for our children," I say. "Do you think this body-hop will stop Moremi from killing my family?"

"If it doesn't, the game continues, no?" he says. "We still fight it, except in different bodies, until we find a way out."

I nod, saying, "First, we pick up Mama. Then Moremi's grave is where we excavate the whole truth."

18:33 /// THE DARK MOUTH

Biophilic skyscrapers rise into the misty skies as the evening traffic heaves onto Mobuto Drive. My ears pop as Jan focuses the steering wheel, throttles us forward, and our car soars above into the minimal air traffic. Surveillance and Wi-Fi saturate the air, suffocating, stinging. Mama's flight. If Mama dies, I will be considered her murderer, too.

The pain in my heart dissipates into my limbs. I see the image of her face pressed against my eyelids, the generosity sparkling in her eyes. I feel it surface, like dregs from the bottom of the ocean. The way Moremi died last night is the way Mama might die today, as if by the same hand, by the same modus operandi. I'll be considered a serial killer now. I could be talking about a stranger, someone you hear about on the news. But it doesn't click that I'm talking about me. Me. The murderer. My fight for survival is taken as an intentional act to kill. If I hadn't killed Moremi, Papa would still be alive.

No, I need this grief out of my bones. But my poor mother. She doesn't even know her husband is dead. Married to him for forty years. I've kidnapped her son, her firstborn, who we've moved from the trunk into the back seat and still remains unconscious. She hasn't even been given the chance to grieve.

No, she won't die.

I *will* save my mother.

The shadows of passing air vehicles blip against our windows. I could fling open the door, throw myself out to be trampled by air-pods. I peer down the sides of an office tower to the traffic below on a six-lane, cable-stayed swing bridge crossing over the Gab River. Vertigo digs into my gut, and I grip the seat.

The interior of the car is too leather-scented. My heart races, and I can't seem to bring myself to open the door.

Far in the distance, a trickle of smoke paints the air between the sky and the towering treetops with a look of pristine detachment. Silence and wind chill the air. We're blocked on both sides by two two-seater mini-pods and a slow-moving sedan-like pod in the front.

"Bliksem, damn driver." I lean across the console and punch the car horn repeatedly, startling Jan. "Move out of the way!" I wave my hand to the drivers beside and in front of us.

Jan revs the car, and our front bumper jerks against the sedan. I catch the old woman's cold, hard stare in her rearview mirror. I lean hard on the horn again as I dial the airport officers, sending in a complaint about Mama's flight. The car slides to the left, the old woman with the thick horn-rimmed glasses slows down to probably exchange numbers, insurance details, and wait for the traffic police, but we zoom past. She flips us the middle finger, taking down our number plate.

A horn wails, followed by a loud sound that scrapes the side of our car, spinning us toward the glitzy façade of an apartment block. My body snaps forward, the seat belt restraining me. My hands slam against the dashboard when our car freezes a millimeter from a balcony. A throng of friends stand back wide-eyed, hands gripping ciders and wine glasses, kwaito music blasting from their speakers. One walks to the balustrade, smacks our hood, and swears, "Fotseke!" Jan apologizes, reverses, and joins a lane.

"The car stopped," he says, face wan. "But last night, your car didn't stop. It *hit* her. If it malfunctioned last night, why's it working today?"

"I don't know, Jan," I say, exasperated. "I don't have time to process that."

"We may have been drunk," says Jan, "but I swear last night she jumped right in front of the car."

6:39 p.m. I slap the dashboard. "Just overtake him!" A white SUV-pod hoots when Jan cuts into their lane. Then dismay—a standstill. The traffic is a long snake, unbroken, unmoving. Time continues even though we don't. I can't remain bound in metal when Mama could die.

I must run.

"I need to get there before Moremi," I say. "Join the ground traffic."

Jan eases out of traffic toward ground level, waiting for a gap so he can join. As the car slips into ground-level traffic, I unclip my seat belt and throw open the door. "Call the flight control unit. Tell them there's a bomb or serial killer on the plane—anything!"

I check the updates Mama's been sending on our online chat.

Mama: Flight attendant says we're arriving shortly.

Me: I'll be by the "International Arrivals" doors. Don't go anywhere else. I'll be there.

My footsteps are faster than the seconds raining on my shoulder. A torrent of desperation mixes with the intoxicating pain of the lactic acid pumping through my legs, my skin slippery with sweat. A motorbike zips past me, striking my shoulder. A motorbike is faster than running. I lurch forward, grabbing for the biker's hood with my prosthetic arm—a slip of hope loosens in my fingers like strands of hair as his hood escapes my grasp, and he zips forward. Fuck. Only five minutes. I punch the tarmac with my feet, chest painful, needing the soothing hand of oxygen, calm and slow. I will breathe later. Cars honk in my direction. But what will I do if I get there and the plane hasn't landed? Moremi can't possibly reach her. But what if she lands before I arrive and just stands in the waiting area? Surely Moremi won't kill her right there in front of everyone.

The airport's exoskeleton is like a sharp-boned ballerina, freeze-formed in action, the echoes of her fluid movements caught in a steel frame. I stream through the parking lots, through the sliding-door entrances, across the waiting area toward the doors labeled *INTERNATIONAL ARRIVALS*. Inside the international terminal, geometric, flowing spaces lead to a high-ceilinged hall with large windows, light streaming in. Outside, the tarmac bay hosts idle aircraft like masses of ships. I bump against an old man pushing a cart, a kid skipping by the metal seats. My eyes scan the flight information board. I part the line leading to the check-in counter as I run to the observation deck, to the curtain wall staring out at the expansive runway; its glass is slashed by diagonal bracings, cutting the view of the sky into trapezoid pieces.

Below the blurry cirrus clouds, I make out the shape of the aircraft, Mama's flight, slowly nosediving toward the runway. A sigh of relief. As soon as it lands, I will hold Mama in a tight hug, never let her go. I heave in breaths, fingers sweaty, and pray to some god.

I scramble past people, pushing them aside, needing to see, to see Moremi's life, bleak in these spaces, fall like lightning. I stop, noticing something, a shape smaller than the jet engine, hunched over the plane's left wing. I step forward, cupping my mouth. The thing crawls toward the fuselage, one of the window seats. Too far away to see. My nose against the window.

Moremi. On the wing. No, no, no. This isn't supposed to be happening. If Moremi wants to frame me for the murders, why would she attempt to kill Mama somewhere I can't possibly be?

I bang my hands against the glass wall. "I'm not on the fucking plane!" I shout.

The plane's getting closer, closer, closer—Moremi is a shadow edging to the window; just as quickly, she smudges away into thin air. She's no longer on the wing.

I hold my breath, counting. No. Mama will step out of the plane. She will hug me in her kindness. The plane will land before Moremi can do remarkable damage. Trembling, I try to dial Mama. I text nonsensical words, telling her to run, but where? *Try staying in a room with no doors or windows, they will still get inside,* murderer Tshekiso said.

Sounds invade my ears: the churn of time, coffee-makers spritzing liquid into mugs, chatter, the airport PA system, echoey, suffocating, footsteps quiet and clip-clopping. She's chopping Mama's head off, I imagine, isn't she? Insanity has gone and slain me. I start screaming, pointing at the plane. Everything twirls around me, screens screaming, dizzying.

I grab a butter knife from the counter of the coffee shop. "Someone save her! I can't take it anymore!" I aim the knife at my chest, my neck, to slice open my throat—for my death to save Mama and all my loved ones. People scream and thrust away from me, watching me, this spectacle.

A security guard grabs me. Eyes seize and manhandle me. My chest tightens—there is no breath in my lungs. The ground, my knees. Ears silenced by my palms. The knife clangs to the floor. "Mama!" I struggle with them. "Let me go! I have to save her. I have to kill myself to save her!" The airplane taxies down the runway. Time is nulled, holding its breath. I grab the guard by the collar, yelling, "God, please save her!"

The plane stills. Seconds, seconds, seconds. The door opens, the aft stairs unravel like a tongue lolling out a dead animal's mouth. The plane barfs up a mass of passengers down the airstairs; they're screaming, agitated into a melee, shoving others over the balustrade onto the tarmac, crushing them with their hooves. Their gut-wrenching screams—they must've seen something, to be so afraid, as if what they saw—the death, the blood—will poison and haunt them. All the passengers run toward the terminal. Hope is crisp in the air as I rope it around my fingers. My eyes scan the rolling crowd—Mama, Mama, Mama, nothing. Emergency vehicles scuttle to the plane, the lights blood-lit, dashing across my face. I don't need to hear it. I know it. Mama. She's dead. She's dead.

Chatter radios in. The guards stop heaving me around like a loose doll. We stare. Security officers pour out onto the hot tarmac. They've let me go now, the security guards. There's something more important than me. A death on an airplane.

The scene eclipses, a shadow scudding the sun. The dark mouth of the plane. Then the last passenger appears at the threshold, a woman bloodied with revenge. Teeth raw and sharp. Pupils large and hungry. It's her. Moremi. My knees buckle. My gait slackens. The cold glass against my hand. No, please, no. Moremi steps forward, a reveal. Her three-fingered hand holds a bulbous object, her fingers snug in its eye sockets like a bowling ball. Her. Mama. Her head. In Moremi's hand. Human innards gleam down her blood-soaked arm.

Her eerie voice reaches me: "I know what you feel, I know how you think—*I* have your essence in my blood. Killing makes me faster, stronger. I am not bound by the laws of physics."

Moments later, a gurney, the black bag of death. Darkness bevels me.

18:48 /// TRICK A DEVIL

A torrent of cold slicks down my back, the blade of a knife. Someone walks over my grave. My throat is tight. My nails grip into my thighs as my mouth screams for oxygen. I cough out chunks of suffocation, despair, anger, my cheeks hot, blazing hot. Jan dragged me from the commotion. We now stand in a conference room on a high-level floor.

They brought the body out. I didn't want to see it.

The airport has been cordoned off, outgoing flights delayed, no one allowed to leave or enter the facility. Through the glass walls, we see flight marshals and police officers halting the flow of people and vehicles at every entry and exit on the ground level. An orange-tinted gas blossoms from the air vents, hovers above us, around us. I feel nothing but light-headed. We hear heavy boots stampeding on our floor.

The door slides open, and a soldier wearing a protective suit sticks his glass-globe-clad head in, sees us. "Very well." He shuts the door and leaves.

Jan stares at me with raised eyebrows, takes curt steps to the door, opens it, and disappears for several seconds. He reappears with beads of sweat on his forehead, panic in his eyes, and a shaking glass of water in his hand. "There are bodies everywhere. Collapsed in place.

Lying on the stairwell, caught in the elevator doors, on the floor, on the tarmac—and every authority's wearing protective suits. There's orange gas everywhere—it must be something in the gas, but why isn't it affecting us?" I rock back and forth. He continues, "There was an old woman moaning on the floor. A woman in a protective suit approached her, said, 'This will counter your experience of this traumatic event.' Then injected her. She passed out. What the hell's going on?" He closes in on me. "We have to get out of here. Love?"

"Is that all you care about? My parents are dead," I whisper.

He pulls me into his arms. Settles me down on a chair.

"I can't breathe," I moan. He slides open the glass doors to the balcony. Cold, crisp air. He pats my back. He wipes the tears from my face, hot to touch. "I'm so sorry." He massages my shoulder.

I throw the glass against the balcony's wall; it cracks and darkens the wall with water. "Stop saying you're sorry! My mother and my father are dead! We're holding my brother hostage. How the hell does a sorry fix that?" I grab his collar. "*They* are dead. I told you we should report it. Everyone I love is dying whilst *your* family is safe. *You* convinced me to bury her, yet I'm the only one being punished. My family is being punished because you—*you*"—I shove him—"*you* convinced me!" I punch his chest. "You manipulated me with all that public-opinion bullshit. You had big strategies then to keep us out of prison. Where the fuck are your big ideas now? Prison is no fucking slap on the wrist, *you* said. We're free, but this is worse than prison. Do you feel better now? They always said your family is as corrupt as they come. Your father raped women, and now *you* kill women."

He stumbles back like I've clocked him. Steadies himself. Swallows. "I-I—" His voice breaks. Inhales. Anger pummels him, stretches his pain across his face. "I am not my father."

"Yes. You. Are." I punch him with the words.

His face tightens. He screws his eyes shut. Holds his breath as if that will pause his heartbeats. "I'd kill myself if it would kill him," he whispers.

"My parents are dead," I say, "my baby will die. Do you even know what that feels like? Do you even care about your children? Or it doesn't matter because they're not on the list, and you've never had to worry about losing anything with the power in the Koshal name, huh? It's not like your wife's going to win custody. Probably why she's stuck to your father is because she knows he's more powerful than you. Is that what she's doing to keep her children?"

"I'm on *your* list," he whispers, eyes downcast. "I'm going to lose my life. The Koshal name can't stop that."

"Hello, darlings." A voice. Moremi. She appears straight through the wall. Head tilted. Smirking.

Jan steps back, mouth hanging open, fear trickling into his eyes.

Moremi eyes him. "It's time. Welcome to the finish line, Jan."

He points, staggers back. "I-I-I can see her. What did we do to her? No, that can't be us. No. She's walking toward us," he says. "Does that mean I'm next?"

"You bastard, you can see me if I've decided to kill you next," Moremi says, approaching us, licking Mama's blood from her fingers. An anger far worse than anything boils deep in my belly. A poison of fury emanates from her eyes as she glares at him. "I despise animals like you. We're going to have a good old time: I'm going to rip your balls out and ram them down your throat, see if you like how you taste. I will deliver death very slowly to you. I'll fry your penis and feed it to your little princesses. What kind of world do you think you're creating for your little girls when you murder a 'little girl'?"

Jan pleads with his hands. "I'm really so—"

"Save it," she says. She walks a circle around us. "The women always have to fall because of a man. Are you sure about this man, his love for you? He fucked up your life just to fuck you. He's clean, his family is still alive. He was able to save his skin last night and make you kill me. Now he can't come up with a strategy to save *your* skin. But imagine the terrible things he'd come up with to save his family if he was in your shoes. Here we are as women, fighting each other, whilst the man is free—an unfortunate, disgusting pigeonhole we find ourselves in. He's fucked up three women's lives. You. Your mother's dead. I'm dead. Your daughter will be his next victim, his next little girl."

Jan turns to me. "Love, no, don't let her get into your head. I know how it sounds and how it looks, but it's not true. I love you. *I. Love. You.* Please believe me. Trust me."

"Ha!" Moremi's mouth opens into a large wound. "The cheapest trick a devil gives a woman. A mouthful of poison. You were just a woman who kept saying 'no' to him. And he won the challenge: He took you to bed over and over. He owned you. Now *you're* losing everything."

He turns to her. "If you hate these toxic roles you're forced into so much, then change it."

She pins him against the wall. Her fingers steel around the brittle fragility of his bones. "You have no shame to kill me then demand to save you."

"I'm not in it for sex," he says, eyeing me. Then to Moremi, "Maybe your exes ruined you, destroyed you. You worked for my father. That sexual harassment case from three years ago—are you one of the silent ones? Not every man is the same."

Her body stills. Becomes *too* still. No chest rising, no eye movements, not a sliver of her bodily mannerisms stir the air. Her cheeks are sunken in, flesh devoured by death. For a brief moment, relief encapsulates me: maybe this is how it all ends. But the wound in her face yaws open, says, "What's your name?"

"Janith Koshal."

"Your father is Aarav Koshal?"

He hesitates. Then: "Yes. Whatever happened in his firm, I know nothing. But I'm sorry. I'm sorry for what happened to you and the other women."

"Is your apology supposed to heal me back to life or rectify what your father and his colleagues continue to do to us?"

"Continue?" Confusion furrows his eyebrows. "I only know as much as was reported in the papers. But you stopped working for him."

She hesitates, like a glitch in a system, then her eyes dull. Something takes over, and she robotically responds, "I am here to avenge my death." She rams his head against the wall. "I am here to avenge my death. I am here—"

"You can't do anything, can you?" I say. "You're just as stuck in this as we are. This is not your fault. You're not evil, but something evil is running your body."

Jan stares at her in pity, blood trickling down the back of his head, staining his collar. "I understand."

A piece of her escapes, face weeping. "You should've been the one to kill me last night. Now I'm here killing innocent people. Men like you, like your father, deserve a far worse death."

My voice is gentler now, hands easing her arm down, and she backs away. "But you're still in there," I say. "And this is not you. Something happened to you. We can work this out together. Tell us, we can help you. Fight through this control. You can do it."

She's almost convinced. Then I realize my hands around hers, sticky with blood. Mama's blood. How could I find something in a ruin of evil after what she's done? Anger refills my veins. She killed my parents. I wrap my hands around her throat, throttling her from behind, staggering us toward the balcony, and she plummets over the edge into the deafening air, smacking hard into the pavement. Gravity reverses, siphons her like a pulley system to a standing position on the balcony. She doesn't slap me. Doesn't punch me. Just smiles. An evil snake of a smile on her torn lips. And this is the evil that Jan thinks holds kindness.

"Turns out, you actually loved your mother," she says, voice playful. "Your mother tastes delicious." She smiles, steps toward me. "Does it hurt now? Has the pain of what you've done kicked in?" She leans in, sniffs me. "I truly know how you feel. Stop lying to these people."

"I only killed one person," I say quietly, a tremor of anger like a ravine in my veins. "You can't keep taking more than one life."

"I am worth many lives," she yells. "I gave you time, yet you wasted it. Do you understand how selfish of a request that was? Do you understand that when I give you time, I am resisting my urges and their pressure, and the closer I get to my death? The closer you get to winning this?"

"Winning? What does this have to do with winning when you're killing my family?" I ask.

"Oh, you'll understand soon enough. What did you think you'd discover, sniffing behind my back at other prisoners? Wasn't your father's death a serious enough sign that I mean business, or are you expecting your darling mother to wake up from the dead and kill you in revenge?" She cackles, smacking her broken knees. "So that's the big idea? To get her to kill you and everything stops, huh? Because you're too much of a coward to follow through. Wrong." She tilts her head. "Your mother is no longer your mother—she will be ruthless. Now you realize why your father killed himself. He didn't want to be a murderous ghost. Except, how would he know the rules? Daddy dearest isn't so innocent, is he?"

I burn. Glare at her. "What did my father do?"

"You don't deserve anything from me. Not even the truth." She steps closer. "Is it painful now?"

"Tell me what to do to stop this, and I'll do it."

"Well, there is one thing that you could do," she says, and the way she smiles produces sick in my mouth. "My mother has lost me, a daughter."

"Your mother's gone," I say.

She holds up her hand. "That's not the point. My mother lost a daughter, so it's only fair that you pay the same debt. Then all this stops. I'll vanish. Imagine, you get to walk away with a clean slate. To get that clean slate: kill your daughter the same way you killed me. If you don't, eventually I will."

My daughter. I sway, sunlight too strong, the sun a coin sparkling in the sky. I have to keep them alive. There's no other way out. Jan says something. My cloak. Inside it, the gun. My fingers reach for it. Point it to my head. Pull the trigger without a second's hesitation.

19:12 /// THE LONG HAUL

Red. Red. Red. As if the sun sears through my eyelids. Tinged blood. Is it heaven's light or hell's fires? A lush of light. A voice. A tug.

My vision flickers with static. My loose lip on the floor, the bloody flesh of my torn tongue. Dismembered words tumble in my mouth. Salty liquid gurgles in my throat. My scalp howls with pain, and my fingers scuttle at my forehead to scrape away the agony but there's a hole, a mushy hole vomiting lurid fluid, pouring it down my eyes, into my mouth—it's so full with the bite of salt. God, help me. The silhouette of sounds ebbs from my ears. I try to gather the voices with my hands into me, but my nerves are screaming; the soul-part of me that resides within the body perforates what used to be my skin, the boundary of me. I am everywhere at once, and a volcano of sickness terrifies my gut. I fold into a pinpoint of bone and skin and scream out the bile from my stomach. Finally reality stills, folds around me, and life and breath expand my lungs. I hyperventilate, drinking in the abrasive, cold oxygen.

"Am I dead?" I cry, woven around my knees. "Please, can I rest now?"

"Wakey, wakey," the murderous ghost says, appearing in my vision.

Words slur from what is supposed to be my mouth. Jan kneels beside me. His tears wet my face. His hand cups the back of my head, part of what remains. I blew my brains out. "Why am I not dead?"

He frames my face with his hands. "Love, breathe. Focus on your breath. I love you. Please stay. I'm so sorry."

The pieces of my tongue and lip lying on the ground squirm, wriggle, and crawl toward me. I tremble in fear, trying to inch myself away, but the pain hogties me into paralysis as Jan watches with terror-filled eyes. The mutilated pieces of my flesh climb across my boot, onto my knee, crane open my mouth, enter the jaw of my teeth and knit themselves across my open lips. I groan in disgust as these worms of my flesh writhe in my mouth, until they've sewn themselves whole and my mouth's no longer a wound.

I cram my fingers into my mouth, desperate, repulsed. "Get them out of me, please!" Blood leaks down my face. "A bullet," I cry, "there's a bullet in my head."

Moremi says, "Shem skepsel. You think you can run away from this with a little bullet in the head? There is no way out of this, sweetie. Not even suicide. You will live with the consequences and make the hard decisions until I kill you. I want you to suffer more pain than I'm suffering. My pain just grows and grows. It won't stop," she says, eyes a frightening focus. "I am hungry."

I'm shaking. Immense pain drives through my veins. In this feverish nightmare, I catch a glimpse of Moremi, a truth of her, her hunger for something besides revenge. As if an umbilical cord of a curse ties us, I feel her overwhelming loss and its desperate dearth of belonging. There's an emptiness in her that desires to be sated and washed by the holiness of love she can't fulfill with killing; I wish to slip through that weakness like a knife and finish her off.

"Love," Jan cries.

A tightening in my gut. I convulse. Nothing comes out. My vision blurs, and my body trembles. My palms press into the cold, hard floor. Nails scrape and drag. The pain is akin to a stillborn birth. I scream. A cacophony of pain like a vat of acid screams into my forehead, then a pin-drop silence: my forehead spits out a bullet. It clinks onto the floor, slicked in blood. The cracked splinters of my skull's frontal bone ricochet into form. My fingers reach to what was once a gaping gunshot wound, and is now merely sealed skin and smeared blood.

"It hurts. My head hurts," I cry.

"Take a fucking painkiller," Moremi says, leaning forward. "Consequences. You shot yourself—now live with the migraine. You think you can just die without atoning for your sins? A different god runs this show. When you murdered me last night, the world changed. *Your* world changed. I am here, risen for a purpose. There is no easy exit. You will not fucking kill me, then dismiss me by trying to die." She throws her head back, cackles. "Get off your ass and face your wrongs. Kill your daughter or watch me kill everyone you love."

"What if I kill someone else, someone else but my baby?" I ask.

"Unfortunately, I didn't have the option yesterday to choose someone else to be a victim instead of me, did I?" she says.

Jan interrupts us. "Okay, how much time do we have to figure out who put this microchip in you?"

Moremi eyes me. "Why are you so keen on saving a fetus? It's not even born yet. It's not a person. You haven't had a conversation with this thing or made memories with it, so why are you so hellbent to save something that could give you freedom? You didn't give me this respect yesterday." I note a tone of jealousy in her voice, and I wish to pry that emotional wound wider; perhaps that is something I could use to control her, although I must be careful, for she is quite vigilant and ruthless.

"I know you lost your mother," I whisper. "I'm sorry. But, please, don't let another child go through what you went through."

"Is this what it means to have a real mother?" she asks, eyes gleaming with sorrow.

"My children . . . died in my womb. Four of them," I whisper. "I-I-I can't kill this one, too. I love her—you can't understand. Please, she's just a baby."

She looks at me forlornly, and I'm awash with relief that she may understand, but she says, "I almost feel sorry for you. But you taught me one thing last night when you were killing me: 'If you don't die, I die. If you die, I live.' That's what you said to me. I'm not here to just kill. I'm here to live again."

It hurts to understand her, to process her words.

"What?" Jan asks, perturbed.

Her lips twist into a smile. "It is fun taunting you two. More fun than you had last night. *You* decided to play the second you killed me. You could've walked away. Now you can't escape me."

Jan and I stare at each other, speechless. I am powerless. I can't bear that my daughter will die, whether I kill her or not.

"Cheer up, love," Moremi says, upbeat, disorienting and sickening me with her chirpy smile for something so morbid. "Upsy-daisy. On your feet." She yanks me up by my elbow. "Try and see it from my point of view. I was a successful creative; how can I fulfill my career goals when I'm dead? But I think you can be smarter than this. You're running out of time. Unfortunately"—she grabs Jan by the collars—"time's up for this accomplice."

"What? No!" I shout. I can't be alone. I can't do this alone. "Take his skin, just don't kill him, please."

"I decide what I take," she growls. Throws him against me. Turns to leave.

"Oh, God, where are you going?" I yell, advancing to her. "Who's next?"

"One. Hour."

I grab her marred hand, and she hisses at me. I draw back. "Please, not my daughter. Anyone but my daughter."

"Who knows, maybe whatever you find out might stop me." She winks.

I scream, fall to my knees, clutch at her feet. "Then take him! Please take Jan, just not my baby."

Jan crams his fist into his mouth. Moremi tilts her head. Caresses my face. Raises my chin. Her eyes shimmer with pity, and a glistening tear rolls down her skin-torn face. Have I reached the rational part of her? She wavers, and this is my challenge to change everything, my only hope. If she gets her truth, then my family can survive. Sometimes the only way is through, like a bullet; through, not around. I will pummel through this adversity. I will. There is more to this murder, to this malfunctioning microchip. I'm not the only one.

"One hour," Moremi reminds me, and thin, cold air dissolves her into nothing.

19:22 /// COMATOSE STRANGERS

I have until 20:12.

"You shouldn't have pushed her," Jan says, eyes focused, jawline tense. "You were this close to cracking her open. She's still in there—a good part of her still resides in her. She's just trapped in this avenging thing. If it were down to her, she wouldn't do all of this. You were this close, and you pushed her. Now the evil part's taken over again. I don't think we'll have another chance to get close like that."

"I'm in this mess because of you," I say above the migraine noise. "I said no. But you kept approaching me. I'd be home with my husband now if it weren't for you."

"You'd be home alone. You weren't happy in your marriage. You're blaming me for loving you."

"None of that matters now," I say.

He raises his hands. "I'm not mad, okay? If saving your daughter means me dying, I'll die a million times for her."

His warm words barely perforate the migraine burning at the edges of my scalp. I want to scathe it out with a knife, anything to stop its terror.

The door clicks open. Two soldiers in protective suits enter the conference room. They raise their guns. "On the floor. Hands behind your back. Cuff them."

My knees give. Not what we need now with a ticking time bomb. Jan and I get on our knees, stare at each other. The other one approaches us, locks our hands behind our backs. They move about the room.

Once checks the storeroom. "Found two females and one male," one says.

"Is anyone conscious?" the soldier asks, face in glassy, bulbous headgear.

"Negative."

He presses his neck, radios in instructions. "Increase security at all entrances and exits. Is there anyone in the east wing?"

A response: "No activity. All occupants down."

"We have the targets contained. Evacuate. Shut down serum."

The barrel of a gun stares at me. "Up."

I swallow. Stand.

The gun presses into the small of my back. "Move."

One soldier exits first, followed by Jan, me, and the soldier behind. We move down a hallway fogged with dusk-tinged smoke, swirling and twirling, obscuring the walls. On the floor, bodies. In doorways, bodies. Immobile. A little boy with a teddy bear clutched in his arms lies diagonally in the hallway, unconscious.

I back against the soldier behind me, crying. "I can't. Is he dead?"

"Move."

Jan stops, stares at me, having sidled past the body.

"Please help him," I cry.

The gun punches my back. I fall face first on the body, crumple myself against the wall, and slide myself upwards away from the little boy. Jan tries to help me but can't manage with his handcuffs.

"Move," the soldier announces.

I stand, follow Jan and his guard. Several more bodies, strewn on the floor. The elevator doors far ahead ding against an old woman lying between them, dress revealing brown pantyhose. They mentioned a serum. Why have they done this to people?

The soldier ahead clasps his hands around her ankles and drags her to the side, nudges her head with his foot to make way for us to enter the elevator. Mirrors hem us in.

He dials his cochlear. It turns bright red then green when someone answers. "We have them secured. We found a man bound in their vehicle. He's been identified as the brother. Command noted. Yes, I have confiscated their phones. Should we blindfold them?" He shakes his head to the soldier behind me.

The soldier answers, "Yes, we have the girl with us. She won't be a problem. We can handle her."

Girl, me. I cringe.

"Two policemen will chauffeur them over. ETA twelve minutes. I've taken control of the situation here."

The elevator descends, circumvented in glass, into a macabre show of collapsed bodies. People at café tables, lying face down on their plates of food. The waiting area filled with sleeping visitors. A mass of heavily geared officials moving in and about the high-ceilinged terminal. The elevator doors ding open into a hallway layered with comatose strangers.

The gun pushes me forward. They guide us through the hallway, and Jan presses his body against mine, his shackled hands reaching for mine.

Outside in the cool breeze, two vehicles wait for us, hovering slightly above the ground.

The gun prods at my lower back. "Get in."

Jan stares at me as he's handled into the second vehicle. We're separated into glass-tinted pod-shuttles, a capsule of a thing. I struggle to lift myself into the vehicle. The soldier gathers me like a child and throws me into the passenger seat. I land on my side and slide my way up into a sitting position. Inside awaits an anonymous driver. A police officer.

"Time is not on our side," the soldier directs the policeman.

He nods. "On it."

The car door slides downward, and the lock mechanism slides into place. The vehicle hums, lifts into the air, hovers northeastward of the city, out of the city, far away from the southward police headquarters in Main Mall. I watch Jan in the other pod-shuttle, wrists cuffed, head bowed to his knees. I stare at the clock on the dashboard. Time is slipping through my hands. My daughter's life is slipping through my hands. My heartbeat quickens. I don't have time for this. To just sit here whilst Moremi is out there causing havoc. This could be the only time it's easy to escape. Wherever they're taking us could be heavily barricaded.

"Please," I cry, "you have to help me. A woman is after my family."

He stares straight ahead as if I haven't spoken.

Just yesterday, my life before today, I was normal: a wife, a soon-to-be mother, established architect, ticking things off the grocery list, overseeing design work, sneaking around with my lover.

Crime rates may have fallen over the years, but how many of us women have been murdered, pitted against each other, our voices muzzled? I feel strange: the weight of fear has dissipated from my body. Dying has fine-tuned my intuition, my valor. I feel everything. I see everything clearly. I feel Moremi's pain. But I'm exhausted of seeing different versions of me—slim, sexy, fat—lying plain, breasts opened, our vaginas as storages and hospices for silly paraphernalia, and being cut to pieces. I'm exhausted of seeing women's victimization stories slovenly splashed across all news outlets, nothing but a mangled body poised for the scandal, that juicy byline for a writer seeking journalistic stardom, and she, poised like a model for the camera, the story in aesthetics. Her blood like lipstick across her body, nothing but a prop, murder dressing her as an exotic corpse. Because it's always the women who die, buried with their silences. But they *have* a story, a name, a soul, more than we could ever have. At least, *I* get to be reborn, wreak havoc, enact change.

It is my power.

This is not where it ends.

This is not how it ends.

We are reborn for a purpose, Moremi and I. Maybe, just maybe, I can change our situation. I have to do better. For my daughter. For Moremi. We don't just get to die and shut the fuck up. The world will feel our fury. Our bodies are wombs to bear murder.

Now I'm longer terrified of myself. Of how I think. Using whatever is near as a weapon, doing things I'd never imagined, things that had never crossed my mind. Like that my only weapon is I can't die, but I can possibly kill the man driving me to my incarceration—because where else would they take me? If my only escape is his death, how can I make it happen quickly? How long will it take this pod-shuttle to crash and burn as I try to incapacitate this man?

Right now, they expect little from this normal-wife-soon-to-be-mother. I must do what I fear or fear will rule me. But I'm in the passenger seat, hands cuffed, harmless, female. Less muscle, but I pack a punch in my joints—the elbows, the knees. A driving force, my trainer once said, that is your advantage. The driver sits on my right side, where my robust prosthetic is fitted. If anything, this is far worse. I'm restrained. Moremi is out there. Seconds are milled furiously fast. Soon, my baby, my husband, my brother—one of them is quick to death. A thorough liquidation whilst I'm restrained.

My only weapon is I can't die, but I can kill the man beside me.

I stare down at the passing view of Sebele Valley, open fields and the open road. Counting my breaths, readying myself, infinitesimally rolling my shoulder, weighing the momentum in my arm. I can do this. I can do this. I can do this. The last thing he expects. A fire. A fire. Even if we crash, even if I burn, I will wake. *He* will not. I will be free to finish this off *with* Moremi.

I am a little girl.

I am a monster.

I jam my steeled right elbow into the side of his head. *Hard*. Over and over as he reaches for his gun. Grapples with me. Pain jams into my right shoulder, the back of my head, my neck from his hands and nails, and I am scared I am scared I am scared.

I am an animal, a creature, hungry, rabid, biting his hands, chewing at his skin. Blood blood blood guzzles down my throat. The pod whizzes, like a drunk person struggling onto the road. I jam my foot into the computer's dashboard to block the sensor and stop the autopilot from taking over. No dent. I twist my body, face my back to him, jam my elbow into his throat. Reach for his gun. Aim at the dashboard. Shoot. Kill the autopilot mechanism.

The pod zooms down toward a forested region past Mochudi. We're plunging, plunging, plunging. Alarms scream into my ears, into my mouth, into my chest, waiting for the impact. The ground nearing at a meteoric speed. Nerve endings frayed with pain, fear. A searing nuclear blow. Darkness explodes in my eyes, my bones, my skin. My soul, ensnared by an animal of fire.

Flames dissolve me, and I am finally dead, floating in an ocean of fire, marooned from my imprisonment.

19:38 /// WHITE AS CLEAN BONE

I am risen. Entombed in darkness. Life is a painful fluid quickly trickling through my veins, sight untouched yet, buckled by immense death—my body, my womanhood deceased. The smell of wet moss.

A heavy shield of metal embalms me in flickers of smoke and embers. I grunt, gnawing through debris with my fingers, seeking light, seeking sense, seeking remorse. Finding none. My skin is a flaming organ of pain, dissipating by the second, healing at every inhale. Oxygen, molten and viscous, burns my lungs, every cell of me desperately clinging to it, all the while trying to eradicate it.

Sunset is only a few minutes away. Something inside me grows, a foreign new innate thing. My arm is backward, the slingshot of my clavicle brittle. I press my arm upward, lifting the metallic wreckage keeping me buried. It creaks backward, clatters onto the remains of its wiry cartilage. I heave myself into a standing position, knees bent backward. I rise from the sea of flames, only but a warmth of pain. Then light. Sheer light sprinkles like a fountain of youth into me, *through* me. I feel something below my left knee, a pain of some sort, signaling a warning. When I look down, the bulbous juts of my knees are the wrong way round. I try to remedy the situation, but my fingers are bent at the joints, wrong way up. Something loose in my mouth, like pebbles—my teeth; my jaw hangs loose. The volume of pain rises as my bones right themselves, knocking, knitting themselves anew, the music like crunching stones. I cough.

The pain is beautiful, the pain is delicious.

Chunks of black dust and motes of skin quiver into the strips of daylight pouring through the treetops.

Nothing but trees, expansive ground, mildew, and birdsong. And I, the centerpiece of a destroyed pod-vehicle mottled with flames. Tatters of my clothes smear into my skin as it forms a continuous membrane, eclipsing my skeleton.

Beneath this wreckage, blood fans out like dark oil into the earth. Smoke, a trickle of silence, a halcyon. The mangled body of the officer is strewn partially out, arms liquid matte, half his body torn off, the other half chewed by the damage. He lies lifeless on the ground, one eye propped open by death, one eye gone. One eye looking at me, cameras at each corner, tinny red lights blinking. I can hear the twitching sound of a camera as it zooms into my face. It stares at me. I stare at it, the air saturated with tiny droplets. Peace, quiet—the migraine's gone, killed.

Twigs crack. I spin.

Ashes, dust, sunlight—eight guns flick through the air, aimed at my head. "Move, or we *will* shoot." Heavy-booted soldiers surround me. Anonymous heads contained in glass and bulletproof suits. The sun sparkles through birdsong, a rising tempo.

My clothes are burned and I'm completely naked. No fear stirs in me. Not a flicker of worry or embarrassment. "You can't kill me."

"We know," the cold, hard voice replies. "Not shoot to kill. *You* are vulnerable to bullets; they can maim you, slow you down. One wrong move, I will shoot you where it hurts the most. Try surviving this through a damaged leg or wounded kidney—*take* your pick."

He aims straight at my left breast.

I peer through the tinted glassware of his headgear, see nothing but dead eyes boring into me. Eight guns encircle my head. I don't have a piece of cloth nor a weapon on me, but I'm the most dangerous, powerful being here. The realization stuns me. I am naked of all materialistic things that have never served me. To imagine I wasted time clinging to superficial ideals with a desperate want, because I was terrified of losing things, afraid of the outcome, afraid of upsetting my husband, my family or my associates. Afraid of being alone, a single unmarried woman, afraid of being a failed business owner, trusting the love of a man I'm having an affair with, and believing in myself. Afraid of taking the next step, because "What will people think?" as if it were death. Here I am having lost everything, having died, yet I am *still* alive, still burning with existence. The gravity of the universe refuses for me to die, yet why did I allow myself to die under the ideals of others? Give them the power to kill me? Why did I spend my *whole* life chloroforming myself with people's beliefs and ethos? It got me nowhere trying to be perfect, tweaking and manipulating myself for them. I lived with shame and guilt, judging myself for being infertile and not being the perfect mother, wife, or daughter. I allowed my culture to inform the type of woman I must be, erasing me. No more. I am becoming my own culture now. I considered myself immoral and thought not to judge men similarly while they committed far more sins than I did. I judge myself no more.

I am not guilty. I have no shame. I will be no man and no woman.

I absolve myself.

I absolve myself.

I absolve myself.

Why must we always die in order to be seen? I rise for all the dead women, killed for unrighteous beliefs. I rise from the fire, weightless of conforming, of fear, of unbecoming. Death has distilled me, has refined me into the purest of me: undiluted and impermeable to this city's conditioning.

I will continue to die and kill all that does not serve me.

Without fear, I am whole.

My senses are now attuned to the fear others perspire. They don't look at me as something to possess, to conquer, to abuse. An object to desire. They *see* me, finally see the power in me. Not as an equal, but far superior. And something delectable paints the air: sweet, sticky with a bit of shard. I step forward, pieces of broken glass cracking beneath my soles, to inhale this delicious scent, smack at it with my tongue to the roof of my mouth. I swallow. The scent buckles, staggers backward. Fear. This beautiful smell is fear. I smile. These men are afraid of me.

I walk toward the man with the gun, and a bullet spears through my side from the other soldier's gun. I falter, drink the pain like cocaine, step forward, and several more shots spiral through my body. I stagger under the weight of this bodily destruction, empowered by the raging pain, until the barrel of the soldier's gun is pressed to my chest.

"Your fear tastes delicious," I whisper, voice crunching, grating, not yet set. "Let me have some."

Heads tousle with disarranged thoughts. He stares at me with disgust and horror. A metallic leash shackles my neck, and someone kicks me to my knees and ties my arms. A bullet to my head, rebirthing me again. Blood, oh, blood. Better to be rebirthed than to give birth.

The pod-vehicle hums nearby. For once in my life, I disgust men. And it is with glorious delight.

He wavers. "Get. Into. The fucking vehicle," he spits.

The vehicle hovers above the treescape toward the Matsieng Fertility Fund building; it has a cast-in concrete roof, pure white, undulating like a bent petal in flight. Glass revealed, the building is surrounded by a pseudo-lake, sitting on a forty-nine-hectare site. It is like a feline building growing from the earth.

A sentry of trees buffers the site from view, and on either side of it, a soft line of rocks rises from the ground leading to the heritage site. The rocks swirl across the site in a stratum of browns and reds, and punched into them are the deep grooves of shapeless waterwombs that, they say, mankind and the ancestor of Batswana rose from, their footprints hardened into the copper rocks.

The vehicle points to the green fields behind the building where a series of tall concrete walls grow down toward the earth. A cavern-like entrance flanked with long strips of water ponds and a walkway that the vehicles settle on, under the shelter of a curved metallic roof supported by tusklike structures, white as clean bone.

The pod hisses as the doors slide up. "Out," the man says.

Agony rips through my limbs as I step out of my vehicle, naked and smoke-marred, onto the paved ground of the portico. Jan exits the second vehicle, stares at my state with widened eyes.

Is this where they torture criminals?

“Move,” they tell us.

“Where the hell are you taking us?” Jan asks as they prod us forward with their weapons.

We descend a series of stairs, flanked by tall copper walls like I’m walking through the boulders of a cave streaming with blood. Thin strips of lighting are fitted into the folds of the surfaces. Four men behind us, two beside us and two before us. All armed. Arms muscled. I feel their palms prickle with sweat as fear’s clammy fingers tighten around their quick heartbeats.

Jan halts, shouts, “What the hell are we doing—?”

One hits him with the butt of the gun on the back of his head. His knees crack against the hard floor. Blood, yet again, trickles down his neck where his hand stumps it.

“Shut up. Get up and move,” the soldier says.

Jan gets up. Walks. No escape. Even so, the bullets will certainly kill Jan. But if he’s bound to die by Moremi’s hand eventually, there is no point in saving him. The exit light is now but a pinpoint, an insurmountable distance away.

“This way.” The soldier guides us into a narrow, bulb-lit passageway with the title above: *CLEANSING UNIT*. He slams open the door to wood floors, wood walls, wood ceiling, and warm light. “Dump your clothes in the recycling chute.” He taps a metal opening in the wall with a flap. “Then enter the next room.”

They’re not incarcerating us. He’s lying. This is not a cleansing unit—they’re going to burn us.

I backpedal into the soldier. “I’m not going in.” Jan folds himself across my back as the butt of the soldier’s gun aims for the back of my neck and instead cracks into Jan’s spine. He grunts, falling against me, and I attempt to hold him up.

“This is an order, not a request,” the soldier says as the other two take off our handcuffs. I massage the marks of pain away from my wrist.

"Uh, sir, this is one cleansing unit," says one soldier. "Shall we take the man to the other?"

"What's there to hide? She's already naked. Besides, they're having an affair. They will cleanse together." He prods Jan forward with his gun. "In. Clothes off. Legs apart and arms spread wide. Then step into the next room. If you refuse to comply, we'll have to invade your privacy to enforce the clothes removal process."

The door is glass on the upper part, which means they'll see everything. They're going to incinerate us and watch us burn.

Jan steps forward. "We're not getting into that room until you tell us what's happening."

"How about this?" The soldier aims his gun at Jan's forehead, and Jan's jawline throbs throbs throbs, chewing on anger. "She can't die, but you can. Nelah, follow the protocol, or we kill your accomplice."

"Pull the trigger," Jan announces. "If you're going to burn us alive, I'd rather meet my end with a bullet to my head." So he's thinking the same thing as I am. "Unless," he adds, "we're not really here to die."

The soldier rolls his eyes. Aims the gun to Jan's foot, pulls the trigger, and the bullet slams through my hand when I shove Jan aside. I yell into my fist as the pain ricochets through my bones. My hand comes up bloody. Bone shrapnel pokes out from my palm. I chew against my fist, but the pain rings through my veins and blurs my sight.

"Good thinking," the soldier says, cocking his head. "Your boyfriend will be a liability with a limp, huh? And you don't need that. Unfortunately, now you're wounded." He gestures with his gun. "Shall I rectify that with a quick death? Trust me, your bones will be back to normal once you're revived."

"Fuck you," I spit, disregarding how knowledgeable he is of this strange phenomenon Moremi's death has fused into us.

The soldier lowers his gun. "I'll take that as a no. Unfortunately, your counsel doesn't agree." The last thing I see is a barrel like an eclipse, a thundering noise, and blackness invades me.

19:49 /// A MUSEUM OF PEOPLE

I wake on a cold wooden floor, staring at two light-brown eyes, my head on Jan's lap. He brushes my braids aside, fingers, thumb against my palm. "Your hand is healed." I sit up. "How do you feel?" he asks softly, worried I might break.

I stare at my hand, clean of damage. My migraine, gone. The handprint burn mark on my shoulder blade, gone. The skin whole on my forearm. Pain is a strange, foreign thing. The sensation for it dissipates with each death. Before, the physical and emotional effort required to process my pain and grief depleted my body—now, it feeds my body. Instead, I devour the velocity of pain's explosion, I guzzle its cataclysmic terror as it spreads through my nerve endings. I understand Moremi now, how violence satiates her anger, confines her meekness, avenges her hurt since no one will rise to the occasion as effective as a vengeful dead woman.

"Babe," Jan says, caressing my cheek.

"I've died three times," I whisper. "I've lost—I don't feel bad. Bad for everything that I've done. The guilt is gone or going, but a large part of it is deceased. I feel . . . good. Is this how serial killers feel? No, not serial killers. But doing something terrible, feeling no remorse but a good high? I did nothing terrible but murder and bury a young woman, yet I lived my life as if every day I was sinning. My parents believed that the sins of the flesh are tied to the sins of the soul and kept themselves from sinful acts to keep themselves pure. I've never been strictly religious, but I know God is out there, that our souls depart to heaven or hell when they cease to exist through our reincarnations. My flesh was attracted to ill will and vices; it's the sin of my flesh and not my soul. I wonder if this is what it feels like to have transcendence into enlightenment, to be absolved of everything. I feel surprisingly spiritual, and my body feels like a vessel, a spaceship I'm traveling in. A body has never felt like this to me. Reincarnation and body-hopping don't feel like this, do they? Is it because I've tasted death? I thought I'd see God's light or something. But I feel the more I die, the more death transmutes me spiritually, possibly bringing me closer to my spirit form, to Matsieng. I feel this deep desire to enmesh myself in Xem. The way society speaks of Matsieng, it's sometimes in demonizing tones, but Xe is our ancestor, and Xe is us. I can feel Xem in my blood, in my breaths. We've been clinging to being governed by this city's laws rather than a higher consciousness."

Jan stares at me, perturbed. "I . . . Your parents died."

"Death is not real, Jan. It's a journey to another world," I say. "The pain is there, a bit, the grieving, but it's not as strong as before."

He frames my face. "I don't want them to kill every good part of you. Don't leave, please."

"I had to interfere, otherwise you'd have a wounded leg," I say. "At least I can heal quickly."

"Through death," he says. "That is a very dark, occult place you're going to. Don't interfere anymore. I will handle what comes to me. Listen to me: never do that again."

"I want to," I whisper, "if it'll remove all this pain, the burden. Do you know what this means for us? I can survive anything; I can do anything without a second's hesitation. Hesitation wastes time. Difficult decisions need to be made, decisions that to you may seem evil, but are for the right purposes. The more I die, the more I can take on Moremi."

"Your child," Jan says. "What about *your* child?"

"I will protect my child from everything and everyone. *That* will never change."

He pulls me into a hug. "You're still there. You're still you. Please don't leave, please." He rubs my back. "We have to use the cleansing unit. I don't know what they mean to do with us, but I have to disrobe—"

"They're cowards taking advantage of their power if they watch us," I say. "Let's get this over and done with."

He stares, surprised and concerned, effortlessly removes his clothes, and we step naked into the next room. The room is dark-embalmed. Two meters by two meters, ribbed flooring, ceramic-tiled walls. One entry door and one exit door, opposite each other, like a sally port. On either end through the glass part of the door, warm light bathes wood-paneled walls. I hug my body.

"Legs apart, arms spread out," the soldier yells.

Cold air prickles my skin as I raise my hands. It snags at my thighs, stomach, and breasts. Jan stands close behind me, buffering me from their prying eyes. I don't give a fuck. I pleasure myself with the sounds their bones will make when I shatter their lives.

One of the soldier snickers on the PA system. "Bastards," Jan mutters.

A hiss and a strong, cold spray of water and disinfectant pours through every opening in the walls and ceiling. Water, like death, transforms our physical appearance but can't scour our crimes. Several minutes pass, being tossed by the cold froth. A buzz. The cold-water spray stops.

"Please approach the door, exit, collect your newly furnished clothing," a disembodied female voice says.

Jan and I approach the sealed door, sandals on the ground. We enter a cubicle room similar to a sauna. Clothes fresh and laundered and folded on the seat. We get dressed in beige cotton pants and cotton shirts and enter a foyer-like space of light where the soldiers await. As they handcuff us again, I register the time on one soldier's watch. 19:57. Fifteen minutes left. Who's next? Terror clutches my throat, and I'm sickened at my thoughts: Please let it be Limbani.

"Sorry, forgot to release the warm water," one soldier says, smiling. "This way."

We turn down a narrow hallway. What is going on? They usually evacuate you from the body, or are we going to be tested on like the other prisoners? But why clean us?

We turn into a wide doorway with a plaque hanging on its rectangular arch: Museum of Life. Inside, empty. Edges of light, branded with steel. What seems like a long hallway is a room with white, face-up displays on plinths, running the length of the room and separated at intervals. Each display unit sits opposite a sheet of wall with brushed-steel doors and clear, rectangular glass punched into the upper-top section, exposing a sleeping face. I freeze, blood thudding in my ears, my eyes taking in the scene.

Millions of doors.

Millions of faces.

Repeated across the wall's long periphery. A museum of people sleeping in the walls. Trapped. The display shoots sharp, bright light into the ceiling. Jan and I recoil. Four men block the second exit.

"Sit," a voice says. "You must be tired."

I jump. A woman appears from a hidden door in the wall. I gasp. Prosecutor Serati Zwebathu, in formal wear, a tablet in her hand. She points to a shelter in an alcove with three cushioned seats, a table, and a strand of lights hanging in the center. "Take off their handcuffs. These are our valued visitors."

The soldier's eyes bolt out. "Ma'am, she crashed—"

"I heard. That's an order."

"Ee mma." The soldier removes our cuffs, his jaw tightening with fury.

"How many are left?" she asks him.

"Her daughter, the husband, and a brother," he responds. "And the lover."

"The brother, he owns a multimedia newspaper, you said?"

"Yes."

"That's a liability."

"We're processing him. He's under the serum. We'll return him to his house before his wife and kids arrive. He shouldn't remember any of today when he wakes up at his home."

"Good, the last thing we need is a news media rat spilling its guts," Serati says. "They could sway public opinion in the wrong direction."

Blood rushes to my face. "What the hell's going on?" I shout. "Why are you talking about my brother?"

"Are you arresting us?" Jan asks, rubbing his wrist as I ask, "Is my husband here?"

"Nothing of the sort," she says, staring at Jan, ignoring my question. "But we do need to talk." Turns to me. "Nice to meet you again, Nelah." I stare at her hand, the watch, the time: 20:03, and I'm dizzy with anxiety. She shrugs. "Mr. Koshal." Shakes Jan's hand. He stares at her, stunned. "I was really looking forward to that weekend braai your husband invited us to. He was at the office—I bumped into him leaving to see your daught—"

"Get the fuck on with it," my panic shouts just to get her to finish her spiel.

She sits down, crosses her legs, stares into the space above us as if she can see a beautiful memory whilst Jan and I glare at the seats as if they are electrocution chairs.

Serati cocks her head to one soldier who forces us to sit with the heavy prod of his gun.

Serati raises her palm. "As per our protocol, we don't inform microchipped persons of our preparations to remove their microchip. Instead, we process them through a trial to ascertain their purity. A Murder Trial, we call it. Without them knowing, they can't trick the system. Generally, with human nature, when the walls are down, and no one is looking, they are who they are. When they know they are being tested, like with the CBE, for example, they put up a different—most often false—version of themselves to prove to society their capability."

I take a deep breath, and the weight of all my sins settles on my knees.

"Each microchipped person is given a criminal scenario, and their response to that scenario determines if they are pure or criminal," she says. "That is how we determine the removal of a microchip, certain that this person is safe for our society."

Jan shivers beside me, and I steel myself for the reveal.

"You were one of the selected microchipped to undergo removal. You were fourth on the list." She pauses, and I clasp my hands into fists, to hold myself together from the overwhelming inevitability. "What that means is the three microchipped people before you passed. Pure. They were given the exact same scenario: a hit-and-run in a discreet location."

The words hit me like bullets.

A nuclear bomb of terror climbs my spine.

Bile claims my throat. *It's over. It's all over.*

"You failed dismally," she says. "Instead of reporting the hit-and-run, seeking medical care for your victim, you killed her and buried her with your lover."

I close my eyes, shutter myself in darkness, away from reality.

Then: "We know everything you have done," Serati delivers. "You are guilty of the murders of Moremi Gadifele, your mother, Magetalene Bogosi, and your father, Loeto Bogosi, and the illegal disposal of their bodies, as well as the assault on your brother, Limbani Bogosi."

I am unhinged, the seams of my skin unstitch themselves, and I am falling, falling, falling apart.

This isn't happening. This isn't happening. Tears flame my face. *My daughter. My daughter.* But the silence is jarring and unsettling. I expect commotion, to be processed and for my consciousness to be suctioned out onto a Mind-Cell disk.

I look up. Serati's eyes shimmer with delight, and an unrecognizable fear clings to my skin with sweat.

"The deadline is Sunday," she says.

Incomprehensible words sputter from my mouth. "D-d-deadline?"

A smile slices across Serati's face. "Moremi has to kill your family by then, or you must have obstructed her to win."

20:04 /// AN HONOR

My head swarms with confusion. I can survive this? No prison? No microchip? Am I trapped in another forensic evaluation? Is this a test, the way they tested me with my husband in the simulation? If I am complicit in her statement, does that mean I fail this test?

I stare about our surroundings, waiting for the walls to fibrillate, come apart, and sow me to the sky.

"Welcome to the Murder Trials," Serati says, "city-sanctioned purification rituals that every microchipped person undergoes. I am the leader of the Murder Trials, a section under Crimes and National Security. Our headquarters are based here, a heritage site, a place where the earth birthed life. I believe we're in the same department and this ritual you are going through is for our heritage, for our continuity."

She tilts her head, studying me.

"Hang on," I whisper. "This is all too much, too fast."

Reality is a sickly concoction I can't stomach. I rise, gag, heave. Nothing.

Serati tuts and Jan pats my back, speechless.

"It's been a wild day," she says. "A lot of private members have lost money, but some have made money. They bet on you"—she points at me—"like a racing horse. Though they can't stomach the scenes, which is a prerequisite to the job: viewing everything."

My skin is filthy with sweat as everything sinks in. *They've* been watching us this whole time. But other people in my position did better. I failed. I can't tell whether I'm disappointed or not. "You just watched my parents die. *You* watched. Did nothing."

Serati muses. "We've never had such a public showing. The others, they did it in closed-up spaces: your typical cul-de-sac homes, offices, derelict facilities, the bundus—oh!" Someone hands her a mug. "Thanks for the latte. It's soya milk, right?"

Her errand boy nods.

I collapse back into my seat. Jan rakes a hand through his wet hair. And I realize now it must be their doing that made it convenient for Jan and I to find the answers we needed from the murderer's report at my office building.

"We can't see everything since Moremi's energy field destroys all communication feeds from your microchip," she says. "We only get glimpses of your actions outside it." Serati takes a sip and continues, "The Murder Trials are quite frankly a cultural heritage ritual our country's been upholding for years. Through it, we've seen a very low crime index. The victim sets the rules that mysteriously emanate from Matsieng, and we deal with the aftermath. It's the way it's always worked. Whoever wins receives financial rewards and no prison sentence; if the victim wins, they are revived and offered financial reparations."

"My husband—"

"Hae, shem skepsel. Poor thing has no idea what's going on," she says. "He doesn't have the jurisdiction." Serati observes me with curious eyes. "Here's what happens next: We've reached a stage close to the end where protocol mandates we interrogate you to prepare entities for the final resurrection."

My mind spins, unable to settle on a consistent emotion, fear or elation, clashing inside my body. "What?"

"Moremi has already selected her new body, should she win. Yours."

"Win?" I growl, clenching my hands into fists. "This isn't a fucking game. *This* is our lives on the fucking line."

The soldiers step forward. To protect her. From me. She raises her hand and they back away. My bones tighten. I can't move. What does that mean? Will Moremi own my identity? Become the mother of my child, that's if she doesn't kill her? It terrifies me, that words leap from my mouth forcefully. "No, I will never allow that. Never."

Serati gulps her latte, sets it down. "The child is determined to evict you and possess your body despite our arguments against it—your body is filthy with criminal tendencies. Our in-house ancestral historian is assessing possible loopholes in hopes of finding her a pure body and perhaps freezing this one as a souvenir. We are hoping for the best outcome."

I need to concentrate, steady myself, because this is good, right? "What do I get when I win?" I ask.

"If you win," she adds bitterly, "we relocate you into a new identity and incinerate your current body. We'll hold a conference to report your former identity's criminal actions against your family and your instant incarceration. Society will believe that you have been imprisoned for your wrongful acts whilst you get to live free. But you will no longer be a citizen of Botswana. You will no longer be one of us. We normally dump people like you in some other continent. Sometimes on rare occasions, you might reside somewhere else in Africa, but you are banned from stepping foot on Botswana soil."

Dump? Like we're some garbage? Fury eclipses any rational response within me. I want to burn this facility down.

"Other countries abroad run things differently," Serati says. "We do have foreign bodies that we can transplant you into a new identity, in a witness-protection style, which requires a feat of labor to navigate the finicky immigration policies. This has required us to spread out our agencies worldwide to deal with transporting our people onto foreign lands without raising eyes."

"So you've been trafficking Batswana who've won the Murder Trials?"

"Trafficking is such a dirty word. This is a much cleaner process of providing you a new life," she says.

I gather my breaths into something calm, a pretense to extract anything useful from Serati. "But how do you decide the winner?" I ask. "Moremi said if I kill my daughter . . . then it all ends."

She sighs. "That's the deal most victims put forth: suggesting something the murderer will find inconceivable, impossible to do. If you fulfill that deal, it activates their final passing."

Who would do that? Kill their baby to save themselves? The silence climbs my back, and I'm too afraid to ask, but I need to know. "What happens if I win, and I've managed to keep my husband and my baby alive?"

She shakes her head. "They are no longer yours. You lost that right. They are dead either way."

I drop my face into my hands, into darkness, everything inside me caves. I won't ever see my baby. I look up. "How is that a win?"

Jan huffs. "What about the people at the airport?"

"They won't remember a thing. We safely disseminated a serum concocted by one of our revered ngaka ya Setswana within the facility."

"So you have Moremi's body?" Jan asks. "I mean, you recovered it from where we buried it? What are the full rules of this trial?"

She shakes her head. "We're not to interfere with the crime scene until the trial is over. The rules are made by the victim. We never fully know what they are, and even if we did, we are not at liberty to give them to you."

"How is it possible that you're able to lead us into these scenarios?" Jan asks, hands raised. "You couldn't have predicted that Nelah and I were going to meet that night or take a drive out on the Oodi-Modipane Road, or that Moremi was going to take a midnight walk. You couldn't have predicted or made certain all those events would coincide into an accident. You just couldn't. It's impossible."

She leans back in her chair, watching me. "Firstly, your microchip was manipulated to control you to cause the accident. Then it's all left to you how you respond. Secondly, the microchip is connected to a database where the AI sorts the list of people into similar attributes. The AI knows you thoroughly, fed from all your daily patterns. It knows what you crave and when." She stares down at her tablet. "*Ginger tea, madombi, and oxtail,* to name a few from this report—your favorite sex position, your mannerisms, speech patterns, when your period starts, when you're ovulating. It leans heavily on hobbies to pick a scenario—your hobbies particularly based on your late-night drives, drunk and sloppy, with your lover."

I feel myself cascading into a swirling abyss of grief, pain and rage. I'm exploding behind the walls of my skin. I want this nuclear bomb of anger to hurt Serati the way it massacres me, so she can understand what I feel, understand it enough to change things for the better. But, no. People like her destroy lives and continue seamlessly with theirs. Hatred is a burning hell, a furnace cremating me, and I'm so scared because soon every moral part of me will vanish. I don't want to become a monster.

"And what if you got to the fiftieth person and no one committed a crime?" Jan says, teeth clenched.

A smile twists up Serati's face. "We never get that far. Statistically, within the first four on the list, one of them is always a killer as per our AI's probability calculations and ranking. Then the next year, we go through the next four. The victim is generally picked from citizens who aren't microchipped."

I was at a disadvantage from the beginning. My consciousness was downloaded into this body, yet there are real criminals out there, without microchips, doing God knows what.

She pins her eyes on Jan. "Unfortunately, Jan, you became an accomplice. You weren't part of the plan."

"What does that mean?" Jan asks, exasperated.

The devil sprawls himself along Serati's smile and I want to drag my nails across her face. "I'm glad you asked. Come this way. What you are about to see is majestic."

Serati walks toward the end of the room, which was obscured by the display units. Jan and I follow her. In the center is an almost circular gorge in the floor. I wonder whether its design is meant to imitate the copper tinge of the Matsieng rocks until I realize—

"That's one of the waterholes," Serati confirms, watching me. The flooring changes from concrete to copper rock. Viscous light blossoms from the deep hole into the ceiling where several spotlights are affixed. "We call them Matsieng. Isn't Xe beautiful? Every death, every killing fills Xer water holes, which act as the urn of our blood, our brothers, our sisters, our brethren," Serati says proudly, and I believe she's seriously fucked in the head. "This is how we keep our crime index so low, particularly homicide. From four thousand three hundred and forty-six homicides every year down to less than ten annually."

Jan and I peer down into the deep crevice, running as a wound in the earth. A deep abyss of blood swirls in the dark. There's an alien hum emanating from its flow, from the throat of this blood ravine, and it travels the length of my neck and arms, warm and inviting, offering a sense of peace, a sense of power. It sends vibrations into my bones. I can't stop myself. I peer further in—strings of whispery screams float from the abyss, choking me with despair, crippling me with a desperate want to tear out my larynx, offer it like a sacred urn to the voices so they pour themselves into it and make a home out of me. My blood throbs against the front-facing parts of my body, the parts facing the crevices, and pushes me toward them. Serati grips my back, and I'm free of its hold. "Stay back. Xe's normally very hungry during the Murder Trials." She glares at me. "Sin is attracted to sin."

I swallow. Step back, shaking with shock. It's like staring into myself. Though I wouldn't consider Matsieng sinful, except that the Murder Trials committee fills Xem with sin or uses Xem to enact evil.

"We give our blood, and we are protected," she says. "Matsieng has every citizen's blood, from when they are born to when they die. This blood has protected our country for years. Has blessed us. We acquire peace through it. A victim, yes, is sacrificed without consent, but their sacrifice is valuable to us. We do everything through Matsieng. Beautiful, no?"

How long has this secret been hidden from the public? Some evil lurks there, sends chills down my back. How long will it take until they can't restrain its excessive hunger? What will happen to us if this tsunami of terror flows into our land, into us? It has my blood. *My* blood. My baby is in her Wombcubator on this same land.

Serati's eyes are steadily focused on me. The hum of blood feeds around us, hums and grows warm with our bodies as she speaks. "Prehistorically, from this waterhole once came a giant. Now it breathes nightmares from the killings and the blood we shed into its lining. Part of your death, your blood, is in here. It knows you very well. It knows

Moremi well. This is what's keeping Moremi alive. This is what keeps you alive until the ritual is over. From the nightmare comes heaven."

"From the nightmare comes heaven," her soldiers repeat at attention.

"We keep discovering new uses for Matsieng's blood. We found over time that Matsieng's power is enhanced more by consuming morally corrupt people's taboo acts rather than ethical people's," Serati says, "hence why we needed to recycle criminally prone bodies. Better yet, society will agree with us to impinge on its privacy by installing these impure people with an AI microchip to secure our safety. In the end, we protect our citizens through Matsieng's power."

Jan clenches his jaw around his fist.

My chest heaves, trying to contain me with some semblance of sanity, but I'm slipping, leaking from the seams of my skin. "This is wrong," I say, trembling. "We never signed up for this."

"We are creating a safe haven for our people," Serati says. "*This* nightmare is the only price we have to pay for that."

"*You're* not paying anything," I say, my voice wobbling with anger.

"I offer certain parts of myself to this urn every week."

I grimace. Step close to her. "Have you offered your father, your mother, your children?"

"I placed my firstborn daughter in here as an inauguration ceremony for my esteemed role as prosecutor."

That, I never expected. "You're sick. Disgusting," I spit, and it's my mind that leaves my mouth, quaking from its cranium. I truly am crazy.

"My firstborn has created a better place for her siblings. She has performed a bigger job than man, and for that, I am proud of her, *will* always be proud of her. People have gone through this rite, and now you are one of the chosen. They have done right by us, and you have to do right by us. I know, it's startling at first, terrifying and traumatizing and confusing, but you will reach the point where your belief is as ours. *This* is an honor."

Anger erupts inside me. If I could rectify things, I would certainly put her on a list for elimination.

"These rules that force us into this kak situation, were they created by the Murder Trials committee?" I ask.

"Not us," she says. "They emanate from Matsieng. We find new discoveries when we experiment with Matsieng's blood. We saw a fascinating phenomenon of using Matsieng's blood in the tower's chemicals to sniff out homicide in the city. We learned we could extend people's lives through science and Matsieng's blood, and we thought we could use the blood to help lower crime, but there were unpleasant results, so we had to set up a committee to manage the practicality of the Murder Trials. For example, we can't see everything since Moremi's energy field destroys all communication feeds from your microchip, an unwanted occurrence resulting from Matsieng's presence in Moremi. Hence, we need to monitor everything when the communication is blocked since we still have access to you. So in a way, we have insurance that should anything bad happen, we can better prepare and protect ourselves." The staccato of her heels echoes as she walks around the waterwombs. "As I mentioned, the victim sets the rules that mysteriously emanate from Matsieng. We haven't yet established how to manipulate these rules, only how to design the purity tests around them. This was conducted through trial-and-error experiments, which helped us understand these rules. From thereon, we proceeded to structure the purity test, and used a system to pick the players, etc."

"What experiments are these?" Jan asks.

"We know culturally that a spirit can't transcend on to the ancestral realm, heaven or hell, or whatever you believe in, if its body was killed or if its life was interrupted in a foul way," Serati says, "so we know the spirit lingers on earth as a ghost—sepoko, as we call it. We studied certain corpses, which were some of our employees who volunteered themselves as experiment subjects—"

"Stop the bullshit jargon," I say. "You mean people who offered themselves to be killed for these experiments."

She ignores my interruption and continues, "Matsieng knows every citizen intimately because we feed Xem your memories and blood. These structures vary worldwide per each country's culture. Back in the day, if someone was killed, people used dingaka tsa Setswana to find the culprit, and through these traditional doctors' spiritual assessment, they would curse the killer, for instance, to reveal themselves by becoming ill or acting mad. We found that Matsieng works in a similar fashion. Now through Matsieng, the lingering spirit is visible to the killer, devout to its vengeance as its goal to transcend, and this is the beautiful part: if the spirit wins, *we*, through Matsieng, transcend the spirit into a new body. Every ghost has its varying ways it can be appeased, which has led to some unpleasant situations we can't control, such as your signal being blocked when Moremi is within your range. So we must watch should any problems arise that might lead to our endangerment."

"Basically," I add, "that will help you should you need to save your asses quickly."

"That's one way to look at it," she says, clasping her hands behind her back. "We must monitor whether the rules change every purity test. This is a risky business because we never know what we'll encounter with every Murder Trial since Matsieng manifests through every ghost in a unique way—but the payoff is huge and worth it."

"A unique way?" Jan asks.

"Every ghost generally acts in the same way," Serati says. "We are unaware of the communication, if there is, happening between the deceased and Matsieng. We have attempted our investigations on the ghosts of our valued employees, which involved one being the murderer and the other the victim—this occurred in a safe, enclosed setting."

I scoff. "Safe."

"But the experiments brought us devastating results because we were interfering with the crime scene and its player," she says. "Members, who are valuable memory holders of this country, suffered a terrible death with no option to reincarnate them. So we've adopted Matsieng's wrath as a law not to interrupt the crime scene."

"Memory holders?" Jan asks. "Care to elaborate?"

"I care not to elaborate. That's very confidential information," Serati says, turning to me. "Your memories are in Matsieng, so you are affected and are part and parcel to the lingering ghost's need to transcend, which in this term allows us to repackage and transcend them into a new body if Moremi wins."

I fold my arms against my body, shock rendering me speechless.

"You all wanted to live in a peaceful world," Serati says. "Unfortunately, peace isn't free. Go on and tell the whole world that the woman you murdered is haunting you, is killing your family. Empathy, I trust, is not what you'll get from them." Then: "Cheer up. You were born at a disadvantage; but that doesn't mean you have to live your life at a disadvantage." She leans forward. "Now you get to rebrand yourself, get an entirely new body, a new identity, start over somewhere else. This time, *you* choose. *Only* if you win." She sighs. "You were chosen for something holy. Some are even grateful for this selection, this blessing. I've heard some revere it as an ancestor's calling."

"It's not a blessing to watch—"

She raises her hand, angry. "Enough." Spit smacks my face. "Fucking deal with the consequences. We have work to do." She crosses her arms. "The deadline is tomorrow. Matsieng's wrath will find the killer and victims, and will burn you both if you don't fulfill your goals and transfer your consciousness. Your arena is defined by the location of its victims. Wherever they go, Moremi follows. They could be in Iceland or on the fucking moon. No location obstructs Moremi's movements, as you've seen."

"But she must have a weakness. *Everyone* has a weakness," I say. "What is hers?"

"This is not some TV game show where you're given the option to call in a favor," Serati says. "This is the fucking Murder Trials. Figure it out. Moremi isn't just a pretty face; she's giving you the illusion of help. People must be careful who they bury before they kill them. There are two of you, yet this girl alone is in the lead."

Jan and I stare at each other. Moremi seemed desperate to find out what happened to her, so of course, I believed she was helping us.

"What about the award committee?" I ask. "They've scheduled me for a forensic evaluation tonight."

"We'll handle them." Serati swipes her palms against her pants. "Follow me."

Jan and I follow her to the steel doors with faces exposed by the glass casing. "Our facility holds a roster of bodies to choose from. If you win, we will process you into this body. Here stands shell one, male, twenty-one years old, five-foot-six, Black, health good, fertile;

shell two . . ." She continues until we reach shell fifty-eight. She stares at Jan with disgust. "To answer your earlier question, unfortunately, you're a hybrid: a murderer and slated victim. But seeing that you are the victim's victim, you are ineligible for a new identity. She is slated to kill you. There is nothing we can do. You chose your path, and this is your only fate." Serati turns to me. "Matsieng's only provided you an hour to decide before Moremi resumes her killing. Then you are free to go. No authorities will interfere with your tasks until the ritual ends." She turns to leave, pauses, says, "Consider this a commercial break from everything. In the meantime, you are free to order a meal of your choice. I'm sure you are in need of some nourishment. If you decide in less than an hour, the clock starts ticking again. Remember: only one person survives, the victim or the murderer."

20:54 /// THREE DEATHS

Serati turns on her heels and disappears. The soldiers stand at all exit points. "Their steak is good," one of the soldiers says. A clock sits on the wall, felling the seconds.

Earlier, I blamed Jan for manipulating me into killing Moremi. I wonder if he regrets now that I'm technically the killer. But he wouldn't want this curse, or else his children would be dead.

"This is fucked up," Jan says. "I can't believe they consider this honorable."

"At least your family is still alive," I say.

"At least, in the end, you'll still be alive," he says.

"Does that sound like a win to you, Jan?" I yell. "With my family gone, my child, my husband? You are the worst mistake of all my life-spans. If I hadn't—if we hadn't . . ."

Jan clenches his hands into fists, anger boiling through him. "You do realize that all this while I'm Moremi's target, I could have run, left you alone to spend the last of my time with my children. All this while I've known I'm going to die. I watched your father die, thinking that I'm next. I saw your mother's body, then it was my turn. How long do I have to wait to die? I stuck to your side, sick with guilt, listening to you doubt me, compare me to a rapist. This isn't just happening to you—it's happening to me, too. I fucked up, yes, but we fucked up together. I gave you a choice that night—to report everything. *I* said I'd follow you, for fuck's sake—but you chose wrong, too." He rakes his hand through his hair.

Emotions still glimmer inside me, despite my three deaths. Tears glob down my face, and it hits me hard that I didn't want to face up to the full blame. It felt safer to put it all on him. "We did something terrible, but we are walking different paths, going through different emotions."

"I've been proving myself to you for over a year, but still nothing counts to you." His lips twist in disgust. "You're hurting, but I can't allow you to keep hurting me with your hurt when we're both suffering." He turns around, facing away from me, covering his face with his hands in frustration.

A soldier steps forward. "Would you like to leave, then?"

Jan looks up from his hands, surprised. "What?"

"It's mandatory for the murderer to remain. You, Koshal, are free to go—well, until Moremi comes for you. Where shall we drop you?"

I turn away. Stare ahead. Swallow. Close my eyes. He will go. And that is fine. He will go. I'm lying to myself, of course. I won't be okay. A cold heaviness drafts through my chest. And the only thing I can think is he's going to leave me alone. Now he's truly going to leave me alone, and I struggle to coalesce the new me with the old me because I feel my old self fall into the next dimension of fear, drown in its viscous shadows. She's suffocating, her body is heavy, dragging the new me down, and I want to kill her, remove myself of her weight. I will have to deal with this alone, and there's nothing more frightening than—

The soldier straddles the gun with his legs, rolls his shoulders back and forth. "Mfetu, you should've just killed the girl," he says and my blood curdles, storms my bones with a freezing, burning anger. "It'd have saved you a whole lot of shit. 'Least then you'd have a chance at winning. Most men who enter the Murder Trials leave richer than they were before because they killed a fucking bitch; there's still more girls to go around anyhow. What's losing one compared to the value you carry. You won't believe how many of us are out there as free murderers in new bodies just 'cause we made the right choice: Killed. A. Fucking. Bitch."

The debris of overwhelming rage extracts itself from my body, an invisible force that revolves around me tornado-wise, and I am in the calm of its center. My voice is dagger-sharp, slices through my lips, sweeps the air aside: "What was her name?"

Irritation narrows the soldier's eyes. "Who?"

"The girl you killed."

His eyes bolt, protrude with fear. He waves his hand. "Behind us now."

My fingers tingle with the static of unrecognizable loss and hurt. "What's *your* name?"

He tilts his head. "Why?"

"I want to remember it when I come for you."

He smirks. "Mxm, mma, you ain't shit just cause you can't die."

The anger returns into my body, settles into the vortex of my spirit, changing me at a molecular level I can't begin to understand, tightening its nucleus, waiting to split and cause mass destruction to things like this man. If only I was that powerful. This, I believe, is the hungry vengeance that overwhelms Moremi. And killing my family will never satiate her.

"Anyway," the soldier says, "where would you like us to drop you?"

"Is that what you would do?" Jan asks the soldier, his face unreadable.

"I see no point in staying," the soldier says. "In fact, I'd consider myself lucky not having to deal with this mess. I'm sure the sex was good, but it's not worth it. Too much baggage."

"Too much baggage? Do you understand her child will die? Her parents already have, and her husband and brother will soon follow suit."

"If she wasn't sleeping around behind her husband's back—"

"I did it to my wife, too."

"That's different."

"Correction: Neither of us were sleeping around. We just slept with each other."

"Women get themselves in these messes. Let them deal with it. The others did exactly that."

"The others?"

"Men like you who were lucky to not have initially liquidated their victim. Sure, you have children and responsibilities, but this is the only time you have to live out whatever fantasies you have."

Jan pinches the bridge of his nose. "What is it about superficial people thinking they and I follow the same principles? Women don't get themselves in these messes; men like you fuck them up so they can't trust an honest guy." He exhales. "No. I will accompany her until the end of the trial. It is my trial as well."

I turn my head to him, but he's not looking at me—*won't* look at me, *can't* look at me. He's just been given an opportunity to be with his daughters with the little time he has, and he's sacrificed it to stay with me. And those poor girls will never see their father again. *Never*.

"I made this mess, too," Jan says. "She can't leave, I *won't* leave." His morals shock me.

The soldier scoffs. "Well, your funeral."

"I've decided," I whisper, cutting off the soldier's chuckle, and he stares at me surprised. Everyone's head turns to me. I point at the fourth steel-brushed door to the right, a woman with dusk-brown skin, eyes sealed in peaceful slumber. "I choose shell ten." Black female, twenty years old, fertile, healthy . . . "We will leave now. To visit your children, Jan. But we won't be able to stay for long."

"Any time is more than enough," Jan says.

A time that will afford us freedom, a murder that will heal us into new lives.

21:21 /// A RABBIT HOLE OF TERROR

Amid their divorce, Jan and his ex-wife-to-be still cohabit for the sake of their twins. Our pod-car drives southeast toward their Extension 12 residence, a brick-faced estate towering in what used to be four independent residences which he bought to his wife's liking, demolished the luxurious homes, consolidated the four plots to build their one home. On the way, he called his lawyer, confirmed that he'd update his will after he'd signed it.

The iron-wrought gates slide open, and Jan stares quietly at the florid, landscaped yard. Two German shepherds bark, approaching and sniffing the pod-car. A woman sits in the garden, under a mulberry tree, reading a novel, drinking a cocktail. Two children in a blue plastic garden pool, splashing and laughing. A bit late for such. Don't they have a bedtime?

Jan steps out of the car, turns to me. "I shouldn't be long." His eyes are wet. He takes a deep breath, crushes his eyes shut, seals himself completely. When he opens his eyes, his expression is clear and calm. He pushes his ochre-black hair back from his forehead, wipes the sweat with the sleeve of his shirt. The dogs follow him eagerly as he offers them a scratch.

His wife looks up, studies him, looks behind him, eyes riveted on me. If she's thinking something, I can't tell what it is. Although, she looks at Jan with less concern and more irritation. He passes her toward his kids, drops to his knees, stares at them. His shoulders quake and I realize he's crying, face crashing into his hands.

Startled, his daughters crawl toward him, reach to his face with their chubby fingers. They stand together and wrap their arms around his brawny form, and they, too, start crying, unable to fully reach his back with their fingers. A tot's hug is tiny in its form, but I've always marveled at the feeling of being held by small arms, the impact large and freeing. Tears prickle my eyes, and I can't watch anymore.

His wife gets up, and I expect her to approach Jan, to take control of this situation. Instead, she heads in my direction. Stomps. Stops outside the pod-car. Stares long and hard, blue eyes burning into me. "So, you're the homewrecker? The pisser around my husband." Pisser. Jan's father must have lodged that into her mouth with some kiss.

"I wonder what your mother-in-law has to say about that," I say, and she narrows her eyes, confusion burrowing wrinkles into her forehead. "Who's worse?" I ask. "The bitch sleeping with your husband or the bitch sleeping with her husband's father?" I raise my hand, dismissing the topic. "Your babies are crying, and *I'm* your concern? *Your* babies are crying." My voice breaks, and tears flood my face. "*Your* babies are crying."

She steps back. Stunned. Shakes her head, and a ringlet of blond curls falls across her freckled face. She turns her neck, watches them, the back of her neck free of any microchip interference. "He and the father are the same, you know," she says. "Jan's far more sinister, although he tries to rein it in, to hide it. I always told him he's just a dormant volcano that'll one day wreak havoc. Why else do you think I'm divorcing him?"

No, I won't backtrack again. I won't doubt. His only weakness was last night's strategy. "*He's* divorcing you."

"It's not my fault I fell in love with his father. It's *his* fault." The loaded statement hits me hard. It's not what she says, but how she says it, like he designed their affair. "He might as well have sold me to his father," she adds, incredulously open about the affair.

"Is that your strategy in the divorce proceedings: your husband prostituted you to his father?"

"It helps that the father had a prior sexual harassment lawsuit." She stares at me, blue irises a burning flame the dark night keels over. "Even though you're literally wiretapped"—she gestures to the back of her neck—"there are many ways to read our conversation, say if they were to subpoena footage from your microchip storage."

I've never met someone who could compute diabolically in this manner by using an unplanned encounter with me as part of her arsenal. She points at Jan now, and my eyes follow her finger—skirting over the wide-angled glass of the front of the house, the watered lawn glistening under the garden lights, the rose bushes—what could literally be a viewing displayed in a courthouse. "*That's* why I don't want him around the kids. *That's* why I'm fighting for full custody."

The scene shows a disheveled man breaking down in front of his children, his mistress nearby. And I wonder what else she has documented when he was at a low, and what type of lows he's had. He's not just about to lose his kids to custody, but he's losing his life, losing his kids to this type of parent.

She gestures wide with her hands. "For him to bring his lover to the house, in front of his kids. Aren't they going through enough? And *you*." She jabs her finger in my direction. "You came willingly, not even thinking about them? You don't understand what it means to be a mother." An octave lower, "No wonder all those babies died inside you. There's nothing in you to give."

I clutch the fabric of my coat in my hands. There's no point to arguments and acerbic statements. "Please," I whisper. "Your babies . . . your babies are crying."

She tuts, retreats into the shadowy garden, a hub of birdsong mingling with the girls' soft cries. Jan kisses his daughters on the tops of their heads, their crying closing to a quiet, and he walks back stiffly.

The gates creak open. A glare of lights. A sleek black car silently pulls in. Several men rush out toward the back seat's door, night cladding their faces and suits. A tinted window slides down, and the interior lights spill out, revealing the serpentine trail of smoke from a cigar tucked into a man's wrinkled, plump fingers, spotted with age. The chauffeur opens the door. A shiny patent leather shoe steps out onto the paved ground, connected to the hefty leg of an old man. Aarav Koshal. Surrounded by five bodyguards.

His eyes switch to our car, Jan and Mel and his twins, and me.

"I did warn my son of the consequences of pissing around the likes of you," he says, voice deep and dark. "Cunts like you always regret saying no. Remember? That 'no' has taken you down a rabbit hole of terror."

Questions explode in my mind, but only two hold unequivocal terror: *Does he know what we did? Is he the reason we're in this position?*

I find my hands crushing his collars, shouting, "Did you do this?"

Several men hike their rough hands under my arms and haul me away from him.

"Bitch!" Aarav spits, shaking a rubble of fat clinging to his jaw. "Do you understand the hell of a mess you've placed my family in? My entire business? The whole fucking industry? Because of your fucking need to fuck."

Jan sidles to my side, hustles the men from my personal space. "What the hell's going on?" He spins around. "Ba?"

"I'll handle him." Aarav raises his hands, a direction for his guards to back up. Comes up nose-to-nose with his son. Fury lit in his eyes. "I've been cleaning up after you for years. When will you learn to piss right?"

Jan's jawline ticks. "What's this about?"

"The girl," he intones. "Where did you bury the body? I don't care about what you did. Tell me, where is the body?"

Jan's fingers twitch, and my breaths jam in my throat. If Aarav went to despicable lengths to provide his son two new bodies and halt his life sentence, could he—no, he can't have a hand in what happened the night of the accident?

"I am on the fucking Murder Trials board," Aarav says, upper lip trembling in anger. "Screwing in the fucking bundus with a wiretapped bitch? Burying a fucking body. You thought we wouldn't see? I gave you the safe option of a roster of women you could screw, yet you decided to let this woman take our name to hell?"

"A roster of women who are your employees," Jan says.

"Willing women," Aarav emphasizes. "We wouldn't have this headache."

I wish Moremi would tear his limbs apart. I'd watch her eat them.

Jan crosses his arms. "If you were watching, then you should know where we buried the woman." Jan taps his chin. "Unless you're not. Another of your lies. For the first time, your power can't walk through a closed door. Which of the board members snitched to you? *Who* are the board members? And that threat you keep hanging over my head is invalid now—you can't force me to do what you want anymore. I'm good as dead."

"You have brought nothing but shame to this family," he spits. "After everything I have done for you, you unappreciative—" He glares at me. Considers Jan. "That girl has something that belongs to a lot of powerful people. Our investors are worried, the type of people you don't want to ruffle. Think about the consequences of your actions—you're good as dead, you think? You have twins, and they won't be destroyed. They'll have to live with what you leave them.

"Where is the body, son?" His eyes flick to me, cold and dreadful. Then back to Jan. "Son, I can protect you. Not this woman, but you. You still want to see your girls grow up, don't you? Then tell me where the girl is." A sprinkle of sweat coats his forehead.

"No," Jan says. "Not until you tell me what's going on."

Aarav appears desperate. For a second, I expect him to fall to his knees and beg Jan. But just his shoulders slump.

"If you must have it that way." Aarav removes his cuff links, cocks his head to the side, and his guards are alert. "Restrain them. Melissa, take the girls into the house." Melissa hurriedly collects her children from the pool and tracks into the house without a look back.

"Search their car." Two men grab Jan, and two men grab me. The rest open our car doors and hunt inside. Aarav rolls his sleeves to his elbows, revealing hairy forearms. Bends low to Jan, who's brought down on his knees. "You're as good as dead, eh? I can still save you. Same deal as before. Procure you a new body, a different identity. Just work with me, son."

"Save her and her family, too," Jan says. "That is the deal. Then I'll give you everything you want."

Aarav's eyes burn me. He wants nothing more than to crush my life beneath the soles of his shoes. "Son, you have unleashed a monster. I do not have the power to stop Moremi's murder spree and the power of Matsieng's blood. I only have the power to transfer you into a different identity."

I flinch when he calls out her name. Why is Moremi so important to him?

Jan sighs. "Then, unfortunately, you are useless to us."

"Damn it, Janith! Forget about me. But think about your twins. If you let this nuclear bomb of a problem escalate, it won't just kill you, it'll kill your daughters. *That* is what we're dealing with."

"What does Moremi have on you that has you so afraid?" Jan asks. "What have you done this time?"

Stunned, I stare at Aarav. His lips smack out incomprehensible words, and I'm fearful of the crimes that could be far worse than the sexual harassment cases.

"Sir, we found something." The guard procures the satchel from the back seat, ruffles through it, and decants the brass humidor, the pills, the quantum computer, the chiffon pouch of microchips. My heart kicks against my chest.

Aarav closes his eyes. Exhales. Relief dissolves the sweat from his forehead. "We have what we need." Tilts his head to the right. "Incinerate them."

The guard freezes. "Sir, the board member warned us not to interfere, or we'll face Matsieng's wrath."

"Fuck her wrath. Burn them."

"No, no, no, you can't burn those," I shout, kicking up my legs as the men tighten their hold around my arms. "I need those to convince Moremi not to kill my family."

"I don't care about your family," Aarav spits.

The bodyguards drag us as he follows the guard to the backyard garden where a fire pit stands among a mass of concrete cut into the form of a hemisphere; a hollow space resides in the center where the burning takes place. Old ashes cloud its oval metal husk. The guard removes the spark screen, places tinder and wood inside, ignites the fire with a long-stemmed lighter, and a fire crackles.

“Stop!” Jan shouts, but his father ignores him as he grabs the microchips and humidor and throws them into the fire. Its tongues lick and stretch across the only thing I have to save my family. Jan throws a punch, but his father blocks it, shocked. Spits insults at his son: “You spoilt fucking brat.”

“Let me go!” I scream. The fires twist and bend the surfaces of my saviors. What am I going to tell Moremi? How am I going to stop my unborn baby from dying? Moremi’s going to think I was pulling one over on her.

“You decided to risk your family’s life,” Aarav says, tipping Jan’s chin up. “For that, you are no longer my son. Unfortunately, your daughters will have to grieve your death. Good day, Janith.”

His guards release us.

Pure animosity saturates my muscles, pours through my skin. “You will pay for this,” I shout. “I swear you will pay for this.” I drag my nails into his face. He spits, throws a punch, and Jan blocks it. Three lines scathe his stubbled cheek, which he pats with a white handkerchief.

“My baby,” I whisper. “I have to save my baby.” I run to the fire pit, clamber onto its concrete surface, dig my fingers through its flames. “My baby, oh God! My baby! I have to save my baby.”

Aarav climbs into his car, and it sweeps out the gates as I dissolve into the flames, unable to die.

21:39 /// THIS HORRID REALITY

Jan retrieves two shovels and several floodlights from his garage. Places them into the trunk of the car.

The fire has died down. All that remains is the brass husk of the humidor and broken pieces of microchips, nothing retrievable, in the fire pit. My back against it. Jan on his knees, arms surrounding me. I smell of smoke, me, a woman always burning.

"It's over," I cry. "This was our only hope. My baby, oh my baby. How am I going to save her?"

Jan wraps his arms around me, kisses my forehead. "We still have the microchip to collect from Moremi's body. *This* time we'll be careful of how we contain the evidence."

He gathers me up.

"Your father," I whisper. "How can people like him exist? How can they share the same air as us and continue to enact evil? How many Matsieng are there in the world, ignoring our plight? Xe could empower these elements to stop him, yet Xe won't. Why? Matsieng drinks our blood, feels our pain—why won't Xe do anything?"

"This is the world we live in," Jan says. "Murders, xenophobia, racism, terrorism—"

"No, that is not how the world will remain after I die." Something flashes in my gut: anger and hatred, making me come alive. "Your father has to die. I sacrifice myself for that."

A short gasp from Jan.

"I murdered Moremi with no other choice," I say. "Now I choose. I will murder your father. I will murder people like him. I will save my daughter first, then kill him—I don't know how and if there will be time to do both, but *that* is the legacy I will leave for my daughter. I will die by killing."

Jan freezes. Swallows. Nods. Holds my hand. Peace and acceptance smile across his face. "I concur. I will be your accomplice."

The crime scene. Disturbed soil, upturned earth. It's astounding that last night's horrid occurrence happened out in the open. The makeshift grave is but two steps from the side of the road, shielded by a barrier of thorn trees. Beside new tracks from off-road vehicles, I can make out a sludge of patterns leading to the grave from where we dragged her, Jan's footsteps and my bare feet going back and forth. We never thought, *never thought,* to clear up that trail. I don't know how we managed to push through the thorn trees unscathed because it's difficult finding a gap to walk through, until we use the barrier of our clothes to mask our skin from any scratches.

Using the floodlights, the scene almost looks daylit.

"Do people really find this honorable?" Jan asks, eyes wide. "Killing people to save people? They're actually rewarded for it?"

Unable to answer, I stand in front of the grave. The surrounding area is level except for this convex bit of sand. And a second grave. Papa. She buried him here.

Jan squats, pats the lump of earth. "How'd Moremi manage to get your father's body here?"

Guilt forms thickly in my throat, making it difficult to speak. "Same way she reached Mama mid-flight, I suppose."

He watches me watching the grave. The first time he's looked at me since our argument at the Murder Trials headquarters. I want him to touch me, to tell me that it'll be okay.

"We don't have time." He bends on one knee, begins digging.

I fall to my knees, cradle the gravel covering Papa's body. I swallow, mumble, "I don't think I can do it in the light." To exhume her from the grave, then excavate the microchip from her decomposing body.

Jan's hand slips around my neck, and his thumb carves circles along my microchip. "It'll take longer if I do it alone. But I can do it, if you can't."

I nod. "You're right." I get on my knees and rake my fingers through the soil, hard stone and thorns scribbling my palms.

"I'm sorry," he whispers.

"I'm sorry, too," I say.

"Do you still regret it?"

"It would have happened either way, with or without our affair."

"But do you still regret it?"

"Us? I don't know. Don't make me lie to you," I say.

"Would Moremi be dead if it weren't for the system? Would you be a killer if it weren't for the system setting this trap?" He stops digging, leans on his knee. "I grew up here. I used to be so proud of how safe it is, how the crime numbers are almost zero for rape, murder, for theft. I've felt safe knowing my girls don't have to walk around the city watching their backs. Only to realize that what's bankrolling this illusion of peace is a fucked-up system that sacrifices us based on some AI that cherry-picks who will be a victim and who will be a murderer. To make matters worse, the fucking discrimination. Already you're branded rotten if you're microchipped, and your odds are already low that you won't be a murderer. And without a microchip, you're basically a victim."

My fingers scud loose rock, trapping soils in my nail beds. And it hits me as I say it: "How long will it take them to remove those dividing lines, to pick whoever they want? To eliminate what *they* don't want? If they've been hiding this secret from us, what else have they been hiding?" I stare up at Jan, watch the shock dance with the lights in his irises, watch him shiver. "We're just two people, Jan. What uprising could we ever accomplish?"

His upper lip trembles. "I can't go like this, leave my girls to grow up in such a system. Who will protect them?"

Something cracks inside me; its tornado threatens to drag me into its depthless depression. If I lose myself, I won't have my faculties to take me through, to save my family. I gather my thoughts desperately, something to ground me, to take me away from the pain.

"Would you have over four thousand three hundred people die every year or just ten?" I ask.

Jan's eyebrows spring up. "Don't tell me you're in support of this?"

"I'm not in support of how it's done, but it's saved many lives. In our old traditions, there were more respectable ways for *animal* sacrifices, feeding their souls and essences to a god of some sort for benevolence to fight against drought, famine, war, to obtain fortune and miracles. I guess this is the dirty upgrade: *we're* the animals. Since they've elevated a level up, they're able to achieve this utopia through an altered nightmare and . . ."

"They could be obtaining more that they're not telling us," he says. "Grading us in some form to attain a higher level of something since certain bodies are valued low for body-hopping schemes—the same process could be established by the Murder Trials committee."

"Disgusting. We're like cattle, corralled for slaughter," I say. "This nightmare is so well-built to force the players into its game. I can't just sit and do nothing. I mean, I can, but everyone I love dies. I can't kill myself; I'm revived. Moremi, too, is trapped in this nightmare. It's not that she wants to kill. She's driven to avenge her death through violence, whether she likes it or not. I feel terribly sorry for her because it's our fault she's in this. We ruined her life, and she deserves to be saved if possible. But the only way to save my daughter is to defeat Moremi, and the only way to defeat Moremi is to kill my daughter. There must be a way to save both, no? In such a way that allows us to finish Aarav."

Suddenly his eyes grasp me. "We *can* do something. We have to. For our daughters. For Moremi, so there are no more people going through what she went through. We have to find a way."

"Earlier at the airport, Moremi mentioned something about her winning and getting closer to death if she gives me more time," I say. "She must've been referring to the Murder Trials. I think she has the power to give us more time but at the sacrifice of herself. Maybe if we convince her enough, we can find a balancing act where she gives us more time without risking her dying."

Jan laughs. "I'm sorry, love, but I've negotiated many difficult deals, and Moremi is a hard sell. She's addicted to death to get her revenge. The only way to convince her of anything is if you kill your unborn daughter—she won't budge on that."

I sigh, musing. "I'll still think of something. We have time before Moremi goes for my daughter, so for now, we can focus on figuring out Moremi's life and—I hate to think this—but that may give us a clue on how to defeat her should I have to save my daughter. But Moremi's life could also give us a clue on how to save both. And whatever gap in time we have, we handle your father."

"That's a perfect plan," he says, then noticing my expression, he asks, "What? What's wrong?"

"I just realized we're going to find out more about Moremi while I've little information about the history of my body," I say. "I mean, I had to accept that I'd never get answers, and for a while, I got over it, got used to not knowing. But it hurts terribly that I may die without knowing about my body and what happened to my family. And the only living person who can give me the truth is my brother, whom I know will never, ever give me an inch of the truth, and who may die before he does."

"Perhaps we can threaten him, given that Moremi will harm him. At this rate, whatever crime we commit is null. But," he adds, "should you win the Murder Trials, perhaps you may have the privilege of receiving intel on this body."

Speechless, I nod. Quickly, he resumes digging.

Last night, our feverish panic masked how difficult it is to dig a grave. We burrow through the earth with our hands, like animals, scraping off time, carving rock, splintering our nails. Hot breaths chug from our mouths. Sweat rains down from our foreheads. Our effort hasn't brought us any closer to Moremi's body. But I can smell it, through the dirt: a burning, sickly sweet scent saturating in rotting meat. The odor crawls like maggots up the alley of my throat, pools on my tongue. I gag. Nothing. Spit.

I slump onto my rear, panting. "It didn't take so long last night."

Jan persists. Sheer concentration. Face glistening. Digs, digs, digs. I fold over onto my knees again, continue. Finally, our fingers scrabble upon her body. I stop, wipe the sweat from my face. Moremi. Discolored. Stiff. Cold. Blisters in her skin. Her half-lidded eyes, exposed sclera, stained with splotches of tache noire. Jan sways, clasps his mouth. She's unrecognizable from the monster we know her as. The slippage of her skin beneath my fingers makes me sick.

The stench of death rots into my nostrils. I look elsewhere as we turn her stiff body over, search her pockets hoping to find other stuffed-away items, but zilch.

"I'm not cutting out that microchip from her neck," Jan says. Swallows. "Peeling her . . . skin . . . was . . . I can't." His face greys like he's about to be sick.

"Are you okay?" In all of this, I've never wondered how he was holding up.

He's startled. "I don't know. I've locked parts of myself up, inside myself, but they're finding their way out, and . . . I don't know."

I rub his shoulder. "I understand." I hug him. "It won't be okay, but it's okay now."

He exhales.

"There's no need to remove her microchip," I say. "We just need to dock a quantum computer to her neck. It'll upload everything, and we can watch it."

Holding my breath, I inch toward her neck, marked with livid bruises, stained a greenish-blue hue, where her blood has come to rest. There's a code on her microchip which corresponds with its reader.

"Fuck," I whisper.

"What?"

"This microchip has to be read by a specific quantum computer. It's for security purposes."

"Might she have it?"

"If she has a bunch of microchips illegally, then she must have a quantum computer to read them. Which your father destroyed."

"A backup, then?" Jan pauses. "Kids are noisy. When it goes quiet, peaceful, you know they're doing something they're not supposed to. You look for them, and you find them making a mess in your bedroom."

"What's your point?" I ask.

"It's been suspiciously quiet. Where is Moremi all this while?"

"I don't want to think about it. My daughter is number one, so Moremi can't reach her yet without going through everyone. You're still alive—that's my barometer for now. If you're still alive, then my daughter is alive."

He nods. Muses. "Whatever was on those microchips was enough of a threat to my father's legacy," he says.

"What if your father found her home and destroyed it, too?" I ask. "That night we hit her, she must've been running or planning to do something with those microchips. She was running away from your father."

"What if she has a secret home that no one knows about?" Jan says. "If she went to great lengths to obtain these microchips and flee, she must have a safe place to hide *other* things."

"Your father didn't burn everything," I say, making my way to the open car, retrieving her journal and screenplay. "Her journal."

"It's scribblings for her creative work," he says.

I page through it. "The residence listed here is Kgale Estate. She's scribbled, 'home at 8:00 p.m.' and various times for other days. Wait, isn't that the gated community where your father's employees live?"

"It is, but she stopped working for him," Jan says.

"At the office. Not outside work hours."

"Jesus. We can't go there. Even if we did, we'd find nothing. They own it. They have access to it."

"Well, the character in this screenplay lives at *that* gated community," I say. "Moremi noted down times when she left the office, times she got home. Between those gaps, she's written 'black hole' in caps."

"What's the time gap?" Jan asks.

"Five hours plus. Her character has no recollection of what happened within those five hours."

"Something disturbing is going on. What if the screenplay is a ruse in case someone chanced upon it?"

"Then we need to find out where her real home is," I whisper.

He stares at the body. "Figure she might tell us?"

"No, she's going to make this difficult for us. Anyway, seems like she has amnesia. The only thing she seems to remember is her accident and her desire to avenge her death. Wait. Her cell phone."

"What about it?" Jan asks.

"We can retrieve her movements from it. Previous movements that might lead back to her real home."

"Her cell phone was not on her person. I checked," he says. "Besides, I doubt she'll go to a secret location with a technological device that could identify its exact location. A device that people like my father could infiltrate."

"You're right."

Then it occurs to me that we only searched her clothes and backpack. Not a thorough search if we don't include her body. I kneel and start unbuttoning her torn jacket and clothes.

Jan grips my arm. "What are you doing?"

"Maybe there's a clue or something on or in her body that might help us."

Jan steps back. "You want us to undress her?"

"We don't have time, Jan." I hold my breath from the fusty enclosing smell of the decaying body as I probe my fingers along her arms, abdomen, and legs, looking for anything perhaps sealed into the skin.

"There's nothing," Jan says.

"Help me turn her over," I say.

He grabs hold of her ankles as I hoist my hands beneath her armpits, and we flip her onto her front.

"Hold her leg," I say.

"This is . . . an intrusion of her privacy."

I glare at him. "We're way past that, don't you think? Hold on." I peer up along her thigh. Beneath the band of her panty line is a tattoo, a series of numbers, one set with a negative number and a house number reading 45083.

"Coordinates," Jan notes, tipping his head back from the smell. He types them into his wrist, where a hovering hologram displays their corresponding location: "Phakalane, roughly twenty-five minutes away. Why'd she tattoo *that* onto herself?"

"What if that's her secret residence?" I say. "But why? Most importantly, should we risk going there?"

He checks his watch. "We left the Murder Trials headquarters at 9:15 p.m., which means Moremi's next killing's at 10:15 p.m. It's 10:00 p.m. We only have fifteen minutes."

I swallow. "I'll take that risk."

"Are you sure?"

"My daughter's not next, right?" I say, desperately. "You're not next, otherwise Moremi'd be here. That's what matters now."

"Okay."

I tug his hand. "Jan, what if she left this behind on her body because she knew something might happen to her?"

"Maybe she was leaving a message behind for authorities if her body was found." He nods. "This has to be it."

Jan quietly wraps her back in her clothes, wipes the grime and blood from her neck, stares at her face, starts to cry. "Forgive me," he whispers.

"Jan," I whisper.

"We never really think about our actions when we're thinking about ourselves," he says. "You were right last night. One day a man could do this same thing to my daughter, kill her and reason the same way I did to protect his daughter."

"We have to break this cycle," I say, brushing aside the hair sweat-matted to his scalp. "And we will. This is how we pay for what we did."

He kisses my fingers, smiles softly when he remembers the dirt in them. "Who'd have thought I'd still love these fingers even after they buried someone."

I pull them away and kiss his lips instead. The warmth, the heated hour on our backs, the fatigue in our bones slows down in this kiss, removes us from this horrid reality. Our breaths, connecting our lungs, are the only drugs allowing us sanity from everything.

He leans his forehead against me, hand cupping my neck, eyes peering deep into mine. "I love you," he whispers.

"I love you, too."

We stand, and I stare at Moremi's body. Is there a way to communicate with her using her corpse? I lean forward to her face and whisper into her ear, "Moremi, it's me, Nelah. I don't know if you can hear me. But we're here. We've found clues to a secret location you had written down. You want the truth, meet us there." I stare at him now. "We're taking her body with us."

He muses. "What other choice do we have? We *may* need her biometrics to access her home."

I jump. Point. "What's that?"

Jan spins. Further out, a night-clad figure in the withering dark walks toward us.

"Hurry," Jan says. We raise Moremi into the trunk. The figure closes in. Mama. I dump myself into the passenger seat. Jan keys the ignition. The car revs.

Mama picks up her pace, starts running. A cheetah on the loose. The car soars into the air. She leaps onto the hood, smashes her fist through the windshield. Jan yanks the wheel manically side to side until the car flings her to the ground, headfirst, where she skims to a still.

She rights her loose head. Wipes off dirt. Stands. Stares at us. Bestial rage crucifies her face as we disappear into the dark.

22:25 /// TRUTH BOMB

Our car winds through a narrow Phakalane road hemmed in by thorn bushes and paloverde trees. My chest's heated with remorse. My crimes have desecrated my mother, forced her into a horrifying role. How can I ever repent for what I've done? And now we're ten minutes late.

"You sure this the right place?" Jan whistles. "This is high-end real estate."

I shrug as I pinpoint the house number in a suburb of privacy, modern architecture, lawns, and driveways. Rosebushes and kids' scooter bikes are bumming it out in the scatter-rained gardens.

He slows onto the driveway adjacent to the garage of a brick-faced double-story, lined with a strip of grass. There's a wall on either side of the gabled house that separates the front yard from the back. The front windows are dark, no lights on.

Jan switches off the ignition. "I'll jump the wall and break in from the back to open the front door for you."

"No time. Break down the front door."

His eyes widen. "How are we going to carry a dead body into the house without getting caught by the neighbors?"

"It's 10:00 p.m. Looks like a geriatric neighborhood. They're probably passed out."

"Which is where young couples hunt real estate: for the quiet."

"Look, who fucking cares? It's not our problem," I say, stepping out of the car, clicking open the trunk. "That's the Murder Trial Committee's headache. They want us to participate in this sick game of theirs as they watch with their booze and bets, then they'll have to deal with the mess."

"Good point."

I gather Moremi's feet, Jan shimmies his hands under her armpits, and we hoist her out. Opposite us, a car trundles onto an identical driveway. Doors swing open. A young mother is surrounded by two toddler boys with party hats and party blowers jumping out from the car with squeals, the streetlights like dancing candles around them.

The mother carries a box of birthday presents from the car's back seat. Her smile freezes. She stops short. Watches Jan kick down the front door, and both of us promptly carry a decomposing body inside. Her box falls to the ground when I return to collect Moremi's journal and screenplay. I wave, and smile. The woman runs, hustling her boys into the house, locks the door, sweeps open the curtain, and stares at me with a phone to her ear, hand trembling. The authorities will remedy the situation by tampering with her memory.

"What if Moremi doesn't live alone?" Jan asks, standing by knee-height woven baskets decorated in zigzag patterns that remind me of mud huts and the patterns that were imprinted onto their façades. We hesitate in the hallway, can't see much through the side-lit windows. Jan picks a poker from the fireplace, stands adjacent to me under the dining room's arch as he bounds through every room, leaving the doors opened.

Returns, smiling. "She has a cinema room. Fucking brilliant. She has everything we need down there. You've got to see this. I think she was working on something."

I sigh in relief, staring at the ebony African masks hanging on the wall, surrounded by wood scents from the flooring and exposed rafters. "We can upload the contents of her microchip."

A neat, luxurious home, with an open-plan kitchen with black-grouted subway tiles, living room with a beige sectional couch, a modest office, blond wood shelves crammed with books, a spacious garden with a hot tub surrounded by fir trees, and an upper floor with two bedrooms. No framed pictures.

The cinema room. Humble. A starlit ceiling. We stand at the back, moving down a set of thick-carpeted stairs flanking one side of the three rows of plush leather seats draped in greys and black colors. The screen, shadowed and blank, upfront with a game console and a satellite feed. Of course, she's a cinephile and gamer. Has she housed any of her private slasher films here? Who are her closest friends? Who does she spend downtime with in this home? Told her deepest secrets? Has anyone even tried to reach her? What was she before we destroyed her life? I feel despicable because we've annihilated a woman and everything she's worked hard for.

Jan picks a tablet from a front-row seat, flicks on the home automation system's interface. Switches on the lights. The screen glares blue. One wall is clad with hundreds of famous film posters, genres ranging from thriller to horror, encasing the cliché typical frozen pose of a screaming woman, blood-dabbed in pop art colors. Moremi, a horror auteur, is now stuck in a real-life horror show. What does she think of that? Consider this a satiric spin on the final girl? It is, after all, contained in my microchip's footage. What if, centuries later, this footage will be used for documentaries to expose our government, the corruption—everything we've done to Moremi and all that has been done to us? Either way, both victim and murderer are *always* supported by obsessive fans.

The cold dark huddles around us, reeking of death, rotten skin, and mildew.

Jan lies her face down on the floor.

My phone rings. Eli.

Deep lines of frustration scathe Jan's forehead.

I click "answer."

"Hey, babe, how'd the site visit go?" Eli asks.

"What?"

"Your Mahalapye project."

Oh. "Sorry, it's a bit crazy down here. Workers used the wrong concrete mix. That's a financial headache and screw-up we're remedying."

"It's after ten. Don't tell me you're still out there."

"Talking to one of the suppliers—no one sleeps in this industry," I say.

"Right. Well, I'm almost done reading the fairy tales. I never thought it'd be so peaceful reading to our unborn baby." A pause. "I miss you. Let me see your face."

I stare at Jan. Spin toward a plain wall. Activate the video call. Smile.

"Where are you?" he asks.

"One of the barracks."

I signal to Jan, who interrupts from behind the phone, "Boss, there's a problem with the foundation—"

"Have to go," I say. "Talk in the morning. Sleep well."

"I love you," he says. My guts squirm with bile. I hang up.

"What?" Jan asks.

"I just got a strange feeling from that call."

"Nothing regarding him can be worse than our predicament," Jan says.

"I don't trust Eli. He's always up to something," I say. "There's nothing I can think of that can give him a leg up on us."

"Do you think he knows that Moremi is after him?" Jan asks.

"He'd be dead by now if he did. The victims don't know until they see Moremi. But Eli works for the police. Surely, he must have someone giving him confidential information."

"Well, there's no evidence to prove that," Jan says, raising his hands in frustration. "We've nothing to worry about except getting distracted by *worrying*. Surely, I hope that Moremi will go for him before me. If she were to kill me before him . . . I mean, you can't love that cockroach more than me. I'm stuck in this with you, not him."

"Hae, Jan, whom I love is not important—"

"People are dying," Jan says, "your love is worth my life right now. The less you love me, the earlier I die."

"Jan, of course, I love you."

"You just don't know who you love more. How fucking great."

I press my hands to his chest. "No, that's not—"

"Let's get on with it." He moves toward a workstation adjacent to the screen. "I found an identical quantum computer to dock onto her microchip. To move forward, we need to experience her memories." Jan's breath is uneasy when he speaks. "How the fuck does this work? I've never had a microchip."

I bring up the screen of the quantum computer. "Press your thumb down at a ninety-degree angle. It'll snatch DNA data from your fingerprint scan. This will connect us wirelessly and, with the help of her pills, it'll put us into the simulation by manipulating our brain and forcing us into a deep sleep."

Jan plants his finger onto the screen. "How do you know all of this?"

I smile sadly. "My husband used to do this sometimes when he'd assess my memory files for undetected infractions. Sometimes we'd watch them on our Plasma."

Jan's eyes widen. "Jesus. You do know that wasn't necessary, right?"

"I know. But better him than dealing with some police officer."

Jan cups my cheek. "I want you to win."

"I want both of us to win." I smile and resume explaining. "Eli would say 'the DNA is the storehouse of all your information,'" I say, mimicking my husband whilst placing the coal-black handheld quantum computer into the projector's dock for instant connection. It doesn't need to be physically connected to Moremi, as it seems she's used it previously. A neon-blue light zips along the slim edges. "And the microchip gathers biometric data from it." I point at the quantum computer, which long ago used to be the size of a low-income home, but now is a portable, handheld device. "The computer will be able to recognize her DNA and interact with it, gathering her data, transmitting and altering it into digital files and potentially showing us any other stored files, which it'll use as material for the simulation."

The door swings open, pouring in the hallway lights. We shield our faces, and Jan steadies his grip around the poker. Moremi. Disfigured hands, newly bloodied. In one hand, she's holding the foot of a man, dragging the comatose body. I cringe as she inhumanly walks down toward us, the downlights careening off the shadows and planes of her peeled-skin face. Jan grimaces, unaccustomed to this sight I've seen a dozen times up close.

I hurry toward the unconscious body, face congealed in blood. "That's my brother. What have you done to him?"

"You owe me a thank you. It was either him or your daughter," she says. "You wanted more time. This is how I buy time. You called me whilst I was in the middle of something. This better be good." She licks her fingers. "Can't say much about your brother. He's halfway to death as we speak. Soon as we're done, I'm going to finish him off."

I exhale. "His wife and kids—"

"Oh, nothing to worry about," she adds with a seductive lilt. "They're still asleep. It was a quiet affair. Although, it was an effort to bring him along."

Jan says, "I'll go find something from the rooms upstairs to rest him on."

He exits the room, returns ten minutes later with a dishrag, pillow, and a blown-up mattress which we place Limbani onto. I wipe the blood from his face, listen to the little breaths leaving his mouth. Eyes sealed into sleep, he looks peaceful, a contrast to his acerbic nature. My brother is still alive. I have to keep him alive. For Mama. For Papa. That leaves Jan, my husband, and my daughter.

"Do you remember why you were in the middle of the road after midnight?" I ask, getting to the point.

"No," Moremi answers with death-burned eyebrows. I can taste her hunger for the truth of what happened to her.

"Or why my father is looking for you?" Jan asks.

"Your father is not important to me," she says, voice harsh. "But, you, oh, I can't wait to lick your nerve endings and munch your penis off."

I gasp. She's playing the monster effectively; her creative well is brimming with morbid ideas.

Jan squirms, adjusts his pants. Clears his throat. "There's a reason I'm asking. It seems that you've upset a lot of powerful people. You have secrets that can destroy a thousand men. No one wants a woman that powerful. They sent my father after us to clean up this mess. He burned the microchips we retrieved from your bag."

Her eyebrows rise. "What microchips?"

"Jesus." Jan thumps his head.

"Death has erased her memory," I note.

She jolts forward. "You caved my fucking skull in with your fucking car. What the fuck did you expect?" Her anger trills the air. The more people she kills, the less we can contain her vengeance. "I should finish you off right now. Fuck this list, these rules, this truth."

I raise my hands. "Moremi, stay with us. Hold on, please. Come, let me show you something." We walk toward the front-row seats, the large screen. "We're going to plug ourselves into the footage from your microchip. You'll be able to watch."

"Why can't I come with you?" she whines.

"You're a ghost," Jan says, losing patience.

"Unfortunately," I add softly, "the technology is not advanced enough to interact with incorporeal people."

Jan makes several selections on the computer's screen. A message appears on the cinema's screen, signalling its connection to Moremi's microchip, giving us visual access to its contents.

"Now we've connected your microchip, let's have a look," I say.

Moremi narrows her eyes at the screen, not understanding what she's seeing.

Jan scrolls his hands across the cinema's screen, which responds to his gestures. There's only one folder titled "Truth Bomb." "Truth Bomb?" Jan asks, staring at Moremi. "Does that ring a bell?"

Something flickers in her eyes, then she doubles over, palms on her head. "It hurts. The memories, they hurt. *Stop!*"

"I don't think she's meant to process any memories prior to the accident," I say. But even when we're alive, we can't process memories from our previous lifespans. We're no different than dead women: everything is *always* stolen from us, men are our death. And Matsieng is a female god, oppressed beneath the earth, fed evil to subside Xer wrath, drinking women's murders and our blood.

"It won't stop." Her hand throttles outward, wraps around my neck, and she gains some solace, some peace it seems, for she's no longer breaking down from the torture of the onslaught of memories. Then it hits me: I am the painkiller to her pain. The only way to stop the painstaking retrieval of her memories is for her to deal with the task she's assigned: killing, avenging her murder. Attacking me.

"That's why you can't remember," I whisper, "because you've been killing and killing. Any moment of rest allows you to remember. The curse doesn't want you to remember."

"What's important to remember other than *you* killing me?" she shouts.

"Because your body was infiltrated with an illegal microchip," I say, "against your wishes. That's far worse than what we've done. Whoever did this to you, you can't even remember them. Don't you want to know what they did with your body?"

"No, no, no," she cries. "You—*you*—killed me!"

I raise my hand to Jan, stopping him from interfering. "Open the files." And to Moremi, "I understand what you're going through, the pain. If you want the truth, you have to steer through it. We're here. You're not alone. Look, we have to work together. We're on the same team."

"There is no us or team here when you're not fucking dead," she says.

"Fair enough," I say. "But I'll *eventually* be dead, and he'll be dead, but we're trying to do something bigger than our lives. *You* need to help us because this will help you, too. Now can you let me go?"

She considers. Releases her grip. Forces her hand down to her side, where it trembles under some undeniable force. Steps back into the shadows. Watches. My stomach twists. *Can I really trust her not to kill us?* She clenches her jaw, trying to steady herself, to cling to this one thing we're trying to do.

"Jan, we don't have much time," I say. "She could kill us whilst we're under."

Her cheekbone-hung skin quivers when she grumbles, "Fingers." Shaking, she doubles over, carves her nails into her jean-clad thighs. She cranes her neck, cocks her head to the side. "Fingers." Her voice, coarse at the edges.

Jan shakes his head. "W-w-what?"

"*You* can't kill him," I bargain.

It's too late. Moremi snatches him by his arm, her teeth clamp his fingers—smash, chew, and crunch. He growls and screams, floundering about. Imprisoning him into place against a wall with her free hand, she stretches her head outward, yanking the bony meat restrained by stretchy veins from Jan's pain-screaming hand. The elastic fibers snap from the pull, dismembered from their three lost fingers lost in the bone-crunching synth sounds of Moremi's mouth as she chews, chews, chews. She spits out the soggy mess of a thumb, index, and middle finger. Jan falls to his knees, hammers his fist into the carpet, stares at his decapitated fingers, no longer singular, individual forms, but mush.

Moremi sighs with ecstatic relief. "I feel better now. That should buy us some time." My pity for her drowns me, and I reach forward to smear the blood off her lips. But something sharp and biting prickles between our skins, and she steps back at the sudden foreign fondness trickling from my body into hers.

Jan's crippled moans dissipate into silence, into his tense jawline, biting down on the pain. I exit the room into the guest toilet and rummage through the counters looking for a first aid kit and return with alcohol and kitchen towels from the kitchen. I stumble down the cinema's stairs and pour the clear alcohol onto his wounds and he screams into his fist, digging his head into his shoulder. He raises his head, swallows a bunch of painkillers as I apply pressure with an absorbent cloth around his raised hand. The white cloth quickly colors red as beads of sweat collapse from his face onto my working hands.

I brush his sweat-slick hair back. "Hold on, okay?"

I gather new towels and tie them tightly around Jan's hand.

Moremi observes us with bloody, brown skin, eyes beady and black with hunger. There is no time to mourn lost limbs when they're the cost of clinging to our lives. Efficiency is our *only* currency to secure our survival. But I understand why Jan stares at me incredulously like I'm some heartless bitch when I say, "Let's get this over and done with before you pass out."

He wipes the sweat from his face. Swallows. Eyes pale with life, he rises onto his feet. Exhales. "You're right, straight to business," he says.

Dizzy with shock, he sweeps his hands across the screen, opens the Truth Bomb folder. We find over a hundred video clips labeled with names and numbers of chronological order. Names of men, women, and the positions they hold: graphic designer, intern copywriter, creative director, secretary, CEO, editor, marketing director.

"Who are all these people?" Moremi asks. "Why do I have these files?"

"That's what we're trying to figure out," I say. "We found ten unbranded microchips in your backpack that Aarav destroyed, but these must be the backups. Luckily, Aarav didn't destroy the other items we found: your journal, screenplay, and a set of pills—"

"The pills." Recognition flickers in her eyes. "The pills take you to a dream world."

"Dream world?" I ask. "You mean they assist with the simulation?"

"They connect you to a dream world. I don't want to go back there, please, no." She slaps her palms against her face. "Too painful to remember."

I place my hands on her shoulders. "Moremi, you're not going back, wherever that is. Everything is going to be okay." I turn to Jan. "We'll consume the pills to initiate the simulation."

He nods, points at an icon. "Moremi, it seems you've been editing the footage from your microchip. This one, for example, prefixed with VER 39 is the latest version which I believe we should watch."

He double-clicks "1_VER 39_MoremiGadifele_graphic_designer," and a video enlarges, projecting the healthy glow of Moremi's living face on the screen. The ferocity in her beauty-taut face, supple with youth, is brown-stitched with a long-gone naivety.

She staggers back. "That's me. I . . . I look so different . . . from now." She stares down at her body, hands feeling the texture of exposed cartilage on her face. "I was so alive." She presses her back into the wall, fear flickering in her eyes.

The Moremi in the video either sits or stands against the dim grey background. No other features. No desk, no plants, no window. Braids tied up high. Brown eyes flicker with vulnerability and fury. "Hello," she says. "I am Moremi Gadifele, and this is my most personal docu-film: the truth. I hope it reaches the masses before the monsters find me. Their faces will show in the reel, their names will show in the credits. Either way, some of you know these people personally. As most fans know, I'm an IT consultant and film student, and I run a horror circus show that simulates live feeds of our most horrid nightmares into entertainment, films, and games. You enjoy being simulated into my work, being one with the characters. Unfortunately, this nightmare started when I was twenty years old and has been my reality for three years. Not only mine, but my colleagues', my friends salaried elsewhere, and strangers bootlegged to multinational corporations by our own. Three years I've been working, filming, and editing this project in the only seconds of freedom I've got. No one knows what happens in the establishments that run our cities or the stories behind our irises. They've made us prisoners in our own bodies. The only way you can understand me is to be in my skin and behind my irises."

The video cuts to black. Jan and I stare at each other. Moremi is a mangled confusion between the seats and the screen.

Jan asks, "*Who* are you?"

"I don't know," Moremi cries, falling to her knees, gripping at air's fabrics. "I don't know. Who am I? Please tell me who I am." Her eyes glimmer in the soft lights, childlike.

I kneel, wrap my arms around her, press my fingers down her braids. "Shh, it's going to be okay."

She grips my shirt. "Something bad happened. Please, you have to find out."

I swallow. "I promise we will."

Jan clicks open the folder titled "Behind Our Irises." In it, we find similar videos, hundreds and hundreds of them. He clicks the one titled "Moremi Gadifele."

Jan hands me the chiffon of pills to untie. He pops one onto his tongue. Swallows. We're back to the beginning. Drugs and fantasy. I slide one onto my tongue, chase it down with my saliva. I'm nervous of what we're about to slip into. Quickly dizzy, Jan and I sit, side by side, holding hands.

The air is deep-freezer cold. The screen flicks to blue, revealing the preface:

BEHIND OUR IRISES
SEASON 1 EPISODE 1
Description
A sci-fi docu-fiction anthology series. An entry-level employee in a global enterprise experiences harrowing terror in an exploitive workplace that catapults her into a violent reality that sees her imprisoned in skin-tight abuse. Physically controlled by the power dynamics in her life, she lies in wait in her body for the freedom to rampage hell on the complicit, on the abusers, to expose the heinous success behind leading international firms and how they use extreme measures to chloroform their victims into silent and subservient roles.
Genres: psychological, sci-fi, mind-bending
This show is: ominous, dark
+ MY LIST

I gasp and stare at Moremi, anxious. "Jesus, physically controlled, imprisoned in skin-tight abuse, chloroformed into subserviency—what does all this mean?"

The reflected words on Moremi's face warp. "I don't know," she says.

"If we're going to live out your experiences in your body, I'm seriously afraid of the abuse we're going to go through," I say.

Jan tugs at my hand, squeezes once. "Are you ready?"

"It'll be just like a dream," I say. "No, a nightmare."

He nods. Presses play.

Black and white lines scratch across the cinema room's screen, zipping back and forth as it processes through the reader. My eyes roll back and forth, making me drowsy. Jan's hand loosens in mine. We sink into black. Even as we know the simulation dream has us under, our minds slip us into a new reality.

22:53 /// EPISODE ONE

A shifting camera. Braids caught in the wind. In the unfailing trek of the mountainous region of reality, I gallop. I'm a chassis of skin and bones tied up in a bow of melanin, chugging out breaths. The POV snaps, and sunlight dissolves into my skin. Eyelids unfurl, eyelashes untie. I wake. Not out of me. A scratch, a tick, and the POV's back in my mind. Moremi's thoughts wash through the simulated landscape like honeyed sunlight: *Sometimes when I blink, I wake into a different reality, a different time zone, and I realize we're here again. At the beginning, again. And then it slips out of my skin away from me. And I can't remember anything. I'm unstitched, caught in a state of unrest. Caught in a loop.*

I wake up in an ocean of dread and panic in a high-storied building, sitting in a conference room surrounded by glass walls and the city's metallic skyline. Clouds skip-scatter across the sky like a dazed track shot. Across from me sits a brown-skinned woman, dressed in a mauve suit, a sleek smile, and a shorn head. Her name tag reads "Manager: Neo Leago."

"This is all we can offer." She slides a glossy sheet of paper across the desk toward me. It's a contract pertaining to graphic design services.

Stunned, I look up. The reflective surface of the ewer shows me trapped in Moremi's body. Tidbits from her mind trickle into me, framing our time: it's three years ago on a blazing hot October and she's twenty years old just when Eli and a twenty-five-year-old me had met, cocooned in our infatuation. Nothing in the room distinctly identifies the name of the firm except the contract. I stare at it, and written in bold is "Koshal Holdings Inc.," and in italics: *agency for your brand*. Aarav's firm. My lip sticks out in a sour pout.

Moremi's thoughts ascertain her—no, our—no, *my* situation: Rent is due tomorrow. I need to buy tampons, pads, pills for the migraine and the ever-fluctuating hormones that fuck my emotions up. I need food. I need transportation fare, health benefits—which one is a priority? Shit, it's not like I can forego periods. Hunger scathes me. Anxiety paralyzes me. A smokestack is trapped in my chest. I'm burning, God, what will I do? Because all they can offer barely covers my rent.

"You are free to look elsewhere," she says.

I've looked everywhere in every firm. Failed interviews. No callbacks, no responses. Except, Koshal Holdings Inc., the most internationally established market research firm. Located in Fairgrounds, in Fairscape building, fiftieth floor. "No, no, no. This is fine. Given my experience, could you review my salary?" Could? It shouldn't be an option. I've already given her the power.

She smiles, says, "We'll be hiring you on a part-time basis, seeing as you're an undergraduate student. Last year, is it?"

I nod.

She smiles. "We'll review your salary at the end of the probation: six months. Unless . . . you're not interested."

Six? Half a year of my life gone just like that. He did say the salary wouldn't do me justice, but in time the experience would elevate me. He pulled strings to get me this job.

He? Who is this man? Moremi's memory forfeits nothing. I lean forward, attempting to force my hand back from signing, but it scathes the pen's ink across the dotted line.

"This way," she says. "Let's get you acquainted with our office."

Moremi forces me to stand. Out of the conference room, I follow Neo as she towers on high heels through sleek floors and marble walls. Approaching the glass entrance door, she nods her head at the scanner. I press my thumb against it. It stings, and the door slides open. She smiles. “Now you’re part of Koshal Holdings Inc. Our scanner has assimilated your details into our system.”

I suck at my thumb, tasting the salt of blood. Did the scanner take my blood?

Her eyebrows furrow, not a wrinkle in sight. “Is everything okay?”

I might sound fussy if I interrogate their technology. “Of course.” *No, Moremi, it’s not alright!*

We swim out into a high-ceilinged room with a cluster of desks in an open-plan layout, like everyone’s sitting in transparent toilets, watching everyone else’s shitty business.

“Our London head office advises this spatial planning is best for space and work efficiency,” she says. “Inspires an open, warm, collaborative space, which is how we like our team—working together.”

“It’s very beautiful,” I whisper. “I love it.”

“Everyone does!” she quips, and her smile glitches into terror, then a smooth smile in a matter of seconds. I dismiss it as involuntary muscle twitches. *Fear smacks me because the woman is afraid and it’s leaking from her mannerisms—why can’t anyone see that?* Her hands hug the back of an ergonomic chair overlooking a translucent screen. “This is your workstation.”

Next to it sits a young man with shoulder-length braids and a meek smile, his hands making inscriptions and drawings on his screen. “Keaboka Letang.” He offers me his hand. “Welcome to our family. We hope you enjoy your stay.”

I laugh at his introduction, then, realizing how rude that is, thank him for the warm welcome. Everyone in this firm appears rich, wearing high-end clothes, manicured hands, hairstyles brand new. I don’t fit in with my pale, old clothes.

Days, weeks, months, I’m locked inside Moremi, her mannerisms shackled around me. I can’t breathe, can’t speak. All I can do is watch and slip through her limbs through broken sunlight, dealing with design intel for clients, briefs, negotiations, meetings, disgruntled clients, revisions, late-night sessions, weekend sessions, starvation, walking the dangerous line of a life with no health benefits, smoking on the balcony with my colleagues.

The day before my probationary period ends, for our late lunch, Neo takes Moremi and me down to the cafeteria to wind down and congratulate us on our hard work. The elevator brings us to the ground-floor restaurant overlooking a garden with fountains, birdsong, and trees. Within thirty minutes, we've allocated ourselves into cliques at a long dining table, overflowing with chatter and mouthwatering cuisine: Several mini-grills that a couple of my coworkers are already laying into. Swaths of nicely marinated boerewors and sticky chicken pieces they wolf down whilst chugging bottles of cider and beer. One coworker, hazy-eyed and slurring words, chews on a biltong and laughs at a stupid joke that Neo lodges. There's a crock filled with chakalaka, bamboo bowls with steamed madombi spattered with an assortment of herbs, bowls and plates of couscous, several cobs of corn, a steaming stew of mogodu—

"This is all so appetizing." My coworker Puleng Maiteko interrupts my hungry, ogling eyes. She raises the decanter and fills her wine glass. "Might as well get stupid drunk."

I don't have to worry about an empty fridge and dinnerless night, so I scatter some sticky chicken still glistening in marinade onto a mini-grill and it sizzles. Puleng tugs at an earring, hanging like a beaded chandelier from her ear, which is a habit of hers when she's concentrating on something bothering her. She's half-Indian and half-Black but prefers to lean into her Black culture for fashion and language.

"What's wrong?" I ask, chewing on a spoonful of chakalaka. *I can't breathe. I'm suffocated with anxiety stuffed with panic and so many claustrophobic emotions heating the cool air.*

"My grandmother once cooked this for our family's usual weekend potluck," she whispers, breath perfumed by the scent of wine.

"Okay . . . then what's the problem?"

"These exact same meals . . . from three years ago." She shakes her head, which is elegantly wrapped in a richly colored Ankara-design tukwi. "It's just hit me like a bad case of déjà vu. It tastes *exactly* the way she does it. No one in our family has been able to replicate the taste of her recipes." A tear slips down her face. "My grandmother passed away five years ago. This . . . just felt like she was alive again."

Puleng drinks three bottles of wine before sunset, and Neo advises the company driver to take her home.

I've also guzzled too many glasses of wine, and even though I'm not in as bad a state as Puleng, I hurry to the office's unisex bathroom to relieve my protesting bladder. I stop when I find Keaboka bent over, his head dipped into a sink full of water, hands grappling with the rim. I yank him up, and his faux locs slap me. What the fuck's going on today? *Pity overwhelms me, Moremi's naivety chloroforms me, paralyses me—why can't I move her hand?* He gasps for air. Stares at himself in the mirror with dark trails of mascara running down his face. He's crying. I'm whiplashed like I'm at a funeral-cum-party. *Inside Moremi, I shake, trying to break free from the restraints of her skin—something bad is going on, and she can't see it.*

"Are you okay?" I ask, forgetting my need to pee.

"It's the only way I can deactivate them. It only lasts three minutes. I don't know why. Listen to me." Keaboka grabs my shoulders, his eyes wild and frantic. "You can't see it, but they . . . They've been selling us to their clients."

I giggle and burp, thinking he's making a joke. He speed-talks nonsensically, staring at his ticking watch, unable to find his cell phone, muttering, "Where the fuck is my phone?" He looks up at me. "They use us. These bastards feel too safe and comfortable with this thing they installed in us. I'm going to fucking kill them when I get the chance!"

"What?" I stagger back, tipsy and confused—stunned also because he's generally a quiet person who focuses on his assignments, managing the social media pages of our clients and photo shoots, booking influencers and models.

"What are you talking about?" I feel terribly sorry for him and offer consoling arms. "Hey, whatever happened, we can probably sort it out with—"

"You're not listening to me." He grabs my shoulders again, wrings them, and I expect myself to crack like an egg and spill all over the bathroom floor. "Get out. Do not renew or upgrade your contract." *Yes, yes, yes, tell her! God, please listen.*

"What? But I need this job. My probation ends today. I'm due in for a review tomorrow."

"For fuck's sake, listen to me! You're better off without a job. Don't sign anything. They have a pipeline where they sell *us*—we are the products—it's those fucking updates—"

The door slams open. Security guards thunder in. Keaboka starts hiccupping and floundering in their grips. *No, no, no! I lurch forward, bump against Moremi's front skin-walls.*

"He'll be alright. He has a condition and is sometimes unwell. We're taking him to the office doctor," they say to me as they gather Keaboka out. *They're lying, can't you see that they're lying? Why won't you hear me, Moremi?*

One guard remains, making sure I don't follow them. "This must be a shock to you. Why don't you rejoin the others?" *Get out, Moremi! Go!*

By Monday, the trauma of my coworker still has me shaken when Neo calls me from my desk. "Mr. Koshal wants to see you." *Panic rises in my bones, drowns me, buries me. I can't steer her to safety.*

I stumble from my seat. "Oh, God, like *Koshal* Koshal, my boss?"

My colleagues laugh along with her. "Yes."

If I'd known, I'd have dressed better than this cheap blouse and pantsuit. I've never seen him before, not even leaving the premises. He exists in the upper floors like God because he knows everything about us: I've only seen his name in our correspondences, but he sends us condolences regarding deaths in the family; at one point, he emailed me wishing me luck on my midterm exams; and he once assigned me to a foreign film director given my study and obsession with film.

My stomach plummets as the panoramic elevator rises into the skies. *I sink to the bottom of her feet, terrified.* Neo comes along with me because my fingerprint only gives me access to specific places. When we pass the floors, some are retrofitted like a luxury hotel—"For visiting clients," Neo explains, hands tucked into her suit. Their hallways look out through velvet-curtained windows, chandeliers dancing in the trickling sunlight, lush carpeting, wood-paneled walls. *Did you hear that? Someone screamed. What are they going to do to us?*

We pour out into a lobby manned by a young woman with a Peruvian weave. I'm astounded at the empty space of glamour, thrice the size of my bedsit, with views of the cityscape, towering buildings shadowing pod-vehicles weaving in and out.

Who would hear anyone scream from a floor this high up?

Why would I think that?

Because it's me, Moremi. Run! Leave!

Neo nods. "This is where I leave you." The elevator doors slide closed.

The receptionist signs me into Mr. Koshal's office, where he sits, back toward me, facing his picture windows. His office is lined with dark wood, seats a plush leather, and a meeting table waits across a wall of shelves.

"Moremi Gadifele, a pleasure to meet you." He stands, tall and broad, hair a dark shade of night. *Hatred, pure hatred reels forward, punches him, but falls through him, returns back to me.* "I like to personally welcome permanent employees to our firm." He directs me to the conference table, circumvented with dark leather seats. "Here's a glass of water."

"I'm not thirsty, thank you."

He smirks. *I want to rip his lips off.* "You'll need it." Pushes forward a glossy sheet and holds back a shiny metal container. "Your *new* contract."

I pick at it with sweaty fingers and gulp. I'm to be upgraded to consultant! With benefits! A better salary! Housing benefits, medical, and more! Jesus, he was right. *Who was right, Moremi?* My fingers stumble looking for a pen to sign.

"There's one clause," Mr. Koshal adds, peering at me with bright brown eyes.

I stare at the stipulation and read, "I'm to be 'installed with a new, noninvasive pill-form technology InSide'—wait, what?" *No, no, no! Run!*

"Developed by one of our prominent clients. If you agree, you keep your job. If you don't, then your current contract runs its course."

Runs its course? It ends today! I'll be jumping back into the hungry ocean of the unemployed. I have two months' worth of pending rent. I've no savings, no belongings, nothing substantial to my name. My landlord has been threatening to throw out my belongings whilst I'm at work. This job is my oasis. *I'm drowning, I'm powerless. I can't save her, I can't save us.*

He slides an enveloped package toward me.

"What is this?" I ask.

"Keys to your new vehicle and a new home in our gated estate. Neo will connect you with our stylist for all your wardrobe and hair needs."

My eyes bolt out. *He* was right. Six months is worth this promotion. *Who are you talking about, Moremi?* Words are glued to the back of my throat. I clear it. "May I have a pen to sign?" I whisper.

Mr. Koshal studies me intently, pulls out a device with a scanner. "Scan your finger. That's how we sign our agreements." At this, he pushes the metal container toward me, a compact thing with a cushioned interior and a pill.

I poise my finger above the screen—*I muster all strength to pull her hand back, to move her feet, to make her run*—momentarily remember the door scanner's prick when I started work here, and Keaboka's words slam into me: *These bastards feel too safe and comfortable with this thing they installed in us. I'm going to fucking kill them when I get the chance! Get out. Do not renew or upgrade your contract.*

Mr. Koshal raises his eyebrows. "Is there a problem? Unless you're no longer interested in working with us?"

"I . . . uh . . ."

"It'll be worth it in the end," he says, adjusting his tie. He has a balding hairline, stocky fingers, and a certain kind of confidence that intimidates me. "It'll make your life so much easier. We're partnering with a highly esteemed technology company, InSide, that's offering our employees a free subscription to their app. It will help you increase your productivity and streamline your life. You will be the best *you* that you can be. You're valuable to us, and we'd hate to lose you." He leans back in his chair, his hazel eyes boring into me. "We're looking to expand our company into several countries: Zambia, Dubai, South Africa, Nigeria." He counts them off with his fingers as if they're already conquered. "And we want to use this year to groom you because we see you eventually heading customer relations in Dubai, once you've cut your teeth in the region. That is, of course, if you stay with us."

I swallow deeply at the thought of living in what is widely regarded as the world's most technologically advanced city and reaching the summit of the corporate ladder. I should probably get the contract reviewed, but *he* recommended this firm to me, he knows them very well, and he's a policeman—he wouldn't entrust me to duplicitous people. I *trust* him, so I trust them.

A policeman? Jesus, who? Why can't I get her memories to name this mysterious man?

I stare at the envelope, at the riches that could fund my career and take me out of the hell of poverty. It's just a fucking pill. Nothing harmful. My colleagues must have gone through the same procedure and they look perfect, happy, and rich.

I press my finger on the scanner and swallow the pill. *I'm falling, falling, falling into the dark abyss of her cavernous body, fear-struck. What if I'm forever imprisoned in her?*

That same day, I'm moved into my new home, located in the gated estate of Kgale Hill. A two-story townhouse with a garage and my shiny luxury car, two bedrooms, living room, open-plan kitchen, and a huge-ass garden. I'm scheduled for a day at the spa to be scrubbed, manicured, hair treated and plaited into thick box braids, and clothes styled to my personality ready for hand-delivery to my wardrobe. A chef who works at the gated community restaurant has delivered a mouthwatering supper. A personal trainer equips me with a weekly three-day routine I must adhere to for our personal sessions. And I wonder at the level of detail observed and funded for in our lives. Who would ever leave such a firm?

That night, when I get home, I feel odd. A surge of anemia and fever overwhelms me. I steady myself with the walls of my new home, wading through the heavy dark until I stumble into bed, out of breath. I've little energy to do anything to nourish myself or call an ambulance. I feel wrecked with an exhaustion that I pray sleep will solve.

When the bright morning sun opens my eyes, I'm urged by a tightening in my gut that rushes me to the bathroom to vomit my entire self out. I sit propped against the bathtub, wiping sweat from my face. Then I see it, in the two mirrors before and behind me: the glinting piece of metal embedded into the back of my neck. I touch it, and it burns with pain. How, what, when? A headache slams into my brain, stands me up, makes me turn away from the mirror.

"I feel better," I whisper, tranced. Brush my teeth. Have breakfast. Shower and go to work. I have the best workday I've ever had in my life, in my new clothes, new hairstyle, skin feeling brand new. I love my colleagues. We work together. Live together. Spend weekends together. Carpool to jols and vacation homes and work trips. *The pill has sedated me, turned my thoughts, my voice, into a sloth. They're conquering us. They've already conquered me. Fight. I have to fight.*

After my twenty-first birthday and over the following eight months, I'm agonized with blackouts. The workload is intense, and I stay late at work. At 10:00 p.m., I'd be leaving the office, waving to the security officials in the lobby, unlocking the car, hands opening the driver's door—then nothing but a complete deep abyss in my memory leading to my 6:00 a.m. alarm blaring. *I'm locked away, can't see, can't feel. But this body was terrorized last night, they've left demons on our skin.* I wake up in bed feeling sore like I've spent the previous day in a HIIT cardio workout, unable to recount where I was the night before or how I got home.

After five months of this routine, I knock off one night and stand in the dark foyer of my home, crumble into a pile of skin and bones on the floor and cry, heaving hot breaths, not knowing why I'm crying, but a deep chasm of hurt somewhere in my chest throbs and throbs with pain. I reach for my cell phone, but my front door flies open. The security guards of our estate. With flashing lights and heavy boots. "Everything alright? We heard the alarm."

"Alarm? What alarm?" I ask.

They gather me up. "It's going to be alright. The doctor's on her way." Lay me on the living room couch. A woman appears. In her gown. Spectacles and sleep-swept hair. My neighbor, Dr. Farahani.

What? She's in on it? Oh, no, no no!

Something glints in her hand, reflecting the slim shape of moonlight sliding through a crack in the curtains. A syringe. "Shh, it's okay, sweetie. This will help." The guards' hands tie me back as I struggle. A sting. An urge. Slowly, I become swallowed into a current of sedation; my eyes slip me into a prison of dark. I glimpse the doctor's handheld device, its glass displaying a map of our estate, little dots with all of our names. Some green. Some red. I am red, changing into amber, changing into green as I fall into a forever-deep slumber. And then I am gone. And my body becomes theirs.

In the morning, I get up. Breakfast. Shower. Dress. Carpool with my colleagues in a state of silence to work.

At 10:00 p.m., when I'm leaving the office, I'm jittery and anxious as I approach my car because somehow it triggers my blackouts. I've called a trans-pod cab, but before I reach the revolving doors, I'm drowning in blackness, gone.

I come to in a glitzy hotel room, my thighs straddling an old, hairy, and pale naked man. Mr. Koshal. All I can do is remain still as pain rattles my body. Inside the shackles of my skin, behind the bars of my bones, I'm screaming, "No! Somebody help me! Get the fuck away from me! I'll fucking kill you! I'm going to burn this building down!"

No sound escapes my lips. But a split second of autonomy. A plate of food on the bedside table. A serrated steak knife. I grab it and dig it deep into him, into his manhood, and he explodes and screams and kicks me off him. A sharp point of the bedside table cracks against my skull, and I'm gone.

The dark clears. I slip in and out of my reverie as my surroundings stabilize their form. Concrete floors. Concrete walls. The airy mouth of a windowless room. The ventilation system hums.

I'm standing barefoot, wrists and ankles cuffed to a workstation. Still trapped inside Moremi. I gather my consciousness as unknown shadows flex and wane against the walls. A long hallway made of steel walls bends and breaks the strips of reflected light as if it were metal bars. Two people appear from the dark, foggy vapor that shifts at the end of the hallway. One slim, one bulky. Dr. Farahani. Mr. Koshal.

I shout, struggling with the handcuffs. Gulp. Opposite me is the glassy prison of the CBE; it glints in the dim light. No forensic panel. It's not the police headquarters. But the room's identical to the evaluation room, except subterranean, voices echoey and gluey.

"Patient is female, twenty-two," Dr. Narges Farahani says. "Yes, it works similarly to the CBE, but we'll be able to monitor them remotely. *He* says the microchips are undetectable."

She's twenty-two? Jan's secretary informed us that Moremi stopped working for Aarav when she was twenty-one, but they kept her longer than that. I eye the glass house. Stare at the wall painted a subtle rose color where the fluorescent lights dance, the wall bends and whittles, rotoscoping me to a cold summer, a cold floor, and a knife warm against his scrotum. Aarav. *I hope we castrated the bastard.* I rest my eyelids over my sight, feeling dizzy, overwhelmed, and stack up the walls. *Let us go!*

"We don't need any more allegations," Aarav says. "Bad for business. He said these were bona fide microchips. Either he's lying, or you're screwing up."

"He," again? Who?

Dr. Farahani says, "It won't happen again."

"She almost fucking sliced my penis off—what the fuck you mean it won't happen again? She ran off. This was too close. If she ended up at a police station, your mind right now would be incinerated."

"This is unchartered territory, what we're doing. It's all trial and error."

"That's not what you marketed to us. You think I want to lose my organs in a fucking trial and error. What the hell are we paying you for?"

"Calm down," she says.

"I don't need another bitch singing." *This is how he got away with it all. My veins fill with adrenaline but not enough power to blow this room up.*

"They won't sing," she emphasizes, irritated. "We control everything. We censor unwanted behavior to avoid that."

"Well, you're not keeping your end of the deal because this bitch daggered me. You understand the reputation we have to uphold with our clients? They want them pliant. It's part of the service. That's why they sign with us. You're ruining our business, the whole fucking industry! Without us, this country would be nothing." He closes into her face. "I know you have a wife and shit and believe in all these people's rights who are confused about who they are—maybe that's why you're slacking for this girl 'cause she's one of you—but we've got to straighten this lesbian up, or it's our life that's kaput, you hear me?"

Her jaw twitches. *She's a sellout. Again. A fucking sellout. Of all people, she should be protecting us.*

Dr. Farahani says, "I'm right next to you. You don't need to yell."

He knifes her shoulder with his finger. "I own you, you hear me?"

"You don't own me; this is a partnership." She eyes him. *The pause is long and poisonous and I want to noose it around their throats.* "I've been very vocal about how much I detest you. You will never respect me, I get that. But touch me again, and I swear I will do far worse to you than what we do to your employees."

"If your revenge is as bad as your service, I doubt I'll suffer much." *He leans close to her, and I can smell his stale breath painted by his acrid cologne.* "We don't want them macheting us; we want them sucking us good. Fix her, him, whatever the fuck she says she is—make her become what I say she is. Now!"

No one cares how we label ourselves if that label can't protect us from this treatment.

She shakes her head. "I told you, I don't want to hear about these heinous escort services you procure for your clients. That's your business. I'm in no way a part of that."

Why does the darkest part of the world fuse sex and power into this addictive crime we fall victim to?

"Please don't hurt me," our voice says. I pinch my waist-length Yaki braids, freeze, cradle myself.

Dr. Farahani moves me about despite my movements slowing Moremi down. It must be something they gave us. My hand gets scanned. I step into the chamber, disrobed. Inside, a toilet, shower, and bed. A mirror shows my reflection: I am Moremi Gadifele, trapped in a one-year-old memory. And something horrible is happening to us. Where is Jan? Why am I alone? Something is wrong. The pressure in my lungs. The tight drawing of someone sipping oxygen from the room. I am a lit flame, a candle stuck in a vacuum, slowly diminishing.

"Stay calm," Dr. Farahani says. "It'll be over soon. Just routine procedure. If you behave, let us in, we'll let you out."

In the morning, getting ready for a work trip to Joburg, I press the pill onto my tongue, like pressing a play button, just as Mr. Koshal and Dr. Farahani explained. The day clips forward, and I hurriedly swerve my car out of the driveway of my townhouse.

Summer pulses down mirages on car tops and parking lots as I wind through midtown traffic. Thirty minutes in, I'm finally throttling the A1 highway at 140 km/hr. Oceanic beats of house music flood my car. I'm singing at the top of my lungs. The speedometer ticks higher and higher, matching my pitch, and—something snaps. Metal crashes against metal. The ground gives in. My voice singes my larynx, scatters what little of this reality remains.

I wake up into my body, barefoot and breathless, wearing nothing but my skin, my hair in a pink Peruvian wig, so unlike me. Eyelids slowly unfurl, reality leaks into my irises. *I stumble back against Moremi's spine, torched by fear.* No car seat beneath me or steering wheel in my hands, but a knife with its serrated edge licked by a bathroom's fluorescent light. Outside, the air is dark, fragrant, and back in my body again, sinuous.

Reality sneezes me to the car then stills to the small bathroom. I stare wild-eyed at the bathroom, the place of terror, where outside the door a woman stands. A naked woman I don't know, whose thighs I woke up between.

"No, no, no, no! I don't want to be here!" I shout. But it's Moremi's voice and my voice, conjoined, splitting, breaking.

I drop the knife, and it clangs to the pale ceramic tiles. There is no out. The walls bulge, sliding inward. The knife is in my hand again. I throw it against the wall. It bounces back to the steady fold of my hand, forcing me to use it. In the mirror, I see the woman watching, smiling.

"No!" I scream.

My bones are tied to the knife by an implacable force as it drags the sharp point to the fearful eye of my wrist. My arm refuses the instruction, and I scream against it. Moremi, stop!

The world view hiccups. I slam into my autopilot body, sat in front of the wheel of my car. I'm on the A1 highway again, an approaching truck wailing its horn. I swerve to the shoulder of the road. Fling my door open. I gulp all the air I can manage, touch my arms and body as if to make certain it's still there. Dust and the smell of burnt tire sting my nose.

"What the fuck was that?" I scream.

I dial Dr. Farahani. Straight to voicemail.

"Bitch!" I scream to the sky. Birds scatter. I've never been good with anger. I apologize to God and try again. Voicemail. Wait for the beat: "What the hell was that? You lied to me! I'm still stuck in this simulation."

Dr. Farahani's voice rains from the sky: "If you behave and let us in, we'll let you out."

The view changes.

"Just let us in." Dr. Farahani's voice points over my shoulder to a normal hallway. Its walls buckle and whip aside to be quickly replaced with individual rooms that the hallway races past like a high-speed train. The rooms are a blur of scenes, the doorways like film frames into a seedy motel. Vertigo-overwhelmed and losing my balance in this dolly zoom, my perspective focuses into these rooms, each with contained scenes and tracking shots from dark episodes of my work life: me with different men and women I don't know, doing things I have never done before.

"Stop, stop, stop!" I scream as the rooms whiz past me.

The scenes freeze.

"What have you done to me?" I cry.

"You need to behave, or we won't let you out," she says.

"Who are these people?"

"Stop harming them, and we'll let you out."

"No, no, no!" I shout.

I stand in a room without a door.

"None of them have doors," she says. "We believe in transparency. But you haven't been transparent. You haven't been a good employee."

Inside, an old man with pitch-black hair, stubbled chin, brown eyes lies on a bed. I sit on his lap and ask, "Is this how you love it, Mr. Koshal?"

"Dance for me," he says. "Spin, baby."

From the doorway, I grip my hands to my eyes. "This isn't happening. Hey, stop that." But the people inside the room can't hear me.

My fingers trace the architrave, lined with trauma. The room slaps me back with a jolt of electricity.

On the floor, my body jerks, fighting the last current flowing through my veins. *I sit back, against Moremi's backbone, quivering in fear.*

"Stop misbehaving, Moremi," Dr. Farahani admonishes. "That's another tell to determine candor. This memory has a lot of repressed, electrifying energy. If you continue to touch the architraves of these rooms and *they* continue to electrocute you, you have failed because you refuse to accept us, to let us in."

Time is at mercy's shadow.

"If you keep failing these tests, you're going to lose your job," Dr. Farahani says.

"I don't want it. I quit," I cry. "I forfeit my salary. Let me out!"

"You can't quit. We don't hire quitters. You're in it for the long haul. You should appreciate what we're doing for you. Many people out there are dying for employment."

"I resign, I don't want to work for you—"

"If you don't behave and let us in, we won't let you out."

The scene changes. I come to in the glass prison, shivering inside Moremi's bones. The air exhales a cold breath. A door just opened. A man walks in. The glass is opaque. Can't make out his face.

I reach out to the glass, but my hand slips through it as if it's water, and I slip out of Moremi's body. I walk closer, the floor burning cold into my soles. I must not stop. I need to get closer to him. To see. My skin. My skin is burning. I stare down. Smoke wafts from my feet, swelling into my face. No, it's only a trick of the mind. When I wake up, there will be no burn scars on my feet. Keep going.

I cry, fall onto my knees. I'm burning. No. I need the truth. I crawl toward Dr. Farahani's swivel chair, grab onto it. My hand falls through. A sharp pain cracks my skull. Blood. The salty tang of it fills my mouth. I force myself to stand. Barely. I rub my eyelids, but my vision won't clear.

His voice surrounds me: "I managed to retrieve new microchips."

Voice, familiar.

I gasp, pinwheeling.

It's

my

husband.

23:29 /// EPISODE TWO

Elifasi's hand rests on Dr. Farahani's shoulder, wedding ring glinting. A familiar feeling ripples between them as she stares up at him.

"Good job," he says. His teeth are too exposed. A smile I've never seen. It melts down his face. He is melting. Fire. Smoke. Colors burning. I'm spinning, falling into darkness. Light breaks. More images, like a polaroid, are thrown into disarray against the screen of my eyeballs; film reel, snapping, shooting. The scene is swallowed, then just as quickly fades into a new scene in a bar. The air, drunk, sways me. The smell of beer, sweat. There's laughter. A jet-rush of drinks pouring into glasses. My husband. Moremi. A memory before Moremi started working at this global enterprise.

Time shimmies to outside. Streetlights, a slip of light in the dark. The night air is warm. Moremi's staggering with loose lips, slurring words. Her skin is wrapped around my bones. Her arm is my arm, flung around my husband's shoulder as he holds us, steadies us. We're unable to walk. Too much alcohol tonight. Where's he taking us?

"Home, kiddo." He heard us. "I'm taking you home."

We turn, stare around at the stars as if they poked us. We laugh, the alcohol turning everything funny. We fall forward. We laugh at how tipsy we are. The naivety is slain from our mouth. The tarmac is rough, scrapes us badly, the heel of our stiletto broken.

"Normally, I can handle my beer," you and I speak. "I'm sorry," we cry. "I wish you were my real father; you've taken care of me for so long. The rent. The recommendation letters. With the internship. How could I ever repay you? I have no family except you."

We start weeping, grateful to have him. Him. In our lives. Our mentor. *Moremi's sickening gratitude straitjackets me, and every one of my struggles tightens the confinement.*

I'm a silhouette clung to her body. She looks up with a hazy sight. Stares at my husband. Only sees the hand he offers to help her up. Only sees his smile, the warmness of it; doesn't see the sharp teeth, the protruding evil salivating his lips.

A scream spews out of my mouth, nothing like vomit.

Time. Time has come and gone, one scene hemorrhaging into another. Elifasi's not there. We're not drunk anymore. The dark is rain-splattered. The sky wails. A dark street. A woman crosses by. She looks about, checks the coast. This street should be lined with townhouses, cars parallel-parked on either side of the road. The woman stops halfway across what we expect to be a road. But there is no road, just a tarmac of dark sky. The woman shakes off the feeling of someone watching her. Picking up speed, she moves. A man appears. Meets her. They're the only light in the street. The dream, the nightmare, the laws it makes in its world are its own dialect, murky but real, time nonchronological.

The Indian man with the crew cut. The woman with the Afro. They kiss, wrap themselves around each other. They kiss without breath. Move without air. I'm watching them through someone's camera, through someone's eyes. The person I'm watching them from breathes heavily, a trance noosed around her brain. She moves forward, pushed forward. I feel this, that Moremi's body is not her own tonight. The closer she gets, the more familiar they look.

It is me and Jan.

At our townhouse, walking into it. *He knew? Shock bows me down to the bulbs of Moremi's knees. He knew.*

The eyes I'm watching through see themselves in a broken pane of glass on the ground. It is Moremi, someone playing God with her, watching through the feed in her iris. My husband. He knew. About Jan and I, during the second year of our marriage. I feel the heat of the microchip overworked in the back of her neck, like the day Elifasi dropped the remote. The day I didn't feel like having sex, the day after the accident.

I hover in the dark like fog, realizing my husband infiltrated Moremi's body with a microchip, but why, why, why?

Moremi's thoughts, fury-filled: "They're having an affair. He's using me to spy on his wife. Using me like an object, a recorder. An unwilling PI. I trusted him. My mentor. My father figure. He's angry, burning in hatred."

The scene dissolves back to the CBE, becomes steadier. Dr. Farahani appears in my vision. She and Elifasi. "Good girl. You're behaving." I can't scream or speak with volition; they did something to me whilst I was trapped in the memory.

"Now we can let you out."

For the next months before I turn twenty-three, I'm awake in my body, but not totally awake or in control of it.

Every eye in Koshal Holdings Inc. runs surveillance programs behind its pupil. Connected through the authenticated enterprise cloud network to its central servers. Able to detect corporate theft, infraction, abuse of work assets, and more. Much more. In that unsurveilled split second when the company automatically upgrades our microchip, when all their restraints loosen, I try to scream.

I'm standing in the conference room, presenting concepts to a client, when I see him. My mentor, Elifasi, shaking hands with Aarav in the glassy hallways. Countless times. The fucker is supplying them with the microchips to brand us like cows. I trusted him. I trusted him! How could he do this to me? Why? How much are they paying him? *Moremi's anger finally matches mine, finally it has power to do something.*

Only half a decibel of my scream escapes as a gasp. The microchip takes control. I compose myself and seamlessly continue with my presentation on Zulu motifs and geometric shapes to use as patterned stories on their textile range. The client is a burly old man with several subsidiaries on the continent, aiming for trendy and inclusive. He is pleased with my proposal to make his product more accessible to their target demographic: hip, female, mid-twenties to early thirties.

My next meeting comes at lunch. A foreign furniture designer with staff and seventeen operations in African countries, but whose profits for his furniture sector are experiencing a stiff dive due to a burgeoning rival: a local competitor. He wants to add a look of diversity to his furniture range and asks which tribe I'm from. Bangwato.

He muses, thinks it'll be interesting to color the themes of his work with this mentioned ethnic background. I try to protest, but the sounds don't come out of me, choked back, like my scream.

After the meeting, I resign to my desk, chew on a chicken sandwich and swallow a protein shake, clicking, tapping, drawing out designs on my screen. In that split-second update, I see it all. The microchips hidden behind our chiffon and silk and wool.

It's funny when something irrefutably terrible happens, and people say, "How can such a thing happen?" But evil flows where it flows. Through gaps and loopholes and human beings. Indifferent to legislation and policies.

Nothing halts it, except, sometimes, a sacrifice.

Each one of us is a well-oiled cog in the workplace machine. There's the odd concerned citizen, who occasionally notices something off about us. The weird gropes. The frozen smiles. The doe-eyed expressions. The unprovoked tears. The silent hallways, offices, lunchroom. Our persistent abnegation posing as customer service. Then the reporters come. Then the police come. We smile mildly and reveal nothing wrong in this fine establishment. No matter how much they investigate every nook and cranny of the buildings and emails, they can't find the secrets stacked in our bodies. What they find are good benefits, fully paid housing, medical aid, a travel allowance, good hospitality, educational grooming, and very loyal unmarried employees who occasionally *love* to sleep with their bosses. But our minds and histories are contained in a database monitored by the data analysts and employee management consultants of Koshal Holdings Inc., which suckles our diversity from our DNA and nervous systems, spools and aggregates it into its network to create 100 percent authentic indigenous products, used for concepts in fashion shows, architectural designs to win tenders. *This could've been me. When Aarav came to my office, seeking services—he would've held me captive the same way as his employees. Relief balloons inside me, but so does disgust as well.*

They don't need to get close to us to have us open our mouths—they are already inside our bodies listening to every thought pattern and whisper from even our grandparents in the genes of our bodies.

The firm is touted for being revolutionary. They mine our stories to flavor just the right amount of diversity in their clients' products which accounts for their sky-high profits. They mine the minerals, diamonds, and jewels of our very thoughts and histories and cultures that have been buried in our brains; the emblems and cultural motifs are woven with the dialect of our pain into their indigenous furniture designs, patterned textiles. It's all the market research they and their clients ever need.

In our heels and short dresses and with men the bosses fancy, we shuttle from our desks to the managers' offices, to hotel rooms and secret getaways. The directors, the managers, the clients have nothing to fear. Their technology sits in us, maims our voices so that our mouths may never betray them, intercepts the neuromuscular signals shuttling from our brains to our vocal cords. It lynches those muscles in our throats just when we want to scream and cry and bleed truth.

I have authorized this technology, agreed to the terms and conditions.

Now: I can't move, I can't breathe, except under the dominant hand of their technology. They are our voices, and we are their voice. Their face. Their ambassador. We are locked behind our irises, and I find my skin feeling artificial, my legs stacked onto a platform, frozen wide eyes staring out into a stream of satisfied customers.

But when the next update comes, I'll get another glimpse of freedom, and that narrow gap in time keeps widening and widening. I have the footage; in our silent freedom, my colleagues and I have talked, we've shared, we've planned: we need to remove these things, expose them.

10:00 p.m. like clockwork. I don't bother leaving the premises. I know where they take me, might as well take myself. The guards smile when the elevator shoves me onto floor thirty-one, into their resort, where they take in clients and us. *I'm so, so high from Moremi's fury. We're fired up, ready to explode.*

A blackout ensnares me. I wake with my limbs pirouetting around a fixed pole, dressed in knee-length boots and skimpy clothes. I stab the boots into his throat, whoever he is. Stab, stab, stab the scene into a bloody haven, take advantage of this malfunctioning microchip they thought they had fixed. Walk out as per the usual. No one observes me, as is the routine. With our temporarily deactivated microchips, we flee, discarding our work phones, our cars, anything they can use to track us.

It's after midnight, but it feels like we don't have time in our bodies. Our tech colleague who's helped us widen the deactivation window said it'll only last six hours before it activates again, and they can pin our location. His cousin, a surgeon, will remove them, but it's very dangerous. We could die. "Why not go to the police?" the surgeon asks.

We can't trust the fucking police! Don't you understand? We can only trust ourselves. We want to leave forever—

The scene cuts,

a microchip glitch,

voices pour out from the microchips into our ears, into our minds, livestreaming a conversation, catapulting our minds to the CBE-like room:

Moremi and my mind hover in the ceiling, watching as Elifasi and Aarav await the entrance of a woman, who slips in and bangs the door. The monitor that authorizes access to us stares at them blankly.

I groan. The woman is Serati. "Have you found them?"

Elifasi and Aarav shake their heads.

"No one must know I am here," Serati says. "I have a solution for how we can get rid of employees like them."

"It's Moremi who's been a problem from the start," Aarav says.

Serati nods. "What I am about to tell you stays between us. I'm committing treason by telling you this. Getting disbarred is the least of my worries. We don't need to look for Moremi."

Moremi's microchip is a live feed of their conversation.

"She is out there with evidence that could take us to hell," Aarav yells.

Serati raises her hand, silences him, expounds on the secret association of the Murder Trials and Matsieng, which takes them a long time to absorb.

"Whatever issue we have, we prostrate ourselves to Matsieng's altars, the waterwombs, spilling our prayers for help. Matsieng has needs we must fulfill—we have found that offerings made to Xem in the form of memories, deaths, and blood keeps Matsieng quietly submerged belowground lest Xe devour our world with destruction; different forms of Matsieng exist throughout the world, specific to each country's culture. We have no scruples in meeting Matsieng's needs to keep us safe. Xe is the god of our beautiful country. Which brings me to the next matter," she says, steepling her hands. "There's something else that can find Moremi for us, kill her for us before she reveals us. I just have to enlist her as a victim, and she'll be gone. Then we can rectify this and avoid any more of these employees singing. Death erases the memory, especially women's, which is very convenient for us. We have a roster of potential murderers picked, and victims we vote on. The final decision is observed by the judge. I'll enlist Moremi as victim. Several members in the police force are privy to this information. No one will ever know. Someone will kill her for us."

Elifasi's eyes widen. "Isn't there a strict protocol to this selection?"

Serati says, "It's AI-based, but everything is easily rigged once you understand the system." *A tornado of terror grips me, spins me, shuts me down.*

Elifasi muses. "If you can elect the victim, can you choose the murderer as well?"

She tilts her head. Nods.

"My wife," Elifasi utters. "She may have seen some things that could compromise us. I've tampered with her microchip and memory, but I'm uncertain of how effective it's been."

Oh, God. This isn't happening. I can't drink anymore of these new revelations—I am full to the brim, spilling all over the floor.

"That cunt refused to work with us, and she's pissing around my son," Aarav says. "We've got two people we need to eliminate, Nelah and Moremi. My team managed to get a hold of the people who fled with Moremi."

"And?" Elifasi asks.

"Apparently, Moremi was working on a documentary film that has very confidential footage of our most esteemed members in compromising positions," Aarav says, "members who have crucial positions in this country. You are also captured in this footage." His eyes point at Elifasi, who swears under his breath.

"I did nothing with her," Elifasi says.

"The evidence shows the 'victims' you groomed and handed off to us," Aarav says. "Not only has she hacked her microchip to edit this footage, but she's also obtained all the other employees' microchip data."

"Fuck," Elifasi says.

"According to the person my team captured," Aarav says, "Moremi was planning to showcase this documentary to the world, to expose us."

"The only way to eliminate this evidence is to eliminate them," Elifasi says, sweat speckling his forehead.

Aarav looks at him like he's sniffing him up. "I'm surprised no one could figure you out with all the sneaky shit you've been up to."

"I played the game right," Eli says, "played my part as a mid-level bureaucrat so no one could smell what I was up to, unlike you, Aarav, who can't fucking leash his son back so that I had to find out about the affair from a low-level employee who was transcribing up my wife's fucking confession from the forensic evaluation."

"So you knew about the affair since before the accident." Aarav tuts and says, "I can only hold up an argument with a man who can control his woman."

Eli narrows his eyes, and only fury is uttered from the glance. Then he glares at Serati. "You were on her forensic evaluation panel and didn't think to tell me about the affair? We're supposed to be fucking working together."

"Handle your affairs, men," Serati says, arms folded. "My existence is not here to babysit yours. I only honor you both with my presence to deal with business. You're lucky that your matters in this lifespan have allowed you that privilege and not elimination."

Aarav steps forward. "Who the hell—"

"Stand down," Elifasi demands, his arm against Aarav's chest.

Serati nods. "Glad to know someone knows his station."

Eli's eyes are the dark shade of fury and calculation, but his face has no ripple of anger.

"There's only so much we can let you get away with," Serati says. "And Moremi is a valuable asset to our creative industry. You can't replicate such talent. But she's too much of a liability—too many important people, some of whom are on the Murder Trials Committee, will be incriminated."

"Is there a way to recover information from her body if she were dead?" Aarav asks.

"Once she's deceased, the information will be gone," Elifasi says. "It often occurs with the cases of convicts we have, besides some criminal residues left in the body."

Serati meditates on a thought, regurgitates it: "There's a reason why amnesia is tied with consciousness transfer. There's a reason why the Murder Trial victim is transmuted into an amnesiac by death. Haven't you ever wondered why a higher percentage of women suffer from amnesia than men? It's the easiest way to silence them. The only reasons we include memory loss in some selected men is to avoid this whole gender-inequality uprising. Besides that, we obtain significant value from female bodies than we do male bodies. They are birthers of life. They have a quality of strength that men lack."

Eli shakes his head. "How can you agree with all this when you're—"

"A woman?" She raises an eyebrow. "Someone has to uphold the status quo, especially the victims—even me, as the victim, since it serves me, too. If I don't, I end up as one of them. As long as nothing's done to me and my lineage, I'm okay with how the system runs."

Eli and Aarav exchange glances.

"Besides, women are so used to sacrificing and losing parts of themselves from their bodies, like blood and babies. It's an experience that qualifies them more than men," Serati says.

A keening, shrilling scream shouts, "Traitor, traitor, traitor!" I am screaming. The betrayal guillotines me. And this is what Moremi was trying to show me the night we killed her. She was crying to me, the person she could trust, because we wore the same gender. Confined to the same curses. Thinking empathy will save us. I *betrayed her. I'm no different than Serati. The worst evil is the slave that drags its counterpart into the same prison and thinks it is free. The sacrificed women, their blood in Matsieng's waterwombs. No more. No. More. To break free, I must break myself. Shatter this prison to dissolve our wrongs that've killed and enslaved women like us. I can feel their voices, the victims, the vibration of their anger fused to my blood, my blood that also floats in Matsieng's waterwombs, screaming, calling for me. Me, the one who's still alive. I know what to do now.*

Serati continues, "Matsieng feeds from the memories—the blood donations are insufficient to sustain Xem, and so during the process of mind transfers, we donate the citizens' memories to Xem without the knowledge of the patients."

"Jesus," they breathe.

"Of course, the Murder Trials Committee is the exception to this rule. We have to remember everything to protect Xem and our country," Serati says.

"You remember all your previous lifespans?" Aarav asks.

She nods.

"But we were told it was a scientific phenomenon from the mind transfer," Elifasi says.

"What else could we say to the country without war breaking out?" Serati asks. "Only the committee and various politicians are privy to this gift. It has allowed us to control the population and maintain our power; unfortunately, within our social fabric, most of those in these top positions are men. I have tried diversifying this place countless times, but some people are not cut out for it and can't handle the pressure. And most of our members aren't keen on people with uteruses entering such important spaces. Of course, I am the exception. The fewer we are as memory holders, the easier it is to manage all of us. But everything comes with a sacrifice; we have to make the difficult decisions. We are very valuable to this country: we are the memory banks, and we recall everything with succinct detail going back centuries. In that respect, there is something you must know about the girl and your wife."

Elifasi furrows his eyebrows. "What about them?"

Serati says, "According to my records, they're related."

"What?" he asks.

"Spanning back to Nelah's second lifespan, she was a woman called Nthati Molapo. She had a daughter with a man by the name of Gao Gadifele, who had accumulated fifty years in his lifespan, whilst she was left with two years. They were deeply in love. The pregnancy was unplanned. Their love couldn't transcend into her new lifespan, with the lengthy waiting period for a body and the amnesia of mind transfer. Her body expired concurrently with her timely expurgation, and Gao succumbed to depression and narcotics and was indicted by the CBE before he could commit any crimes, which orphaned their one-year-old daughter, Moremi."

Elifasi closes his hanging mouth. "That's, what? Twenty-two years ago?"

She nods.

"And now Nelah will murder the daughter she never knew she had." Elifasi smiles. "I've struck gold. Perhaps now she'll understand betrayal." He stares at Serati. "What do your records reveal about me?"

"You were a low-life scum who swindled every family you were born in," she says calmly.

Elifasi smiles. "Well, that perfectly explains your attitude toward me."

"What do your records say about me?" Aarav asks, on edge.

Her eyes measure him momentarily. "You suffered terribly. A poor, sad life."

"Good thing I made up for it," he says, then notices her weariness. "What?"

"In your current lifespan, you've employed three of your own children from previous lifespans. And, given the nature of your business, they suffer a great deal." She clears her throat. "You . . . have become intimate with one of them, a young woman by the name of Puleng Maiteko. She took her uncle's surname after her mother disappeared."

Puleng, the girl who complained that the work meals resembled her grandmother's recipes—they mined the recipe from her using the microchip.

Elifasi throws him a disgusted expression and steps away.

"Puleng is my daughter? See the fucking problems your memory donations are doing to us?" Aarav spits, inching up to her face.

Elifasi rolls his eyes. "The rapist cries wolf, how ironic. Even if the law increased the period on the waitlist, it doesn't end incest."

"By now, we are fairly acquainted. Cut us into this deal," Aarav demands with a pointed finger. "We want to know and remember everything."

"In your empire, you may be a god." Serati steps forward, every word clipped. "Do not let that illusion fool you into thinking you are above me. I have let you get away with heinous things for the purpose of feeding Matsieng. Do not be mistaken that you aren't dispensable. There are cockroaches of scum like you around. Ones that know not to bite the hand that feeds them." She sighs. "This is how the new world functions. Either you want immortality or you give that up."

"What is the point of immortality if you can't fucking remember your past?" Aarav's voice deepens into anger. "What is the point when each mind transfer kills our past? That is not immortality. That is dying and being reborn."

Serati folds her arms. Stares at him.

Anger spans Aarav's jawline. "Puleng Maiteko. Who's the mother?"

The soft downlight dance in her brown-swept irises. "I am," she says.

The news stuns them, worse how calmly she pulls the trigger, delivers the bullet, soft-voiced.

"Why didn't you protect her, goddamnit?" Aarav yells.

Serati shrugs. "In my new lifespan, she's no longer my daughter. I distinctly separate my lifespans. The past stays in the past."

They observe her with fear, unrestrained terror, and undeniable confusion. It leaves them speechless. What does this mean for them, if she can do this to her own daughter? You can't trust someone like this, a woman like this.

Elifasi shifts from one foot to the other, discomfort splayed across his twisted lips. "From here on, perhaps we should limit our interaction."

"Anything is fine with me as long as the goals are strictly met," Serati adds.

The men wearily stare at each other.

From her pocket, Serati produces a glass ampoule glinting with a dark red liquid.

"What's this?" Eli asks.

"Blood from Matsieng's waterwombs," she says. "We keep finding new uses. Of course, we must be careful, for this blood has immense power and can be fatal. But, if you drink this diluted version, it'll connect us in case there are any fuck-ups that we need to resolve."

They wince, shake their heads.

"If I'm going to drink this blood from this Matsieng *thing*"—Aarav stabs his finger at the vial—"it has to be worth more than connecting us. Any powers we get from her?"

Eli's head bobs up and down in agreement.

"Xem," Serati corrects him. "Do not blaspheme our ancestor." She steps closer to him, a head taller than me, and looks down at him. "Aarav, the committee has advanced certain privileges to your family, given our members' stakes in your companies and the relationship we've had with the Koshal ancestors—"

"Not all of my fucking family!" he shouts. "I lost my memories, and some of my firms assisted with this technology that this fucking Dr. Farahani still struggles to maintain."

"Your technology is a subpar imitation of the one we use in conjunction with Matsieng," Serati enunciates. "Our members were only interested in working with you given the success of your firms, and so we turned a blind eye to how you maintain that *success*. As such, not everyone in your family is awarded that privilege. We can quickly elect a different Koshal to work with."

This shuts up Aarav, and Serati continues, "We've only used Matsieng's blood for other functions, such as the police towers' chemicals, assisting in the body-hopping transitions, etc.—not for your personal use. If you don't want it," Serati says, "I'm not here to convince you. I hope you are ready to face the consequences of that decision." She pauses, stares at Eli. "But *you* can do far more damage with this blood in your system based on your relationship with Nelah."

"What damage?" Eli asks.

She sighs. "Let's hope we never find out. We don't need another complication."

"Fucking hell," Aarav says. "Fucking mess these bitches got us in. Do it, just fucking do it." He screws his eyes shut, opens his mouth and Serati disposes the first droplet of blood onto his tongue, then Eli's, and she swallows the remaining.

"To conclude the meeting," her gentle voice probes, "gentlemen, it is agreed, then, that Moremi and Nelah are our imminent problems?" They nod, and again she delivers the bullet with ease and agility. "Murder two birds with one stone: the Murder Trials."

23:48 /// EPISODE THREE

The images coalesce to a night.

We have to run, be on the run forever, always escaping them. My colleagues and I split into the veld, into the dark of empty roads. The microchips automate. They've found me. My eyes are a shifting camera. Braids caught in the wind. In the unfailing trek of the mountainous region of reality, I gallop, trying to lose them. I'm a chassis of skin and bones tied up in a bow of melanin, chugging out breaths.

Someone's using my microchip now. To control me. Defiling my body. Hogtying my mind so I remain passive. Inert. The scene clips forward, racing as a fast-bound train.

"Kill her." I hear their voices in my microchip filling my skull. Elifasi. Dr. Farahani. Aarav. Serati.

An oncoming car. Headlights, sharp and obtrusive. A sharp intake of dark, and my body flings me into it. A hard sky, dark earth. The hard earth catches my back when I fall—she's harder than I thought. I wake up with a scream torn into my teeth.

Sharp thunder. Pain, so much pain. A woman. A man.

Death stabs, scrapes, and tears me apart. My skin, and beneath it, bones split my sinews. God, it hurts. I'm just a cigarette, inhaling this cancer from the microchip. Lovers who shouldn't be lovers—I feel them panic, pick at me, try to bury me. The soil fills my mouth and covers my screams. Death slings the oxygen from my lungs. The night is all over me, making holes in my skin. Dragging me. Air is painful; it burns as it leaves my lungs. I pray to the air. I pray to the sky. I pray to the land. *Keep me safe. Save me. Please keep me alive. Mama, I'm scared.* I pray to them, but they ignore my pleas. The lonely eye of the moon watches them kill me, watches me die. Land, air, night, the woman and man desecrate my body, arrange my body into the grave.

The job is done. I am char. I am taboo. I am gone.

Dawn wakes me up, lividity in my back. With a tinge of darkness, my memories drip from my body, coagulate with the blood in the earth. I exhume myself from a makeshift grave, cleaved from my physical body. I drag myself from the ditch, panting, feeling for the air that should be gasping from the hole in my throat where a piece of broken glass has slit it open. I grab its sharp eye, yank it out, blood gurgles out. No breath, no heartbeat. I am dead.

Pure, unadulterated anger floods my system.

At 1:34 a.m., I took my last breath.

Something significant tries to come alive, something I was meant to do. People's names sit at the edge of my tongue, but I can't remember them. My memories evade me. Skewered from my skull, they decay on the ground with my dismembered toes. They're not important. I have a new role. I limp the stretch of murram road, parting the forest. Pain licks the jarring bone protruding from my elbow, slipping away. I am death. Anger, anesthesia to the pain. I pled to the person who also wore my gender, hoping that sameness would be my savior. But no, the woman was a demon, as was the man. Merciless. *How could they? I will be the knife slicing through their flesh. My revenge will be their passport to hell.*

I don't need oxygen unless I sip it from the woman's lungs. *I am not reborn for nothing.*

The birds stir. I watch a beetle scuttle across my broken toes. A crow slices the air above the treetops. The foliage sways. I'm dizzy. I cup my hands beneath my dripping blood and drink it. I walk, without toes, without skin, free from gravity's hold.

Incoming thoughts, snapshots of people, the new victims: an old man, an old woman, their son; the woman's husband, her lover, her fetus trapped in a pod.

I know her. The killer. Her accomplice. The people she loves.

I am the secret they tried to maim; I am the secret back from the dead.

CAST

Moremi Gadifele	As Herself
Dr. Narges Farahani	As Herself
Aarav Koshal	As Himself
Elifasi Bogosi-Ntsu	As Himself
Serati Zwebathu	As Herself
Nelah Bogosi-Ntsu	As Herself
Janith Koshal	As Himself

....

Stream in VR again?

NEXT EPISODE ►

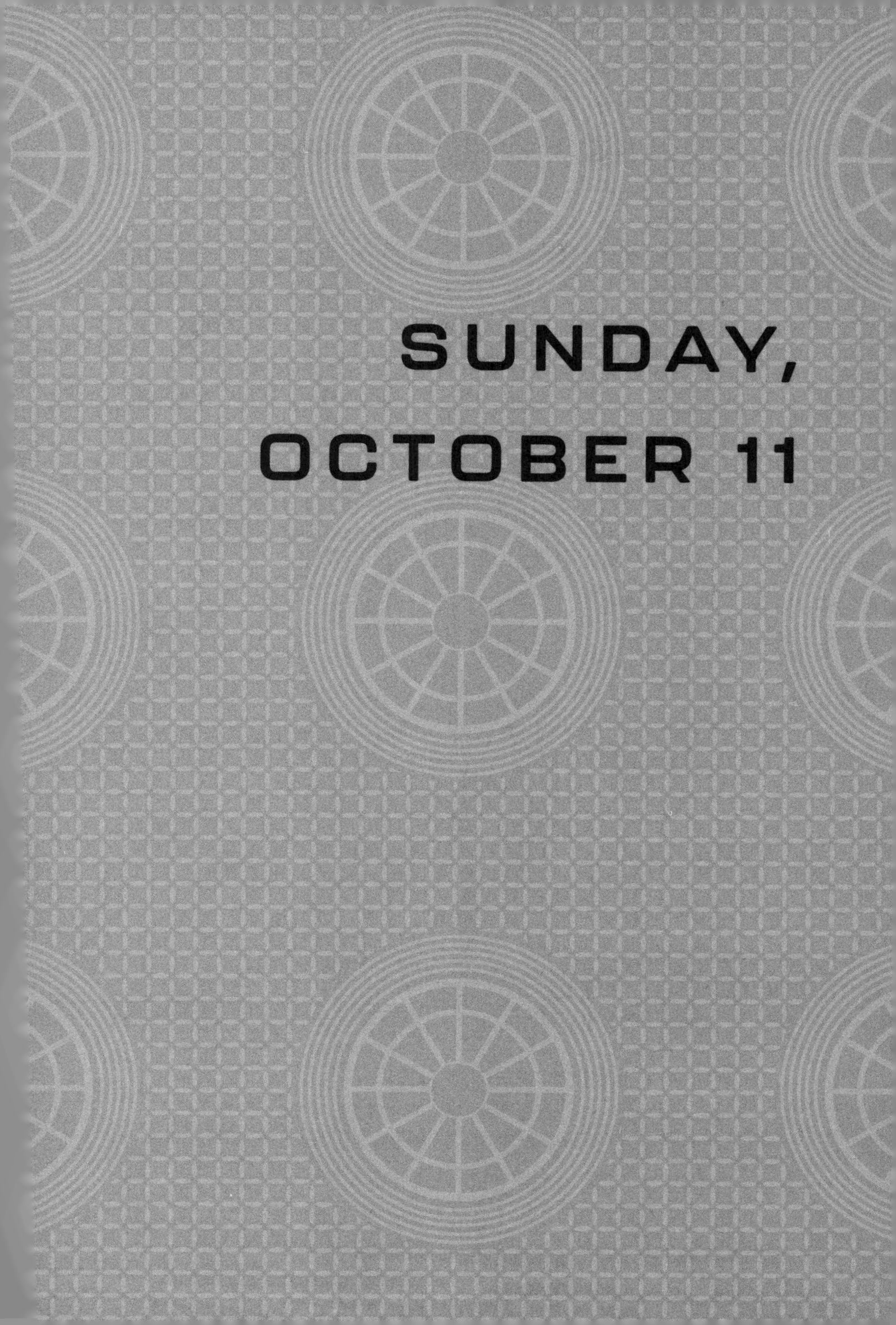

SUNDAY, OCTOBER 11

00:02 /// WHAT KIND OF MOTHER ARE YOU?

Silence flickers, its embers grow faint. The night deepens into a slippery fugue. Jan and I wake, the screen black, the air cold, the words NEXT EPISODE glare across our faces.

Moremi sits, forlorn, huddled into her knees. “You . . . You didn’t kill me. *They* did.” I watch the credits drip down her face as they scroll down the screen. “I trusted him. But he used me.”

“Elifasi was supplying multinational corporations with microchips to control their employees,” I say, bile rising into my mouth. “How could I have not known? Jan, that’s how your father seemed clean after those allegations.”

Jan stares at his hands, into nothing. “He also used the microchips to control and mine data from his employees to get all those contracts he’s been lauded for. How is he my father? How can I be related to something like that? How could they talk so casually about rape and holding people hostage, controlling them? How are they not afraid to kill people? What the hell is wrong with them?” He spins to me. “Have you heard of this company, InSide?”

I shake my head. “It doesn’t exist. He lied.”

“Moremi tried to run away,” Jan whispers, “and *we* killed her.”

I stare at Moremi. I have a daughter. A full-grown daughter. Who’s been alone and hurt for twenty-two years. I have two daughters. Two. Unborn, dead. And I can’t but think what I did to my daughter, having an affair with her boss’s son. The same boss has been abusing her, only for me and her boss’s son to kill her while she was fleeing from her boss’s captivity, only for her to be straitjacketed into a violent vengeance by the Murder Trials, forced to kill. Fuck. How else would I expect anyone to deal with this trauma when coerced to face their killer? She was orphaned, and the world fucked her over. If this life was dealt to her, it would obliterate any idealized future I imagined for my unborn daughter. The life I didn’t want my unborn daughter to inherit is the life she will live. The same issues I fled from with my parents and brother manifest themselves between us, reincarnated. Regardless of how much I distance myself from my problems, they will always orbit my life, rebirthing themselves and finding a way toward me. The only solution is to submit myself to the things I haven’t wanted to face. I must do better than my parents and Limbani regardless of whether Moremi accepts me; I will understand if she rejects me.

I gingerly touch Moremi’s shoulder, afraid she’ll disintegrate. She looks up. “You’re my mother,” she says, and weeps. “They knew. That prosecutor knew. Didn’t do anything. Let me grow up without a parent. How many of us are out there? Alone. With nothing. No hope. No home. Being lied to, told we’ll be safe. By the government, the ministers, the social workers.”

“Do you remember?” I ask softly.

Tears brim in her eyes, fall to the floor. She nods, shakes her head, buries her face into her hands. “I’ve been trying to fight it, not let it claim me, but this changes everything. I’m caught between my insatiable desire to kill and the pain of memories spilling into my mind. I am burning because I’m remembering.”

I can only imagine that the recent revelation and events are like a sun, the rays burning against her memories, exposing them. They run amok in her body like a river of fire. I want to douse myself in them, to set myself aflame if it could unyoke her from the Murder Trials. A rivulet of remembrance quivers through her body. Her pupils dilate as she gives herself wantonly to the pain; for a second, the surface of her skin shimmers, and her body grows fuzzy and evanescent, as if caught between being erased and staying. In that glitchy moment, I see how to defeat her. Her weaknesses are her memories, wolves waiting to devour her. This is the opportune time to save my unborn daughter by submerging my other daughter into the fatal waters of her memories. But I can't come to terms with saving one child by killing another. How different would it be for my child to be born to this legacy and its secrets than to the life I was reincarnated into? Not my child, but any child. My altruism isn't solely based on maternal instincts. No one should go through this. *No one.*

"What happened to your father?" I ask, aware that I'm guiding her toward a feverish dissipation, but my fingers grasp hers to keep her tied to the fabric of our reality, and it burns burns burns—for in such close proximity to her I, too, close in on my death.

"I was just a year old when Mama's lifespan—*your* lifespan—expired. Papa was sad, *always* sad. He went for his CBE and never came home. Then our home was taken, and I bounced from relative to relative."

"Oh, nana." I pull her into my arms, and my exposed skin begins to hiss smoke from our contact; it's as if my self-preservation has been tangled up in my need to save her, and the fusion has become a delicious torture. "I'm so sorry. I am here now. I will protect you. You hear me?"

She cries into my chest. "You should've protected me in the beginning—from him." She points a finger at Jan.

"If I had known," Jan says, pauses, stares. "I didn't know, but that doesn't change what I did."

"Jan and I were complicit," I say.

"*You* hesitated, but he didn't," Moremi says. "But I begged *you* that night. How could you not tell from the core of your soul that I was your daughter? I cried for my mother. I cried. You carried dead babies in your body, and you couldn't tell. What kind of mother are you? *How* could you not know me?"

My insides tremble and break. "I-I don't know. I . . . I should've known."

Tears flow down her face. "You've been killing your children and getting away with it."

I shrivel inside myself. Swallow. The air, dead in my lungs.

Jan kneels beside us, holds my limp hand. "She didn't know. That doesn't make her a terrible mother. You saw what they do with our memories. She lost you, and they stripped that memory from her."

"She should've held on to the memory of me," Moremi whispers.

"What's happening to all of us is a grave injustice," Jan says. "Under the circumstances, we did heinous things to cover our tracks. It's inexcusable, what we conspired to do. The guilt is my hell because it was *my* decision, she—*your* mother was manipulated by my decision."

"No." Moremi glares at him. "*She* manipulated you."

The words slap my face. Jan's grip disappears. The lonely grasp of the air helms me.

"What?" Jan's pain, his voice, his shock scrapes at my skin, closes my lungs. "What is she talking about?"

"The microchip," Moremi says, and I gasp, "No!"

She peers at me. "Then tell him. I know everything you felt that night you killed me, from your essence."

I knit my fingers through each other and whisper, "You always protect me. That night I knew you'd find a way to help me—*us*. I believed that although the microchip didn't stop me, it was still recording. I thought if anyone watched the footage in my CBE evaluation, they'd see I was manipulated, fed drugs, and by some miracle, I'd get the same deal I got last time, which is probation and a year's worth of therapy. *That* intercepted my journey to virtual incarceration. A deal that was engineered by my husband."

The heat from his anger flares against my face. "And what would happen to me?"

"Your father would save you like he's done before."

He scoffs. "And everything would be back to normal?"

"Yes. By some screwed-up logic manufactured by my panicked mind, that's what I truly believed."

"And your husband is the savior in all of this, nè? The man you stick to." He laughs. "I'm so stupid, so dom. I sold a portion of my shares for you."

I look up, stunned by the information he's disclosed. "What?"

"I made a deal with someone who had the power to change your verdict when you failed your CBE. To save you. To engineer that same interception you so wholly believed your husband was behind."

His revelation hits me hard. Sends a jolt through my bones. *This* never occurred to me. My mind jams as I try to compute how Jan could have found out. How he pretended to not know. Why he did it. *Because he loves me,* like he's mentioned before. Then everything stills. A warm feeling slips inside me, and his love is all at once tangible, filling my chest, flowing through my veins. "But why didn't you tell me?" I ask.

"Because you would've felt guilty, like you owed me, like I was buying you, which was never the case." He stares at me, but his gaze goes through me as if I'm not there. "I've never meant anything to you. I've just been a sex toy. An object you can use for your purposes."

"No. That's not true."

"Then why didn't you tell me about your plan?" he asks.

"Because it would hurt you, Jan. I hated myself for thinking that. I *never* wanted you to know. You must believe, I am not the same person as the night of the accident."

"And I am not the same person who loved you."

Pain cascades inside my gut, up my spine, through the veins in my neck.

He looks away. "The unfortunate thing is I can't stop loving you. It'll take some time to go away, to leave my body."

"I love you," I whisper. "Please, don't give up on me now."

His eyes bore into me. Pain tracks tears down his face. "*You* gave up on *me*. Many times. How do I trust a love like that? I'm imprisoned by my love for you."

"Give me time. To fix what I've broken."

"I've no time. I'll be dead."

I grip his face, lean my head against his until our eyes kiss. "I love you, Jan. My love will keep you alive. Us alive. Our love will keep us alive. Keep us floating in this life. We will not be shipwrecked from reality. Please, baby, believe. *Asseblief.*"

He closes his eyes, seals himself in darkness. Breaths tremble from his lips, and I sip them as we sway in this seesawing reality, this unknown truth.

"We've murdered, but I can't murder our love," he whispers.

Moremi groans. "How can you still support her? After everything. What about me? *Who* supports me? Protects me like the fetus you've been obsessed about?"

I pull Moremi into our embrace. "Whatever happened, you're my daughter. You are under my shield; nothing will touch you. It's time we take them down. We can only do this if we work together. We have to work together. But you have to tell us everything you know. *Everything*."

Her anger subsides. "You're not lying," she whispers. "I can feel it, your love. For the first time, I can feel the truth. I wish I had this sense when I was alive. Then I wouldn't have trusted him. *Your* husband . . . but your family is not so innocent. No one is. I guess that's what makes us human."

Jan stirs. "What did they do?"

Moremi looks at me. "Well, Mama's . . ." She pauses, catches herself. "Is it okay if I call you that?"

A deep pain of love wakes in my heart. I've been dying to hear that word from a child of my own. "You can call me whatever you want," I say, and a tear slips down my face.

Moremi wipes it with her fingers. "The last time I said that I must've been a year old. It feels strange saying it: Mama. But I like it."

"I love it, too," I say, gripping her hand. Everything feels warm and perfect and I don't want it to end. I want to stretch this time with my hands, pull it around us, sit in it and find out everything about her.

A smile gnaws its way up the tightly exposed cartilage in her face, and sadness explodes inside me. *We* did this to her. And Aarav, what he did to her, I want to make him pay.

"Your husband is not as financially incapable as you think," Moremi reveals, staring ahead in concentration. "He has money hidden from bribes he's taken as well as his dealings with Serati and Aarav."

"That fucking thokolosi," I spit. "We'd argue for hours about money, even to pay our daughter's maintenance fee for the Wombcubator. I can't believe him." My lips stutter, and I feel shock shred my body into senseless anger.

"I'm afraid of people like Elifasi," Moremi says. "Jan's father is openly immoral. But a man like Elifasi, who is quiet and obedient-appearing, makes knives out of his bones that you never see he's already stabbed you with."

Jan perks up. "Does Eli have something he can use against us?"

"I can only see him when I need to kill him," Moremi says. "But nothing I can sense."

From the space leading to the stairs, my brother stirs. Wakes. Sits up. Cups his hand around his neck, stopping the flow of blood, his skin lined with dried-up blood. "Where the hell am I?" His eyes catch Moremi. "Get away from me!" He's not halfway to death as Moremi claimed. He shakes his head. "No, no, no, it's happening again. No. Why does this keep happening? I did nothing wrong."

"Happening again?" I ask. My heart pounds. Fear rattles inside me. Confused, I turn to Moremi.

She frowns and the world's slit open and thrown into the fires again when she whispers, "You're not going to like this, Mama, but your father participated in the Murder Trials." Her voice's sheathed with sadness. "He was hunting. Shot a twelve-year-old kid by accident. He failed their test, and just like you"—she steers her eyes from me, resurrects the courage—"he buried the body. Buried the secret."

00:12 /// MURDER, GODSENT

Papa participated in the Murder Trials. The words settle in my mind with dizzying effect. I stand, feet frozen to the ground, unable to understand the meaning behind my daughter's statements.

Jan exits the cinema and returns with a glass of water for Limbani. "Take a few breaths, man, we're just trying to figure everything out. Moremi won't hurt you."

My brother glares at him. "She terrorized me in the bathroom before knocking me out."

Moremi folds her arms, scoffs. "Ag, please, you're still alive, aren't you? Besides, I believe you are familiar with this kind of practice . . . well, as a victim, that is. Unfortunately for you, today we exhume the truth about your family."

"A victim?" My mouth hangs open.

Limbani throws the glass at Moremi. It spears through her, shatters against the wall, darkens it with water. He attempts to stand but Jan pushes him back down. Limbani shakes, pulls his knees close to his chest, muttering, "Not again, not again, not again."

I come to, at the fear trickling from Limbani. I take a deep breath, walk toward him. Squat next to him. Touch his shoulder gently. Regurgitate everything that's happened: our parents' deaths, the Murder Trials, their rules, our predicament. His irises dilate at every reveal, but at least his trembles dissipate. He grips his knees tighter—childlike, terrified—eyes focused ahead as his mind slowly chews the startling news.

"Your father's list was eleven people long," Moremi says. "Three cousins murdered in a span of seconds. Two brothers murdered in a span of two days. Four sisters murdered in one day. His parents murdered early dawn. *He* was nowhere to be found until dusk, when on the farm grounds, his daughter was assaulted by the ghost. To save his wife and two other children—"

My knees buckle. "Two other children?"

Moremi side-eyes Limbani with disgust. "There were three of you. Two sisters and a brother. You had a sister, the firstborn, Nalia."

My insides curdle with cold, confusion, fury.

"Your father was in hiding," Moremi says. "Although the ghost knew where he was, it was pissed off. At his cowardice. Before activating its final passing, nothing can stop a ghost from killing until it feels it has inflicted enough pain on its victim. So it went to his pride and joy: Nalia." The air is sewn tight into our lungs. Claws of sadness climb our spines. Pity saturates our exhales with death. "The attack occurred on the farm grounds, at sunset. Limbani and the original host of your body witnessed it, tried to save her. The ghost threw you back—"

Limbani crushes his eyes closed. "Your horrifying, shrilling scream. An auger had got your arm. She was only thirteen at the time, and I fifteen."

Moremi peers up at me, eyes shiny with tears. "And . . . it's how you lost your arm."

Grief beckons me. I stare at my arm, terrorized by guilt for having harshly criticized this body, never knowing the immense pain it suffered. I poisoned it with my toxic thoughts, but it wasn't less perfect or less of a person. It was beautiful, held many lives, carried us through grief and loss. This body of mine is powerful, with or without limbs.

My brother's eyes evade mine as he cuddles himself.

"This is the second time Limbani's almost been killed by a victim," Moremi explains tragically, and I feel terrible for him. "That's how he got those surgical scars on his neck." I was always told it was from him wriggling through a church's fence. "As Limbani tried to pull you from it," Moremi says, "your father came and finished the killing. Killed Nalia to save you, Limbani, and his wife. The sunrays dissolved the ghost into its final passing for it was satisfied."

Limbani huddles into himself, cries, "I can still remember that ghost standing in the fields, drenched in blood, just watching us as the sun burned him. I couldn't understand what was going on."

The room inhales, exhales. Sits in its grove of mourning.

"Papa killed his own daughter to stop the Murder Trials," I whisper, disgusted. I face Moremi. "You made that offer to me."

Moremi blinks. Looks away.

I stare at my hands, clear of blood, but not sin. "'The devil's come to collect my sins. My punishment has come. I will be redeemed for my sins.'" I stare at Jan. "Papa's last words. That's why he killed himself. To stop the pattern. But he just saved himself." Revulsion toils in my gut. I peer at my daughter. "How do you know all of this?"

She shrugs. "I have access to your essence, your DNA, and the family connected to it, including their secrets and histories, which I'm to use to my advantage as part of the Murder Trials."

I take a deep breath. "Serati told us that if I win the Murder Trials, I lose my identity and citizenship, so how come Papa was able to keep his?"

"Every victim gets a different deal," Moremi says. "You're a woman and microchipped, and he was a man. Given that he was unfairly forced into the Murder Trials, the committee's decision considered that. They didn't take anything about your history into account."

I stare at her. "You kept this from me this whole time?"

"We were enemies—I saw no reason to tell you." Moremi's face fills with pity. She reaches for my hand. "I am sorry. I want you to know the truth."

I nod. "So, Papa was microchipped?"

She shakes her head. "A mistake was made. He was supposed to be a victim, but somehow he was selected as a murderer. The committee was quite smaller at that time and was error-prone. Before they could remedy it, it was too late. That's the Murder Trials—nothing stops them—not even human errors."

Jan fists his hands, colors his face with a deep red fury. "They make mistakes, and the citizen pays the cost?"

Moremi nods, continues, "Mama, that's how *your* family became wealthy, from the proceeds of the trial award, basically hush money given the Murder Trials Committee's error. Your father never disclosed to the family the real reason for the deaths in their family. As part of his reward, he requested that no reports were made of the killings. There was no one left to fight for the truth except him, his wife, and his two children. Your father was haggard and traumatized," Moremi says. "Sleepwalked, had nightmares and hallucinations of the boy returning again as a devil to punish him. Said not a word—"

"Until three years later." Limbani snatches the story from Moremi; his cheeks, layered in anger, grumble out the truth. "Tortured and stalked by this hallucinatory child-demon, Papa broke down and told us everything. When my sister realized what had funded our family ranch, the expensive cars, the lavish clothes, the private schools, the trips, was not our family business, but the murder of a young boy. That's how . . ." He clams his mouth with his fist, eyes tear, stares away. Limbani inclines his head, and an avalanche of sobs wrecks his body.

Moremi folds her arms. "Well, the daughter wanted no more attachment to the family name, so when she turned eighteen, she disowned her family, donated her body, and became a carer to survive." She throws a glance at me. "That's why the second owner of your body was considered an Original but struggled to live in this body, and within three months, her consciousness died in an alleged accident. The body was intact but she'd opted for cremation but was declined, and a third owner was placed into your body, but within three months, they committed a crime that got them evicted from your body, and that's when you, Mama, became the fourth host of this body."

I stagger back. "What?"

I'm not the third host, I'm the fourth. There was another secret trapped in this body. *My* body. I glare at Limbani, who sinks his face into his hands.

"Jesu, what do you mean alleged accident?" I ask, staring at Limbani.

"She had suicidal ideation, and we put her through therapy. She'd had a car accident—some say she jumped into a moving car, but the video footage from the surrounding area says otherwise. Her consciousness was unable to be saved—the doctors tried, but the body rejected it.

The body was still functional for another host, so they pulled one off the waiting list, who ended up committing a crime in the body."

I'm silent, astounded at the feat this body has undergone. This body at the age of eighteen had experienced so much, three deaths and the loss of three hosts.

"A family secret they were desperate to keep buried," Moremi says. "It's easy to maintain this perfect façade, when hell is burning inside and no one is putting out the fires."

"And the blood money? That's where the wealth of our family comes from?" I whisper.

Limbani stares shamefully at his hands, uproots the grief from his body with each word of confession: "That's how I developed my media company to where it is. Sometimes I despised myself when I'd watch you build your firm from hard work, clean money, and success. It reminded me that my company was powerful today because we profited from the death of children and relatives."

A coldness of shock fills my chest. "I thought you were jealous of my success—do you know what that did to me, all this hiding? Would it have truly killed you all, to be honest with me? What good has it done to keep these secrets? Look at us. Papa and Mama are dead!"

"I know, I know," he cries. "We thought it was best not to tell you. It pained Mama that we lost Nalia, and all the other Nelahs. Mama believed their daughter's body was haunted and punished by the sin of my father killing Nalia, hence why your body's hosts were easily swayed into wrongdoing. The week Mama was planning to serve Papa divorce papers, you arrived. She stayed in the marriage for you. If she left, she didn't know who would fill that spot and perhaps ruin you. Abandoning the marriage would expose you to horrors she didn't want to imagine. She knew she'd done no wrong but sentenced herself to that marriage to save you. It was her sacrifice for you. Mama felt your innocence and wanted to protect its purity. She never wanted to taint you with our dark history—that's why they stalled in giving you the inheritance. They were protecting *you*."

Silence is grave around me. "This whole time, I thought our parents didn't want me as their daughter. If you were honest with me, my doubts wouldn't have crippled me this way."

Limbani stares at me teary-eyed. "Through several years, Mama worked on forgiving Papa. It was her idea for you not to inherit the blood money, which to her meant that you wouldn't inherit the curse. Instead, she poured all her love into you, her faith that she wouldn't lose another child. Deep down, that hurt me because you received the love I always wanted, and I handled it wrong. So I used my businesses to distract me, and I just kept getting more of our parents' money to extend the outreach of my company, hoping to use it for good even if I wasn't good."

"Why? All these lies," I say. "And you terrorized me for years!"

Limbani wrests his face from his hands. Stares at me, eyes red with anger, voice sour-tinged. "I was angry with you because I was angry with myself! With what my father did. Losing my sister. Your existence symbolized how trapped we were because you were free of all these secrets. You were family, profiting from our inheritance but not carrying the baggage that came with it. *You* were protected. A fucking stranger. *You* became their hope. And I was supposed to just deal with it. Be a man. I was called a pussy for breaking out in tears. Lauded for acting cold. How could I love you? How could I accept you when what I was feeling wasn't accepted?" He hangs his head between his knees, destroyed, burned. "This fucking family, this trauma has stained our DNA."

I'm devastated by the truth, that Mama stayed in a marriage that had betrayed her to save her child, neither was she ever bitter or hostile to me. Why must women push themselves to endure marriage, forcing themselves to forgive their husbands for a heinous act? Why must it be up to them to save the marriage, to save the children? Her love may have not stopped this curse, but she was my shield, and I must now be the fruit of her faith and take this curse by the throat and slay it.

"This is where we cut the damn tree down," I say, staring at Limbani. "This is where we change the pattern, you hear?" I step closer to him. He's also the victim in this, conditioned to accept it. "No more generational trauma. We will not be cowards of our fate. It's only you and me left. *We* are in control now. If you want to cry, cry. Let it out. But we have to kill our old toxic selves to become better people. We need to fix this, or it'll only get worse."

Limbani blinks, stares.

"Is that why Mama was having nightmares when I was young?" I ask.

"Ja, it triggered her, and she'd distance herself from Papa to recover," Limbani says, and I recall how Papa would give Mama space, but now I understand why. "She was still having the night terrors before passing on. It hit her the most."

"We can't move forward if there are still secrets," I ask.

"None," he answers. His dark-brown eyes focus on mine. "I didn't expect you to respond . . . so calmly. I thought you'd be angry, fight, seek revenge."

"*That* hasn't solved anything so far," I whisper. Look away. "I killed my own daughter—who am I to shame?"

"You didn't kill me," my daughter says. "*They* did."

Limbani whispers, "Is it . . . okay if I hug you?"

My breath catches. "Ja."

He limps forward. Wraps his arms around me. I rest my face into his chest. Ten years we've been siblings, and this has never happened.

"Nelah," he says.

"Yeah?"

"I'm really sorry for everything. The things I said, the things I did. I am sorry."

"I am sorry, too." Peace almost seems foreign in my body. "This may be wrong to say, but you're the first Black man who has authentically apologized to me."

"Culture conditions us to not seek forgiveness from women," he whispers. "That we do no wrong, that women are to blame for the damage we impose on them. Forces us to castrate our emotions. My marriage is in tatters because of that. I want to be a better man."

"Strange, isn't it?" Jan says from my side, his palm on the small of my back. "Something horrid had to happen for us to recognize the wrong, to mandate a change."

Limbani and I pull apart and laugh. "Murder, god-sent?" I say. "Let's not go that far."

We stand, folded in silence.

Limbani stares at Moremi. "I didn't know you had a daughter."

"From my previous lifespan," I say.

He smiles. "In the past, we'd say from a previous marriage." He scowls. "You scare me," he tells her.

"I'm sorry," she whispers, and sinks her head into my chest and I hold her.

My voices muffles against her braids. "Where's Mama?"

Moremi pouts, casually says, "Limbani. She'll be coming for him in one hour, so I can deal with the next person."

Limbani backpedals, eyes prised wide by fear. "You have to stop her. Please . . . I can't see her like—" He begins to cry.

Moremi's pity enfolds him. "I'll try." She looks at me. "There's something that the Murder Trials Committee hasn't been transparent about to you," she says, and my stomach curdles with sick. "The way they obtain international identities for some of those who win. Over the decades, they've been able to station several of their agencies abroad in collaboration with some human traffickers to obtain bodies and smuggle Batswana citizens into those identities and ultimately into that foreign country. The upside loophole for them is that they don't need to forge passports and identities, since you will be smuggled into the country's citizenship, and since there's no technology developed yet to discern if a foreign consciousness has been swindled into a country's native population, the Murder Trials Committee can get away with these acts. Sometimes these bodies belong to sex workers or the destitute in foreign lands. There are horrible stories where sex workers are picked up by a client, thinking they will offer their services, only for their bodies to be kidnapped. Some sell their bodies willingly so the money can go to their family. So far, the Murder Trials have inseminated themselves in Pakistan, Qatar, Seychelles, Swaziland, Ireland, Brazil, Australia—and they're losing their foothold in some places while they're trying to penetrate other countries."

"Fuck," we all say.

"This is a very networked hell," I say. "This is bigger than us. The whole world would need to end."

"I can't process this," Jan says, sitting down and cuddling his bloody arm.

"There may be a way out for us," Moremi says, "but you have to hear my idea first."

00:26 /// MONSTER'S PAWN

"In the end, your father paid for his sins," Moremi says to Limbani and I, "like a generational curse, handed down to you and I, came for him—no one is ever truly free. They come for you, your sins. Now I have blood on my hands that I'm afraid I will have to pay for in the future. So, what exactly are we winning, besides freeing the authorities from Matsieng's wrath?"

I nod, feeling so proud of her. "We're saving them instead of saving ourselves."

"I am confined to these actions and nothing else," Moremi says. "It makes me powerful, less hungry, but I don't want to do this anymore."

I hold her hands. "Moremi, you're not the monster. I'm not the monster. We're just a monster's pawn."

"Exactly," she says. "But we need a plan to overthrow them. We'd have to destroy them and our history to avoid anyone ever choosing us again. That's how we got selected in the first place, from the database. Destroying the committee and anyone who knows us will destroy the very link that ties us to their world."

I nod, facing my brother. "You have to download this footage and use your media company to broadcast it live. This is the only way we can expose them. But that is the backup plan, because fuck indictment, we must deal with them. Everything ends when they end," I say. "Our job is to protect the people from them. What's to say they won't do this to another group of people again? We will create a safe haven for the people. We were on their hit list, so the cast members of Moremi's film and the committee are our hit list."

"The cast is long," Jan says.

"Hell has space," Moremi says.

"Where is the committee located? Their base?" Jan asks.

"The Matsieng Facility," Moremi says. "It's a cigar lounge of sorts where they gather specifically for the viewing. I was roaming around the building during your meeting with Serati. That's where the Murder Trials Committee is hosting their viewing."

"How can we access it?" I ask.

"The hallways are heavily armed with autonomous weapons and guarded," Moremi says.

"You both have powers. A bullet in me will kill me," Jan says.

"We are your weapons," Moremi says. "Your bulletproof vest."

"I need to be useful for something," Jan says, cradling his blood-soaked hand. "We need everyone who's on our hit list, localized; we won't have the time to scatter ourselves throughout the city. We don't know the whereabouts of my father or your husband. But given the gist of our new predicament, should they matter at all now?"

"What they did was wrong, Jan. I won't let them get away with what they did, hurting people and families, it affects everything," I say. "We can lure Aarav to Matsieng with a lie that he didn't erase all the data. We won't need to tell him where we are since he was able to track us before."

"We've discarded my phone and all other trackable devices," Jan says.

"Except my microchip," I whisper.

"Is the committee watching us right now?" Moremi asks, stepping back.

"Your presence interferes with the signal," I say. "It cuts off all visual and auditory access. I'm going to need you next to me, so they don't see what's coming."

"What about your husband?" Jan asks.

"I'll threaten him with the information we have. They're expecting this to be over soon because we're supposed to die, but this information won't die with us. He'll have no choice but to come." I pause. "Can we reverse the curse of the Murder Trials?"

"One has to win, one has to lose," Moremi says.

"They said the rules change. What are the rules for you to win now?" Jan asks. "They are subject to your desires. Well, sort of, since your desire to kill is incited by Matsieng."

"As it stands, I have a hunger that will only be satiated once your pain and suffering are commensurate with mine," Moremi says. "The only way I can win and get to live again is if that hunger is fed."

"Then let's do that only if my baby stays alive," I say, wondering if perhaps her offer to end my daughter's life has changed.

Moremi says, "Our pain will only be equal once I kill your daughter. That is the one thing you least want, which is an unstoppable hunger to to me. Unfortunately, I can't switch it off."

It strikes my sternum like seismic force and I wobble, bones unhinging themselves from my skeleton. I know I'm just imagining that my body is breaking, but I can't let my baby die. "You can't kill my baby. If you *have* to kill anyone, kill me."

Jan steadies me, his eyes focused on Moremi. "*They* are the murderers. Why hasn't that changed your rules?"

"They worked within the rules." Moremi looks at me. "Technically, you killed me, with your hands. You buried me, snatched my breath away."

I gnaw on my lips as I try to gather myself together. "I get it, I get it," I say. "But she's a baby—doesn't that stir any sympathy in you?"

She stares solemnly at her missing toes. "Death changed me. Robbed me of all empathy or morals, except for vengeance. You killed my innocence. *They* killed my innocence."

"Moremi, you're not killing *us* anymore," I remind her, hanging onto her with desperation. "Only the enemy."

"No more killing," Jan repeats. "Remember that."

But her eyes roll back and it seems like we're losing her. Jan runs his hand through his hair. "Moremi, there're only four people left on the list: Nelah's daughter, her brother, her husband, and me. Nelah and

"Well, how will bringing a zombie apocalypse upon our land solve anything?" Jan asks, perturbed.

"Besides the people trapped there, it's also the spirits who lost the trials," Moremi says. "Well, anyone who's not a man," she clarifies.

"But where do the spirits of males who lose the Murder Trials go?" I ask.

"They are placed in the virtual prison or the body-hop waiting list for an indefinite term," Moremi says, "but most have the privilege to pass on naturally. That angers the spirits trapped in the waterwombs because they don't have any of those rights."

"Does the Murder Trials Committee know this?" Jan asks.

She shakes her head. "No, they think it's Matsieng they've been feeding the deaths. Matsieng may have our memories, but it's the spirits who feed from the deaths and blood, mutating the rules to one day free them from the waterholes, and it's making me powerful, too. Matsieng can overcome them, but Xe's leaving the world to its demise and letting it die of its own hubris."

"Shit," Limbani says.

"This is a volcano of angry spirits waiting to erupt," Jan says.

"I've noticed over time that there are moments when I gain autonomy in my power because those spirits are mutating the rules; they're blocking Matsieng's power because they're being fed evil. The other ghosts before me had less power than me, and it seems they become more empowered as more and more Murder Trials take place; the same is to be said of the killers because no other woman who preceded you has had the same connection that you have to Matsieng—if you fail, whatever that failure involves, then it will be up to any of the succeeding female participants of the following Murder Trials to either tilt the scales toward evil or good. But I'm still restricted and have yet to attain the full power I need to have complete control." She looks up at me. "Perhaps if there'd been more Murder Trials before me, I'd be more powerful than I am today. But if am this half-powerful, and you are that half-powerful, our pairing, which the history of the Murder Trials has never seen before, could revolutionize this system. I can't touch anyone who's not on my revenge list, but you can, Mama," she says. "You are already empowered with the revivals you experience from each death—each time you die, you're instantly reborn. Your connection to Matsieng is the loophole. Both death and life flow in Xem. Xe operates under different laws. To sacrifice yourself to Xem is irrevocable, but Xe will empower you with every weapon you need. That is how I have strength. That is how I am able to move with such speed, to defy gravity. To defy the laws of nature. I gained that through Matsieng. It's very difficult to smuggle anything from my reality into yours, but not the other way around. Now, this is a calculated guess, but I believe you could gain more as a sacrificial lamb."

Jan folds his arms. "What does that mean?"

"Well, that's my idea," Moremi says. "We should infiltrate Matsieng so Mama can bury herself in Xer waterwombs to gain power to overthrow the committee."

Jan's eyes widen. "How do we know you're not lying again, that your need for revenge isn't still driving you?"

Moremi stares at him, hesitant. "The same can be thought of you, too."

"Hey, we're on the same team," I say. "What weapons will Matsieng give me?"

"I don't know, but there is immense energy in there," Moremi says. "Out of this world. Blood from centuries ago. From ancestors. It ties to different realms. Matsieng . . . Xe is like a god. Xe could be the kill switch to this curse, and it could reverse everything. That's how powerful Xe is. And Mama, to come into that power, you'd need to take the fall for everyone's sins and give yourself to Matsieng. That might change our lives."

"This is a huge risk," Jan says. "We don't even know if it'll work."

"I should be killing you right now," Moremi says. "I have a clock in me, a time bomb I'm fighting every second. Do you understand what I am risking not killing you this second? I am losing myself, losing the trial. This is me trying to cooperate with you."

"Why must we always take the fall?" I ask, clasping my hands to my face. "Why haven't previous targets thought of this?"

"Like I told you, the previous ghosts lacked the autonomy even to try," Moremi says. "I'm certain the ghosts in the next Murder Trials will be much more powerful and free than me. I don't know how many Murder Trials it would take for the ghosts to gain complete autonomy.

You can imagine how terrible that will be for our country. Matsieng will not stop the ghosts from overflowing onto our land as punishment to us. If humans had just left Xem alone, the ghosts wouldn't be able to do this."

"Why do you trust me?" I ask.

Her eyes stare steadfastly at me as if inhaling me. "I have your essence, and I can sense your honesty. It changed how I saw you over time, when you started to see and empathize with me. It felt like love. But I still had to remember myself and not let that obstruct my mission. This still aligns with what I want: vengeance."

"Then I will do it," I say, taking a deep breath. "I'll sacrifice myself to Xer waterwombs."

Moremi's half-torn lips split wider with shock.

"Hang on, let's think about this clearly," Jan says. "We don't know what we're dealing with. What if you die in there?"

"I'm not going to let my daughter die again," I say. "Jan, you have committed sins even if you may feel guiltless about them. Limbani, you've committed sins. Papa has committed sins. Everyone has committed something. I can no longer judge myself or you. Matsieng *should* be the arbiter. Not greedy people on the Murder Trials Committee who use human trafficking for their own gain. Now, if this is the only chance to redeem our sins, to right all our wrongs, to save us, and I am the only one who can do it, then I'm going to do it. If I can die and rise again—if Moremi can kill after death—imagine what we'll be capable of if I fuse myself to Matsieng. I can save my daughter, and I can save Moremi and take care of people like Aarav. Saving my children could translate to my death, but sometimes death is freedom from hell. Don't you get it? Death is a different language from what we know it to be. I'll be transcending into Matsieng. We don't know what the outcome will be but, like the Murder Trials, I have no choice but to participate. And this is how I choose to move forward."

Jan rubs his jaw, and my brother stares wide-eyed. Something dings, and he looks up. "I've downloaded the footage," Limbani says.

"Good," I say. "You must remember that your life is in danger. We can't protect you. The signal is sunrise. If by 5:00 a.m. you haven't heard from us, we failed."

"All our lives are in danger," Limbani says. "I could be picked next for the Murder Trials. Or my wife or children."

"Then we need to find a way to get inside Matsieng," Jan says.

"We better hurry," Moremi says, a casual lilt to her voice. "Your mother will be here in ten minutes."

Limbani starts shaking, and clutches his mouth as if he's going to be sick.

I nod at my daughter, graze my fingers across her cheek. "The committee will be suspicious once we're on Matsieng premises and they're no longer receiving feedback from my microchip. That alerts them you're with me instead of killing your assigned targets. So this is where we separate—"

"Actually, I have an idea of how to gain access to Matsieng," Moremi says. "It involves blood. A lot of blood."

"That doesn't surprise me," Jan says.

I smile. "Let's hear it."

Glancing at her reflection in the cinema's mirrored wall, Moremi says, "Prior to our arrival at Matsieng, Jan, you will drive like a crazy man to Serati, plead for her to save you. Tell her that I am after you, that you witnessed my attack on Mama, et cetera. Then I will arrive with your body, Mama, where I will force them to prepare your body for me since that's the body I chose to live in once I win the trial. That will be the opportune time for you to succumb to Matsieng."

"That's a smart plan!" I say.

She looks at me now, apologetically. "I will try not to throw a hard punch. But we need the wounds and blood to convince Serati. Otherwise, she'll be suspicious."

I grimace, staring at my brother's injuries. "I've survived a car crash and a gunshot wound to my head. I believe I can stomach anything."

Limbani winces.

She looks at me. "You understand seasickness? In this case, you'll get time-sick when you journey with me to Matsieng."

I chew my lip. "I don't understand what that means, but I'm prepared for what may come."

Jan taps his chin, nods. "For what it's worth, it *is* a good plan."

Moremi says, "I wasn't hunting for a compliment nor for your permission."

The right side of his smile springs up. "I know. I hope one day you will forgive me. I truly am sorry."

Pity flickers in her eyes. "I'll think about it."

Everyone is tired. We are all tired and want this over. I stare at my watch. "The deadline is closing in. The sun will find us in five hours."

"There's a mistake," Moremi whispers. "The deadline isn't Sunday's sunrise—it's when you killed me."

"What?" Jan asks.

"I died at 1:34 a.m."

"That leaves us with one hour." I stare at them. "We don't need much else."

I have killed, and I have died. More is to be mined from this curse. Somewhere in my body lies a metaphorical womb, waiting for the seed of murder—the fallopian, a passage of rite. No guilt will exorcise this evil that impregnates us with its gory deeds.

I spin around. A sound. "Did you hear that?"

"No." Jan shakes his head.

A shadow, up the stairs, fills the doorway. I gasp. "Eli."

00:37 /// RUN

Eli. Gloved. Sweat-speckled. Loose shirt, dust-pocked pants.

"Bothered not to send me the memo, babe?" Elifasi says, head tilted, eyes focused on the streamlined edge of his gun aimed at Jan. A glimmer of gold; light flicks across his wedding band.

"Concrete mix fuck-up, you said. Out of the city," Eli says.

"What are you doing?" I ask.

"I knew something fishy was going on. Might as well stop the act." He takes two steps down, swings his gun at each one of us. A smoked voice, sharp and malignant. "Serati informed me that you've disappeared from their monitoring screens for quite some time, which can only mean you're with Moremi. If she isn't killing, then what the hell are you rats up to, we asked ourselves. This area was the last location pinged on your microchip." He stares at Jan, lips twisted in disgust. "This tsetse fly has been getting on my nerves. Fucking *my* wife. Your father threatened me with his goons if I didn't rein my wife in. Him and his hoodlum guards and I have been hunting through houses in this neighborhood for the better part of an hour. Got us running around like a pack of dogs, Nelah. Then I saw your car parked outside. You shouldn't have left it out there. And now I see your little consortium gathered to invade Matsieng and broadcast us to the world. How stupid are you to think you can get away with this plan?"

"Is that why you called me earlier? Showing false tenderness for our daughter to discover what was happening with us?" I spit. "You bastard."

He smiles. "There she is. At the end of the day, I wanted to come home to a cold beer and a warm pussy, but you were busy fucking this tsetse fly, so I had to resort to this tool." He shakes out a remote control from his pocket.

I blink. It's the the same one that fell from his pocket the morning after we killed Moremi. Eli had asked for sex, and I'd said no, then changed my mind. In the pantry, he thrust into me. I wondered why I was consumed with the need for sex. *My wife,* he'd said to Serati, *she may have seen some things that could compromise us. I've tampered with her microchip and memory, but I'm uncertain of how effective it's been.*

The realization hits me as I whisper, "You used that to control me, to force me to have sex with you."

Eli smiles, eyes bright. Suddenly, he frowns. "This remote has been rendered useless by Moremi's energy field. I can't control you anymore, Nelah. I'll have to resort to the manual way of solving things."

He stares at Moremi, not realizing that being able to see her means he's an instant target. My blood's overflowing with pure ecstasy.

"It isn't that fucking hard to kill, to work your way through the whole family. You've always been a disappointment," Eli says.

How did I marry such a man? Moremi stares silently, but her eyes are daggers, her thoughts venom leaking with the need to devour this monster, this thokolosi of a man.

Elifasi waves his hand as if she's a casual thing to dismiss. "Never mind, bygones et al. Except, Moremi, I'm glad you're here. This is perfect. I can take care of everyone without getting caught on your microchip, Nelah."

"Even if you kill us today," Jan says, "you can't murder the truth."

"Shut up!" Elifasi shouts. "And actually, I *can* murder the truth. Starting by exterminating this backup plan."

He aims the gun. Pulls the trigger. The bullet sweeps through the air, separated by a second from my brother's forehead. Moremi growls, yanks him out of the way with the sweeping force of gravity. Limbani smacks back first against the screen, topples to the ground in a fold of distorted limbs. Alive. Knocked out.

Gunsmoke shrivels the air. Huffs of anger expel from Moremi's mouth, revving a chestful of hatred. Her lunges rip through the air as Jan and I take cover behind the seats.

A swarm of bullets rocket through her, past us. She digs her nails, her serrated teeth, a bomb of serrated anger into Elifasi's body, tongue stripping the sinews and cartilage in his arms and chest. She draws back the skin from his face, licks the bone structure with the flaming purity of hatred as his screams pulverize our mercy, our sympathy.

She is done talking.

She is done negotiating.

She is done listening.

Moremi sits up on her haunches in the puddle of Elifasi's groans. "I will leave the rest of you for Mother." Her head rotates on the neck of her hunger, blood hanging like a torn fabric of skin down her jaw. "Mama, it is time."

A tsunami of blood lies in her path. It stuns me that Elifasi is still alive. I stand, walk up the stairs toward her raised fist. Jan follows suit, dark hair amok. His sleeves are pulled up to the elbows, veins tense like ropes.

Face still twisted by the adrenaline of anger, Moremi mouths, "I am sorry, Mama, but this will hurt."

I wince, close my eyes, wait for the damage—the pummeling of fists constellated across my broken skin. She is bullet-fast. I'm strewn on the ground, spluttering blood onto the carpet. I watch her through a swollen eye as she raises Elifasi lengthwise onto her shoulders. Drags me by the leg. Half-turns to Jan, and whispers, "Run."

00:52 /// THE ROPE OF TIME

Moremi is an advanced transport system; she's beheaded reality, tunnels us through the dark space of time, pulling apart its fabric as she drives us through this dark tornado of a distance spun into a shorter journey. The breath of a breeze soul-sweeps through my skin. Vertigo ensues. Pressure exerts itself against my lungs. Time is strange, covered in the viscous husk of ectoplasm—it makes me sick, makes me dizzy, makes me death-kin.

The amniotic fluid of this dark matter hugs us, compresses us deep into ourselves, and just when I think my bones will fracture, it spits us out, a meteoric birth onto the winding garden paths of Matsieng's heritage site. Past the fertility building that sticks out like a shard of earth's bone, Moremi continues to drag me across the paved lanes by my leg, the sky snatching screams from my throat. Blood-mottled vomit sprays from my mouth. My hand slams against the herringbone-set brick, leaving a feverish handprint of blood.

"Time-sickness," Moremi explains. "It certainly aids our ruse."

She arrives at the entrance, death-bound, covered in spilled screams, spilled souls, blood-sewn. Far beyond, a smoking car, hood slammed into the fist of a baobab tree. Jan. He's already at the entrance battering Serati with pleas, his shirt torn, blood dripping down the side of his forehead, strands of hair burned by fear; it is uncanny the level of destruction our emotions have on our bodies that they could set us aflame if we give into them.

Around us, a wooded private garden serenaded by a linear fountain flanking the entrance. Six guards stand sentry, three on either side, rifles at the ready. Jan freezes. Turns around. Shock stretches his eyes at the sight of me while my mouth is scraped by unknown things.

Moremi drops my leg, and I crawl away from her, grabbing Serati's pant leg. "Help me, please," I cry. Her eyes scorn down at me. She kicks off my grip. Black liquid weeps from my eyes, down my cheeks. I am rotten. I want to do terrible things to her, tear her tongue out, flay her skin. I am sin-saturated. I am evil. I accept it.

Elifasi hangs like a shawl around Moremi's shoulder, coming to, moaning, intoxicated with time.

Serati's nose flares. "What the hell is this nonsense? This is authorized access only." She directs her smoking glare at Moremi. "Do you realize how much of our section's budget you're cutting into to clean up your publicity stunts?"

"Twenty-four minutes remain before the trial ends," Moremi announces, "and I have a lot of work to do. I have brought the body that will be my new home, which you will prepare for me whilst I quickly kill these two men before I move on to the fetus archived next door at the fertility center. I will end the trial by drinking Nelah's soul. I am fast by any standard, but twenty-four minutes is cutting it a bit too close." My heart skips a beat; even though she's acting, she seems serious about killing my baby. "The Murder Trials Section . . ." Moremi steps forward. "Is the new arena . . .?"

"Which contains specialized genetic data worth millions," Serati complains. "Under no circumstances will I allow you to desecrate or potentially ruin years of work."

"Everything I need is within proximity," Moremi says.

Serati shakes her head, folds her arms. "Unfortunately—"

"*You* are interfering with a crime scene, obstructing Matsieng's law," Moremi says.

Serati stares at Jan, who's observing the conversation casually, then remembers his role and starts fleeing, screaming. Moremi throws her hand out, tailspins the air around Jan's neck, pulls him toward us. Serati's mouth hangs open at the evolution of Moremi's blood-hungry vengeance that's gaining potency by the second, perhaps enough to flood all thresholds of time, of laws, and drown Moremi.

For the first time, fear spreads through Serati's eyeballs. Words splutter from her lips. "I . . . We can't . . . It's inconceivable. This is sacred ground. We protect Matsieng to protect ourselves."

"Matsieng is very well capable of protecting Xemself," Moremi says. "The only thing you fear is becoming a casualty because you know Xe doesn't mind how Xe's fed. Serati, you are dispensable. You are obstructing my justice, an action that incites Matsieng's wrath. Matsieng sets the rules. Not you. The victim and murderer are a manifestation of Xem."

The tunnel lights flicker, and the darkness within glowers and spirals like smoke toward us, wintry cold. "Twenty-one minutes left," Moremi says.

Serati blinks, stares aside. Sighs. Arms limp. "We'll provide an off-set training room as your arena and any weapons you require—although weapons in our reality do not work on bodies from your reality."

"No," Moremi says. "The whole arena. Evacuate everyone. Close it down. No one goes in, no one goes out until the trial is over."

Serati's eyes narrow. "We'll secure the building. We will be present to protect significant data."

"Fine."

Serati steps forward. "I will supervise the crime."

Moremi smiles. "Be my guest. You're not my target, but I can't say much for flying stray bullets catching you off-guard."

Serati gasps. "Let them in," she directs the soldiers.

They part for us, for Moremi, shouldering my husband. She yanks Jan with the rope of time and drags me with her free hand into the curtain of dark. Once we enter Matsieng's Museum of Life, the room is dimly lit save for the sleeping shells in their glass-and-steel casings.

"The surgeons will be here momentarily," Serati says, "although I strongly advise you select our most reputable shells. Nelah's body won't sustain you for—"

"Shut up," Moremi says.

Serati nods. Gestures to her soldiers. "Prepare the theatre." They disappear into a door on the left side of the wall, and we're alone with Serati, invaded by silence.

Moremi drops my husband onto the ground. He rolls onto his side, coughs, spits blood at Serati's shoes. "You never thought I'd find out you withheld that *she* was going to kill me?"

"Every war produces casualties," Serati says, staring at him with slit eyes as I stare at Matsieng's cupules, deep craters in the rock, bracing.

Elifasi grunts. "Yet you continued to use me, to find her, to stop all this shit from coming out."

"Soldiers still fight knowing they may die," Serati says, lips twisted in disgust.

"Even though we've been on the same team for years, you've made me into an enemy," Elifasi says. He sits up, guides himself to standing, cradling his broken right arm and wincing as the skin peeling from his face sways. Smiles at Moremi. "Thank you for delivering us here. It is time."

Slowly, Moremi dissolves. Unseen. Gone. This is not part of the plan. Where is she going? Why's Elifasi thanking her? How could this be part of his plan? *What* is his plan? I raise myself from my knees as Jan's body relaxes, freed from the restraint of time.

Elifasi points his finger at us. "Don't take another step. Trust me, I may not be holding a gun, but I have a far stronger weapon. You take a step, and you will regret who it kills."

I hold my breath, stay still.

Elifasi guns a look at Serati. "Don't think about it. I'm part of this trial. Anything I do, you aren't to interfere. Today, I'm *your* fucking boss."

Serati glares, stands back. What a job.

Elifasi hobbles to me. "Serati withheld the fact that I, too, would be on the chopping board, which I learned about when you gave us the blood, so I had to figure out how to save myself because I'm bloody hell fed up of kissing ass just to survive. And, you, moratiwa," he enunciates, pointing a finger at me, "for all that intelligence you swagger about with, your tiny little brain hasn't figured out why my department has been experimenting on prisoners. Homicide, specifically. Jan, you motherfucker, while you were distracting yourself by screwing my wife, your father was instrumental in discovering this piece of intel: his informant disclosed that a select number of members from my department have been secretly developing a part of the CBE—using one of the technologies developed by one of his many companies—in conjunction with Matsieng's blood to manipulate the ghost's killing spree."

"Honestly, who gives a fuck?" Jan says. "Is there a point to this yapping?"

"Mxm, shut your mouth, lerete ke wena," Elifasi shouts. "God! This feels so good. For once, you bitches are powerless. You looked down on people like me as if we were cockroaches smutting your existence. Look at me now." He laughs, coughing out blood. Elifasi turns to me, continues, "Granted, they're unethical, inhumane experiments on prisoners. Instead of sending everyone who fails their forensic evaluations to the Crypt, the department holds a portion of them in this section's basement. It's their own curated jailhouse. Each cell holds two prisoners, and through the microchip feed, they control one to kill the other. The tech team analyses what happens when they use Matsieng's blood on its victim and study them through the CBE while observing the ghost during its killing rampage. That is, in what way that blood influences the Murder Trials—say, if a relative drinks it."

My breath is knocked out of my lungs. "What?" I swallow deeply. He drank Matsieng's blood, didn't he? What powers did it give him?

"Except, Aarav and I only found this out in the last hour through our trusted informant." There's venom in his eyes when he stares at Serati. "You should've disclosed to me the power Matsieng's blood would give me to manipulate Moremi. Do you understand how much easier sharing this information with us would've been? We'd have gotten rid of them a long time ago. It feels fucking great to not have to shut up in front of you because of the power you had. How does it feel now to have to listen for once in your goddamned life without the authority to tell me to stand down?" He raises his hands when she tries to speak. "Shut up. I don't want to hear your lies."

He looks at me now, smirking. "Moremi does decide whom to kill next. But by merely existing as Moremi's victim and being your husband, drinking Matsieng's blood allows me to manipulate *whom* Moremi will kill next and *what* will activate her final passing. For so long, I wondered why. Matsieng's blood fills you with death, and I become part ghost and part human. If I am a lingering ghost, I gain almost the same powers to enact my vengeance as a ghost like Moremi. Ja-nee, and the spirits in Matsieng are all too eager to have their way, their evil. Of course, because Moremi was resistant to them, I allowed them to use me so I could gain the power to manipulate her since she didn't want to be enmeshed in their evil. Matsieng certainly promotes and feeds from immoral acts."

"That's selling your soul to the devil," Jan says.

"Mxm, fotseke!" Elifasi spits. "Bloody fool."

My head swims, and I wish I could lean over, fall apart. He watches me with rabid eyes, studies me with intense passion, letting this sink in. It takes a while, like I've been removed from this environment. When did he find out about this power? After Serati made him drink the blood? It doesn't matter when he found out. Any new information that avails itself to him, he sharpens it into a blade. He always has a trick up his sleeve, the dirty bastard. He always uses everything to his advantage and leaves no crumb to waste. Now I must consume every crumb of power to leave him none.

Elifasi stabs his finger into my shoulder. "I had to protect myself with the one thing in the world that you'd never sacrifice," Elifasi says, spraying me with spit.

My stomach curls in on itself. The air is a sharp knife gutting me. Sweat rolls down my back, pools under my armpits into the grave of my soul. I am sick, sick, sick, seesawing on the last legs of my consciousness.

"Obviously," my husband says, "to get to me, you must kill all these people you love, including our beloved daughter."

01:17 /// SIN-FEVER

"Now," my husband says, undisturbed. "Where'd your sweetheart of a daughter disappear to? Moremi, shem skepsel, controlled by Aarav's company when she was alive, and now she's still compelled by this curse to seek vengeance." He smiles. "She's next door: in the Wombcubator, biding her time. She's very hungry, sweetheart." Elifasi raps my chest with his knuckles, checks his watch. "You have five minutes before you lose yet another one of our children. This pain you feel now is the same pain I felt when I found out about you fucking another man."

A breath of words, soft soft soft pain bleeds from my lips. "She's not even born." Her tiny fingers, her innocence. "Hate me. But not your baby. *Your* own baby girl."

"I can always have another kid." His eyes are dark, pitiless, steady on mine. He circles me. "You would never kill your children—well, except for the first four that your rotten womb suffocated. This is the fifth chance to save your baby. *I* live, *she* lives. That's how I fucking survive the Murder Trials," he spits.

I'm dizzy, hands faint of life. "I thought . . . she'd be safe with you. How . . . How can I leave something like you to exist? This world is full of people like you."

Women *should not* always have to die. Girls should not be born into death. No. No more. Something is happening to my brain. My brain is ticking—panicked, desperate to escape. Desperate. Panicked. My body is ice cold. Elifasi drank death, sold his soul to evil. I will slaughter my soul for a god. My hands fill with rage. This is just a body, and I feel so removed from it, from reality. My bones tighten. I have died thrice, and my body knows new dimensions. I know what I must do now. Nothing is more important than protecting our future girls, avenging what's been done to our dead women. I will not be controlled. *They* will not be controlled. *I* will be the last woman to die this way. The answer hits me, how to manipulate the database:

Serati said, *Every death, every killing, fills Xer waterholes . . . We give our blood, and we are protected. It has every citizen's blood, from when they are born to when they die. This blood has protected our country for years. Has blessed us. We acquire peace through it.*

Moremi said, *In my world, I am God . . . It's very difficult to smuggle anything from my reality into yours, but not the other way.*

A victim, yes, is sacrificed without consent, but their sacrifice is valuable to us.

From the nightmare, comes heaven.

Sin is attracted to sin.

Sin attracts sin.

Sin exterminates sins.

From the nightmare comes heaven.

Matsieng contains every citizen's blood, except men's; *it* is the database. Sin is attracted to sin. *Something has to bring itself into Moremi's world*. Matsieng won't be able to resist the greater sin I am offering: me; my body as Xer vessel. I am every death. I am every killing. The nonconsenting victim becomes the city, and the value of its sacrifice is our sanctuary, our peace, our heaven. *It's startling at first, terrifying and traumatizing and confusing, but you will reach the point where your belief is as ours.* I believe now, Serati. I believe in Matsieng, in Xer power to exterminate all sin through sin. Faith powers the action. Serati was right: *From the nightmare comes heaven.* I become the nightmare—as our government, our city, our leaders' nightmare. A nightmare shall renew the world into a new haven.

We do everything through Matsieng. We acquire peace through Xem.

I will be their blessing. I am their judge and punisher, incarnate of Matsieng.

One minute left. The waterwombs are open. A stream of squalls soar from Matsieng's waterwombs, flutter against the stacked shell-units, the brushed steel doors. Creatures of evil. Creatures of hunger. A fusion of death and life, a union of undivided dimensions. I die for my children. I succumb to Matsieng. In this second that could kill my unborn daughter, my feet carry me forward, hurl me into the bloody waters of Matsieng, into the evil lapping at Xer walls.

I am gone.

Reality evaporates. A fire burns; it blasts screams from the chimney of my throat.

The dark tide of Matsieng's blood rips and tears me apart. I break against the windshield of the murk. Memories, injustices, and immoral behaviors saturate these bloody waters, consume me with their horrid stories from before the times the crime eradication system was implemented because each spirit contains the history of its ancestors and the history of horrors from time immemorial—the system may have abolished those violations, but the traumas still scream on: Men have taken children from the streets to have their children. It's sick. These men, there are deserts in their heartlands. They've learned how to open child-thighs, their mouths spraying evil into the crooks of their knees, breaking the language from them. Men who still fondle the night with their wives hung around their necks. They make a shebeen of children's limbs, turning their hearts into sorghum and dust, teeth nicking their magic from children's milk, children who don't know what it means to be the vessel for birth as death lilts at the cages in their chests. It snows in parts of them that didn't know the sun. There are secrets in our city from ancient times before crime was exterminated. Terrible secrets. Scathing lies. The rage burns in me. In the womb of dark sin, the screams of innocent lives boil to a fever pitch in the ribcage of my soul and from these spirits I gain access to the ancestors' unresolved trauma: I am the Black, the brown, the *other* being segregated and wiped out, *still* being stolen and possessed, that the *color* denies itself. I am the prostitute, the young girl walking through dark streets alone. I am the pregnant woman. I am the young man. I am the person whose gender is mutilated to conform me, to teach me a lesson. I am the liminal, the niece, the daughter, the sister, the mother in seedy hotels, rich houses, back gardens, sewers—meal tickets to sadistic killers and government leaders. Behind closed skins and in eye sockets, they bury themselves in the wombs of little children to carve their names inside them until their bellies balloon to the sky, their hearts nowhere found.

These are the men in power, people made of devil-skins, unburned by God's hands. I see their past, in my mind, in my sight. I see them in our news feed, in our government, in our schools who act as our guardians—these are the people that make a noose out of Bible pages, wrap it around our ears and eyes, and hang us dry. I know these people with starving throats so full of fire; they carved hunger into the bellies of our people, took their children's hunger to dress their dinner tables and parade streets and slums and now the poor suffer.

They are the infertility of this global war. It makes sense now: Evil obscures evil to maintain its existence. I am the grave site of the many women and men. I am the war zone. I feel the victim's pain, the killer's seductive joy. I have sin-fever.

Sun that sees all sin.
Moon that sees all sin.
Air that touches all crimes.
Ground that consumes all corpses.
I exhume myself from this waterwomb, dressed in all elements.
Reality owns me not. *Reality* is shipwrecked away from me.
I feel everything. I see everything. I am Wrath.
Fear is not my dictator.

01:34 /// I AM XEM

I float in Matsieng's waterwombs, a universe of their own, a swathe of dripping vermillion colors swallowing my vision. A siren wails, a cacophony of insanity, a tornado of screams spins around me into darkness, into death. I am burning, burning, burning. Life is sapped from my veins. A swarm of cries from the lives historied in this blood surrounds me, alchemizes me into a fetus of hellish pain as I'm spun, spun, spun—*oh God, when will it end? Make it stop!*

My mind is going to explode as it sucks me into the depths of my past lifespans' forgotten pain, forgotten lives. The climax rises, climbing through me, lobotomizes my every thought into a nuclear explosion, implodes me into a constellation of memories floating mote-like in dire black space.

Peace, *peace*, finally, as I float in Matsieng's universe. I am frozen in the starburst of what I used to be. Satellites of memories revolve around me: Moremi, newly born, enfolded in my arms; me, newly born, enfolded in my first mother's arms; the lilting sway of my unborn daughter in her pod. I am saturated in love, an intoxicating, pure love; just as quickly, it's sullied by the presence of other people, destroyed by corruption, and I am filled with anger. Toxic patterns suckling at our breasts are stripped from our bodies. Given new lives, dead zones. Memories castrated.

Evil does not end because my life ends.

I submit my body to you. Possess me in all your power, Matsieng, and I will feed you.

I rescind myself, purge my soul and my sins to save them. I feed all of me to Matsieng, as Xe unclothes me of my female body, dousing me in Xem, and abolishes the spirits' evil.

The images dissolve. I drop into my body, rising, rising, rising in the blood caverns, the splinter of broken bones snapping into position, and the weight of peace and power fills my lungs, my mind, killing all fear. I am not a murderer; I own what is given to me. I transmute evil to good through the elixir of death.

I am Xem.

I am a god.

The well is dark, cavernous, slippery; my fingers find purchase in the cracks. My leg cranks up, finding a foothold. Then my other leg. My hands scramble for the edge of the waterhole's opening, shrouded in the screams of its past blood holders. My legs fold over my head, climbing me out of the hole until I am standing in my original height almost as tall as all the humans in the room. I am a being without bone and sinew, a form composed of blood and sin.

I stare down at my legs. I am undisturbed that it's not bare feet and toes I see. Instead, I have spindly legs with hooves for feet: dark, hard, and dangerous. My arms are streaked with blood as if my skin *is* blood. I spread my fingers apart, and my hands change form, metamorphosing into claws. The rest of my skin remains stretched across my abdomen, chest, and back as my spine calibrates its structure into something animalistic, something sacred. A horn protrudes from the right side of my forehead with untenable force, pain, and ecstasy. My jaw cranes open, and my canines grow into long spears.

A totem births itself in my bones.

I am the people's totem. I am their sereto.

A smile spreads across my face. I glance at my shoulders; my bones peek out like the scapula of an animal. Once, Matsieng ascended from these waterwombs with our tribes and a herd of animals that became our totems and protected us in the past. Now, I rise, as a totem, like Xem, protector of our new tribe.

A man stands overhead. Points his trembling rifle at me, warns me to get down on my knees, hands behind my back, or he'll shoot. I cut my eyes to him. His mouth yanks itself open, stretches over his skull, and kills him. His death has erased further sin from this world.

I detect tiny eyes of surveillance embedded into the nooks of walls and ceiling. The Murder Trials Committee, at the distal end of the Matsieng facility. A cigar lounge. Dark glasses. Glare and snare. Banter. The cast members. Screams pierce the air. Doors bang open. Smoke, hazy.

The task team in their protective suits stomp toward me, shields out, their sins wet on their faces. Gas grenades spiral past my feet. Guns point in my direction. Threats missile toward me.

I wrench the microchip from my neck. I claw through the nerves and cartilage and tissue and uproot a pinched bullet from my splintered shoulder bone. Bulbs shatter into darkness. The Murder Trials Section, so subterranean, like a grave, earth-tucked.

A spray of bullets from a gun perforates my body. The bullet wounds seal themselves.

"I am the wrath of all your sins." The voice emanates from my new sin-skin by my own volition. Dawn begins to tread into the Murder Trials Section, interrupting our consortium. I raise my hand, halting its movements. "Sun, hide your eye, eclipse your birth from our sins. I am the destruction of this city."

Darkness scuds the sun.

I am Wrath; I am Sin. I am Matsieng.

A mile behind me, through a gap in the columns, a soldier sneaks up, lines up his rifle, telescopes his aim to focus on me.

I don't need microchips to control him. I have his ancestors' blood within me.

The soldier drops his gun. His mouth is slack, his jaw unhinged. He has a knife. He scratches at his skin; he is allergic to his skin. The only cure is death. I rid our city of this pollutant that continues to destroy our world.

A delicious klaxon of screams. I devour them.

My sin-skin whispers, "Men may have not offered their blood to my waterwombs, but because of their relation to the spirits that fill me, I have every citizen's blood in me, from when they are born to when they die. I see you all before you act, before you think, I *know* you."

The soldier beside him points his gun to me—asphyxiation initiates. He crumples to his knees, gone. *Moon, hide your eye, eclipse your birth from our sins.*

The obstacles, protectors of my targets, are done and gone.

Hit list: Serati. Elifasi. Aarav. The out-of-sight sinners from the Murder Trials Committee.

Serati stands where she last was when I entered the waterwombs; she's paralyzed by fear. All the council members emerge from all their holes, in their expensive suits, sweat-soaked and intoxicated from their drink as they watched the Murder Trials. Sin attracts sin. "This is the lung of earth. You have no place here," my sin-skin whispers, and the council members fold to their knees. "You are charged for extortion, bribery, misuse of public funds, eradicating human rights, fraud, murder, femicide, rape—all the crimes committed under your watch. I am all your sins here to reap your sorrows into your corpses. You can't be exorcised."

I count all their sins, transmute them into little demons that scrabble about on spindly legs looking for their owners, tearing through skins, scraping bones with teeth as they wail.

Elifasi balks, a puddle of urine beneath his trembling feet.

The air through Matsieng's power drags Aarav to our crime scene, forces him to his knees before me. The serpentine rope of time shackles Aarav's body. He grovels by my feet. "Naughty or nice?" I ask.

He whimpers. Aarav stretches his hand out to Jan, screaming, "Son, please!" The air burns his skin to ash. He is gone forever, and so will it be the same for Serati, Elifasi, and those like them, for their sins' immortality can't be ceased unless they are terminated.

This is the new world. The purity of silence calms me.

The sun never fails us. Elifasi, fear bridling beneath all that muscle, those dark eyes. A ray of fire knifes across his skin, climbs up his spine, compels him to kneel. He is a burning sin.

I dig my nails into Serati's cranium. Serati screeches, running out of memory; I climax from the organic flow, the slurping of her memories straight into my being. I am a memory bank. I am Matsieng.

Time is bleak, a fast creature.

05:00. It is time for the sun's reckoning.

Here now is the cusp of dawn, when the sky contains a fading moon, a waking sun. The sun, a blazing forensic eye, burns the chemicals exuded by the police tower dangerous only to those who can't be purified. Its probing rays seep into corridors, seeking; into homes, seeking; into bodies, seeking; into minds, finding.

The air is liquid with these transgressors' deaths floating amok, unrecognizable in the debris of their sins—but other offenders, men who escaped being microchipped, who still exist within our world not monitored by the government, and therefore were getting away with harming those considered insignificant . . . They must be found, persecuted. The air is my breath, my eye, my power; the earth is my skin. Every citizen inhales, exhales from the pistons of my lungs. Air is unescapable—it is part of our sustenance, it is God, it sees all. Therefore, I am the vessel of air, and I control its atomic being, for it touches every part of you, sees every part of you, has for centuries absorbed your crimes—not today.

Every citizen wakes. Air, the complicit bystander of all crimes, is no longer mute. It climbs into their lungs and burns all breathing of the unholy, renews their spirit before the transference into pure bodies. The sun, always a dreamer, the punisher, screams fire into their skins.

Air is my sea.

"Sea-rise will be our baptism," my sin-skin whispers. "May the oceans rise and drown everything, for we will be reborn."

Reality evolves to punish them; air, dusk, and earth are my bloodhounds hunting through bloodlines, searching for the sick ones. I watch passersby, the air frying their alveoli.

"Now in death, you are forgiven," my sin-skin says. Outside, the moon is a toxic beauty. "It is time: Sun, moon-stain your bloodied ribs." I raise my arms to my blood holders. "Come, my sinners."

Sleepers leave their beds. For kilometers, cars stop in mid-motion, spilling out their passengers, who dust themselves off and trek distances toward us. Bikes crush fallen leaves as their drivers steer toward us. People in gardens leave their benches and sandwiches, and turn toward us. Office buildings excrete people from all their orifices: the highest floors tumble bodies out onto the pavements. Still, they come forth toward us, rising despite their broken bones, their mutilated knees.

Sun, hide your eye, eclipse your birth.

Our heartbeats are cataclysmic, a big bang.

Tonight, the whole city dies. We exterminate sin to create a new world.

Blood drowns the walls. We stand on the horizon, watching. Architecture is a prisoner of this torn world, unable to run, its feet frozen to the ground. The city has teeth, and it devours the land, the politics, the materialistic gluttony. I listen to the seismic, burrowing screams, a symphony of dying sins. The air tastes like smoke and suicide as people terminate themselves, detonate in their wrongs, lives bubbling in their throats with old blood.

In death, their pure spirits rise; in death, they are forgiven. I press my palms to their spirit foreheads to spill them into sacred bodies made of clay and breath, sacred bodies that clamber out from Matsieng's creation grounds, the waterwombs, as shells devoid of consciousness, devoid of souls waiting to be filled. Everyone gets a new body. Soft rivers run in my throat; volcanoes thunder in my voice. "Live," I whisper. They hobble to the empty shells, some of which were housed in the Murder Trials' Museum of Life; now the shells are awakening, lit by these new souls pouring into them. The doors crane open as other shells leave their homes of brushed steel, sin-nude, standing, waiting to be worn. More empty bodies appear from the waterwombs, created by Matsieng's power to house all the awaiting spirits. Other spirits step forth choosing their body, filling the shells with souls and minds, feet glistening with synthetic amniotic fluid. This is the new world, memories tossed within. This is the new immortality.

I glance at Jan. "Choose your body," my sin-skin whispers. "Like everyone else, you get to remake yourself. Your father always chose your identity. Now you get to be who you want."

He stammers.

"Do not be afraid," my sin-skin says. "I am still in here."

Jan points a finger. A male sin-nude shell approaches us. Jan gazes at its form. Honey-gold eyes, bronze skin, crew-cut, crow-black hair. Fear devastates his lips, his body. Janith Koshal. A sin-smoking motherfucker.

"Your time has come," my sin-skin whispers.

Jan presses his fist against his mouth to stop the screams climbing up his throat, a ladder of hurt. "Take my hand," my sin-skin whispers as my claws change back into human hands. "You are safe with me. But first, you have sinned, and we must cleanse you of sin."

Jan staggers back, shaking. I tear the sternum from his body, unspool his soul to fill the new shell. The pain in Jan's voice trickles through my fingers, a glowing, sinuous viscosity lined with bass, and I helm it with my palms, gingerly pouring his voice into the throttled larynx of his new shell. I watch his irises wake with a new color of brown. Shorn head brims with thoughts, memories, desires. Pale skin wraps tendons and veins surging with life.

Mama appears through a copse of trees, haggard with death.

Moremi appears, jaw unbalanced. She is they, she is woman, she is monster. "The baby is still alive," they whisper, carrying my fast-grown baby. My baby coos and stares at me with dewy-black eyes. I cradle my baby in my arms; her skin is soft, her chubby legs rubbing against me as she sucks her thumb.

Moremi stares about this carnage. Nods. "This is the revolution I wanted. Mama, you have freed me. Bless you. And now I will curate my own body."

Moremi and my mother stare at me, at the macabre image of my baby and me. I reach out: Moremi, Mama, and Jan grasp my hand. We stand on the shores of our sins, in a sea of its fire, fingers entangled, inundated with transgressions like smog around us. The cable of time transmits them into reality, into life, into reborn things. Two shells—melanin-brushed, soft-dawn irises, sharp-boned, heads haloed in a froth of Afros—open themselves to be filled by Mama and Moremi.

New bodies, new lives, branded with virtue.

"You're pure," I say.

We stand on a precipice of a new world. There's existence shimmering in the constellation. There is no god on the horizon; there is only smoke. The sun is a hot eye in the sky, scanning, burning always on a Sunday. Somewhere out there is a crucified criminal being found by the sun, by time, by me, being drawn out to this scene, this asylum of forgiveness. An exodus of citizens arrives at their appointed shells, discards their old bodies and enter new ones of their choice. A clean slate.

Murder hangs in the air, like fine, sweet mist. Now, more than ever, we are Xem, and we *women* will be powerful, invincible warriors and horrifyingly untouchable. In our city, everyone lives forever.

We are perfect; we are pure.

ACKNOWLEDGMENTS

The amount of work that goes into the finished product of a manuscript is mind-boggling, an architecture woven from different hands at different stages, the beauty that flourishes from it. Endless gratitude to all who have supported my every literary pursuit and poured care and peace into me. Thank you to those I can no longer name but who were instrumental in this book.

Cheryl S. Ntumy, thank you for your forever intelligent and deeply insightful edits; thank you for offering patience and mentorship for almost every bad draft of a novel I had to *Womb City*; it was in the early years of being in Botswana, what felt like being landlocked from every literary endeavor, that I finally found you, a local and marvelous author offering me guidance on the craft of writing.

It has taken thirteen years to reach this literary point. In late 2017, after what took five years of writing novels and over 400 rejections, obtaining my first literary agent (what felt like a miracle), and losing them, I'd nothing literary to my name, and I'd involuntarily quit writing from the triggering emotional exhaustion, wondering if it were the work or the identity getting rejected, and what was the point? Three years later, I found it safe to write a novel again, which became *Womb City*, my miracle baby. My deepest gratitude to Naomi Davis for saying yes when I was at the edge of pulling the manuscript from the slush piles after receiving confusing *the writing is far superior to most of the material that crosses my desk BUT* rejections to *I didn't connect to the characters* rejections from agent to agent—it is a miracle I made it through; thank you, Naomi, for your editorial insight and understanding of every scene that it felt as if you wrote it, and a huge thank you to James McGowan who knew we'd be a great fit. To my editor, Sarah Guan, good God, your brain is badass; I love your brain, I loved your editorial notes, you're exceptionally mind-blowing, and your understanding of *Womb City* shone a light in areas that unraveled a world hidden within it—I'm so blessed to have you as an editor. Martin Cahill, thank you for your support and enthusiasm—I don't know how you do it, but thank you! A huge thank you to the Erewhon and Kensington team, Sydnee Thompson, thank you; Samira Iravani, Colin

Verdi, and Leah Marsh thank you for this beautiful, jaw-dropping cover design and art and interior design.

In the space after quitting writing, I dipped my toes into writing short stories—which felt safer and quicker and allowed for experimentation and figuring out my identity—so a huge thank you to the literary magazines and anthologies who accepted my work, to the editors who gave a home for a writer, it is where I found a welcoming community that felt *less gatekeeping*, where I developed my writing; where would we writers be without your support and the work you do.

Thank you to Wole Talabi, who edited my story "Behind Our Irises," which appeared in Brittle Paper's *Africanfuturism: An Anthology*; I didn't realize this story, in its almost entirety, would later form an essential scene in *Womb City*. Gratitude to the Brittle Paper team! I recall receiving my edits from Wole Talabi, and it was probably one of the rare one or two occasions I'd been edited by a Black editor/author (besides beloved Cheryl S. Ntumy) who caught the story's nuances.

Kate Brauning, thank you: during your Breakthrough Writers' Boot Camp, I found the business aspect of your mentorship for authors enlightening; you read the early version of *Womb City*, and your suggestions were encouraging. Aubrey, encyclopedia of all things related to neuroscience and physics, thank you for all the chats each time I had probing questions. Lesego, thank you, one wouldn't have survived certain *shenanigans* without you. Immense gratitude to the bad-ass literary circles I started in: Cheryl S. Ntumy, Gothataone Moeng, Sharon Tshipa—a hilarious RIP to the projects we tried to start, but a thankful embrace to the kinship. My Luls, Luiza, bless you for the beautiful friendship that made Orange warm and your legal introspections that helped me finesse one writing complication I'd written myself into. Thank you, Henneh Kyereh Kwaku, bruv, dearest therapist, dearest friend—for the times we'd forever get lost in our unmasked ND days, weaving through our labyrinthine rabbit hole tunnels of thoughts and topics, how it felt to breathe unapologetically; one couldn't have survived Orange without home in it. Dr. Ainehi Edoro Glines, bless you, and immense gratitude for seeing me into one of my dream-come-true experiences. Silvia Moreno-Garcia, Lavie Tidhar, Cristina Jurado, and Francesco Verso, bless you, and thank you for all your support! I'm so forever thankful to the mentors and those who offered guidance with grace and no self-aggrandizing purposes, especially the marginalized folk who provided help with no strings attached and who didn't burn you to keep themselves warm and seen by your light and reasoning it with absurd logics—what a world, thank you for the grace that still exists in it.

Boitumelo and Omphile, ama-gang gang, tsalulus, choms-erryting, the *eish ja neh* hilarious moments—my life would be dull without you two, my forever-there, forever-safe kin.

Thank you, dearest reader, for visiting and spending time in *Womb City*; wishing you a safe journey back.

Thank you for reading this title from Erewhon Books, publishing books that embrace the liminal and unclassifiable and championing the unusual, the uncanny, and the hard-to-define.

We are proud of the team behind *Womb City* by Tlotlo Tsamaase:

Sarah Guan, Publisher
Diana Pho, Executive Editor
Viengsamai Fetters, Editorial Assistant

Martin Cahill, Marketing and Publicity Manager
Kasie Griffitts, Sales Associate

Cassandra Farrin, Director of Publishing and Production
Leah Marsh, Production Editor
Kelsy Thompson, Production Editor
Sydnee Thompson, Copyeditor
Rayne Stone, Proofreader

Samira Iravani, Art Director
Colin Verdi, Cover Artist

. . . and the whole Kensington Books team!

Learn more about Erewhon Books and our authors at erewhonbooks.com.

Twitter: @erewhonbooks
Instagram: @erewhonbooks
Facebook: @ErewhonBooks